Her Parents' Daughter

Carolyn McCrae

Published by New Generation Publishing in 2014

Copyright © Carolyn McCrae 2014

First Edition

The author asserts the moral right under the Copyright, Designs and Patents Act 1988 to be identified as the author of this work.

All Rights reserved. No part of this publication may be reproduced, stored in a retrieval system or transmitted, in any form or by any means without the prior consent of the author, nor be otherwise circulated in any form of binding or cover other than that which it is published and without a similar condition being imposed on the subsequent purchaser.

www.newgeneration-publishing.com

New Generation **Publishing**

**Also by
Carolyn McCrae**

The Iniquities Trilogy:
The Last Dance
(Winner David St John Thomas Prize for Self-Published Fiction 2006)
Walking Alone
Runaways
Highly Unsuitable Girl

www.carolynmccrae.com

Thanks

Thank you Sylvie and Malcolm Drake
of Pilton, Somerset
for your enthusiasm and encouragement.

And thank you Colin for continuing to put up with my
quirks and foibles.
And for so much more.

Chapter 1
The Murder is Committed

Two elderly sisters walked together out of the churchyard and took their seats, as they did every Sunday, on the bench in the town square. Whatever the weather, they would sit for an hour after the service before heading home for their lunch.

In the winter they would appreciate the peace and quiet, but on hot summer weekends the square came alive with bustle and colour. In August the harbour, almost empty in the winter months, was crowded with yachts whose crews mingled with weekenders and day-trippers transforming the atmosphere of the often quiet town.

"There're lots of people around today." Louise Woods commented, opening the conversation as she always did.

"I should hope so. If the town wasn't full on a lovely sunny bank holiday Sunday like this then we've got real problems." Her sister Vanessa replied tartly.

"Look there are another couple of coaches." Louise continued, unfazed by her sister's unwillingness to engage in meaningless conversation. "They're not supposed to be here, they should be in the car park."

"Stupid." Her sister replied.

Louise wasn't sure whether Vanessa was referring to her or to the drivers of the coaches and decided it was the drivers. "They are aren't they?"

They watched as the passengers climbed carefully down the steep steps of the coaches. Men and women of the sisters' generation, they seemed unconcerned that they blocked the pavements and spilled out onto the streets obstructing the paths of the drivers who were attempting to navigate their vehicles, with varying degrees of skill and patience, through the narrow streets. For several minutes Louise and Vanessa watched the coach-loads gradually disperse and free up the road to a continuous stream of cars.

"Why is everyone always in such a hurry to be somewhere they're not?" Louise asked but Vanessa made no attempt to answer as she concentrated on an over-sized four-by-four being manoeuvred into a parking space that was far too narrow for comfort.

Louise didn't mind that her sister made no attempt to answer her as her attention had strayed to a woman who had walked out into the street without looking.

"What a silly woman. She's so lucky the driver of that car was concentrating. If he'd been on his phone or worrying about finding a parking space he'd probably have run into her." She looked up at her sister. "I'm so glad I don't drive." She added wistfully.

"Bloody good thing too." Vanessa commented sharply without looking at her sister. "You'd be bloody useless, a danger to everyone else on the road. You only see what you want to see and then only when you've got the right glasses on. I'm beginning to notice that you're going deaf as well. You only seem to hear what you want to hear when you want to hear it."

Louise took the criticism in good part, she was used to it. She knew that she would never think of a suitable retort quickly enough to make it worthwhile trying so she changed the subject. "Look at that, two yellow cars parked next to each other. Odd enough to see one, every other car seems to be grey these days, but two together is very interesting." And she settled back to pass the hour between church and lunch thinking her own thoughts.

In The Queen's Head, the least busy of the three pubs in the town, two elderly men leaned awkwardly against the back bar. Each was, for his own reasons, carefully watching the man and woman who were sitting at a table near the door.

For more than sixty years Eric Atkinson and Richard Mackenzie had disliked each other, each actively working to thwart the other's ambitions. Richard had won the earlier battles that had been played out between them but he knew he was losing this last one.

He was tired of it all and he was ill and now Georgina was dead there seemed to him to be no point in fighting any more.

"I should have killed you when I had the chance." Richard spoke quietly, almost conversationally, and without malice. He was simply stating a fact.

"Well you didn't, did you? Just one of your many mistakes." Eric replied. "Perhaps you would have done if you'd known how much trouble I'd cause you, your precious Georgina and the girl."

He spoke as one who knew he held the winning hand.

Richard had no way of knowing what it was that Eric had planned, he just knew that, whatever it was, he would not be able to prevent it.

To both men the woman sitting at the table by the door seemed uncomfortable, fidgeting on her chair, tapping her toes on the stone floor and turning her glass round and round in her hands. They both recognised that she hardly said a word as the man leant back in his chair talking with every sign of confident familiarity and they both understood that when she did speak she was contradicting what the man had told her, repeating the word 'no' clearly several times.

Richard turned his back to the bar and spoke quietly. "You said if I met you here you'd give me my," he hesitated, he did not want to use the word 'gun' in such a public place, "you said you'd give me back what you stole from me."

"No I didn't." Eric smiled, and if anyone had been looking they would have seen that it was not a smile that carried any feeling of mirth or sympathy. "That was always your problem old boy, no attention to detail. I didn't say I'd give you your gun back. I didn't say that at all."

"What are you up to Eric?" Richard asked as he looked anxiously across at Jane sitting with the man he knew to be

David Childs. "You've set something up haven't you? It's no coincidence that that man is here with Jane in the same bar at the same time you told me to meet you."

Their conversation, such as it was, ended abruptly as they saw the woman push back her chair, pick up her bag and sling it over her shoulder. After saying a few words that appeared to neither Richard nor Eric to be very friendly, she left.

All three men, for their own reasons, followed her.

Dr Jane Carmichael turned right into the narrow street and headed towards the square but she couldn't move as quickly as she would have liked because of the group of old aged pensioners occupying the pavement and spilling into the road. She tried to push through them but found she just had to amble along at their pace.

She knew David Childs would be following her and she wanted to get away from him, but even as she finally cleared her way through the crowd she had to avoid cars dawdling through the town as they looked for a rare parking spot or swerved to avoid people walking into the road.

She was only a ten-minute walk from her home but it seemed to Jane to be a very long way away.

As soon as he saw David Childs was following Georgina's daughter out onto the street Richard made his way as quickly as he could from the bar and followed them both out into the crowded street with Eric close behind him.

"Jane!" Richard called, trying to catch her attention, but his voice had no strength as a shaft of pain spread across his chest. He wondered if he would fall to the ground but he managed to stay standing as he gasped for breath.

He could think of nothing but the pain, it filled his body and his mind. He felt as though his chest would explode with the beating of his heart.

He couldn't walk, he could only lean against the shop wall, as he fought to control his body. He fought, also, to see what was happening around him. Where was Jane? Where was David Childs? What was Eric doing?

His thoughts came slowly.

Jane. David Childs. Eric. All in the same place. At the same time.

Richard felt helpless as he tried to make sense of it all.

Eric had stolen his gun. The thought registered through the fog that was his brain. But why? Surely he had guns of his own. It made no sense but it had to. Eric was a clever man, he would not do anything without a reason.

Richard had no strength left.

He could not stop Eric doing whatever it was he had planned.

He knew Eric had won when the heard the shots.

He wondered, in a detached way, why people said guns went 'bang'. Few did and he had recognised the sounds for what they were, two shots from his service revolver.

'Why?' he asked himself. 'Why did Eric have to shoot her? What had she ever done to him? What had Jane ever done to anyone? It wasn't her fault she was who she was. None of it was her fault.' Tears escaped his closed eyelids and ran, unchecked, down his cheeks.

She had been all that was left of Georgina.

He felt the movement of the people in the street around him but with his eyes closed he couldn't tell whether they were running towards the sound of the shots or away from them. And he could not make his eyes open.

He had to concentrate hard on breathing in and out. Surely the pain had to ease.

Perhaps he would be able to help Jane this one last time.

Vanessa Woods, sitting with her sister on the bench by the church, looked around to see what could have caused the unusual noise. Perhaps someone had dropped something, perhaps a mobile phone. She had often commented to Louise that no one of the younger generation seemed to be able to walk anywhere without one of the blessed things pressed to their ear.

But the noise had surely been too loud for that. She didn't recognise the sound and she wasn't sure how many times she heard that 'crack' but she decided it must have been twice and that was what she would tell the police when they asked her.

Looking around to see what could have made the sound she saw a man lying on the ground no more than a few yards away from her.

"There's a man on the ground." Vanessa reported to her sister.

"Has he fallen over? Do you think he's drunk? There are a couple of stag parties in town today."

"He's not drunk. I think that woman's shot him." Vanessa whispered urgently. "Look. There's a gun in her hand. Yes. That's it. She's just shot him."

"What did you say?" Louise was unsure she had heard her sister correctly, but she could just see in the narrow gap between the parked cars and the shop windows that there was someone slumped on the ground and a woman standing over him with something in her hand.

"Right in front of us that man has been shot." Still Vanessa's voice was low, as if she didn't want anyone else to hear.

"Do you think he's dead?"

"Looks like it. He doesn't seem to be moving anyway."

Other people in the square were beginning to notice what was happening. A woman screamed, a father shielded his young daughter's eyes and hurried her away, others huddled around the man on the ground while the woman standing over him did not move.

"Shouldn't we call the police or an ambulance or something?" Louise asked urgently.

"Someone will surely have called 999 on their wretched mobile phones. We'll just stay here until the police come." Vanessa told her sister firmly. "They'll want to speak to us, after all is said and done, we saw the whole thing didn't we?"

Richard felt the waves of pain begin to subside. He pressed his back against the wall to push himself upright and he forced his eyes to open. He saw Jane through the crowd and she was standing. She wasn't dead. He knew Eric would never have missed the shot. He was confused.

He began to walk carefully towards her and as he drew closer he could see his revolver in her hand and the body of David Childs on the ground at her feet.

Through his pain he realised what had been done.

Eric had never intended to do anything as simple as just killing Jane. He'd done something far worse. He was going to punish her. And by punishing Jane he would have his revenge.

After nearly sixty years Eric had won.

Richard knew, as clearly as if he had planned it himself, that Jane would be arrested and charged, tried and convicted, and imprisoned for the rest of her life.

Eric had set her up.

Jane would be punished because, in a lifetime of searching, Eric had found no evidence that she, or her mother, or her father, had been involved in the treason he and his paymasters had convinced themselves had been committed.

The pain spread from his chest to his head. Richard knew there was nothing he could do to save her. His eyes closed as if somehow shutting out the world would shut out the agonies.

He knew he couldn't push his way through the crowd quickly enough to take the gun from her hand, he wouldn't be able to magic her away from danger as he had done so often in the past. She was on her own now. She would have to cope alone.

He became aware of someone standing too close to him. Eric was smiling.

He heard the words 'not just two birds with one stone, old man, this makes it three'.

He felt the pinprick in his neck and knew Eric was leaving nothing to chance.

Richard had always believed that dying was something that should be done in private.

He pushed himself away from the wall and struggled to walk the few yards to his car. No one noticed his distress, everyone who had not left the square was concentrating on Jane and the man lying at her feet.

He pressed the button that opened his car door and he eased himself onto the seat. It was all he could do to pull his legs off the pavement and into the foot well. He pressed the button that closed the door and shut out the world one last time.

As the pain stopped he had one last thought of Georgina as she had been when he had first known her, when they had both been young.

"He was chasing after her. Then they were talking, there, on the corner, by the shop. And then she killed him." Vanessa spoke with the authority she had assumed in every one of the sixty-three years since her younger sister had been born.

"She was right with him when he fell." Louise agreed with Vanessa, as she always did.

"And she had the gun in her hand. That's all we need to remember." Vanessa spoke firmly having little confidence in the accuracy of Louise's memory. Louise had always been a little scatty and Vanessa felt it was important their statements were simple and precise, and identical. They were witnesses to murder and their evidence would be crucial in the trial. She knew this because she was an avid viewer of detective programmes on the television.

"She's just standing there with the gun still in her hand. Isn't that stupid? Wouldn't you have thought she'd have thrown it away and run? Wouldn't you have run?" Louise asked thoughtfully.

"I wouldn't have shot him in the first place." Vanessa was abrupt. "We must just remember everything we have seen."

She knew from the courtroom dramas on television that it was the simple stories that were the most convincing. And they were the easiest to remember. Consistency, she felt, was every bit as important as accuracy in these matters.

"I'd have run away." Louise shook her head in disbelief at the stupidity of the murderess.

"I don't think either of us has the slightest idea of what we'd do, neither, I suspect, ever having been in that situation." Her elder sister answered cuttingly.

"She should have run away, or at least dropped the gun. Just standing there doesn't seem right somehow." Louise said, as if to herself, which was just as well because her sister was no longer listening to her.

Vanessa was determined that she would not be left out of the drama. "We were probably the only ones to see it all. Everyone else was busy doing their own thing, we are the only ones just sitting, watching. They will want to speak to us."

"Are they going to arrest her?" Louise asked tentatively.

"I would be very surprised if they didn't. Now listen carefully and remember everything I tell you."

Vanessa could just see between the people and the parked cars as she gave a running commentary to her sister.

"A policeman is pushing everyone back, another has squatted down by the man on the ground, he's pressing something to his neck, he's talking to someone, perhaps the victim, the other policeman is talking to the woman, he doesn't seem very friendly, though she's just murdered someone so I wouldn't expect them to be really." Vanessa was trying to get as good a look at the scene as possible. "It's all very exciting."

When a policewoman who was trying to clear the crowd away from the square came near them Vanessa shouted out to catch her attention.

"Officer. Officer. We saw it happen. We know exactly what happened. My sister and I saw everything."

"We'll be collecting witnesses' names and addresses as soon as we can." The young woman said, rather too brusquely for Vanessa's liking.

"But we saw it all." Vanessa pressed her case. She was already imagining her role as a star witness for the prosecution in court.

"We will take all the details when the ambulance has been and gone. Stay here please."

"Is he dead?" Vanessa had time to ask before a very loud siren indicated that the ambulance had arrived and the policewoman turned away from her without answering.

"Maybe he's not dead." Louise was beginning to wish they had had nothing to do with whatever it was that was going on. She didn't want to get involved. She certainly didn't want to have to stand up in court and face cross-examination, she knew from watching re-runs of Judge John Deed on the television how aggressive and rude some lawyers could be. She wasn't sure she wanted to have anything to do with all that, especially as, when she thought about it, she hadn't really seen anything at all.

"If he's not dead yet he will be soon. It'll be murder." Vanessa stated confidently. She was taking in every detail, just in case it might be useful in court.

"She looks a bit familiar doesn't she?" Louise asked, doubtful whether she should have said anything.

"I think I've seen her around." Vanessa was dismissive but Louise persevered.

"She does look familiar. I've seen her face somewhere."

"She'll just be a local Lou. You'll have seen her around I expect."

"No. I remember. She's that woman who's been in all the papers. That's it. She's the one who's been in the papers."

"Maybe, maybe not." Vanessa replied dismissively. She was never happy when Louise noticed something she didn't.

"It was her. I'm sure." Louise said quietly and determinedly, in the small voice she had used all her life when disagreeing with her elder sister.

"There's something else, I think I heard him call after her." Vanesa spoke firmly, reasserting her authority.

"I don't think I heard anything."

"Well I did. He said something about silver."

"Silver?"

"Yes, 'come back silver'. And he said 'It wasn't me'. Yes, that was it. 'It wasn't my fault Silver.' That's what he said."

"I don't think I heard him, though I could have done, yes I might have done. 'Silver, it wasn't my fault.' Yes, you're right Vanessa, that's what he called after her." Louise persuaded herself, and from that moment really believed, that she had heard the words.

"We must make sure the police know what we saw and heard."

The two sisters watched as the crowd parted to allow the paramedics access to the victim. They had only a few minutes to wait before the ambulance drove away, its siren silent.

"He's dead then." Vanessa said in a matter of fact tone.

"Why do you say that?"

"If there was any hope they'd have had the siren blaring as they headed to A & E as fast as they could. He'll be dead. And look, they're taking her away."

"That policeman's just walking her away. He hasn't even put handcuffs on her."

"Don't be so silly Louise, of course he will have done."

"I don't think he did." Louise said quietly enough for her sister to be able to pretend not to hear.

They sat in silence as they watched two policemen put up a blue and white cordon around the spot where the man had fallen and then start talking to the few people who had remained close to the spot.

"Officer. Officer. We're witnesses you know. We can tell you everything that happened." Vanessa stood up and headed purposefully towards a policeman who was talking to a young woman with a rucksack on her back. "I am a witness, and my sister. We both saw and heard everything."

The policeman registered their names and address on his tablet computer. "When will you get in touch?" Vanessa asked urgently. "My sister and I have valuable information."

"We will be in touch very soon Miss, er," he checked his screen, "Miss Woods."

Happy that she had done everything to ensure her involvement in future proceedings Vanessa took her sister's arm. "Come on Lou, let's get home. I think we both need a stiff scotch before lunch and there's nothing left to see here."

After taking one last look at the blue and white cordon Louise touched her sister tentatively on the arm. "I don't want to speak to the police, Van. I don't think I'd be a very good witness. I really don't want to get involved."

"Oh shut up Lou. Stop being so silly. Of course you saw it all. You saw the same as I did. We both saw that poor man following her into the square and we both heard him calling out to her and we both saw her shoot him then just stand there with the gun in her hand."

"Really Van, I'm not sure."

"Come on Lou, don't be such a wimp. This'll be fun. We've watched enough murder stories and detective stuff on the television now we'll have a real part to play in this one. That woman, whoever she is, is as guilty as sin. It's obvious for all to see."

As they walked away from the scene of so much excitement they passed the parked yellow car but they were so intent on getting home they failed to notice the old man slumped over the steering wheel.

Chapter 2
The Murder Trial begins

A little under a year later Dr Jane Carmichael sat motionless in the dock, her face displaying no emotion. She was determined that not one person amongst all the assembled lawyers, members of the public and especially the press could glimpse any hint of her true feelings.

Her legal team had given her strict instructions.

She was not to let her attention wander for a moment. She was to listen attentively, but she was to show no reaction to anything that might be said during the court proceedings. She was to preserve a demeanour of dignified and detached interest. Above all, she must be patient and have faith in Gordon Hamilton, her barrister, and let him do the job he was exceptionally good at, however unorthodox his approach may seem at times. As she prepared to listen to the prosecution's opening arguments she had every intention of obeying their instructions to the letter.

Three days had been spent selecting the jury and as she looked at the nine women and three men, all white and in various stages of middle-age, she wondered whether the defence or the prosecution had won that phase of the battle. If anything, Jane thought, they looked like people who would believe that the police could do or say no wrong.

Jane's immediate impression of the lead barrister for the prosecution was that the woman was somewhat younger than she was, perhaps in her late thirties or early forties, with intelligent eyes and a quiet voice that invited people to concentrate on what she had to say. Jane had no doubt that what Gordon Hamilton had told her was absolutely true, Maria Stanley was a highly experienced prosecuting QC and she would be a difficult opponent.

As she stood waiting for the judge to appear Jane Carmichael wondered, not for the first time, why the court case seemed to be about 'opponents' 'winning' or 'losing' rather than establishing the truth.

"The prosecution…" Maria Stanley appeared to ignore everyone else in the court as she began to speak directly to the jury "…will prove beyond the possibility of any doubt that on the afternoon of Sunday the 24th day of August 2014 the accused, Dr Jane Carmichael, deliberately and with pre-meditation, shot Detective Inspector David Childs twice, at point blank range. These shots, to his face and to his chest, killed him almost instantly." She paused, Jane thought for dramatic effect, looking away from the jury to the judge and then back at the jury before continuing in a more business-like tone. "The prosecution will present evidence to this court that shows that Dr Carmichael had had a long-standing relationship with her victim, we will explain how that relationship was ended in the weeks prior to the shooting. We will bring witnesses to describe the events of that horrific bank holiday weekend lunchtime, witnesses to an argument in a public house, to the confrontation in the crowded town square and to the very shots that killed Detective Inspector David Childs. We will bring evidence that Dr Carmichael was apprehended by the police standing over her victim, the murder weapon, the gun, still in her hand. We will present evidence that this gun was one to which Dr Carmichael, and most probably Dr Carmichael alone, had access. We will bring expert evidence that no other weapon could have been involved and that DI David Childs' injuries could only have been inflicted by someone standing exactly where Dr Carmichael, and Dr Carmichael alone, stood. We will demonstrate beyond a shadow of doubt that the accused was guilty of this pre-meditated and cold-blooded murder."

Again Maria Stanley paused, took a sip from a plastic mug of water and carefully placed it back down on the desk before continuing, still addressing the jury as though no other person in the court was involved.

"The motive for this callous murder was a very simple one. Dr Carmichael believed that the man who had been her lover for many years had betrayed her. We will bring evidence to the court regarding a scandal which had been the subject of widespread press coverage in the days leading up to the murder. Dr Carmichael believed that only David Childs could have known the details that were published, only David Childs could have alerted the media and only David Childs could have provided the intimate photographs that were used to illustrate the story. Not only did she feel publicly humiliated by being named as the illegitimate daughter of Lord Grahame Johnstone she was incensed that the newspapers also accused Lord Johnstone and her mother of being agents for the Soviet Union throughout the Cold War. Dr Carmichael blamed Detective Inspector Childs for these damning accusations being made public. We, the prosecution, will prove that in an act of calculated retribution Jane Carmichael murdered Detective Inspector David Childs in front of many witnesses. It was a very deliberate and a very public execution."

As she listened Jane Carmichael watched the people in the court go about their business; the women carefully recording every word spoken, the men in black gowns, some with wigs, some without, moving from desk to desk for no apparent reason, the banks of lawyers, three on her team and four on the prosecution, whispering to each other. To none of them was any of this out of the ordinary yet to her, the centre of all the drama, it all seemed very strange indeed.

She sat back on the uncomfortable chair and followed proceedings attentively, as she had been told to do.

'Would you like to question the witness Mister Hamilton?' the judge prompted the young barrister after the first witness, a forensic scientist, had given his evidence.

"No thank you My Lord."

Over the course of the next three weeks Jane Carmichael sat expressionless in the court.

She watched as the police who attended the scene were called to give their accounts of the events of that Sunday afternoon. She heard details of what she had been wearing, what she had been carrying and how she had looked and acted in those minutes in the square. She appeared to be listening disinterestedly as Paramedics described their attempts to save the victim in gruesome detail and she did not flinch, as did some members of the jury, at the photographs of the injuries that were displayed on the screens around the court as forensic pathologists explained the wounds and the manner in which they had been inflicted. She contained her frustration through the two days of evidence during which Detective Sergeant Anne Hill and Detective Constable Ian Spalding, the detectives who had conducted the initial interviews, read from their notebooks giving their stilted and emotionless versions of what had happened in the immediate aftermath of the murder.

Finally she listened carefully as the sequence of eye witnesses repeated what they believed they had seen that day, a year before, in the town square.

They stories were identical. Yes, they were present in the square; yes, they saw the woman they could identify as the accused with the man they could identify as the victim, David Childs. Yes, they heard the gun shot. Yes, they saw the man fall and die. Yes, they saw Jane Carmichael standing over the body, the gun in her hand.

As Maria Stanley finished her questioning of each witness the judge turned to Gordon Hamilton and every time his answer was 'No questions My Lord.'

He did not contradict the expert evidence regarding the injuries sustained and the weapon used. He did not dispute that the revolver had belonged to Richard Mackenzie and that Jane Carmichael would have had access to it. He did not ask why the forensic evidence stopped short of describing any kind of residue on Jane Carmichael's hands or clothes. Nor did he question the evidence given by the first seven of the nine men and women who had given witness statements to the police.

As the days of evidence passed Jane Carmichael found it increasingly difficult to understand her legal team's tactics.

Gordon Hamilton asked no questions and contested the evidence of not one witness.

Every time he answered 'No questions, thank you My Lord' to the judge's enquiry she wondered whether he was honestly planning to prove her innocence or whether their conversations, during which he had given her hope that he believed in her innocence, had been a charade.

After three weeks she was beginning to lose faith in those who were supposed to be her defence. 'Perhaps' she found herself thinking, 'Gordon Hamilton is one of the enemy.' Perhaps he was connected to Eric Atkinson and whoever it was who was behind his schemes. Perhaps he wanted to see her found guilty.

'If only...' Jane Carmichael thought many times through the long days in court.

There were so many if onlys.

If only David Childs had not spent much of his life obsessed with the idea of the girl he had always called 'Silver Birch'.

If only she had been strong enough to stick to her refusal when he had insisted she join him for a drink that Sunday lunchtime.

But the most important 'if only' of all was one over which she had had no control.

'If only' she thought time and time again as the trial progressed, 'if only, I had not been born my parents' daughter'.

Chapter 3
London, July 1958

'Following the most successful visit of the British Prime Minister in March of this year, and at the personal invitation of Chairman Nikita Sergeyevich Khrushchev, the recently appointed British Minister of Education, Grahame Johnstone, is to make an informal visit to Moscow. Chairman Khrushchev is known to take a keen interest in the education of our young people and is eager to explore ways in which our two countries can cooperate. The Minister will be accompanied on the short visit to Moscow by a small delegation to include Sir Michael Fox.'

The invitation, issued by the Soviet Embassy in London, created some consternation in the intelligence services of more than one country. In the time of the ever more dangerous Cold War every politician in every nation was the subject of intense scrutiny and it was common knowledge that Grahame Johnstone had for some years, albeit before the war, been a member of the Communist Party of Great Britain.

Although he had changed his political allegiance when he entered politics he had had to persuade many people that the views he had held in his youth had simply been a naïve response to the rise of fascism. After his election to Parliament in 1950 he claimed to be as anti-Soviet as anyone in the House. 'Not only have I left communism, communism has left me' he repeated as a mantra whenever the subject was raised.

The invitation also caused considerable interest in the Houses of Parliament.

There were malicious whispers in the corridors of Westminster and Whitehall, by those who did not wish Grahame Johnstone well, that it was 'interesting' that it was he who had been invited rather than his well-respected, and far more experienced, predecessor. They also found it 'interesting' that, despite his communist history, he had been allowed to visit the United States. These purveyors of innuendo also wondered why it would be Sir Michael Fox accompanying the newly promoted minister, rather than a more robust politician.

In some people's eyes Sir Michael Fox showed what could have been a dangerous sympathy towards the Soviet bloc. He had been at Yalta with Churchill and had been friendly with Stalin and even after travel between the two countries had become almost impossible Sir Michael had managed to make regular visits to one or other of the many friends he had in the Soviet Union. Many who knew the name but not the man assumed that Sir Michael had been awarded his knighthood for the length of his public service rather than its quality. They were not to know that he had been recognised for his unpublicised role with the British security services.

A week before the planned visit Richard Mackenzie stood outside a heavy baize lined door awaiting the instruction to enter.

He had been a policeman for five years, for three of those as a member of a Specialist Operations group responsible for protecting, and reporting on the actions of, prominent politicians. In the two months he had been assigned to Grahame Johnstone he had accompanied him on his visits to Washington and to Paris but the briefings for those visits had been routine. Richard had never been called to a meeting in the anonymous office block just off the Strand.

"Good morning Mackenzie. Sit down. Smoke?" Sir Michael Fox extended a welcome to the young officer.

"No thank you sir, I don't."

Richard took his place in the only free chair around the low coffee table in front of the fireplace. He knew Sir Michael, of course, but he recognised neither of the other two men seated in the comfortable armchairs and was interested that they were not introduced to him. He had not expected others to be present and he had not expected the meeting to be so informal.

"What do you know of Miss Georgina Carmichael?" Sir Michael asked without preamble, concentrating on closing the lid of a large silver cigarette box.

Richard looked at the other two men mentally assigning them the names Glasses and Redhead.

"I know that she accompanies Mr Johnstone on all his official engagements." The question was the only one for which he was unprepared. He decided to say as little as possible.

"And?"

"She is his assistant."

"And?"

"She is his lover." Richard realised all three men knew and he could see nothing would be gained in hiding his knowledge.

"You will have learned a great deal about Mr Johnstone's life in the time you have been with him?" The man Richard had named Redhead made the statement a question.

"I have been assigned to Mr Johnstone only since April but he does not appear to be an overly secretive man. They are perfectly professional in public but there is more to their relationship than just friendship."

"I can confirm that." Redhead added.

"Detail please." Sir Michael prompted, nodding towards Redhead. "It is important we all are made aware of all the circumstances."

"Georgina Carmichael and Grahame Johnstone met in 1941 at the Ministry of Fuel and Power. Both were gifted mathematicians with similar interests in the field of statistics and were assigned to the same section. Miss Carmichael was only 18, straight out of school, and it appears that Mr Johnstone, only a couple of years older but much more worldly wise and confident, took her under his wing. We are led to believe that there was nothing intimate in their relationship at that time, they simply shared an interest in playing with numbers." Redhead made obvious his disdain for people who preferred mathematics to the study of the classics. "When the war ended and Mr Johnstone began his career in politics Miss Carmichael joined him as his assistant. She worked in his constituency office in Hampshire and now also in London. There was never any indication of any liaison between them until this past Easter when they spent a weekend together in Devon."

"Good, good." Sir Michael said thoughtfully. "As I thought. Mackenzie? Your view?"

"I was not assigned until after Easter so I am unaware of the Devon trip but I can say that they spend two evenings together each week, every Tuesday and Thursday, at her flat in Putney." Richard confirmed. "He appears to be careful, he never stays through the night, always leaves soon after midnight and walks back over the river to his home in Chelsea. I have never seen him take a taxi or a bus, in either direction though it must be a couple of miles or more."

"But you are sure they are not simply having a meal? Listening to the wireless or watching the television?"

"I have seen no shadows on the curtain, sir, so we cannot be absolutely certain, but I can think of no other reason why he would visit her flat so regularly and until the small hours of the morning and then be so careful as to have no link with the area."

"You're probably right. He lives alone?"

"Yes. He has a woman to clean and cook for him but she is only his daily."

"Do you believe Miss Carmichael to be his only mistress?" Sir Michael asked Redhead while Richard wondered why the meeting seemed focused on Grahame Johnstone's love life.

"I wouldn't describe her as his mistress, not in the strict sense of the term, in that she is not kept by him. As far as we can see no money changes hands. Miss Carmichael has always paid her own rent by cheque. She has a bank account into which her monthly salary cheque is paid by Johnstone's constituency party. She is not unduly highly paid, even after her recent pay rise, at £60 per month. She also does some freelance work for which she is paid irregular sums but we know the source of those." Richard thought Redhead showed a great deal of knowledge about Georgina's life and wondered why she was so important.

"Very interesting. We shall call her his 'lover' then. Are you able to tell me whether he has another 'lover'?" Sir Michael prompted tetchily. He did not like being corrected.

"Laura Cromwell." Redhead said firmly.

"Really? Sir Michael said thoughtfully. "They sleep together?"

Redhead nodded.

"How do you view this Mackenzie?"

"I agree. They meet in London but are never seen out together. Also in the last month Mr Johnstone has been invited to two weekend house parties at her parents' home near Arundel in Sussex, weekends to which, I should make clear, Miss Carmichael is never invited."

"Nor would she be." Redhead added.

"Is he perhaps courting Miss Cromwell more formally, with a view to marriage?" Sir Michael suggested.

"We sincerely hope that that is the case." Glasses spoke for the first time. "Miss Cromwell would be a far more suitable spouse, being a member of one of that small number of families that has run this country, in one way or another, since Tudor times. Miss Carmichael, for all her talents and attractions, cannot be allowed to be his wife, not with the career we have mapped out for Grahame Johnstone."

"And what is that, just for the benefit of our less politically minded colleagues?" Sir Michael asked.

"He is to be Education Minister for only a year, during which time he will raise his profile on the international stage. He will be promoted to Foreign Secretary in the next reshuffle. After the next election he will be Chancellor of the Exchequer and then Prime Minister, probably in two general elections time."

Richard briefly wondered how many elections, both public and private, would be rigged to get Grahame Johnstone the career that was being planned for him by unknown men in secretive meetings.

"But there is a fly in the ointment. The Cromwell family won't have him if they get a sniff of his involvement with Miss Carmichael and I'm afraid we cannot allow that. In fact it is our preference that that relationship, on any level, comes to an end as soon as possible." Glasses showed no embarrassment in acknowledging his power over the lives of others. "It is not only in the party's interests but also, I think we are agreed, those of the country that no one in society or in Westminster or, heaven forbid, in the press, learns of the intimacy between them. "That is where you come in Mackenzie. You must make sure they are discreet until we can bring the liaison to its inevitable conclusion."

Richard nodded as he wondered at the conceit of men who so arrogantly dictated the relationships of others. Glasses, he decided, was a party man, a political fixer, planning the next twenty years of government, probably with the collusion of many who should be politically neutral. He thought Redhead had to be a member of the intelligence services, probably MI5.

"We are all agreed it must end but our reasons are different. Whereas the party which this gentleman serves wishes to protect the career of Mr Johnstone it is our duty to protect Miss Carmichael." Sir Michael continued. "Mackenzie will need to know why." He spoke to Redhead who turned towards Richard for the first time.

"You must know that Miss Georgina Carmichael is one of us."

"One of us?" Richard asked, unsure what was meant.

"She works for me."

"This is the 'freelance work' she gets paid for?" Richard asked.

"It is a measure of her skill that you had no idea." Redhead looked towards Sir Michael who nodded so he continued. "Miss Carmichael first came to our attention when she applied to the wartime Civil Service. Thorough checks were done, as you would expect, and it soon became clear that 'Miss Georgina Carmichael' did not exist. You may read this to learn her background." He handed Richard a thin buff coloured file.

The room was silent for the five minutes it took Richard to read the two closely typed sheets. When he finished reading he passed the file back to Redhead.

"Now, where was I? Ah yes. We were attracted by the fact that she speaks several dialects of Russian as fluently and flawlessly as she does English, a skill that has been extremely useful to us in ways I will not explore with you today."

"I had no idea."

"Her long friendship with Mr Johnstone, and the trust he reposes in her, was an unexpected bonus of which we have taken full advantage."

"She spies on him?"

"I wouldn't put it quite that way but she is, inevitably, able to report more of his thoughts and actions than you are."

"She is one of us, Mackenzie," Sir Michael repeated "and it is most important that you keep her out of harm's way. It would be difficult to overstate her importance to this country as it fights its corner in this Cold War. You will not let on to her that you know anything of this but you should know that Miss Carmichael is as much your responsibility as is Grahame Johnstone."

"We require two things of you in Moscow." Redhead continued. "Firstly you must ensure that Miss Carmichael and Mr Johnstone do not find themselves in any compromising position. Embassies are dangerous places, no one can be trusted, the slightest snippet of gossip is magnified by their siege mentalities. Secondly you must ensure Miss Carmichael does not find herself in any situation which may be misconstrued or misinterpreted as compromising her loyalty to this country."

Sir Michael stood as if to end Richard's involvement in the meeting.

"One final thing Mackenzie. It has been decided that this Moscow junket is an opportunity to confirm Grahame Johnstone's loyalty to his country. Some, it seems, require evidence that he will not compromise them at some later date in his career. They seem to think him unsound and that he must be discovered before they are too much associated with him. Sometimes we have to serve our political masters. A test has been put in place."

"What test?"

"It is not necessary for you to know the details."

Richard stood up, nodded towards Glasses and Redhead and walked towards the door.

"Remember Mackenzie, it is your job to keep Miss Carmichael safe from those who wish her harm."

As Richard left the room he could have no idea that that was to be his lifetime's work.

Chapter 4
Moscow, July 1958 Day 1

A week after the meeting in London two identical limousines with blacked out windows led the small convoy of vehicles that sped down the wide and empty boulevards of Moscow towards the British Embassy.

Sitting comfortably in the back of the lead car Grahame Johnstone and Georgina Carmichael talked with the familiarity of their long friendship while the third occupant of the car, Sir Michael Fox sat, his eyes closed apparently unconcerned and uninterested.

"The roads are weirdly quiet." Georgina said as she peered through the darkened windows out onto the street.

"I don't suppose many are allowed to own cars." Grahame answered reasonably.

"But there are so few people walking about and the weather's lovely."

"I believe only party officials are allowed cars, though that might be a bit of a politically inspired exaggeration."

No one watching them or listening in on their conversation would have thought them anything other than long-standing colleagues.

"There are a few people sitting at the tables outside that café. But there aren't many walking around. It looks like a really lovely city to walk around. Do you think we would be allowed to?"

"What do you think Sir Michael?" Grahame looked across at Sir Michael to see if permission would be granted.

Without opening his eyes Sir Michael answered. "It might be difficult to arrange."

"It would be nice to have just half an hour or so doing something other than being whisked around in limousines and doing exactly as we're told." Georgina said rather wistfully. "I'd love to actually see Red Square and the Kremlin after all that we hear."

"Do you think it might be possible Sir Michael?" Grahame pressed.

Sir Michael opened his eyes. "I'll certainly ask. You have a full agenda but perhaps there will be some leeway."

"Yes please do, Sir Michael, it would be lovely." Georgina turned to Grahame and smiled. He had no idea she was doing exactly as she had been instructed.

In the second limousine Richard Mackenzie sat opposite an old adversary, Eric Atkinson.

The two had had a mutual and deep-seated dislike of each other from the days when they had first met at the National Police College. They had been equal in achievement and, since they had both been highly competitive, they were in conflict with each other through much of their training.

"Fancy seeing you playing nursemaid to that piece of shit and his tart."

"Nice to see you too Eric."

Eric Atkinson held the official position of third cultural attaché in the British Embassy in Moscow despite having no interest in the arts of either his countrymen or of the Soviets. In 1956 he had answered an obscure advertisement in the London Evening News. Two months after an interview he felt had gone well, he was invited to join MI6.

"All that kowtowing. Not what you trained for was it?"

"No doubt you're doing something far more suited to your talents."

"You'd be surprised what I get up to."

"I doubt it."

Eric Atkinson did not presume to know why this visit had been engineered but he was sure there was more to it than just developing educational links between the two countries which were, after all, practically at war with each other.

He had made it his business to see a list of the members of the delegation and make his own enquiries. Just in case he might find anything that might be useful to him.

Eric had been told by people he believed that there was nothing suspect about Sir Michael but he had checked up anyway.

Grahame Johnstone's love of communism through his school and university days was well documented but as Eric read through newspapers and less public documents he became convinced that there had been no change of heart. Grahame Johnstone had been at school with, had gone to university with, or had been friends with, a number of men who were turning out to be traitors. Eric was going to watch the minister very closely in the next two days and if he could expose him doing anything suspicious it could only be as good for his own career as it would be bad for Grahame Johnstone's.

Unexpectedly, Eric had found his research into Miss Georgina Carmichael the most interesting of the three.

The flaws in her official history were not obvious but he had found them. And he had seen the way to kill two birds with one stone.

Trap her and, because of her close association with the minister, he would be condemned too.

It was going to be so simple.

One way or another they would leave Moscow wishing they had never been.

Richard was unpacking his case in the room he had been allocated for the two nights he was to spend in the Embassy when the door opened and Eric walked in and sat down in the only chair in the room.

"Is he fucking her?" Eric asked conversationally as he reached inside his pocket for his cigarette case. "She's getting on a bit now for that sort of thing. If I were him I'd move on to something a bit younger."

"Come in, make yourself at home why don't you?"

"Still the sarcastic lying bastard then?"

Richard did not answer.

"Well is he?"

"Is he what?"

"Still fucking her."

"What makes you think he is?"

"Fucking obvious mate. You just have to see them together. You're supposed to be a policeman. Surely even one as brainless as you can't have missed it."

Richard was not going to let Eric make him lose his temper. "They are just good friends."

"Fucking good friends if you ask me." Eric laughed at his own joke.

"I didn't."

"What about security?"

"Security?"

"Well wouldn't that sort of thing lay your precious politician open to a spot of blackmail. It wouldn't do his career any good either if Joe Public found out he was fucking his secretary."

"First off he is not fucking her, as you put it, and second off Georgina Carmichael is not his secretary, they work together, she is his assistant if you have to give her a label."

"Have it your own way." Eric continued, enjoying himself. "Anyway, apart from her being a bit past her best what do you know about our Miss Carmichael?" He patted his pockets, searching for his matches, showing that he had no intention of leaving Richard on his own for a while.

"Enough." Richard stayed standing, apparently concentrating on adjusting his shaving kit around the basin in the corner of the room. He didn't want Eric to think their conversation was going to be a long one. He was wondering why Eric wanted to talk about Georgina Carmichael rather than Grahame Johnstone. Had Sir Michael known that that would happen? Is that why there was that strange meeting the previous week? He would have to be on his guard.

"She's been vetted presumably?" Eric's dry tone showed he didn't believe that the process undertaken by some people was always as diligent as it should be.

"Of course, she'd have to have been. Why?"

"When?"

"When she joined the Ministry of Power or whatever it was called, in the war. She was a civil servant before she worked with Mr Johnstone."

"Bloody wartime recruit was she? No wonder it wasn't done properly."

"She will have had her annual assessments."

"Fat load of use they are."

"Do you think there might be the problem then?"

"Things get missed." Eric replied slyly. "We can't take anything on trust, especially not the way things are here."

"Here?"

"Moscow, mate. Can't trust anyone to do anything right, so I ran my own checks."

Richard knew that Sir Michael and Redhead would be interested to know how much Eric had discovered about Georgina.

"OK. And what did you find?"

"Far more than whoever it was that did her checks."

"I suppose you're going to tell me whatever it is you think you've found." Richard sounded irritated.

Eric said nothing while he lit his cigarette and exhaled in exaggerated fashion, blowing a steady stream of smoke across the room. "Why would I want to do that?"

"Because you have always wanted to show how bloody clever you are. You just can't resist it can you?"

As Richard sat down on the edge of the narrow bed Eric smiled, slowly took another long drag on his cigarette and blew out another stream of the pungent smoke across the room. Eric congratulated himself on winning the first round in their encounter, 'the prat couldn't get rid of me. That's one nil to the home side'.

"What have I learned about your Georgina Carmichael?" He began.

"She is not 'my' Georgina."

"You'd like her to be though wouldn't you?" Eric looked slyly at Richard to see if he had hit home, and knew he had. "You fancy your chances with her? You're even more of a fool than I thought. You're nowhere near her league, even if she is past her best, what is she? Thirty-five? And she's probably desperate for a husband, but however desperate she might be she's not going to go for a runt like you. Not in a million years old son."

Richard was not going to let Eric provoke him and he said nothing.

In the silence Eric took a long drag on his cigarette before beginning to answer Richard's question. "I've learned that your Georgina is a bit of a mystery."

Still Richard said nothing.

"What do you know about where she comes from, who she is, you know the stuff a minder should know about his charge?"

"She's not my 'charge' as you put it, Mr Johnstone is."

"Same difference as far as I'm concerned. What do you know about her?"

"Not a lot because it hasn't been my job to know." Richard was happy to play the game.

"Well the first thing I can tell you is her name's not 'Georgina Carmichael'. She probably got that off a gravestone somewhere. Her real name is Selina Schreiber."

"Who?" Richard had to find out how much Eric had learned about Georgina.

"Selina Schreiber. She's the daughter of Hermann and Alexandrina Schreiber though I should say 'was the daughter' as they both copped it in the blitz."

"She's German?" Richard hoped his voice betrayed curiosity.

"Not exactly."

"Not exactly what?"

"Not exactly German."

"So? She's from Eastern Europe." Richard deliberately misinterpreted Eric's statement. "A great many people escaped Poland, Czechoslovakia, Hungary all sorts of places like that before the war and have been perfectly good citizens, contributing to the war effort and the recovery since."

"Calm down. Of course I know they did. I'm not as stupid as you'd like to think." Eric stubbed out his cigarette in the ashtray on the small table that separated them and immediately lit another before continuing, enjoying his feeling of having a hold over Richard. "The Schreibers were ethnic Germans..."

Richard continued to interrupt. It was important that Eric should not pick up on the fact that nothing he was saying was news to him. "And the Germans are no longer our enemies, they are our allies in this Cold War. You really must move on Eric. It's the Soviets we're all worrying about now or hadn't you understood that?"

"Exactly. I said the Schreibers were ethnic Germans, not Germans. They were *ethnic* Germans. They didn't come from Germany, they came from Russia."

"Russia?" Richard had to accept that Eric's investigations had been rather too thorough.

"You will know, of course, that a hundred years ago thousands of Germans were encouraged to settle on the plains of Russia. Despite holding on to much of their German culture they became, to all intents and purposes, Russian."

"So Georgina's parents were Russian?" Richard thought Eric would expect him to ask such a question.

"They were. But very conveniently all their documents were destroyed when their house was bombed."

"And her parents were killed." Richard thought that that might have been considered more important than the destruction of identity papers.

"Very convenient that."

"You think they phoned Hitler and gave them their address so Georgina's papers could be destroyed?"

"Don't be so fucking pathetic."

"It's just that you seem to suspect her of something. What? And why? There are millions of immigrants in England, perfectly good citizens, just doing the best they can for their new country."

"But there aren't so many working quite so close to the centre of government, not being fucked by a man who thinks he is a future Prime Minister."

"You are wrong there."

But Eric ignored him. "Selina Schreiber isn't just any old immigrant. She was born a Russian. Even you will understand why that is of interest to us now she is back in the country of her birth."

"You think she's a spy?"

"Come on Richard, no one used the word 'spy'. I believe she's a traitor gathering what information she can from her pillow talk and feeding it back to Moscow. Even you can see she's wangled herself into a very nice position to do that very effectively. Where's she been already with Johnstone? Paris last month? Washington before that? Here now? Where next? Bonn? Very handy."

Richard was trying to work out if Eric really believed she was an agent for the Russians and, if he did, would that be more or less dangerous than his knowing the truth. He decided that Sir Michael, Redhead and even Glasses would not want MI6, for whom Eric undoubtedly worked, to know that MI5 had suspicions about Grahame Johnstone.

"She's British." Richard said firmly. "She was brought up an English girl. She has lived and worked in England for practically all her life, she's proved her loyalty by working all through the war and since. And she is not Grahame Johnstone's mistress. I really don't see what you're getting at." He felt Eric would expect him to support Georgina.

"Just because someone lives in England doesn't make them English."

"Of course it doesn't. But she is."

"Immigrants keep to themselves don't they? Ghettoes of them, sticking together, keeping themselves to themselves."

"Possibly some, not all."

"Well the Schreibers did. When they first arrived in England they lived and worked with other Russians."

"So?"

"The Schreibers had lost everything in 1917 but they weren't against the revolution."

"You are saying they left the country even though they were Bolsheviks?"

"Do I have to give you a history lesson?"

"If you must."

"They were just one family amongst thousands who left their farms because they'd have died of starvation if they hadn't."

"You can't blame them then can you?"

"Many of their sort made it to America where they reckoned they'd have the freedom to spread their socialist revolutionary ideas. More fool them. Anyway the Schreibers only got as far as London, Hammersmith to be precise."

"Were they Jewish?" Richard was still pressing to discover the extent of Eric's information.

"No. They had no religion. They were communists, that was all they believed in."

"So they were communist immigrants. That doesn't make them traitors to their adopted country."

"Well it bloody well gives them a head start. In 1928 they somehow got hold of birth certificates and papers and managed to hide their past. That's not the act of innocent people is it? No. They did that because they wanted to disappear."

"So they changed their names? No one wanted to have a German name then, not even the Royal Family."

"Yes, there was quite an industry in finding new identities. It's made it quite difficult for us to track who some people really were and where they really came from.

I struck lucky with the Schreibers." Richard noticed he didn't say how. "They may have changed their names but there was one thing they couldn't change, and that was their politics."

"Their politics?"

"Their communism. They organised a communist cell."

Richard felt he could justify their position. "So what? Communism wasn't illegal then, it isn't now."

"Possibly not." Eric sounded anything but convinced. "But they didn't just join the Communist Party, they were activists, organising, and recruiting for the cause."

"How could Georgina have been an 'activist'? She couldn't have been more than a child."

"They catch them when they're young. By the time she was 14 she was as active as any adult could have been. She was a very clever girl, your little Selina-Georgina."

Richard chose to ignore the scorn in Eric's voice.

"If you condemn Georgina and her family for being members of the CPGB you'd be condemning most of the civil service and half of today's House of Commons, not to mention, in all probability, the odd member of the Royal family. Intellectuals, industrialists, all perfectly respectable and responsible members of English society, were communists. They saw it as the only way to beat fascism and prevent another World War. And who's to say they weren't wrong when you see how things turned out?"

"People like Grahame Johnstone?" Eric said pointedly.

"Times change. People change. Mr Johnstone may have been a member of the party when he was younger but now he's no more a communist than you and I and Miss Carmichael is no traitor."

"I say they both need careful observation."

"I suppose you've got evidence of all this?"

"Oh yes. I've got evidence. It wasn't difficult once you knew where to look." Eric took another long drag on his cigarette. "But don't think for a moment I'm going to share any of it with you."

"I don't believe you have any evidence at all. You've found out what you think is her history and your paranoia is making up the rest. You have no proof simply because there can be none because she is not what you say she is."

"No? You've never thought it might be possible?"

"No. Never. Why would I?"

"You wouldn't because you have no nose for these things. You are, and always will be, nothing but a babysitter."

"Whereas you are a spy-catcher?" Richard loaded his voice with sarcasm.

"I will be." Eric took the question at its face value. "Maclean and Burgess escaped justice but what of the others? There'll be others won't there? Of course there will. There'll be a third and a fourth and a fifth and a sixth man. Aren't you worried who those men, or women, might be?"

Eric left the question hanging in the air as he took another long drag of his pungent local cigarette then stubbed it out inefficiently so the room soon filled with its sharp fumes. He carefully extracted another cigarette from his case and lit it, daring Richard to stop him.

"You think Grahame Johnstone is one of them?" Richard eventually asked, knowing it was a risky question, but one he felt he should ask.

Eric didn't reply, simply looking squarely at Richard and blinking slowly.

"Everyone knows Grahame Johnstone is now as much a part of the establishment as it is possible to be." Richard continued.

"Not everyone thinks that."

"They should."

"Why?"

"Because he is beyond suspicion."

"You might like to think so."

"I am not alone in knowing so."

"You're very sure."

"I am."

43

"You shouldn't be."

"I am. You're wrong Eric, totally wrong. There is absolutely nothing suspect about either of them."

"So you say, but while she's on my patch I'll keep a very close eye on her and I'm cleverer than she is. Your little Fraulein Schreiber will make a mistake. And I'll get her."

"Don't call her that."

"What you think and what you do when you are in England is no business of mine but while you're here I'd appreciate it if you did your job."

"What do you mean by that?"

"Well it seems that that bumbling old tosser Sir Michael Fox has informed us we are to arrange for your Mr Johnstone and his fraulein to leave the Embassy and go for a little walkies tomorrow evening. Apparently they want to see Red Square and the Kremlin. Don't you think that just a tad suspicious?"

"Are they going to be allowed to?" Richard asked. This was news to him. Sir Michael had said nothing, but then they had arranged to meet later that evening so perhaps something was to be said then. Perhaps this was something to do with the test that had been prepared by Sir Michael for Grahame.

"It seems so. As long as they stick to a prescribed route and don't dawdle or chat to any of the natives."

"Presumably they won't have much chance to do that as you'll be keeping an eye on them."

The look Eric gave him said that he was stupid even to consider the possibility that they would be allowed to leave the Embassy without a great deal of company. "Oh yes, I will certainly be doing that. Don't you worry, I'll be keeping a close eye on them and so will you. And you'll have to tell me what you see them doing and if I see something that you don't tell me about I'll know you're in it with them won't I?"

"You're a paranoid bastard Eric. You always have been and no doubt you always will be."

"Well I don't trust you, or him, or her, and I'm not the only one."

"Who else?" Richard asked. It would be useful for him to know.

"Anyone with any sense." Eric said dismissively.

Eric stood up, made a point of slowly stubbing out his cigarette and left the room. Richard got up from the bed and opened the window, looking out through the bars at the rose garden idyllic in the sunshine, and breathing fresh air.

An hour later Richard was in Sir Michael's office.

"Well?"

"I've had a long chat with Eric Atkinson."

"And?"

"He knows all about Miss Carmichael's origins."

"I thought he might. And?"

"He has his suspicions that she is only playing the role of innocent personal assistant. He says she is an agent for the Russians, listening to what Mr Johnstone says on their pillow and reporting back to Moscow."

"He does, does he?"

"I don't think he has anything that could be called hard evidence. I think he just has vague and circumstantial suspicions. I don't think he has any idea what kind of work she's really involved in. I thought it better that he thinks she's a Russian agent rather than one for MI5."

"Quite right too. We don't want anyone knowing who we're keeping tabs on do we? What has he on Grahame Johnstone?"

"He believes he is still a communist and is probably part of the university espionage ring. He won't be able to prove that, of course, but he could easily incriminate him through Georg..., that is through Miss Carmichael."

"You didn't...."

"No. I didn't. Every time he said that they were.... well, every time he seemed to be trying to get me to confirm they had a relationship I said they were just friends but I'm sure he doesn't believe me. My guess is that he'd love to catch either or both of them in some incriminating or ambiguous position. I'm not sure why he has such an interest in them."

"He's an ambitious one. I was told he was like a Jack Russell terrier, snapping and yapping at people's heels until he gets what he wants. Two probably perfectly innocent assistant secretaries have been returned to London because of your friend Atkinson's persistent suspicions."

"He's no friend of mine."

"You knew him though? At Police College?"

"I did. We never got on."

"I did wonder when I saw you were there at the same time."

Richard wondered whether he could ask Sir Michael why he would be interested in the minute details of the careers of two lowly officers but before he could say anything Sir Michael smiled. "Nothing, Mackenzie, is ever left to chance. Your acquaintance with Atkinson could be useful or it could be a hindrance. I judged it would be useful as his animosity towards you might lead to his showing off and giving away more of his plans."

"Atkinson did say that they are going to be allowed to take a walk out into the city tomorrow evening."

"Yes. It has been agreed that they are to leave the Embassy at six and have half an hour to walk over the river to Red Square. This is to be our opportunity to check something of Grahame Johnstone's loyalties. A verbal message and a sealed envelope will be passed to him. He knows nothing and is not expecting it. We will find out much about him. If he says nothing to you, or if he hands over the envelope having opened it, then we will know that he has something to hide. It will not be proof, but it will be some sort of evidence against him. Very little is ever proof in this game."

"It might give Atkinson a chance to do something tricky though mightn't it?"

"We cannot back out of our arrangement now."

"And Miss Carmichael knows about this?"

"She does."

"Aren't her loyalties going to be divided? I mean she won't want him disgraced will she?"

"I beg your pardon?"

"I mean she's in love with him isn't she?"

"Is she? Whatever makes you think that?"

Richard thought for a moment before replying. "Then she's a bloody good actress."

"Miss Carmichael is a complete professional and she will not succumb to any female emotional entanglements."

"She has me convinced."

"She is well aware that we hold all the cards. If she steps out of line we can rescind her right to stay in Britain. She cannot risk that."

"She won't then? Step out of line I mean."

"She has not, so far, shown any sign of doing so, but it is as well for us to have the whip as well as the carrot. She is too useful to us to allow your Mr Atkinson to be successful in whatever it is he has planned for her. For the time being at any rate."

Richard thought for a few moments before asking what seemed, to him, to be a perfectly obvious question. "But won't the giving of the note and the passing of the verbal message be an opportunity for someone to misconstrue Miss Carmichael's role? Exactly the situation we are trying to prevent?"

"The contact and the location have been carefully chosen and no one who wishes her ill will be watching at the precise moment the encounter takes place. You should know that the letter contains nothing of great importance, we simply want to see if Johnstone hands it over unopened. However, we really do need to know what the man making contact says to them. You should know that the contact, we shall call him Berndt, is a very important participant in this game we play."

In a room on the other side of the Embassy Eric Atkinson was making his own arrangements for the following evening.

His plan was a simple one. As Grahame Johnstone and the woman walked over the bridge a man would go up to them, engage them in conversation. Another man, with a long-range camera, would photograph this interaction and within hours of their leaving the country those photographs would be in the hands of the BBC and every Fleet Street news desk. No facts would be necessary, no details would be required, the innuendo would be sufficient to bring Grahame Johnstone's career to an end.

Eric Atkinson had no doubt whatsoever that Grahame Johnstone was a traitor and if it meant fabricating evidence to get him out of the position where he could harm his country then that was what would be done.

Official charges may never be brought, but Eric saw no problem in that. Once his plan had worked Grahame Johnstone would be out of government and Fraulein Schreiber would be denounced and deported as the traitor she undoubtedly was.

'Two birds with one stone' Eric thought, satisfied that his simple plan could not fail. 'And perhaps even three.'

For while he would be believed and would be given the recognition, and the promotion, he deserved Richard Mackenzie would undoubtedly be dismissed the service.

Chapter 5
Moscow, July 1958 Day 2

"Today you will be visiting two technicums where you will allow yourselves to be suitably impressed. Technicums are like British technical schools, one up from a secondary modern school but not quite a grammar, though here in the Soviet Union it is the brightest children who are chosen to have the best education, unlike in Britain where, however clever you are, you will be at the bottom of the pile if your family hasn't got any money."

Eric Atkinson gave Grahame Johnstone and Georgina Carmichael his briefing on the day's schedule as they were driven through the empty streets to their first appointment. School had done nothing for him, he'd learned everything he needed in the army, and now he was telling a government minister what he had to do. He was enjoying himself.

"You will be expected to comment favourably on the social skills of the students. They believe the English school child is innately ill-mannered and ill-behaved and that they are beaten into toeing the line by the birch and the ruler. Here they never have to resort to corporal punishment as every student values their education." Eric paused to check that they were still taking notice of him and that they both realised that he believed the Soviets were absolutely right on that.

"Odd as it may seem, in this country they seem to value educating girls to the same level as boys so make sure you comment on the work of at least one female student. Personally I think it's a waste of resources educating them, how can they be useful in industry and science?" He looked squarely at Georgina. "Women, after all, don't get where they want to be because of their brains do they?"

He ignored the look from Grahame Johnstone that told him he had overstepped the mark and continued to give his instructions for the day.

"Ask the questions we sent you in your briefing notes, and make sure you ask different questions at the different establishments, there will be discussion on every aspect of your visits long after you have returned to London."

Eric settled back in the limousine happy that he had complete control of the situation.

The day went to plan as the Education Minister and his assistant allowed themselves to be shown everything their hosts wanted them to see. They sat in the front of classes where well-rehearsed pupils of both sexes recited obscure sections of Shakespeare then followed up, in perfectly accented English, with detailed comparisons of the workings of diesel and internal combustion engines and suggestions for their improved design.

As they walked back to the limousine after their final visit Grahame and Georgina were able to speak for the first time that day with no one to overhear their conversation.

"You know what's different about Moscow?" Georgina asked, resisting the impulse to tuck her hand in the crook of Grahame's arm.

"Well pretty much everything, but what in particular did you have in mind?" Grahame smiled as he replied, relieved that the day had gone so smoothly.

"They've all treated me as your equal. They've shaken my hand first more often than not and they've spoken to me as often as to you."

"So?"

"They would never have treated me like that in England."

"No?"

"No. Have you never noticed? In England they ignore me. I am invisible because I'm a woman."

"I'm sure I have no idea what you mean but remind me to do something for the position of women when I'm Prime Minister." He tried to laugh her comments away.

Having made her point Georgina changed the subject. "That ghastly little man from the Embassy seems intent on showing you how important he is."

"He's a nasty little creep, certainly, and I wish he'd made it marginally less obvious that he thinks my visit is a complete waste of time and effort."

"I don't trust him." Georgina ventured.

"Forget him. He's not important. What is important is that I'm seen to be open to talking to the Soviets."

"Is that why you were invited?"

"That is why we accepted. I was invited so that I could take the message back to the West that the USSR is now a very modern country and is having no problem keeping up with the West in the field of technology. I'm here to report back that Soviet education is infinitely superior to ours, that their students are more intelligent and better informed than ours and that their future is brighter."

"Unfortunately I suspect that all that is actually true."

"We can certainly learn some things from what I've seen today."

"Such as?"

"Encouraging science education for girls?" He grinned and Georgina squeezed his arm as the driver opened the door of the limousine.

"Seriously though, the most important part of my trip yet to come."

"The reception tonight?"

Grahame nodded. "There will be important people there, people I will need to charm, people who must know that Britain is not war-mongering but that we will stand our ground if forced into a corner."

"But before that we've got our walk. I'm looking forward to that."

Their opportunity for more private conversation ended as Richard and Eric Atkinson took their places in the limousine.

"I'm looking forward to our walk." Georgina repeated brightly as she walked with Grahame into the Embassy foyer "We've got just enough time before getting ready for the reception."

A man who Georgina did not recognise came up to Grahame and whispered something she could not catch and walked quickly away.

"I'm so sorry, I'm going to have to disappoint you." Grahame turned to Georgina. "I have papers to sign, that blessed red box! The department has taken so much trouble to get it here so I cannot ignore it, now can I?"

She knew it was an excuse. He would have known all day that there would be a box of cabinet papers waiting for him. He could have gone on the walk had he chosen to. She wondered why he was backing out at the last minute.

"Still here?" Sir Michael strode purposefully into the foyer. "I would have thought you would be out enjoying this lovely evening sunshine."

"There's been a change of plan." Grahame spoke almost too brightly. "I have my box to attend to so Miss Carmichael will be going for her evening stroll alone."

"Is that wise?" Eric said, rather too quickly.

"I will be fine." Georgina said firmly. "I don't want to lose the opportunity to see something of the city, and it's such a lovely evening."

Rapid re-calculations were being made by Sir Michael, by Richard and by Eric. All were annoyed that Grahame Johnstone had, perhaps deliberately, wrong-footed their plans.

"I'm sure that will be acceptable." Sir Michael said smoothly. "I'm certain that we will be able to guarantee Miss Carmichael's safety as she takes the evening air can we not Mr Mackenzie? Mr Atkinson?"

Richard nodded. "Yes Sir Michael." The plan would still work if he made sure Georgina saw Grahame privately as soon as she returned and passed on the message and the unopened envelope to him.

Eric Atkinson nodded. "Yes Sir." If he had the evidence to implicate Georgina it would hardly take his newspaper contacts much imagination to tie in Grahame Johnstone. It was risky, Grahame Johnstone might be able to wriggle out of having any knowledge of her activities, he could say there was no relationship between them or that he had been duped. It was not as watertight as his original plan but it would have to do.

Half an hour later Georgina walked out of the Embassy and headed along Sofiskaya Quay towards the bridge over the Moskva River.

As Georgina began her walk she knew that Richard and Eric would not be the only ones following her and she immediately spotted the two men, she presumed from the KGB, one on either side of the road. There were a few other people on the wide pavements across the bridge but as she passed by she made sure she made no eye contact with them.

When she had reached the riverside gardens on the north side of the river she stopped to look out over the water knowing that she would be seen to be disobeying Eric's explicit instructions.

No one close enough or with a lens powerful enough to focus on her face could have interpreted her expression.

No one could tell from her face how she felt. Moscow was four hundred miles from where she had been born but she felt at home. The voices she heard spoke a language she had known since her earliest days. She thought of her parents and wondered what they would make of her being in Moscow, staying at the British Embassy and doing what she was trained to do.

As she looked out over the river she felt inconsolably sad that she could never be who she really was.

After five minutes Georgina opened her handbag and pulled out a small, neatly folded, handkerchief. It was a very humid evening, she had every reason to be dabbing her face free of perspiration. She carefully replaced the handkerchief, closed the clasp of her bag and turned to retrace her steps looking around her at the bushes and the trees in the unexpectedly attractive gardens.

As she neared the street a man brushed into her.

"Excuse me." The man said, in good, if slightly accented, English.

"*Ya khorosho govoru po-russki.*" She answered 'I speak perfect Russian."

The man didn't comment, he simply continued in English. "You are alone?" He had been expecting her to be with a man.

"Yes." She answered, without explanation.

"Are men following you?"

"Undoubtedly. There are two on the bridge and one by the gate." She spoke quickly. She didn't look at the man so she could not notice how closely he was observing her.

"Drop your bag."

She unquestioningly and immediately did as the man whose name may or may not have been Berndt told her.

He bent to pick it up but with sleight of hand worthy of a magician he undid the clasp, removed the handkerchief and placed a small envelope in the bag and redid the clasp before handing it back to her. No one could have seen what he had done.

She said nothing.

"*Ty prekrasna. Videt' vas snova.*" "You are beautiful. I will see you again."

"*Proschchaniye.*" She said quietly, her back to anyone who would be watching. "Farewell." He smiled quickly and was gone.

She walked back to the Embassy, arriving exactly twenty nine minutes after she had left.

"Nice walk?" Eric was waiting for her by the Embassy door.

"Lovely, thank you." She answered conversationally. "I'm afraid I didn't do quite as you told me. I had to stop to look at the river, the light was so beautiful, so I didn't get as far as the square."

"Did you have company?"

She raised an eyebrow as if to say his question was too obvious. "Undoubtedly."

"Did you speak to anyone?"

"Oh don't be ridiculous." If Eric, or one of his cohorts, had seen her speak to the man in the park then so be it but she trusted that man. He had known that there would be people watching and he had chosen his spot well.

Richard interrupted the exchange as he arrived in the foyer. "You'd better begin to get ready for the reception. You have an hour or so but first Mr Johnstone would like a quick word."

Of the two men's plans only one had worked.

In the hour before the reception Georgina gave the envelope to Grahame and he gave it, unopened, to Sir Michael and was rewarded with a warm handshake.

"It was strange, Sir Michael, Georgina said that the man handed her this envelope as if he had been expecting her."

"Thank you Grahame."

"Thank Georgina. Did you know this would happen? Did you know someone would try to talk to us?"

"I had my suspicions and was rather afraid your red box would prevent the contact. Did Miss Carmichael say whether the man said anything to her?"

"Yes. He told her to drop her bag."

"Did she?"

"Yes."

"Did the man say anything else?"

"Yes. He said she was very beautiful and that he would see her again."

Sir Michael looked thoughtful. "Did he now? How very interesting."

"I suppose that all means something?" Grahame asked, curious.

"I suppose it does." Sir Michael replied enigmatically.

"One other thing she thought was odd."

"Yes? What was that?"

"He took her handkerchief. Out of her handbag."
"Really? How interesting."

In a room on the other side of the embassy Eric was shouting at two of the men on his team.

"I couldn't get the shot." The first man argued.

"What do you mean? How easy can it be to take one single fucking photograph?"

"How could I take the photos of her meeting someone when there wasn't any meeting."

"What do you mean 'there wasn't any meeting'? Of course there was a fucking meeting. Why do you think the bitch went for a walk?"

"You said someone would talk to her on the bridge. Well no one stopped her on the bridge so I couldn't take the shot could I?"

"Well what's your excuse?" he shouted at the second man.

"She wasn't in the square. How could I take a photo when she wasn't there?"

"Oh fuck off out of here. Both of you!"

Eric was angry. The opportunity had been missed.

And in his mind the only person who could have sabotaged his plan was Richard Mackenzie.

The reception that evening was a formal one and Richard sat with Eric, both in ill-fitting dinner jackets, watching elegantly dressed Russians, whose clothes cost more than many of their countrymen could earn in several years, talking to the men and women they regularly met on such occasions.

Richard saw Eric's eyes following Georgina around the room. "You really don't trust her do you?"

"No. I don't trust her or that Johnstone shit. They're both as bad as each other."

"We're back to London tomorrow, leaving you in peace."

"I'll still be keeping an eye on them." Richard didn't ask how Eric would do that, they both knew men who would do anything, anywhere, if paid enough. "And don't think I won't be keeping an eye on you too."

Richard said nothing. He was watching Georgina as she made animated conversation with a dull looking middle aged couple.

"Men who screw tarts tend not to ask themselves why the tart is allowing herself to be screwed." Eric continued as if voicing a deep philosophical insight.

"They've been friends and colleagues for years and no one has ever accused them of being lovers."

"They will be. If you insist they aren't yet they will be one day."

"If she was like that she'd have tried it on years ago wouldn't she? If she was a gold-digger she'd have caught him by now wouldn't she?"

"Not necessarily. That's what they do isn't it? They wait. They are patient. There will be a reason why she's waited. If she has waited. They wait and only do what they're told to do when they're told to do it."

"They?"

"Moles."

"You've been over here too long Eric. You've absorbed the national paranoia."

They continued to watch the room carefully in silence.

Richard liked to see the way Georgina moved in the slight fabric of her evening dress. He watched as she moved with Grahame from small group to small group with the confidence of a professional diplomat.

"Your little Fraulein is acting a little above her station don't you think? I wonder if she is really deluded enough to think that she will be Lady Grahame Johnstone one day."

"You think he'll be knighted one day?" Richard decided to respond to the easiest of Eric's snide remarks. He was disappointed in himself, he should not have let Eric read him so well.

"Oh yes. He may even get to the House of Lords. Grahame Johnstone's got all the hallmarks of a man with ambition in a party full of nonentities. I bet you ten quid that he'll be Prime Minister one day but she won't be anywhere near him."

"Why do you think that?"

"He'll be warned off. Someone will tell him, if he doesn't already know, that she isn't reliable."

"Of course she's reliable. She's as reliable as they come."

Eric ignored the interruption. "Didn't you listen to anything I was saying yesterday? And once he realises that she won't ever be accepted by society he will drop her like a stone. Believe me, his ambition will be far stronger than any affection he feels for his little fraulein. There'll be a society lady with a good family somewhere lined up for him."

Richard's eyes followed Grahame and Georgina as they worked their way around the room. His face showed nothing of the anger he felt.

Two hours later, as the evening drew to a close, Richard still couldn't decide whether he was angry because Georgina was being used by the Minister and by MI5, or because Eric Atkinson had read the situation so perfectly.

Chapter 6
London and York, 1959

"You can't marry her."

"Why not Prime Minister?"

"Because she would hold you back."

"I beg your pardon?"

"You know what we have planned for you, Grahame, but all that just won't be possible if Miss Carmichael becomes your wife."

"Why ever not?"

"There are very good reasons, some of which you may not be aware of."

"I beg your pardon?"

"How much do you really know about Miss Carmichael?"

"I know enough."

"I doubt that."

Grahame was unsure how to reply. He had to admit that he didn't know much about her life before they had met in 1941. "I know she's kind and loyal and very, very clever."

"What about Laura? Have you been leading my niece on for the past few months?"

"I'm very fond of Laura, of course, I am, and I do understand it's what her family have been wanting."

"Of course it's what we want. You are my chosen successor, you need someone with a flawless background at your side."

"And Georgina's background is flawed?"

"I'm afraid there are a number of question marks surrounding her family and if you married her the press, and others, would become very interested. Apart from any harm it would do to your career it would be unfair on Miss Carmichael to put her under such scrutiny. You must see that."

"But she's pregnant."

"Ah." The prime minister paused and raised his hands in a gesture of acceptance. "That is undoubtedly unfortunate."

"Up to a few moments ago I was feeling rather pleased."

"Well it's up to you Grahame. If you marry Miss Carmichael you can wave goodbye to your career. I dare say you might be able to continue as an MP but even that is doubtful with today's press being what they are."

"A stark choice."

"Well, dear boy, simply by saying that you have made the decision have you not? If you truly loved her there would be no question of there even being a choice."

"What will happen to her?"

"Just like that? You have put her behind you that easily? I'm impressed with the level of your ambition." The Prime Minister looked across his desk at Grahame Johnstone and not for the first time was pleased that the party had chosen this ruthless young man to be his successor.

"Can we do something for her?" Grahame asked tentatively.

"The best thing you can do for both of you is to send her to one of those private clinics. Even when you marry Laura, which you will do my boy, and soon, having a love child will be one hostage to fortune you, and the party, do not need. The press is quick enough to make scandal even where there is no basis, imagine the damage they'd cause if they ever got hold of this."

"I don't think she'd do that. She's not far off forty so I suppose time is running out for her. And she wouldn't let on to the press. She just wouldn't."

The Prime Minister carefully un-crossed and re-crossed his long legs and formed his hands into a church steeple, a habit he had when he wanted to give the impression he was thinking.

"Leave it to me Grahame. And I look forward to seeing the announcement in The Times of your engagement to Laura before too much time has passed."

The Prime Minister pressed a button on his desk, the door opened and Grahame was ushered out of the office which he believed would one day be his. A few moments later Sir Michael Fox was settling into one of the comfortable chairs next to the fire opposite the Prime Minister.

"So he won't be marrying her?" Sir Michael asked.

"No. He won't."

"Did he fight hard?"

"No, not at all, in fact I was rather impressed by the strength of his political ambitions. He cast her adrift in no more than the blink of an eye."

"He may not wish to protect her but I'm afraid I have to."

"You know she's pregnant? Of course you do. Do we know anyone who would marry her? Make her a respectable husband?" The Prime Minister asked.

"I suspect it's rather too late for that, Prime Minister, the child is due in March, and that is only five months away."

"I think it best if Miss Carmichael leaves the scene completely."

"She's been at his right hand for nearly twenty years. Questions will be asked in all sorts of quarters if she disappears."

"I'm sure you will find a satisfactory explanation."

Sir Michael had been extremely annoyed when Georgina had told him, two months before, of her suspicions about her condition. She had been apologetic, explaining that she had been taking precautions but that they had failed. Now she was pregnant, however, she was adamant she was going to keep the child. Sir Michael told her not to tell Grahame for as long as possible. Time was needed for arrangements to be made.

"What do you suggest we do with Miss Carmichael?"

"She has done a very difficult job very well for a number of years. We owe her something."

"We owe her? What a strange thing to say. We owe nobody for anything."

"Perhaps I have not put that well. She may still be useful to us."

"That is better! There was me thinking you were going soft Sir Michael!" The Prime Minister chuckled.

"Under normal circumstances I would say that money would do, set her up with a regular income and a comfortable house somewhere in the Cotswolds where she can play the role of a widow or some such out of the public eye."

"And these are not normal circumstances?"

"No Prime Minister. Would you want the world to know that we had had close political colleagues under observation by the intelligence services?"

"No, indeed I would not."

"Would you want Grahame to be exposed as the father of a bastard child, when he will, no doubt be married to your sister's daughter?"

"Indeed I would not, nor, I suspect would any of the family."

Sir Michael allowed a few moments of silence while the Prime Minister imagined the impact such a scandal would make.

"In some circumstances she would take her own life out of shame or meet with an untimely road accident but I am reluctant to go down that route. Too many people would ask too many questions. It is not as easy to control inquests as it used to be."

"No. You are right."

"And she has skills which may still be of use to us. And not just with regard to Johnstone. You will recall her facility with languages and with the interrogation of defectors?"

"That of course, cannot continue."

"Of course not. Not for a while at any rate."

"So you say we should not be too harsh on the woman?"

"Not harsh at all."

"But she will disappear?"

"She will."

"For as long as we need her to be out of sight."

"Indeed."

The Prime Minister was persuaded. "Does Grahame need to know anything?"

"No. He must know nothing. As far as he will be concerned she will be in Canada. We will let it be known that Miss Georgina Carmichael has resigned in order that she can join her brother in Montreal, his wife is very ill and someone has to look after his children. It will all be very open and above board. She will, of course, not be the one going to Canada. We did think about that but decided against it. We need to have her close to us, we have to be able to check on her. She must disappear in the eyes of the world but not in ours. She will be given a new identity and resettled but we will always know where she is and what she is doing and be able to call on her if we need her services again."

"But what will stop her going to the papers, making money out of her story when she sees Johnstone in the public eye?"

"Miss Carmichael would not do that."

"You are very certain."

"I am."

"You had better be right."

"I am. I am more concerned that she will be targeted by rogue elements from the service who would expose her for money or from some misguided sense of justice. There are some who believe she has been batting for the other team."

"Working for the Russians?"

"Indeed."

"What are you doing about that?"

"We have re-assigned Richard Mackenzie. They know each other and he will, amongst his other duties, ensure she comes to no harm."

"So everything will be sorted out with the minimum of fuss?"

"It will Prime Minister."

"And I have no reason to worry about Miss Carmichael again?"

"None at all Prime Minister."

A little more than three hours later Georgina Carmichael sat patiently in the passenger seat as Richard Mackenzie put her cases in the boot of his Hillman Minx.

She had been expecting the telephone call.

When Grahame had told her that he was meeting the Prime Minister she had known it would all be over. He would be talked out of the marriage she had known all along would be impossible. He would marry Laura Cromwell and his career would progress as the party planned.

"Where are we going?" She asked Richard as he started the car.

"York."

"I've never been to York."

"It's a very pleasant city."

After that brief exchange she was grateful that Richard did not make unnecessary conversation. The hours of silence allowed her to think. She was not afraid of being alone, in many ways she had been alone since the death of her parents. Even as she had allowed Grahame Johnstone into her life she had never been dependent on him. She had done what she had had to do but had never committed herself to him. She had never, whatever anybody had thought, expected to be his wife and she would not pine for him. It was having to give up her work that would leave the greatest hole in her life.

She had enjoyed every aspect of both her jobs since the war. Acting as Grahame's assistant had given her responsibility and challenges and she had travelled to many places she would otherwise never have visited, but it was the work she had done with Sir Michael's office that she would miss the most. Using her skills with languages she had felt involved in activities that were important to her adopted country, far more important than politics.

Now that was all in the past. Her future was as a mother. She would have no other job to occupy her mind. She was not looking forward to knowing no one and living in a city of which she knew nothing.

She sat in the passenger seat staring out through the windscreen.

"Would you like to stop for a cup of tea?" Richard asked as they approached Biggleswade.

"Only if you want to." She had answered so they had carried on.

They did stop for a short break in Stamford but the conversation was confined to what a nice town it seemed to be.

They stopped again for petrol in Tickhill.

"Aren't you getting tired with all this driving?" Georgina asked as they sat opposite each other in the transport café.

"Not really."

"How much longer is there to go?" She asked after a period of silence.

"Not much more than an hour or so."

"I'll be glad to get there."

"So will I."

It was getting dark when they reached the house, an anonymous semi-detached house in a respectable neighbourhood two miles from the centre of the city.

Georgina walked through the front door and looked around her. The house had obviously just been redecorated. In the front room she noticed that the furniture was modern. It was not what she would have chosen but it looked comfortable enough. Without saying anything she walked back into the hall and through to the kitchen.

"All mod cons." Richard said awkwardly. "Twin tub washing machine, fridge, gas cooker."

"Very nice." She commented then, as if realising how he might misconstrue her silence throughout the drive, she added brightly "It's certainly not what I'm used to but I will be able to make it home. I can't remember when I last lived in a house with stairs."

"Come on, I'll make us a cup of coffee. We can sit down and I'll explain it all."

"You've had the last eight hours to do that."

"You didn't seem to want to talk."

"Can I just get something off my chest Richard?"

"Fire ahead."

"In all this no one has asked me what I wanted to do, or where I wanted to go. It's all been taken out of my hands. It's as if I'm no longer an adult, able to make my own decisions. I mean no one has asked me anything. I understand why I had to leave Grahame and my work with the service, which of course you know about, but someone could have given me one thing that was my choice. Couldn't they?"

Richard shrugged. It would be better he let her talk so he could know what her feelings really were.

"I know I made the most important choice didn't I? I chose to keep the baby." She looked down at her barely swollen stomach. "If I'd agreed to go to one of those clinics I'd still have been able to work but only for a little while. Grahame would never have been allowed to stay unmarried for much longer and he was never going to marry me so I would have left that job soon anyway. But I still could have been useful to the service couldn't I? Surely I could have carried on with that? That's what I find so difficult to understand. Why have I been cut me off?"

Richard was surprised that it was losing her work that bothered her, not being abandoned by Grahame. "There was no other way. Not under all the circumstances. It was all or nothing so, I'm afraid it has to be nothing."

It was some time before she replied.

"I suppose you're right. I just find it rather sad."

Richard put the two cups of coffee on the table and sat down opposite Georgina. "You'll make a new life." He said, trying to sound encouraging though he wondered how she would get on as a first time mother approaching middle age. "And I know you'll understand that there really was no other way. Everyone in Westminster knew how close the two of you were. As it becomes more obvious you're expecting the press wouldn't bother to ask questions, they'd think they already knew the answers. And their answers would be right, and to all their questions, all of them, Georgina, even the ones we really don't want them to ask. And the PM and Sir Michael could never allow that to happen. They couldn't let anyone get too interested in you. What were the alternatives? I'll tell you but you already know, a taxi that fails to swerve out of the way when you are pushed into the street, an overdose of barbiturates and alcohol because you couldn't stand the shame? This way you, and your child, get to live. You must never forget that this really is the only way."

He stopped, embarrassed that he had spoken so honestly.

"Ouch."

She knew everything Richard had said made sense. She knew no one left the job she had been doing easily, questions were always asked and very often there was no one left to answer them.

She stirred her coffee slowly. "I understand. Thank you for being so honest, I probably needed that. Now, you must tell me. Who am I now?"

"You are Elizabeth Wright. It's all in here." Richard reached down, took an envelope from his briefcase and placed it on the table between them. "You're a recent widow. Your late husband, Robert Wright, always known as Bob, was American. He died in September in Vietnam.

You have come to York because he was stationed nearby earlier in your marriage and you were happy here. You'll find all the documents you need, your birth certificate as Elizabeth Gordon, your exam certificates, you were quite clever high grades especially in maths, your marriage certificate, your husband's birth certificate and his death certificate, even newspaper cuttings of the action in which he died. Read up on it."

"What happens about doctors? I mean I haven't seen one and I should have notes."

"When you go to the local surgery you will say you have been putting on weight and always feel tired. You will not say you know you are expecting. Your husband only died ten weeks ago so you've put all your symptoms down to your distress and now you think, you hope, you might be pregnant."

"Nothing left to chance then?"

"I sincerely hope not."

"But I'm on my own?"

"I'll be around but only when and if you need me. I'm sure you'll soon make a new life. You'll have your baby. You'll make friends up here. You're free to do exactly what you want with your life."

"As long as I do it out of the public eye and as long as no one knows who my child's father really is or what I have done in my life since 1941. That's all highly conducive to developing trust in a close relationship with someone don't you think?" She tried not to sound bitter.

"You will be well provided for financially…."

"But money isn't everything is it?"

"You must just find a way to be happy."

Georgina looked up from her coffee to see Richard staring at her.

It would have been difficult to misread the look on his face.

"Does Grahame want to know when his child is born?" She asked deliberately.

"Of course. Just tell me anything you want him to know and I'll make sure he gets the information."

"But I can't talk to him?"

"No."

"This is a totally new life then. I am Elizabeth Wright."

"You are."

They sat sipping at their coffees, neither, for their own reasons, wanting the evening to end.

"There is one more thing."

"Yes?"

"There will be people looking for you. You must keep on your guard and if you ever suspect anyone is watching you you must let me know immediately."

"Like who?"

"You must know what you're up against. As soon as people realise you're not just off sick questions will be asked and there will be people on both sides who will make it their business to find out everything about you. Some will think you've defected, some will think you've got yourself into some sort of trouble but all will want to know what has really become of you and what you've really been doing for the past twenty years. And when they find out, which they will, they'll track you down so they can find out what it is they don't know. And it won't only be the other side, Elizabeth," he used her new name quite deliberately. "It won't just be 'them', it will also be 'us'. You know too much about too many people to be allowed to get away from them."

"So who?"

"Do you remember that nasty little weasel in Moscow last year? His name is Eric Atkinson and he knows a lot about you. He believes you are an agent, sleeping with your boss to get close to the centre of government and pass on secrets to the Russians."

"He thinks that?"

Richard nodded. "At least he didn't understand that this country trusts their politicians so little they set women to sleep with them and to spy on them."

"You've known all along?"

"Since before Moscow, yes."

"How little you must think of me."

"I think you are quite remarkable." Realising she might see the true meaning behind his words he looked away.

"I suppose the press will be interested too. As Grahame becomes more successful, which I have no doubt he will, I can imagine some reporter wanting to track me down."

"And everyone else who has something to gain by casting suspicion on him. Inside and outside his party."

"You paint a very bleak picture."

"I'm sorry if it seems bleak now but it will get easier. You'll become Elizabeth Wright just as you became Georgina Carmichael."

"You know that too?"

"Since before Moscow, yes."

"No one will be able to find me though, will they?"

"We've made it as difficult as possible but you must be on your guard. Always remember they are trying but also remember me."

"You?"

"It's my job to make sure they don't find you. Yes, of course I'm reporting back on what you're doing but that is only routine. My job is to keep you safe for as long as I possibly can. The rest of my life if needs be."

"That almost sounds like a marriage. 'For as long as we both shall live.'" She managed to make it sound like a joke but she realised too late that it was one that they were both uncomfortable with.

"Maybe not a marriage, but it's certainly a commitment." Richard replied awkwardly. "But never forget, Elizabeth, it is one I happily make."

At 9.30 in the evening of Tuesday, March 15 1960 Jane Wright was born.

When asked by a nurse who she could phone to tell about the birth Elizabeth gave her Richard's number. 'He's an old friend of my husband' she explained before turning over and staring at the cream coloured wall as Jane slept peacefully in the cot beside her.

Richard received two telephone calls that evening.

The first, from an efficient nurse in York, told him briefly that Mrs Elizabeth Wright had given birth to a daughter, '6 pounds 2 ounces, a little light but doing well'. The woman had no time to talk so Richard just noted down the details to pass to Grahame. 'Do you know if the baby has been given a name?' he had asked and the nurse had said 'Jane'.

"Good luck Jane Wright. You will need every bit of luck you can get." He spoke aloud to the empty room when he had put the phone receiver down. "But I promise you I'll look after you as I will your mother. For as long as you need me."

A few minutes later he dialled Grahame's number and waited for the answer.

"I'm afraid Mr Johnstone isn't in."

"Miss Cromwell?" Richard asked. "Do you know when will he be back?"

"He's at the House, he should be back in a hour or so."

"I need to speak with him."

"Is that you Richard? He said you might be calling soon."

"Yes? What did he say?"

"He said the baby should be due about now."

"You know about that?"

"Yes. He told me and of course I'll not to say anything to anyone. But he needed me to know."

"I can see that."

"Well? What is the news?"

"A daughter, Jane, born this evening, doing well."

"Oh good. A daughter will be so much less trouble than a son would have been. I find men tend to discount their daughters where they cannot forget their sons."

"No one will ever know there's any connection between the child and her father."

"Good. The less he is involved the better. Tell the mother that we wish them both all the best."

Richard put the phone down knowing he would not pass on that particular message.

It was nearly midnight when Richard's phone rang again. He answered it thinking it would be Grahame. It wasn't.

"I suppose you think you've been bloody clever."

"What?"

"I suppose you think you'll be protecting the Fraulein."

"What? Eric, is that you?"

"Yes. It's me. Eric. The one you got fired. The one whose career you've successfully fucked up."

"The one who what?"

"I knew you were thick but can't you do any better than that?"

"You've been given the boot?"

"Yes. Summarily fired. No reference. No notice. Here's your ticket. Get on the plane back to England and get lost."

"You're in London?"

"Got in yesterday. Took bloody hours to get through passport control. Someone somewhere has got it in for me. So I've been thinking…."

"In a bar by the sound of it."

"…. I've been thinking. The only ones who had anything to gain by getting rid of me were you, the Fraulein, and that ponce of a politician. Between the three of you you've got me fired and now I've got nowhere to live and no job. And it's because of you…."

"I've had nothing to do with this. Why would I?"

"No? Then it's that ponce, Grahame what's'isname. He's realised I'm on to them.. him… her… and he's got me out of the way, well I'll find out the truth."

"What truth? You're drunk and you're talking shit."

"One or the other or both of them are traitors, Russian spies. I know it. I would have been able to prove it if you hadn't got in the way, protecting her, in Moscow last summer. But I'll prove it now. If it takes the rest of my life I'll prove it."

"You're mad; drunk and mad."

"She's a ruski and a communist he was probably a commie since he was at Cambridge with all the others. They're all traitors and enemies of this country and I'll prove it."

"You're repeating yourself Eric, you always did when you were pissed. Go and sleep it off. You'll realise what shit you're talking when you wake up. That's if you remember any of this."

"What have you done with her?"

"Who?"

"Don't play bloody dumb, the Fraulein."

"I don't know what you mean."

"She's left her job. Gone. Disappeared. Done a runner. They told me Canada but I don't believe a word of it."

"What?"

"Where is she?"

"I don't know what you mean."

"Oh come on Dicky boy, you know everything. She's left her job and no one knows why and she's left her flat and the man who lives there now has never heard of her."

"Why do you think I would know?"

"Because she's been moved, and it's been done properly. But you underestimate me, you've always underestimated me. I'm good, Richard Mackenzie, I'm a damn sight fucking better than you are and I'll find her. I'll find her and I'll expose her for the lying fucking bitch of a traitor she is. If it takes me the rest of my life I'll do it. And if you get in my way... Well, I hope you do so then I can bloody kill you."

Richard put the phone down.

A battle line had been drawn.

From now on it would be him against Eric.

As he poured himself a large scotch he wondered how long it would be before there was a winner, and who that winner would be.

Chapter 7
York, 1965

Jane was five years old and had just started at the local primary school when Elizabeth Wright noticed the man as they walked up the hill from the school. Her first thought was that his clothes seemed wrong, no one would wear what looked like a heavy tweed jacket on the third day of the late summer heat wave.

She couldn't be sure he was following them but it was very rare to see a man alone on the suburban avenue in the middle of a weekday afternoon.

She tried not to appear hurried as she headed for home and sanctuary. Sighing with a mixture of fear and relief she shut the door and settled into the usual routine of making tea.

When Jane asked to be allowed to play in the garden it was against her better judgement but Elizabeth said she could, as long as she stayed in the back garden and didn't go out onto the road.

She had known for nearly six years that this day would come. Richard had warned her that night he had driven her up from London and she had been on her guard all that time. There had been moments when she had thought that she was being followed but they had passed. This time, though, it was different. The man definitely had no good reason to be in their road at this time of day.

She had no idea whether he was a reporter chasing after a story about Grahame Johnstone's love-child or someone, more sinister, chasing her for her other career but she was sure of one thing. She had to tell Richard and when she did she and Jane would have to move.

She wanted one more night in the house that had become their home but she packed a few things in a bag and put it by the door, just in case.

Despite it being still light Elizabeth drew the curtains in the front of the house, as she did so she looked out of the window to see if the man was watching. She didn't see him but she knew he was there.

Even when, an hour later, Jane was safely inside and all the doors were locked, she could not relax. No cover was impenetrable, however deep. It had taken nearly six years but whoever it was had found her.

She kept Jane in her bed with her throughout the long night. She could not sleep. Events would move quickly as soon as she picked up the phone and talked to Richard. Then everything would be out of her hands. As she lay with her arms around her peacefully sleeping daughter, she was making a point, if only to herself.

It was her choice that she and Jane would spend one more night before their lives were changed.

The next day she was calm and reassuring as she dressed Jane for school and they set off for the half-mile walk. The day before Elizabeth had felt happy. With Jane at school she had been thinking about finding a job. There were insurance companies opening offices in the city and the references Richard would have been able to obtain for her would have landed her an interesting post.

But that would never happen now they had been found.

As she saw Jane safely through the school gates she turned and had a chance to see the man before he ducked behind a hedge.

As she walked home she hoped that the man would follow her and not stay outside the school. Jane would be a very easy target. She was relieved when she glimpsed him following her up the hill.

Once home, despite the weather, she stayed inside. She put her passport, her cheque-book, all their birth, marriage and death certificates in the bag she had put together the night before. Then she sat on the settee in her living room, the curtains still drawn.

She could not settle and after a few minutes put the contents of the laundry basket in the twin tub. In a few hours strangers would be clearing the house and she could not have them nosing through the laundry.

An hour later she walked through the house spending longest in Jane's bedroom.

She had so many memories of learning how to be a mother in that room.

She then went into the kitchen to drink one last cup of tea sitting at the pink formica topped table.

She did not call Richard. She had decided it was likely whoever was watching her was tapping into her phone calls. She put the radio on loud and spent the rest of the morning watching the clock until it would be lunchtime and then, in twenty minutes, Jane would be in the playground.

She picked up the phone and dialled a taxi company she had not used before. 'Where to Madam?' the controller had asked and she had said 'just to Castlegate, I have a dentist's appointment'. While she was waiting for the doorbell she made sure the back door was still bolted and all the windows were shut and locked.

When the doorbell rang she asked the driver to wait a minute and phoned the taxi company again. 'Can you tell me the driver's name?' she asked. 'Dave.' 'Thanks.'

She walked to the door.

"What's your name?"

"Dave. I'm Dave. You wanted a taxi to go to Castlegate."

When she was safely in the taxi and they had travelled a short distance she changed her instructions.

"Can you go via Brooke School please? I need to pick up my daughter."

When they got to the school she knew she had timed it right, Jane was in the playground. She came when her mother called and in a moment she was in the taxi.

"But I've left all my things in the classroom." She said, not understanding what was going on.

As they approached the city Elizabeth changed her instructions again. "Dave? I'm so sorry. I've changed my mind again. Can you drop us up at the Minster?"

She would make sure she and Jane were never alone until Richard could come to their rescue, just in case the man had managed to follow her into the city. She paid the taxi and hustled Jane around the corner, out of Dave's sight and into a small tea-room.

"This is fun Mummy."

"It's a treat Jane, we won't do it all the time but you've been a good girl and you've settled into school well. You deserve a treat."

When they had settled at a table in the back of the shop she ordered a plate of sandwiches and one of cream cakes. When they were served Elizabeth asked if there was a telephone she could use. 'I just need to make two short calls. I'll pay of course. Oh and could you sit with my daughter? I won't be long. Thank you very much'

Her first call was to the school to explain Jane's absence. She had apologised for worrying them before she realised no one had noticed Jane was missing, it was still break time and the afternoon register had not yet been taken. It had seemed to Elizabeth that hours must have passed since she had picked Jane up but it could only have been twenty minutes. 'A family crisis', and as she made her short explanation she realised it was the truth. 'I'll let you know when Jane will be able to return.'

She put the phone down before the school secretary could question her further and quickly picked the receiver up again and dialled the London number.

"Richard? It's me. Elizabeth."

"What's the matter?" He called her every month to make sure everything was fine. She never called him.

"We're being followed."

"Where are you now? At home?"

"No. We're in a tea room in York, by the Minster."

"Stay out of sight if you can. I'll catch a train and be with you in, what, five or six hours."

"We can't stay here for that long. And we can't go home can we?"

"No, don't do that." Richard had always had a plan in place. "As soon as you can go to the hotel by the railway station, The Royal York, and check in as Mrs Richard Williamson. There will be a reservation. Chat to the receptionist, tell her that you're meeting your husband who's coming up by train from London. Then stay in your room. Have you got what you need?"

"The basics and the paperwork."

"Good girl. I'll see you later." He tried not to allow his voice to betray how pleased he was to be seeing her again but how worried he was that she had been found.

"Richard?" She wanted to thank him but the phone was already dead.

She walked back to the table. She had to be calm. Jane smiled up at her, trusting her and enjoying the treat.

Forty five minutes later she paid the bill and took Jane's hand to steer her out of the tearoom, down the hill over the river, through the break in the city walls to the hotel. She held Jane's hand tightly in one hand and her bag in the other the whole way.

So much was happening and so quickly. So much had been organised in the blink of an eye.

And just as in 1959 their fate was now out of her hands.

Richard knew the man following Elizabeth would be Eric, or someone paid by him, and he spent the first part of his journey from London working out how he could have traced her.

Eric would have picked away at any clue, or bribed anyone, to find out where she was. He would never have given up on his attempts to prove that she was a Russian agent and that Grahame Johnstone was the fifth man in the university spy ring.

As the train drew into Newark Richard decided that the only possible way Eric could have found them was to have followed the trail of the money. It was the only link between Elizabeth Wright and any government department. Money was always the weak link.

Eric must have bribed someone in the department to check on any regular payment arrangements that had begun at the right time. He would have worked systematically through them, eliminating those that could not be to Georgina, until he had found the bank in York which had led him to 'Elizabeth Wright'.

Richard spent the time between Newark and Doncaster identifying the mistakes that might have been made and working out how they could be avoided in the future.

After Doncaster he was concerned with the damage that might have been done before Elizabeth had noticed him. Telephone calls would have been bugged but he knew Elizabeth would never say anything that could be misinterpreted. The main danger, Richard believed, was that photographs would have been taken.

He wondered whether five-year old Jane looked anything like her father but even so, photographs of Elizabeth with a child could be dynamite if used to illustrate the right story.

When he arrived in York Richard didn't head directly to the nearby hotel instead he took a taxi, giving the driver the street number four doors up from the house that had been Elizabeth's home. He had to check whether or not Eric was still watching the house. If he was still there Elizabeth and Jane would be safe for the night.

As his taxi pulled up past the house he could see the curtains were drawn and the changing patterns of light told him the television in the living room was switched on. He smiled. The operatives who had been designated to clear the house were giving a good impression of Elizabeth being at home.

After ten minutes of sitting in the taxi watching the road Richard saw that someone else was watching the house. A car was parked several houses down from

Elizabeth's and the man sitting in the driver's seat had not moved.

'Could you get out and open the bonnet of your car, tinker with something for a minute or two? Make it look like you've had an ignition problem or something?' Richard asked the driver who looked back over his shoulder and smiled. 'Her husband still at home then?' Richard nodded. It was as good an excuse as any.

When they headed back towards the city Richard turned to check whether they were being followed. The road was completely clear. They had, perhaps, until morning before Eric realised he had been duped.

Elizabeth's first question was "Can we go home?"

"No. I'm afraid that is going to be impossible. He's still watching the house."

"Who is it?"

"Do you remember I told you about Eric Atkinson?"

"That odd little man from Moscow?"

"That's the one. It has to be him, or one of his henchmen."

"Does he still think I'm a Russian spy?"

"I can't be certain but after your six years of sacrifice we aren't going to take any chances. He's a man with a mission I'm afraid, and one with an axe to grind. He was forced out of the service under a bit of a cloud. He'd been doing a bit of freelancing and that is frowned upon in our line of business but I'm afraid he blames you and me. He's been working as a sort of private investigator, making quite a good living selling salacious stories to the gutter press. Your story, I'm afraid, is exactly what he would get his teeth into."

"And you think he's after stuff he can sell to the papers. Me and Jane? Anything else?"

"He might want to widen it out a bit, you know, mysterious meetings in Moscow."

"That would make a great name for a film wouldn't it? *Mysterious Meetings in Moscow*"

"Seriously, I'm worried that he might have all sorts of pictures he could write misleading captions to."

"And Grahame wouldn't like that would he? It would imply he had *Mysterious Meetings in Moscow* too."

"I can say absolutely that Grahame would not like that."

"He's doing well isn't he? I see photos of him and his wife and his son and daughter in the society pages." She did her best not to sound bitter.

"Shadow Chancellor and about to become leader of his party."

"Even in opposition, the greasy pole is being climbed then?"

"But we're not moving you to protect Grahame Johnstone's career, we're moving you because that is what we have to do to keep both you and Jane safe."

"Poor little mite." Elizabeth looked across at her sleeping daughter. "She was just making friends."

"We wouldn't be doing this to you if we didn't think it absolutely necessary."

"I know, but it doesn't make it any easier."

They sat in silence for a few moments, both looking down at the sleeping Jane, both wondering what their worlds would have been like if she had not been born.

"I wouldn't be without her you know. She's such a sweetie when she wants to be and she's going to be a very clever young lady."

"I would have thought that was inevitable with her parents being who they are."

"I wonder if that necessarily follows? Anyway, let's be practical. Where will we be moving to?"

"Well your house is being packed up now, I should say they are doing this very inconspicuously. Everything personal is being packed by a lady, don't worry, your clothes and Jane's toys, your books and photographs, all that sort of thing, they will be waiting for you in your new house."

"The furniture?"

"There will be all new at your new house."

"And where is that?"

"A lovely small town on the Isle of Wight. It will be really easy to monitor movements on and off the island so you'll be safer there. It had actually all been arranged for someone else but that, well that sort of fell through."

"You mean you didn't get the person out?"

Richard shook his head. "Neither got out."

"Berlin?"

He nodded. He had often wondered how much Elizabeth, as Georgina, could have contributed in their war in Eastern Europe had she not had to be side-lined. She was astute, intelligent, perceptive and had a sizeable streak of common sense.

"And who will we be? Presumably Elizabeth and Jane Wright can no longer exist."

"No. You can keep your first names, we thought it would confuse little Jane too much to have to change and in any case they aren't uncommon names. You will, of course, have to have a new surname, we thought Somerset."

"Elizabeth and Jane Somerset. Sounds as good as anything would be. E liz a beth Som er set," She spoke each syllable of the name distinctly, "Elizabeth Somerset, is rather distinguished. May I ask what happened to Mr Somerset?"

"You are a divorcee. A painful separation, you are the innocent party and are licking your wounds."

"Isn't that a bit risqué? Though there is, obviously, an element of truth."

"Divorce is nothing like as uncommon as it was. Even quite respectable families experience divorces now it's so much easier."

"I'm pleased I'm the innocent party. I would hate to have to have some lover hidden away somewhere. I don't think I'm the sort to be able to run two men at the same time. One was tricky enough."

Richard smiled. Elizabeth had made the evening so much easier than it might have been and she seemed to him to be taking everything in her stride.

"Which brings me to tonight's arrangements. What are they?"

"I must sleep here to preserve the role we are playing, but as you see, I did specify twin beds."

"I should hope so." Elizabeth's voice was stern.

But Richard noticed she was smiling as she spoke.

The next morning Richard shepherded Elizabeth and Jane into the car he had arranged. They had had an early breakfast in their room and were on the road south soon after eight.

"Where are we going Mummy?"

"We're going on a little holiday, poppet."

"What about school? It's dancing today. I like that."

"Sorry, darling, you won't be going back to school."

Jane's smiling face dropped. "What did I do wrong?" Her lips pursed and Elizabeth thought her daughter might be about to have one of the crying fits she sometimes had that would be stopped only with a hug from Big Teddy.

"You did nothing wrong darling, honestly, it's just that you can't go back to that school. You'll be going to another very soon."

"But what about Annie and Susie? They'll wonder where I am."

Elizabeth caught Richard's eye in the rear view mirror. She had no answer.

"I'll get a message to the school to say you've had to leave York."

"I've sort of done that, yesterday, I had to as I took her out during lunch break. I said it was a family crisis."

"Family crisis?" Jane repeated the words she didn't understand.

"Just be a good girl and watch the countryside. Everything will be fine. We're together and that's all that matters, isn't it." She hugged her daughter to her.

"What about Big Teddy?"

"Big Teddy will be waiting for you when we get to your new house." Richard said as he saw in his rear view mirror that Jane was close to tears.

"Promise?" Jane asked him.

"Promise." He said firmly.

In a few minutes Jane had drifted off to sleep lying across her mother's lap on the back seat of the car as Richard drove them south.

"The car with all your bits and pieces left the house just before dawn and they would certainly not have left someone as important as Big Teddy behind." Richard reassured Elizabeth with a smile.

Both were thinking of the silent trip nearly six years before, when Richard had driven her north.

"Tell me about the new us."

"What do you want to know?"

"Everything? School?"

"Jane will start next Monday. All her records will be sent down, as if from her old school. All you have to tell her is that she can answer any questions her new friends might ask her. She has lived in York but has had to leave because of a family crisis. The teachers will be told it's because of your divorce so they won't ask any awkward questions. They certainly wouldn't dare mention the word 'divorce' to Jane."

"What if someone asks about her father?"

"What have you told her?"

"She's never really asked about him. It's just been normal for her not to have a man around the house so she'll probably just shrug and say she hadn't got a father or at least she'd say she'd never seen him."

"She never asked anything?"

"I've never talked to her about him and I don't suppose anyone else did. She's still a bit young for that."

"It's going to get more and more difficult for you, you know, as she gets older and can ask questions. And she will ask questions, and also, if she's anything like her mother, she won't be fobbed off with vague platitudes, she'll ask you questions and she'll want the truth."

"I know. But I'm putting off thinking about it until it happens."

"I don't think Grahame has any idea what he's putting you through."

"I don't suppose he ever thinks about us."

"He won't have forgotten you, or Jane."

"Sometimes I remember who I was, what I used to be. Seeing Eric Atkinson has made me think of Moscow and how when we were there anything seemed possible but even there I had the feeling I had never been 'me'. I'm not explaining myself very well am I? Sorry. It's just that I'm not sure who 'me' is any more. It really is very difficult which is why I'm not going to."

"Not going to do what?"

"Think about me anymore. My life, from now on, has to be all about Jane."

Chapter 8
Isle of Wight, July 1976

Perhaps it was the quieter island life, or just that they were protected from the mainland by three miles of The Solent, but after their move from York Elizabeth Somerset was less on edge than she had been at any time since before her daughter had been born and for eleven peaceful years their life seemed almost normal.

In many ways Elizabeth was happy, Jane had good friends and was growing into an open hearted and generous young lady but in the long hours she spent on her own she never stopped wondering what her life might have been had Jane never been born. That she had no friends she knew was no one's fault but her own. She found it impossible to trust anyone she met. She had too many secrets for that.

She knew that the mothers of Jane's friends talked about her behind her back, saying she was a little strange. They might have been more friendly had she not been a single, divorced woman. They could never take the risk of inviting her to dinner parties or social gatherings. She had no man with her, and that made it difficult for everyone, especially those who were unsure of their husbands.

She passed the time of day with her neighbours and with the men and women serving in the shops she visited but Elizabeth had no one she could call a friend, apart from Richard.

Once a month, without fail, he called her on the telephone. They would chat for a few minutes and then Richard would ask Elizabeth if everything was OK. And every month she would answer 'Yes'. And he would know she was lying.

Richard knew that Elizabeth loved her daughter and would do anything for her, but he also knew that she, as an intelligent woman who for nearly twenty years had earned her living in the most interesting of ways, hated the frustrations of the life she had been forced to live. 'It is

Jane who is important.' Elizabeth repeated month after month. 'It is my job to make her life what she wants it to be, it's the only job I want now'.

In those calls Richard never told her anything of his own life and she never asked.

He told her nothing about his marriage to the widow of a friend killed in Berlin. He never told her of the birth of his son and, two years later, of his daughter. He was never sure why he never said anything about his family. The only explanation he could give himself was that it didn't seem fair that he had a happy family life when that was something she would never have.

Because he had never told her he had a wife and children he had no need to tell her when they died in a fog-bound motorway car crash after a half-term trip to the zoo.

Their conversations were about everyday topics, about how Jane was getting on, the state of the weather or the most prominent sport in the news. They never mentioned Grahame Johnstone and the hostages to fortune that hung over Elizabeth and Jane.

Richard knew he was nothing to Elizabeth but her minder, the organiser who was keeping her and her daughter safe. It was something he had learned to live with.

At the end of the summer term 1976, Jane's exams behind them, Elizabeth looked forward to the long holidays thinking that Jane would have the best time ever.

Her daughter had sensible and responsible friends and she was growing in confidence. Elizabeth allowed herself the luxury of thinking she had done a good job in raising her daughter.

The summer was shaping up to be an historically hot one and much of the first two weeks of Jane's holiday were spent on the beach. Elizabeth had not minded, Jane's friends were ones she had known since her first days in Primary School. There was no threat. Life was good.

It was, Elizabeth was certain, going to be an excellent summer, the summer when Jane would blossom.

Sitting outside in the shade of the neighbour's tree, dozing off in the quiet of the hot afternoon, she wasn't at first sure whether the phone she heard ringing was hers or her neighbours. It was neither the day nor the time for Richard's call and she couldn't imagine who else might be phoning her.

When she realised it was her phone she rushed in, her immediate thoughts that Jane had had an accident.

She had felt so safe for so long that she was completely unprepared.

"Elizabeth?"

"Richard? What is it?"

"I'm sorry."

It was all he had to say. She knew what was coming.

"No."

"Elizabeth, I'm so sorry but he's found you."

"Eric Atkinson?" The name had never been far from her thoughts.

"He's been seen on the island."

"Oh shit."

"I'll be with you this afternoon. Stay at home. Where's Jane?"

"She's with friends at the beach."

"What time will she be home?"

"She's always home at sixish for tea before she goes out again. Should I fetch her?"

"No need. I'll be with you at five."

Jane was completely unprepared for the look on her mother's face when she returned home late that afternoon after a day on the beach.

"Janey, come in. I've something to tell you."

"That sounds serious."

"Come through. I want you to meet an old friend. This is Richard."

"Richard?"

"Hello Jane."

"Who are you?" Jane looked from her mother to the man and back to her mother, her voice filled with suspicion.

"I'm an old friend of your mother's."

"How old?"

"We go back a long way, since before you were born."

A thought flashed across Jane's mind. "Are you my father?"

She looked from Richard to her mother and back to Richard and wasn't sure what the look between them meant.

"No, Jane, I'm not your father though, I have to say, I would be very proud to have been."

"So you're just a friend of my mother's?" Jane sounded very doubtful.

"Yes, Jane, just a friend."

Jane wasn't sure she believed him. "Then how come, if you're such a good old friend, I've never seen you before?"

"Janey, you will understand one day that friends don't always live in each other's pockets, they are just people who you can rely on when there is a problem."

"And there's a problem now?"

"Sit down Jane. I need to speak to you seriously." Richard had taken over the conversation from Elizabeth and somehow that seemed to make it more important.

Jane sat.

"There's a man who is a danger to you and your mother...."

"My father?"

"No, not your father, just someone who can do your mother a great deal of harm."

"I've always wondered about my father."

"I divorced your father when you were young Jane, for very good reasons. Please don't make me explain."

"Sorry Mum."

"One day I will feel strong enough to tell you about him, no, not when you're 'grown up' you are 'grown up' now." She smiled at her daughter. "I'll probably not tell you until you're middle aged, or even an old woman." Richard admired Elizabeth for making a joke out of it.

"OK." Jane said, reluctantly. "Then what do you feel strong enough to tell me?"

Richard answered in a business like tone, trying to take the emotion out of the situation. "There is a man who knew your mother years ago and, as I said, he is a danger."

"Did you know him?"

"I did."

"What sort of danger?" Jane asked firmly.

Richard wondered how he could strike the right tone to make Jane cooperate without frightening her. He couldn't think of the right words and was grateful when Elizabeth took up the challenge.

"Jane. I did something when I was younger that I really don't want anyone to know about. And this man wants to make a newspaper story out of it."

"What on earth did you do?"

Richard took up the argument. "We have to keep you safe from this man who would happily destroy your mother. Please, you must not fight me, you must help me do what I have to do."

"We need to leave the island, love, we need to move." Elizabeth didn't try to soften the blow.

"No." Jane looked from her mother to Richard and back to her mother. "No. Let whoever he is publish his stupid story. What can be so bad that we have to move?"

"You have to trust me Jane. We cannot let this man find you and your mother. One day you'll understand...."

"Oh that's crap! 'One day' this and 'one day' that. I'm 16. I'm not a child! You've got to tell me what it's all about or I won't go with you. You can run away if you like but I'll stay here. I've got friends here, everything I know is here. I'm not leaving."

"I'm afraid you have no choice."

"I've told you I won't go. I'm staying here."

Jane turned and ran up to her room, slamming the door behind her. Something in her memory was of another day, another move. It was like a dream she could feel but not put exact words to.

Her two black and white cats, Otty and Beavy, were curled up on her bed asleep and she snuggled next to them. She had known there were secrets in her family, she had known that her mother had never been completely open with her, but she couldn't imagine anything bad enough to make them have to move.

It was half an hour before she heard the knock on her door and her mother came into her room and sat down on the end of her bed.

"I'm so sorry, Janey. This is absolutely the last thing I ever wanted to happen. You must know that. We've been so happy here." Jane picked up Otty and handed the pliant cat to her mother by way of a peace offering.

Jane was the first to break the awkward silence.

"You can't make me leave all my friends, everything I've ever known."

"I'm afraid I have to. And tonight."

"Tonight? Why? That's ridiculous!"

"Because." Elizabeth said firmly. It was what she had said every time her daughter asked her a question she knew she could not answer but this time she understood it would never be enough.

"But Mum I'm 16, not far off 17, now. Surely you can trust me now? I mean if you can't tell me now when will you be able to tell me the truth about whatever it was that happened? Surely it can't be that awful?"

Elizabeth knew she couldn't tell her daughter the whole truth. But she also knew she would have to tell her something.

"Come down, it's a lovely evening, Richard's left us on our own for an hour. Let's sit outside, I'll open a bottle of wine, you're old enough to have a glass and I suppose I do owe you something of an explanation. Perhaps it is finally time for me to be a little more honest with you."

Richard had told Elizabeth that they needed to be ready to leave on the ten to midnight ferry but she had insisted on having time to talk to her daughter. She was never going to be able to tell Jane the truth but she was going to have to tell her something to make her accept being uprooted from the only life she had known.

"It's a simple story really, and not that original I'm afraid." Elizabeth had long planned what she would and what she would not say when she finally had to tell Jane about her father. She would be honest about everything other than the real reason she slept with him, the real reason he could never marry her and who he was.

"Go on Mum." Jane prompted, she did not want her mother to back out when they had got this far.

"The one lie I have allowed you to believe is that your father and I were divorced. That isn't true. We were never married."

"I'm illegitimate?"

"If you need to label yourself in those terms then yes, you were born outside wedlock. It's such a horrible term, so demeaning, as if only children born within marriage are 'legitimate' children."

"I've always wondered. I mean you've never said anything about him."

"I knew I'd have to tell you one day, I just never thought it would be to show you that you cannot stay here on the island on your own. You have to come away with me, Janey, you must."

"OK. I'm listening."

"Really?"

"Yes."

"We've got to go back to the war. I starting working in one of the ministries in London when I was 18 and when the war ended I had to find something else to do. I didn't like the idea of having to find a husband, that wasn't so easy after the war anyway with so many more women than men around, so I went to work for someone I'd known at the ministry who was going into politics."

As she listened to her mother Jane thought it sounded like a long prepared explanation. Her mother was showing no emotion and Jane wasn't sure whether that was because she didn't care or because she cared too much.

"That man unexpectedly got into parliament in 1950 and he began to progress up what they call the greasy pole of politics. He became quite successful. I wasn't particularly young and I wasn't particularly pretty but I was efficient and unattached and considered safe so I started accompanying him on trips when he needed a woman to escort. I was well into my thirties and that was considered quite on the shelf then. Everyone I knew thought of me as a career spinster. It was all terribly above board and completely respectable. I really didn't want the relationship to be anything other than professional because I liked him very much and I respected him."

"But you didn't love him?" Jane wanted it to be personal.

"I don't think I ever thought about it in those terms. We were friends, first and foremost, for years. But we grew close and the sex side of things came a lot later. We sort of just fell into it, it just happened, I don't think either of us had ever thought it would."

"When are we talking about?"

"1957. You can't imagine how things have changed for women in such a short time, Jane darling. But they were different times in more ways than that. Everyone in the country had thought that all our troubles would be gone when the war was finally over but the peace was only just the beginning of other problems. The Cold War was a dire time. People understood something of how close we were to complete nuclear annihilation, but very few understood how much this country owed America and how quickly they wanted to be paid back, and how that meant we had to do exactly what the Americans wanted us to do. It was a time when no one had enough of anything, not enough food to eat, not enough clothes to keep them warm through awful winters, not enough houses to live in, not enough of anything. Everyone had expected that 1950's would herald this brave new world. It was a new half-century, everything was going to be put right. But it didn't quite work out like that. It really wasn't an easy time to be in government."

"And my father was in government?"

"Yes, he was." Again, Elizabeth lied and told the truth at the same time.

"And one night it all got out of hand?" Jane prompted, wanting to get away from the history lesson and back to the explanation of how she had come into existence.

"Yes. There was a very late night sitting in the House and afterwards we just went back to his office and one thing led to another."

"Was that when I came along?"

"No. Not for quite some time. It was never going to be a one-night-stand. But once the dam had been breached, as it were, it could not be mended."

"How long?"

"How long did the affair last? Until I realised I was pregnant. That was mid-1959, so just over two years."

"And no one found out?"

"Oh yes. Quite a few people knew about it. He had to tell the Prime Minister, even though he had far more important things to worry about at the time. And the Secret Services had to know because I went abroad with your father a few times. A few others I suppose, but not many."

"So you were my father's mistress?" Jane asked, almost smiling.

"What a wonderfully old fashioned word!"

"Well, were you?"

"I suppose in some ways I was, though I never thought of it like that. I was never kept by him as you would expect a mistress to be kept. I had my own flat, I earned my own living, I was independent; it was just that I went to bed with a man to whom I was not married. No one would think twice about it these days."

"At least I wasn't the product of a one-night's stand."

"Is that what you thought?"

"I have often wondered whether you actually knew who my father was."

"I'm sorry you thought that. That must be horrid. I should have told you more about it earlier." Elizabeth looked, with great tenderness, at her daughter. "Your father was a good man. You are like him in many ways, you have his skill with numbers but more, you have his ability to be quiet and to think things through. Sometimes, when I look at you concentrating on your homework, I see him."

"You loved him?"

"I suppose I did, in a way, though somehow putting a word to the feelings we had seemed unimportant at the time. Now isn't the time to go into what 'love' is and how many different sorts of emotions come under that one heading but I will say I just wish it had been possible for us all to have lived a normal life together. I do regret that we were not able to do that."

"So what happened when you found yourself, you know, up the duff?"

Elizabeth looked at her daughter. She had known that one day she would have this, or a similar, conversation and she had rehearsed what she would say many times. She had hoped to be able to choose a moment when they could have relaxed afterwards, talked everything through, but now she had less than half an hour before they had to pack their things and leave the only home Jane could remember.

She tried not to speak quickly. "In 1959 it really wasn't that easy. Women who got themselves into trouble really couldn't just go to the chemist and get a morning after pill, or nip down to the family doctor and get referred for an abortion. You went through with it either by marrying the father or having the baby adopted. Very, very few respectable women became single mothers. But I had no choice. I couldn't marry your father and I couldn't bear to lose you up to adoption, so we had to find a third way."

"Why couldn't you marry him?"

It was the question Elizabeth had dreaded. She had known Grahame would never be allowed to marry her, not with her background, even under the circumstances of her having his child. But she had not known about Laura and that meant she had failed in her surveillance, a situation that made her feel even worse about what had happened. She should have known. She should have seen it coming.

"I suppose the simple answer, darling, is that he didn't want to marry me." It was the easiest way out.

"Oh." Jane was surprised at the simple answer.

"Perhaps he needed a different sort of wife than I could have been. And at the time, if there had been any scandal, it could have brought down the government and they couldn't allow that to happen."

Jane was sensitive enough to realise she should not push that line of enquiry any further. "So what did you do?"

"I disappeared. One day I was there, at my desk in the department, the next day I was not. One day I was Georgina Carmichael, my real name by the way, the next day I wasn't. I was given a new name, a complete life story really. You must understand that your father had powerful friends and also that sort of thing was easier to arrange before the days of Facebook and everyone in the world carrying a camera around with them."

"Sort of witness protection? We've been studying that sort of thing in Civics."

"Sort of like that I suppose."

"What happened then?"

"You were born and we faded from view."

"Where were we? Here on the island?"

"No. In York."

"I remember." Jane said slowly. "We lived on a hill didn't we? The road sloped steeply. I remember falling off my bike and I remember playing in the garden, in a paddling pool."

Elizabeth was aware time was passing fast. It wouldn't be long before Richard came to take them away, but she knew how important this conversation was to Jane. She couldn't hurry it.

"Yes. We were happy there, I think."

"We left just as I started school didn't we?"

"How funny you should remember that."

"Why did we leave?"

"A man who wanted to do harm to you, to me and to your father had found us and so we had to go."

"Is that what's happening now? He's found us again and we've got to move?"

"It seems so."

"That can't just be because a politician years ago had what they'd call a 'lovechild' can it? I mean they wouldn't keep chasing us just for that would they?"

"That one reporter will not leave the story, that is us, alone. Richard says the longer he has to wait the more determined he is to get the full story."

Elizabeth knew that it sounded bizarre that someone would be that persistent but she had to make Jane believe that she was the only reason this man was pursuing them. "No, Jane darling, there was never anything more than that."

"You won't tell me who my father is will you?"

"You will find out soon enough, if only because I have given you enough clues for a clever girl like you to work it out for yourself."

Jane thought for a few minutes trying to work out who could be so important that a reporter was still be bothering to track her and her mother down 17 years after an affair. Who, she wondered, could be so important that they had never wanted for money, so important that they had never been found.

"Would I know my father's name?" She eventually asked, not really expecting an answer.

"You would. That's why I'm not going to tell you."

"Why not?"

"It would be too much of a burden." Elizabeth finished her wine and moved her chair. "We really need to be getting our things together. Richard will arrange all the big stuff but we need to get our personal things together, and find those cat baskets."

"No Mum. I'll sort that out, but now you're talking to me answer a couple more questions. Please?"

Elizabeth sat back on the chair and tipped some of the untouched wine from her daughter's glass into hers.

"Ten minutes, then we really must get ready." She thought it only fair to give Jane some answers since she was uprooting her from everything she had ever cared about. "Fire away then."

"What about your family? Your parents? Didn't they ask any questions? Didn't they wonder where you'd gone?"

"Your grand-parents died in the war. In 1941."

"In an air-raid?"

"Yes, it was an air-raid. They lived in London and nothing would persuade them to go into a shelter."

"What were their names? Have you got any photos?"

"Why this sudden interest in my parents?" She had been prepared to talk about her daughter's father but had not been expecting a discussion about her own. She could never explain everything to Jane and she had not yet come to any conclusions about what information she could give her daughter.

"Tell me. Please. I want to know more about me and since I can't know anything about my dad and his family I want to know everything about you and yours."

"Their names were Harry and Alexandra."

"Harry and Alexandra Carmichael?"

"Of course."

"And they died in an air-raid. How sad."

"It was. I was at work that night otherwise I would have been dead too."

'It must have been awful."

"It was." Elizabeth hoped that, by using a dead tone of voice, she would stop her daughter asking any more questions, questions that could become awkward to answer. And she had no intention of lying to her daughter any more than she had to. She would fail to tell her everything, perhaps that was lying by omission, but she wouldn't actually lie when asked a direct question.

"Were you close to them?" Jane asked, thinking that she probably shouldn't have.

"Not really. They had been quite old when I was born. The First World War had got in the way of their courtship and so they were in their 40s when I came along, and being in your 40s was old in those days."

She told herself that what she said was the truth, albeit a very limited version of the truth.

"So you haven't any brothers or sisters?"

"I'm sorry. No. I've only got you."

When Elizabeth answered that question she thought she was, for once, telling her daughter the truth. She did not know then that she had a younger brother.

She had no idea that not only did she have a brother but that she had met him, in the gardens by the river in Moscow, one July evening almost exactly eighteen years before.

Jane sipped at the wine thoughtfully. "But since it was so difficult and you had so much to lose why didn't you just get rid of me?"

"As I said, Jane, it was not that easy in 1959 and even if it had been easy I would not have done it. I could not have done it. I wouldn't be without you for the world."

"That's something anyway." Jane said quietly.

Elizabeth allowed a few moments of silence before sitting up straighter, pulling her shoulders back and saying firmly that they had to get ready.

"Now we do have to get a move on. Richard will be back soon and we must do as he says."

"And this will carry on forever?"

"Until your father's career comes to a halt and whatever he may or may not have done is no longer of interest to anyone."

"But that could be years."

"It could."

Jane was silenced as she faced the prospect of never being able to settle down, of never being able to be free of the worry that someone might know who her mother or father really were or who she was.

"One more question Mum, then I promise I'll go and pack an overnight bag."

Elizabeth sat back in her chair and nodded. Jane continued. "Who is Richard? Really I mean. He's not just any old friend is he?"

"That's the easy one!" Elizabeth almost laughed. "He is our friend, Janey darling, he's the one who looks after us."

"He's a fixer?"

"A fixer? What an interesting description. I suppose in a way he is, but he's a policeman. He's a very dear friend who just happens to be a policeman."

"So a policeman's telling us we really have to move?" Jane tried to make her voice sound efficient and business-like, she did not want to show the enormous resentment she felt at being uprooted when it was nothing to do with her.

"Yes. I'm so sorry but I have to go and you must come with me."

"Why must I?"

"Because you can't stay here on your own and, as I say, I cannot stay here at all."

Elizabeth realised she was losing the battle to persuade Jane who was beginning to dig her heels in.

"I know what they do on these programmes, they make people change their names, make them forget everything about their lives. I don't want to change my name and I don't want to forget everything I've ever known."

"I don't know what I can say to convince you other than there really is no choice."

"Just so this unnamed man who is my father has his career saved?"

"There is more to it than that."

"What?"

"I really can't tell you."

"No?"

"No."

"We have to just roll over and do as this policeman says?"

"Yes."

"It's shitty."

"Yes. It's shitty." Elizabeth couldn't disagree. "But the quieter we are about everything when we get there the safer we will be and the longer we can stay."

"That's blackmail!"

"No it isn't Jane. Look we haven't got time to argue. Go and put your stuff in a bag, we have to leave tonight."

But Jane wasn't going to give up easily, she was getting increasingly frightened at the prospect of having to leave everything that was familiar behind.

"Can't you tell me anything about who I'm going to have to be?"

Her mother nodded. "You'll still be Jane and I'll still be Elizabeth."

"And the rest of the name? We won't be Somerset any more will we?"

"Our surname will be Birch."

"Birch? Jane Birch? I really don't like that. Don't we have any say in it?"

"It's all been arranged so, no, we don't have any say in it."

"Don't you mind that?"

"I understand some of what goes into organising it so, no, I don't think we're in a position to tell them anything."

"So where are we going? Will we still be by the sea?"

"We've been found a nice house on the edge of a very nice town in Shropshire."

"That's nowhere near the sea!"

"The house is close to a river, but no, you're right, there is no sea, no beach, no sailing. I'm sorry, Jane. So sorry. But you must know I wouldn't do this to you if it weren't absolutely the only thing we can do."

"I think this is all so much shit."

"I can't disagree but go up and put a few things in a bag, and put the cats in their basket, Richard will be back shortly. Please be nice to him darling, he's doing his best for us you know."

"We can take the cats?"

"As if we'd leave them behind!" Elizabeth tried to make a joke of her daughter's question, but simply the fact that Jane had felt she had to ask made her feel dreadful.

From the moment she had put the phone down after Richard's call Elizabeth had known that this move would be far less easy to carry off successfully than the move from York. Then Jane had been only 5 years old and had accepted everything as only a child could, now she was 16 and was questioning everything and accepting nothing on trust.

"Go on Jane. Upstairs. Please. I'll clear up here." She tried not to show her daughter how upset she was as she took the glasses and the empty bottle into her familiar kitchen.

As she did the last washing up she would ever do looking out over her pots of carefully tended geraniums and the fence covered with sweet peas, just coming into flower, she could not stop her tears from falling. As she angrily brushed them away she wasn't sure whether they were tears of anger at having to uproot Jane and leave their home, at frustration at Eric Atkinson's prejudiced perseverance, at fear of the unknown or simply tears of self-pity.

Deciding it was self-pity she made herself think of what she had said to Richard as they had driven south from York, 'my life, from now on, has to be all about Jane'.

She carefully folded the drying up cloth and placed it on the draining board before heading up the stairs. 'Jane,' she said to herself firmly, 'it really is all about Jane.'

Chapter 9
Ludlow, Shropshire, 1976

It had all happened so quickly.

After she had left her mother downstairs Jane had packed what she would need for two days and had caught the cats and placed them, complaining as loudly as she wanted to, into their travelling basket.

"No phone calls!" Richard had yelled up the stairs announcing his return. "And hurry up, we've only got a few minutes to get to the ferry."

They stayed in the car for the forty minutes crossing of the Solent to Lymington. Jane had wanted to get out and watch Yarmouth disappear, certain that she would never see it again, but Richard was adamant that they should not risk anyone seeing them leave.

"We must stay in the car."

"Why?"

"Someone may see us and recognise you or your Mum."

"And? So? What if they did?"

Richard looked at Elizabeth who shrugged.

"Look Jane. One day…"

"I know. One day 'when I'm older' I'll understand. That is just so much complete rubbish. I'm 16. I'm not a child anymore."

"But you are just proving to your mother how immature you still are. Just shut up and stay quiet."

"Richard!" Elizabeth looked at him trying to warn him that that was not the way to talk to her daughter.

He understood and changed his tone.

"I'm sorry Jane but you must realise that I wouldn't ask you to do these things if I wasn't really worried. Honestly, it's not just a case of an article in a paper. It really is more than that. You mustn't put yourself and your mother at risk by giving anyone a chance to see you."

Her mother added her voice. "Please Jane, understand what Richard is saying."

"But how can keeping in touch with a couple of friends put us at risk? You wouldn't even let me say goodbye. What will they think of me?" Jane tried to continue the argument she knew she was losing.

Richard started to explain, as if to a small child, slowly and deliberately. "There will be people who will be asking all your school friends what they know of you. It really would put them in a difficult position if you tell them anything. Think how much easier it will be for them if they really don't know, and really haven't heard from you. Think how difficult it would be for them if they had to choose between telling these people what they knew, possibly for money, or lying. By saying nothing you are being more of a friend to them."

Jane had no answer to that. So she sat in sulky silence as they drove north towards Swindon.

She may have given up the argument she knew she could not win, she may have been tired and she was definitely unhappy but one thing she knew. She was never going to forgive her mother for putting her in this situation.

Her resentment grew with every mile. She thought back over what her mother had said about her father, about his career, about her grandparents, about the choice her mother had had to make and it seemed to Jane that everything Richard was making them do was to make someone else's life easier. No one seemed to worry about what this was all doing to her.

She stared out of the car window at the blackness and she sulked.

None of any of this was her fault.

She hadn't asked to be born yet she felt she was the only one to be suffering as she curled up and tried to make herself comfortable on the back seat of Richard's car, her arms wrapped around the cats' travelling basket. At least Otty and Beavy loved her. She pushed her fingers into the basket and was rewarded with strangely comforting licks from their rough tongues as she gradually let herself fall asleep.

"Do you remember the other drive?" Richard asked, once she was sure Jane was asleep.

"You mean from York? Yes. Of course I do."

"She was so innocent then wasn't she? I suppose that's the difference between 5 and 16 years old." Richard said, his voice filled with practicality and some humour.

"I suppose it is."

Several miles later Elizabeth continued the conversation. "You know she was so pleased to find Big Teddy on her bed when we got to the new house?"

"She was so sweet then, so trusting and now she's becoming more and more questioning."

"As you once said, she is undoubtedly her parents' daughter."

Richard parked outside the new house in the middle of the afternoon. Jane and Elizabeth peered out of the car windows without moving. The road was a quiet one and they could see the river running alongside, the water level very low in the continuing drought. The house was a two-storey middle terrace made of red brick and it seemed a lot larger than their cottage.

"Is that it?" Jane asked sulkily.

"It is." Richard answered.

"Oh."

"Come on," Elizabeth opened her door, "Let's get unloaded."

As Richard carried their bags and Jane the cats' basket they walked up the path from the road towards the green front door.

"I hope you'll be happy here." Richard said as he held the door open for them to walk into the strange, empty house.

"I doubt it." Jane said. "It's horrible."

She and Elizabeth walked separately from room to room which even in the hot afternoon sun seemed cold and unwelcoming.

"It's horrible!" Jane repeated. "It's all brown. And it smells."

"It has been empty for a few months." Richard admitted. "But someone has been in opening the windows, keeping it aired."

"It still smells as if someone died here." Jane said as she looked in the room that she assumed would be the living room.

"We'll get all your things up from the island as soon as we can arrange it."

"And the pictures from my bedroom wall." Jane spoke with determination. She wasn't going to make this easy for either her mother or for Richard.

"It'll only be a day or so."

"The kitchen's like something out of the 1950s. It's even older fashioned than the one in York." She told Richard as they both remembered that day.

"Then you made me a cup of coffee."

"It was the middle of the night."

"Any chance of a cup of tea now?"

"I'd like one too." Jane added as she walked into the kitchen and sat down at the large pine table.

"There'll be someone along with a better cooker and washing machine. Those should come today but there should be some nice crockery and cutlery."

Richard watched Elizabeth as she opened and shut cupboard doors looking for the things necessary to make three mugs of tea.

"Someone's stocked the fridge." She said taking out a pint of milk. "Thanks. We can put up with this for a while can't we Janey?"

"I suppose we'll have to."

Elizabeth's hopes that her daughter would relax were disappointed when Jane took her mug of tea and left the kitchen without saying another word.

Jane climbed the bare wooden stairs and she looked around the bedrooms, choosing the larger one in the front. She didn't want to think anything good at all about this house but she did allow that this bedroom was larger than the one she had just left. And it was lit up in the afternoon sun whereas her old bedroom had always been a little dark. And, she reluctantly admitted to herself, there was a lovely view across the quiet road over a small river, almost dried to a trickle in the on-going drought, to a field, yellow with grain. She didn't want to feel disloyal to her bedroom on the island but there she had looked out onto the brick wall of the house next door. 'Perhaps,' she thought, 'it wouldn't be so bad.'

But she was never going to admit that to anyone else but herself.

"I'll leave you to settle in then." Richard said when he had finished his tea. "Take care of yourselves. Hopefully it will be some while before we meet again."

He shook Elizabeth's hand formally.

"Say goodbye to Jane. I'm sure she'll come round. It will be strange for a bit but she will make friends."

"I hope you're right." Elizabeth replied doubtfully.

"I'll call on Sunday."

"Thank you."

And he was gone.

Five minutes later Jane walked into the kitchen and announced she was going for a walk.

"No Jane. Not today. Please. Stay here with me. They've filled the fridge and we can get a salad together and sit in the garden with a bottle of wine."

"Just like yesterday." Jane tried to sound ironic but only managed to sound miserable. "Was it only yesterday?"

"Please Jane, this isn't easy for either of us. I've left everything that's familiar to me too, it's not just your life that's been completely disrupted."

"But it's your fault."

"Please don't let's argue. We need to help each other make the best of it."

Jane headed into town early the next morning. Even at half past seven it seemed very hot. She was used to there always being a sea breeze but then, she reasoned, Ludlow was almost as far from the sea as it was possible to get. She would miss the sea. The river she walked along as she headed towards the town was only a dribble and she wondered vaguely what it would be like in full flow. She turned up the hill towards what looked like the town centre.

She had set out early hoping to be able to look around before anybody was out and about, but as she turned into the market place she saw that the town was already busy. She walked up and down the aisles of stalls watching as customers and stall-holders chatted and laughed together. Everything was totally strange.

In Yarmouth and Freshwater she had known all the shops, every broken paving slab and most of the people, but here there was nothing that was familiar.

On the island she had known where everywhere was, the place names on the signposts all meant something. Here she looked at the road signs and didn't recognise one name. She felt as though she were in a foreign country.

And she knew no one.

She went into a café, ordered a cup of tea and sat at a table in the window.

She was utterly miserable.

She knew she should be heading back down the hill as her mother would be worrying about her but she was determined to stay out a long time. She made the last half an hour as she stared through the window at the busy market.

If her mother was worried, too bad, maybe if she was made to be really worried she would understand how wrong it had been to leave the island.

She ordered another cup of tea and a bun.

It was after ten o'clock when she realised the owner of the café was looking at her, perhaps wondering why it had taken her over two hours to drink two cups of tea and eat one bun. So she got up, took her cup and plate over to the counter, said 'sorry', she wasn't sure why, and left.

As she saw groups of boys and girls about her age laughing together on the benches by what looked like castle walls she thought of the friends she had left behind. They would be on the beach and they would be talking about her. What would they be thinking? Would there have been reporters asking them where she'd gone? She rather hoped there would be.

This morning she was supposed to have been meeting them by the pier and then they were all going to ride their bikes round to Colwell Bay. Would they have waited for her? Perhaps one of them had said they'd go round to her house to see why she was late. Perhaps they'd find an empty house, or perhaps Richard's people were still clearing it out.

She wondered how long it would be before they gave up wondering what had happened to her and how long before they forgot she had ever existed.

She didn't think she would find it easy to make friends here in Ludlow. Everyone her age would already have been in a group for years, probably since primary school, just as she had been back on the island.

As she headed back down the hill her thoughts was filled with self-pity and resentment against her mother. 'I hate you. I hate you. I hate you. And I'll never ever think of this place as home.'

Two days later a van arrived with boxes someone had packed for them. As she put her clothes away in the old-fashioned chests of drawers and stuck her posters over the unfortunate wallpaper she tried not to give in to the thought that all her private things had been touched and seen by a stranger, but she failed and spent the rest of the day curled up on her bed with Otty and Beavy. Perhaps they felt as lonely as she did, but then she felt even more resentful as she realised that they had each other.

She didn't leave the house for a week, spending the time sun-bathing in the back garden, reading the trashy romantic novels she had found on a bookshelf in the dining-room and talking to her mother as little as possible.

Elizabeth, who was feeling no less lonely and just as unsettled, let her daughter work through her resentment.

They had lived in Ludlow for a little under two weeks when Elizabeth asked her daughter to go into the town to do the shopping.

"There's a street market today. It might be fun."

"Fun?" Jane remembered the way she had felt that first morning. The way everyone seemed to know each other, the way she was just an outsider.

"Well more fun than just going into a supermarket or even normal shops."

"At least no one knows how ignorant I am in a supermarket. I don't have to acknowledge that I haven't a clue how many sausages there are in a pound."

Elizabeth looked at her daughter to see if she was being serious. "Just ask for what you want, I've put it on the list. Don't be such a wilting Minnie."

"OK." Jane stood up reluctantly. "I'll go."

Many years later, as she sat through the court case listening to so many lies being told about her, she wished with all her heart she hadn't agreed to go shopping that morning. As she sat in court more 'if onlys' came to her mind as she remembered that day.

If only she had refused point blank to go. If only she had stayed arguing with her mother a little longer. If only she'd said she'd do the shopping later, or go to the supermarket as usual.

But she hadn't refused to go, she hadn't argued about it for longer and she hadn't delayed going until later or gone to the supermarket.

So that morning she did meet David Childs.

Jane was in no hurry.

She stood by the bridge watching the ducks trying to keep cool in the shade of the willow tree. She looked at the list her mother had made deciding what else she would get and what she would 'forget'. Then she screwed up the list and threw it into a bin. 'Nothing', she thought, 'was more naff than going shopping with a list'. She gazed vaguely in the shop windows as she ambled up the hill towards the market.

Nothing seemed interesting enough to bother about. There was a wool shop where all the wools seemed to be baby pink or baby blue. Next to it was a sweet shop whose window was filled with old-fashioned jars filled with unappetisingly brown lumps. The flower shop seemed to specialise only in wreaths for funerals so she dismissed her half thought out idea of buying some flowers for her room.

She hadn't been focussing on anything, there was, she thought, very little worth focussing on, when her attention was drawn sharply to the image on the front of one of the magazines in the newsagents.

The magazine cover was a cartoon of various members of the government and as she looked at the drawing she knew that the man in the centre was her father.

She saw the likeness. She wondered why she had never noticed it before in the hundreds of times she had seen his face on the television and in the newspapers. Then she realised it was because the cartoonist had picked out certain features that they shared; the slight bend in the nose, the shape of the eyes, the chin that was quite square, lips that were too narrow.

The cartoon could have been one, albeit a very cruel one, of her.

Now she knew the reason for all the secrecy. Now she understood why she and her mother would never be able to have a normal life.

As she walked around the street, not looking at shops, simply staring at the pavement in front of her, her eyes filled with tears. How could the man she knew had to be her father be so selfish? How could that man Richard claim to be their friend when he was only a dogsbody? How could her mother be so weak that she didn't stand up to either of them? And why did none of them worry about what they were doing to her?

As she walked towards the bright and bustling market place she was determined not to allow herself to be downtrodden like her mother had been. She would not live her life in the way that suited anybody else. She had given in to them too often.

It was her misfortune that she was in a rebellious frame of mind when David Childs blocked her way in the narrow street.

On any normal day she would have told him to piss off and would have brushed passed him as he asked her who she was and why he had never seen her before.

But this was no normal day for Jane.

If it had been a normal day, back on the island in a town she knew, she would have had the confidence to ignore him and get on with her shopping. But it wasn't a normal day and she hadn't the confidence to ignore him and when he started talking to her she didn't tell him where to go. She knew that being picked up walking along the street was not the way to make any friend worth having, no matter how much she wanted to meet people, but she didn't ignore him, instead she stopped and when he suggested an ice cream she walked with him to the van parked by the castle gate.

This was exactly what her mother, and Richard, and her father and anyone would have told her not to do. So she did it.

He said his name was David Childs. 'Now you won't forget that will you?' he had said before asking her what her name was. She could think of no good reason not to tell him but he didn't believe her. 'No one's called Jane' he had said before telling her about all the ideas the name 'Jane' gave to him. She thought he was a bit odd when he started telling her he imagined himself as Tarzan holding her in his arms and swinging through treetops.

He asked her whether she had just moved to the town, she couldn't have lived there long as he would have seen her before, or whether she was just a tourist. Having lived all that she could remember of her life in a place where trippers frequently outnumbered residents she knew she would never admit to being a tourist. When she told David Childs she had just moved to the town he asked her where she lived but she just said 'half a mile outside town'. He was beginning to seem altogether too nosy.

When he asked her back to his place to listen to a record he had just bought her common sense over-ruled her newly found rebellion and she told him she couldn't, she had to do some shopping, she'd already been out too long. 'Another time then' he had said as she stood up, thanked him for the ice cream and walked away.

As she went from stall to stall in the still busy market buying what she could remember from her mother's list, she thought he might follow her but whenever she looked over her shoulder she couldn't see him. Her basket full of things her mother may or may not have wanted she wondered if she would ever see David Childs again and decided she didn't care one way or the other.

He was quite good looking, quite well spoken, but he was also quite creepy.

It was only when she walked past the newsagent and saw the magazine cartoon cover that the thought crossed her mind that David Childs might have seen that magazine cover and, having seen it, might have recognised a likeness and that was why he had picked her out as she had walked along the street. And that was why he had spent so much time talking to her. She could think of no other reason.

As did many 16 year old girls, Jane hated her appearance. She was not tall and slender, her hair was not long blonde and straight. That she was shorter and plumper and far less attractive than her friends hadn't mattered when she had known them all since they were five years old, when they were all in school uniform or jeans and sweatshirts but here, amongst strangers, wearing shorts and a t-shirt she was very aware of her shortcomings. David Childs must have had another reason to talk to her, it could not have been because he had found her attractive.

"Do you think we'll settle here?" Jane asked her mother as she put the shopping away in the still unfamiliar kitchen cupboards.

"Ideally? Yes. Realistically? Probably not."

"I suppose it'll get more difficult as I get older. It must have been easy shutting yourself away when I didn't ask any questions and just accepted whatever you said." She did not attempt to hide the resentment from her voice. "I know who my Dad is." She added, as if as an afterthought.

Elizabeth was not surprised. She knew Jane would work it out after their conversation that last night on the island.

"How did you find out?"

"There's a cartoon on the front cover of a magazine. I saw it in the newsagent. It could have been me."

"You do take after him."

"I think his politics stink."

"So do a lot of people."

"But they still vote for him."

"And as long as the majority want him to be in government we will have to stay under the radar."

"That could be years."

"It was never meant to be this long, you know love, it was only ever meant to be for five or six years. He was going to give up and do something academic but he got the bug for power I suppose."

"But it's been seventeen years now. How much longer?"

"At least another four or five."

"It's not fair. I don't know why you've put up with it. Is he so bloody ashamed of us? Honestly Mum why do you put up with it? Times had changed since you were pregnant. And wouldn't most people say 'good chap' if it did come out that he had a bastard daughter?"

"I agreed." Elizabeth said simply, hoping it would be enough to satisfy Jane. She really didn't want to go into the real reasons for the need for such secrecy.

"Why don't we come out with it ourselves? It would be a two day wonder in the press. It really wouldn't do him any harm. How could it?"

"I told you, Jane, I agreed."

"You agreed in exchange for money. That's it isn't it? If you go public then all the money and the houses and everything will dry up. He just bought us off. You've never had a job have you? All our money comes from him doesn't it?"

Elizabeth was thinking more quickly than it appeared she was. She dried the dishes and put them away methodically but her mind was racing. How much should she tell Jane? How much knowledge could she trust her with? What would be the intended and unintended consequences of telling her the truth? The draining board was clear before she came to her decision. Just as she had told Jane not to tell her friends on the island that they were leaving, Jane must not know the true reason for the secrecy.

If kept in ignorance Jane would never be in the position of having to lie.

Jane must always believe that secrecy was necessary because she was her father's daughter, however that might stretch her credulity, and however low it would leave her opinion of her mother.

"I agreed, Jane."

"So I'm stuck with all this."

"I'm sorry."

"Surely I can make my own life, go to university, get a job. I can leave home and you can carry on with this ridiculous charade."

"I can't keep you prisoner, Jane, but I'm asking you. Please stay with me and help me play the part."

"Whatever the cost?"

"If we stay quiet there won't be any need to move again. We can be settled as Elizabeth and Jane Birch. If no one asks questions about us then we won't have to move on again. We must just keep living quietly and unobtrusively and make sure no one finds out who we are."

"So I'm not to make friends, not to trust anyone?"

"I know it's a lot to ask, especially as you meet boys and want to get to know them."

"Tell me Mum, if Richard hadn't come down to move us off the island would you ever have told me anything?"

"You wouldn't have needed to know."

"So I would have grown up and left home and lived my life not having any idea of who I really was?"

"You would always be my daughter, Jane."

"So if Richard hadn't come you wouldn't have told me anything so I wouldn't be shit scared all the time about saying or doing the wrong thing."

"Are you? Scared I mean?"

"I don't know what I am. But ever since we moved here I'm can't get away from your fear and you don't trust anyone. It's always 'don't go too far' and 'don't be late back' and 'don't speak to anyone'. It really isn't fair."

"No it isn't. I know it isn't. And if there were any alternative I wouldn't be putting you through this."

"And there really is no alternative? I don't believe you."

"You have to."

"So we've just got to wait until this man who found us on the island finds us again?"

"We must hope he doesn't."

"So all this secrecy and all this cloak and dagger stuff is his fault really? No one else is the least bit interested. Is that what you're saying?"

"It's because of him, yes. For some reason he wants to cause as much harm as he can to as many people as possible."

"So you're just the innocent victim in this?" Jane's voice betrayed more than a hint of sarcasm.

"No darling, that's you. And I am so, so sorry. But believe me, there is nothing else we can do now but play the hand we have been dealt and hope that man doesn't track us down again."

"Well I hope Richard knows his job and kept our tracks well hidden. I don't want to have to move again."

And with that Jane went upstairs to her room where Otty and Beavy were lying contentedly in the sunshine on her bed purring loudly. "Oh shut up you two!" Jane yelled and threw a t-shirt at them, the only thing she could get her hands on. They opened their eyes, stared at her, and closed them again.

Jane grabbed a book and left them to it. She would spend the rest of the day sulking and reading in the garden.

She had already forgotten about David Childs.

But David Childs had not forgotten her.

In a town where every boy knew every girl his age because they had all grown up together, a girl recently moved to the town was bound to attract notice but even allowing for her 'newness' David thought there was something mysterious and secretive about the girl who said her name was Jane. In the hours after he had met her he wondered what it was about her that seemed familiar. He spent the afternoon hanging about with his friends, listening to records in Woolworths but he couldn't stop thinking about Jane.

It was only as he walked past the newsagents on his way home later that afternoon that he saw who it was that Jane reminded him of. After that afternoon, every time he saw Grahame Johnstone on the news, he thought of Jane and since Grahame Johnstone was frequently on the news through that late summer and autumn he never forgot about the mysterious, secretive girl.

When she started at her new school in September Jane kept herself to herself, avoiding the possibility of making friends. She found it easy to fit in but be anonymous at the same time. She would smile if she noticed someone smiling at her but she would speak only when spoken to, never beginning a conversation with anyone.

It was a large school and she was sure that, as the end of her first term loomed, most of the teachers and all but one or two of her fellow pupils did not even know her name.

Her efforts to be anonymous came to an end, however, in early December.

It had been decided that a Lower Sixth debating society would be formed as part of the General Studies course and the inaugural debate was to be held against the sixth form of the local boys' grammar school. So many girls volunteered to speak that a ballot was taken, every girl's name was written on a scrap of paper, carefully folded and placed in the emptied waste paper bin. Jane was horrified when hers was the first name drawn out. She said she couldn't do it, that someone else should be allowed to do it, someone who wanted to do it. But she was not allowed to withdraw 'it wouldn't be fair' the teacher said, brooking no argument.

When she got home that evening she told her mother.

"It shouldn't be too much of a problem, kitten, it's not a public event is it?"

"No, just our sixth form and the boys' school. Just like a late class really"

"Well, you're interested in current affairs, you should do well. You must work on the subject, be sure of your facts, be sure of your views and argue with honesty and conviction."

Jane was amazed at how much help her mother was in the days leading up to the debate, giving advice on how to speak in public, how often and when to look at her notes, when to look at members of the audience, when to look at no one in particular. She began to look forward to the evening.

She had no expectations that the girls' team would win the vote as the proposal, that the planned town by-pass should be cancelled, deserved to be defeated. Jane and the two other speakers on her team had been warned that they would certainly lose the vote as it was patently obvious to all that there had to be a by-pass but it would be good experience marshalling arguments in a lost cause.

After an hour of listening to the boys' badly put together and ineffectively presented arguments there was a break for coffee. Jane stood apart from the other girls in the team who had gone to join their friends flirting with a group of the boys. She sipped at the hot weak coffee that had been provided thinking about what she would say in her contribution.

"Hi."

She looked at the boy who she thought she recognised.

"Remember me?" He asked with what Jane thought to be a degree of arrogance.

She shrugged in response. She had recognised the boy from the summer and just remembered his name was David Childs.

"You're Jane Birch. You didn't tell me your name in the summer."

"No. Well yes I'm Jane Birch and no, I probably didn't tell you in the summer. Why would I tell everyone I meet in the street my name?"

"I don't like the name Jane so I'm going to call you Silver. Silver Birch. Get it?"

Jane rather liked the idea, though she wasn't going to tell this boy that. She thought of a silver birch tree as tall, willowy and graceful, everything she wanted to be but wasn't.

"Well Silver do you fancy going out with me on Friday?" He asked with what she recognised was forced nonchalance.

"OK." She wasn't sure whether she really wanted to but she couldn't think of any good excuse to say no. She could always just stand him up.

"We could see a film."

"OK."

And then it was time to go back to the second half of the debate. David had just enough time to say he'd meet her in the café on the Bullring at 6.30.

When she got home that night, after she had answered all the questions her mother had asked about the debate she admitted that she had a date for Friday. She was totally prepared for her mother to say 'No you can't go' and was rather hoping she would.

"Are you sure? Is he, well, you know, is he OK?"

Jane laughed at her mother's reluctance to ask outright what sort of family he came from, whether he was the sort of boy that could be introduced to her without embarrassment. On the island every family had known every other family.

"He's fine Mum! He seems perfectly respectable. He wears polished leather shoes." She said that as if it guaranteed that he meant her no harm.

As they talked about her Friday date Jane knew she really ought to mention to her mother that throughout the evening there had been a photographer from the local newspaper taking pictures. But, knowing how her mother would take that news, she kept quiet.

She hoped that something far more interesting than a school debate, albeit the first of its type in the town, would occur during the week so no pictures would be published, and if it did decide to print one of the photographs they had taken at the school event it would be tucked away on an inside page and be one of the many that had been taken that did not include her.

"Are you sure you want to go?" Elizabeth asked that Friday evening as she fed Otty and Beavy, her back to her daughter. "You haven't changed your mind about going to the cinema with this young man?"

"You sound as if you want me to have done."

"Well, it's just that.... Well I've got a bad feeling about it that's all."

"I won't go if you don't want me but I can't stand him up."

"You could ring him. What did you say his surname was?" Elizabeth had already picked up the phone book. She really didn't want Jane to go.

"Childs."

After a few seconds thumbing through the directory Elizabeth said she could find no entry for anyone called Childs.

"Well that's the name he gave me. David Childs."

"Perhaps his parents are ex-directory." Her mother suggested.

"Or perhaps it isn't his real name. He seems a bit liberal with names. He doesn't like my name, Jane, so he said he was going to call me Silver."

"Silver Birch." Elizabeth smiled reluctantly. "That's really rather good."

"I'm more of a plain Jane."

"Oh don't be so silly."

"If we can't call him I'll have to go won't I? I can't just not turn up, can I? But I'll come straight back. I'm meeting him at the coffee bar. If I can get out of it there I will. Otherwise I'll just see the film and come straight back. I should be back by 10.30, 11 at the latest."

"I know you'll be meeting people and getting to know them, I know that, but I've just got a bad feeling about tonight. I really don't know why."

"Probably because it's the first time I've ever been out with someone you don't know, or whose mother you didn't know. I don't know why I said yes. I thought he was a bit creepy."

"You just come back as quickly as you can." Elizabeth said as she watched the cats gobble up their food. "Ah there's the evening paper. I just wanted to see if….." She stopped short when she saw the front page. "Kitchen. Now."

Jane always obeyed her mother when she used that tone of voice.

"What's the matter Mum? What's the problem?"

Nothing was said as Jane took the paper from her mother's outstretched hand. She knew immediately. "Oh bugger."

"You knew about this?"

Jane nodded.

"You allowed a photograph to be taken that would be printed in the paper? I can't believe you'd be so stupid."

"I couldn't stop him could I? I had no idea there'd be a reporter there! It's not my fault."

"It's the front page story Jane. And look, you aren't just *in* the photograph, you *are* the photograph. And listen to this caption. *'First amongst the young ladies, Jane Birch, 16, argued most persuasively in a lost cause.'*"

"Oh shit."

"Yes my girl 'Oh shit'."

"Maybe …"

"Maybe nothing. That man will be here before we know it. You can't go out tonight. You'll stay here and you'll pack. I've got a phone call to make."

"I'm going." Jane experienced a moment of the same sense of rebellion she had felt that day when she had first met David Childs. "I'm fed up with always having to do what you say we must do. I'm going out."

And she slammed the door behind her.

Jane thought everything seemed to be going quite well with David.

They sat in a booth at the back of the café. She found he was a lot easier to talk to than she remembered. He seemed more interested in her than he had done before, asking her about herself and her family and appearing to be listening to her answers.

When he asked her where she had lived before coming to Ludlow she had answered 'York'. Reasoning that it wasn't a lie and he probably wouldn't know much about the city. When he asked about her family she said she was an only child, no brothers and no sisters.

When he asked her what her father did she smiled sadly and said her father was dead. When he appeared to get flustered and said he was sorry, he shouldn't have said anything, she told him not to worry, he had died when she was a baby and what you never knew you never missed.

She wondered whether he wasn't just a little bit too nosy, didn't look at her a little bit too closely, didn't ask rather too many questions.

Despite her worries she liked the feeling of normality as she sat with a boy in the café where all the other booths were occupied by a girl and a boy all drinking coffee or coke before going to the cinema.

But she knew she ought to get home. Her mother was right, she shouldn't have made the date and, having made it, she shouldn't have come. But she had made the date and she had come, and she decided she would stick it out even though *Midway* was not her sort of film. She wanted to be normal and this was what normal girls did, they went to the pictures with boys on a Friday night. Even though the film was not really one they wanted to see.

She made herself watch the battle scenes and she tried to get involved with the plot but she spent the time waiting for the film to end. With every minute she knew she had made a series of wrong decisions in accepting and then turning up and then staying.

She relaxed a little when she realised David Childs was not going to paw or grope her. He sat without touching her through the whole film and although, at first, she was pleased he didn't try anything on, by the end of the film she had rather wished he had, at the very least, put his arm around her shoulders or held her hand, just to show he liked her a bit.

When he asked to walk her home she accepted, relieved that, perhaps, he wasn't regretting asking her out. She felt unreasonably happy when he put his arm around her as they walked down the broad street towards the river. When he stopped in the dark of the old gateway in the town walls she knew he was going to kiss her.

She had been kissed before but those kisses she considered to have been highly unsatisfactory. They had been delivered either with dry pursed lips or wet open mouths, neither method giving her any pleasure. David Childs' kiss was half way between the two extremes, and, she thought when they eventually pulled apart, an entirely repeatable experience.

She rather liked the feeling of belonging with him as he held her hand the whole time they walked the half-mile back to her house.

"Thank you for taking me out." She said as she turned towards him when they reached her gate. She hoped he would kiss her again and he did begin to put his arms around her and bend his head.

Then she heard voices coming from the house.

Her mother should have been alone. There should have been no voices. It had to be Richard. She forgot all about wanting to be with David. She was filled with guilt. It was her fault. She should never have gone out, this night of all nights.

"I've got to go in David Childs. Goodnight and thank you. I really enjoyed the evening. Sorry."

And she pulled away from him and walked quickly towards the house. She stopped at the door and rang the doorbell. She had a key but she thought it would be better to announce her arrival. It would break up any argument that might be going on in the dark house. She stood resolutely facing the door, determined not to turn and wave to David Childs, as she waited to be let in.

Richard opened the door.

"Come in Jane."

She said nothing, simply walking to the kitchen where her mother was sitting at the table, her head in her hands.

"Mum?"

Elizabeth looked up at her daughter and across at Richard and shook her head.

"Hello Richard. Sorry. This is my fault isn't it?"

"I think perhaps it was. Getting your picture on the front page of a newspaper is hardly what I would call keeping under the radar."

Richard was pleased that Jane had the sensitivity to look sheepish.

"I didn't know that would happen."

"Perhaps it was just bad luck then." He didn't sound convinced.

"I tried to get out of doing the debate but they wouldn't let me and it wasn't my fault there was a newspaper photographer there was it?"

"No, Jane, it wasn't. Though I have to say it's very unfortunate. You've almost phoned every national newspaper in the country and told them where your mother is."

"No one would see it would they?"

"Of course they would."

"And how would he know it was me?"

"Look at the photo Jane." Elizabeth picked up two newspapers, one the local with the photograph of her, the second a national with a photograph of her father."

"Shit."

"Two bloody peas in a pod." Richard added.

"Not quite that." Elizabeth corrected him.

"So we've going to have to move again?" Jane asked, knowing the answer would be yes.

"Yes. We do." Her mother answered firmly.

"You do understand why there is so much secrecy surrounding you and your mother don't you?"

"I suppose I do. But it's just a silly photo in a silly local newspaper. Why would anyone who's looking for us think to look at it and why would anyone link me with him? It's so silly."

"Jane," Richard began wearily, "it is not 'silly'. All the nationals have people in towns like this looking out for stories. Someone will have been on the phone saying 'we've got a girl here who looks the absolute spitting image of Grahame Johnstone, do you want me to check it out?' And the answer will be 'yes'. Nationals will pay a lot for your story, it will get people very inquisitive. So it is definitely not silly. We've already wasted too much time waiting for you to get back from your date. Put some things in a bag. We're off." He said it so firmly and with such conviction that Jane regretted her outburst.

She could not quite interpret the look that passed between Richard and her mother but it looked to her as if they knew more than they were telling her.

"You don't trust me with the truth do you? It's something more isn't it? Tell me."

Still they didn't answer.

"I don't suppose any of what you've told me is the truth."

Richard finally spoke. "It's my job to keep you both safe. That I will do in the only way I know how. I'm sorry you have to move again, it can't be easy for you but believe me, we only do it because it's completely essential."

"What's with this 'keeping safe'? No one's going to kill us are they? No one's going to kill us just because I'm the bastard daughter of some greaseball who cares more for his career than anything else. What would be the worst thing that could happen? A few weeks of the newspapers and shock horror he might have to resign. That's not 'unsafe' is it?"

"Jane, darling, please. Don't be difficult."

"Difficult! I wasn't difficult when we upped sticks and left the island in July was I? I packed and left all my friends just as you told me too. OK I sulked a bit. Who wouldn't? But I settled in. I went to school. I kept beneath the sodding radar. Well now, just as I'm making friends, getting to know people, getting to know the place, you're saying we've got to move again. Well no. I won't go. Not unless you tell me the real reason. I don't believe it's just that I'm, well, I am who I am."

"I really am very sorry, Jane, I will not." Richard did not sound sorry. His voice had a finality and an authority about it that told Jane she was not going to get any answers to any questions she might ask.

"Mum?" She looked for her mother to support her stand. "Tell him to tell me. Or tell me yourself. If you know."

Elizabeth shook her head slowly, not looking her daughter in the eye. "We're going and that's final. Go upstairs and pack a bag."

Realising she wasn't going to win Jane decided to acquiesce with as bad a grace as possible.

"So, whoever's fault it is and for whatever reason we're going to have to move again. We will have to change names. Again." She hoped they understood how angry she felt. "It is absolutely not fair!"

"Life isn't fair and the sooner you take that on board the easier it will be for everyone. Get some stuff together, enough for a week or so. We're leaving in ten minutes."

"What about Otty and Beavy?"

"Trap them here in the kitchen and we'll move them when we get the house contents moved." Richard was uncompromising.

"I want to take them with us."

"Well you can't."

An hour and a half later Jane and her mother were settling into their room in an hotel in Shrewsbury. Neither spoke and the silence was not a comfortable one. Despite it being well past midnight neither was tired and there was no chance either would sleep.

"You haven't told me the truth have you?" Silver sat on her bed her knees up around her chin watching as her mother unpacked what few things they had brought with them.

"What do you mean?"

"They wouldn't be doing all this just because some cruddy politician had a bastard daughter a million years ago."

Her mother made no attempt to answer, simply concentrating on putting their things in drawers. Even if they were only going to be here one night she didn't want to be living out of a suitcase. She felt unsettled enough as it was.

"What is it everyone is so scared about? Scandal? Come on! This is 1976. Times have changed. It's hardly going to ruin his political career or bring down the sodding government is it!"

Still her mother made no attempt to answer.

"It's not the sodding Cold War anymore is it? The Russians aren't going to invade us are they? No one gives a flying fuck about Grahame fucking Johnstone."

Jane tried to shock her mother into making some sort of response, but Elizabeth didn't rise to the provocation and remained steadfastly silent.

"You're not going to tell me are you?" Jane eventually conceded. "You're never going to tell me the truth."

"There is nothing more to tell. Go to bed now. I'm tired even if you aren't. We'll talk in the morning."

But both knew she would do everything to avoid doing that.

As they were eating their room service breakfasts with varying degrees of enthusiasm a knock on the door was swiftly followed by Richard walking into their room. It was obvious to them both that he was not happy. He unfolded the tabloid newspaper and read without emotion.

"*Eighteen years ago an attractive fixture on the Westminster social scene was one Georgina Carmichael.*

Questions were asked when she disappeared in late 1959 but she was soon forgotten. By some. Now she has been found hiding out in a quiet market town in Shropshire with her 16 year old daughter.

Some may say that if a week is a long time in politics then 17 years is a geological epoch but I say that when a politician is still very much in the public eye, a potential Prime Minister, we have every right to know everything about his past, even the murkier parts of it.

You may ask 'Does it matter if a man fathers a love-child?'

I say of course it does if that child and her mother are kept fed and housed and educated by public money, that is taxpayers' money, that is your money.

I say of course it does when that man's policies are so judgemental of single mothers that the lives of lesser mortals are ruined.

I say of course it does when it proves that that man is nothing more than a hypocrite and a liar. More to come."

"Oh shit." Jane was the first to speak when Richard had stopped, very carefully, folding up the newspaper.

"Yes. 'Oh shit'. But this one is somewhat worse." He took one of the more serious newspapers. "They say similar things, though not with quite so much sensationalism, but they have printed a copy of the photograph. Listen to the caption. '*Is there any doubt about who the father is?*'" Richard didn't wait for any response from Jane or Elizabeth. "We need to change your appearance. I'll get a hairdresser here to cut and dye that hair, and you'll need to pluck those eyebrows."

"I've got to change?"

"I think so darling."

"Why didn't they print a photo of you?"

"They wouldn't have been able to find one." Elizabeth answered, perhaps a little too quickly.

"Not even one from 17 years ago? Surely if you were that 'attractive fixture' of the social scene you must have been slapped all over the papers."

Elizabeth looked at Richard for an answer.

"Papers weren't so interested in printing photos in those days. I doubt many were taken and even fewer will survive and those will be in the dark recesses of archives." He couldn't tell Jane that everyone had been very careful not to have any photographs of Georgina Carmichael taken and those that had existed had long ago been destroyed.

The day was spent in the hotel room.

A woman who barely spoke arrived within an hour of Richard's departure and she made all the changes to Jane's appearance that Richard had specified.

In the evening, after she had gone, room service delivered a supper and Elizabeth and Jane picked at it in a silence broken only by the sound of the television.

Chapter 10
West Midlands, 1977

The next morning Richard drove Elizabeth and Jane Bicton to another anonymous house in an anonymous street on the outskirts of Birmingham.

They both hated it on sight.

They had, in their different ways, thought they might one day enjoy living in Ludlow. The house, with its view across the river to fields, needed work and redecoration but they had made a start in the five months they had been there. From this new house all they could see were rows of houses. But then, as Richard had said, they had had to find somewhere quickly and this was all there was that fitted all criteria.

Jane tried not to cry when she was reunited with Otty and Beavy but the tears refused to do anything but fall.

"At least they recognise me." She sobbed. "Oh Mum it isn't fair!"

"We must do what we must do." Elizabeth said. "I've told you why. You really must grow up a bit and listen."

After that, Jane decided to retreat into what her mother called a 'monumental sulk' but which Jane thought was a perfectly justifiable withdrawal of cooperation.

They unpacked without any enthusiasm.

The cats were trapped in the kitchen with the litter tray and their plaintive cries served only to make Jane even more angry at her mother.

"I hate this." Jane said to the empty room as she put the ornaments she cherished on the window-ledge of what would now be her bedroom. She thought it small, dark and boring. She looked out of the window. It looked over the back garden and the back gardens of the neighbours on both sides. At least, she thought, in Ludlow there had been high fences and hedges and no one could see into their garden.

She closed the door behind her and headed for the kitchen.

"This house is shit." She told her mother.

Elizabeth ignored her daughter's language, to have made a point about it would have accepted that she had a point. "I'm sorry love. But we have to do what we're told. There is no alternative."

"What? Just because they pay our bills and rent our homes for us? That report in the paper was right wasn't it? We're being kept by public money just because that man's scared shitless that someone will find out he fucked his secretary."

"That really isn't fair Jane."

"Well tell me what the real reason is."

"I have told you. And please stop rattling on about it. I gave my word we would cooperate. And, by the way, I was never his secretary."

"But why does Richard keep saying he is keeping us safe? That's the word he uses, safe."

"Because that is the instruction he was given."

"And like a good boy he does what he's told."

"Don't be sarcastic. He's keeping us safe from prying eyes, safe from intrusion, safe from humiliation."

"So it's really you he's keeping safe isn't it? Not me. I don't give a shit so it must be you."

"Us. Jane. Us. Because wherever I am you are."

"Until I leave home. Perhaps I should leave now, then I wouldn't be such a problem to you."

"You will not be so stupid."

"No I probably won't. Yet. But as soon as I can I will."

"When you're older you will be free to do whatever you want, obviously. But Jane, please don't do anything hasty."

Elizabeth knew she could never win the argument, especially with Jane in this sort of mood, so she carried on with the unpacking.

"Come on, help me put all this stuff away, at least we have our own pots and pans."

Elizabeth saw the scrap of paper as soon as she opened the box. A quick glance at what was written on it made her smile with relief that the argument would soon be forgotten.

"Look what I've found." She handed her daughter the scrap of paper

"What?"

"Here. A message. Who's it from?"

"The guy from Friday." Her daughter was in no mood to share more information.

"David Childs is the one you went to the pictures with wasn't it?"

There was no answer.

"He must have gone down to see you on Sunday and found the removal van. He must have been very disappointed."

Jane remembered the way she'd felt when he'd kissed her on the way home from the cinema. David Childs was on her side. She knew it, and as she glared across the room at her mother she really believed that he was the only person in the world who was.

"Was there more to it than just the pictures that time?" Elizabeth asked. It seemed to her to be a suspiciously gushing message from a boy to a girl after only one date.

"No. Nothing. I told you. I only met him twice, first time at the debate then the pictures. Oh, there was the time he tried to chat me up at the beginning of the summer."

"Could he have known?"

"Who I am? He never said anything but if I'm so like my father that I had to have all that done to change what I look like then perhaps the whole bloody town knew."

"Don't be like that, Jane, please. Could you have let anything slip?"

"No. I couldn't."

Her answer was emphatic but the question made her think. Had she given anything away as they had talked in the coffee bar before she had left for the cinema or when they had been chatting over coffee at the debate? She didn't think so. She was sure she hadn't.

"You're sure?" Her mother asked.

"Absolutely certain." Jane answered with a certainty she wasn't entirely sure was justified.

"Then you made some kind of impression on him."

"Seems so."

Jane put the piece of paper in her pocket, transferring it to her purse.

For the next two days she barely spoke to her mother. She spent a lot of time in her room day-dreaming about David Childs. Perhaps, she thought, he was one of those lost opportunities of life. Perhaps they would meet again one day. Perhaps she would always remember him even when she was old.

If she had thought about him sensibly she would have realised that she didn't even like him very much but such was her need for someone to hang her dreams on that she built up her feelings for him to such an extent that he became important to her.

As she lay on her bed she allowed herself to imagine meeting him again. He would put his arm around her shoulders again, he would kiss her and she would feel again that sense of belonging.

In her mood of overwhelming self-pity and resentment she rummaged through a bag she had brought with her and found an empty exercise book.

In it she wrote down everything she remembered her mother had told her. About her mother's real name and how her grand-parents had died in the war; about how her mother had worked for her father; about who her father was and what she felt about him; about Richard and why they kept moving house. She wrote about her life on the Isle of Wight and her friends there, and about how she missed them. When she had finished she closed the book and wrote *Silver Birch* in large and ornate lettering on the cover.

She quite liked the name David had given her.

In the week before Christmas Jane visited the school she would be starting at in the New Year.

"I hate it Mum" Jane had said as she and Elizabeth walked across the tarmacked playground to the large modern looking glass and concrete building.

"It is quite big isn't it?" Elizabeth agreed reluctantly.

They asked directions and found their way down the corridors lined with display boards of pupil's work. Knots of boys and girls rushed backwards and forwards shouting at the tops of their voices.

"It's not what I'm used to." Jane said doubtfully.

"I know darling but here it seems they've gone comprehensive."

"Oh." Jane had been proud of passing exams at every stage of her school life.

The Head of Year was brusque and business-like.

"What were you doing at your last school? A levels?"

"Yes, I'd done one term."

"What subjects?"

"Maths, Further Maths and Physics." Jane answered confidently.

"Here're some sample O level papers. Work through what you can over the holidays and we'll see whether you can continue with an A level course."

"What do you mean?"

"Well, if you're being a little optimistic in going for A levels we'll find out sooner rather than later."

"Do you have many girls get to university to read Maths?" Elizabeth asked.

"Is that what you had planned?" The Head of Year asked without enthusiasm. "We'll have to see."

After being shown round the school Elizabeth and Jane walked home in silence. Elizabeth was thinking back to the enthusiasm and thrill of learning that had pervaded the technicum she had visited in Moscow all those years before and Jane was blaming her mother. She had just settled in to the school in Ludlow, she had liked the teachers, she had liked the work and had been doing well. Here, she decided, she would do nothing. She would keep herself to herself, as she had done since leaving the island, but she would not work. She didn't want to do well here where it seemed so little was expected of her.

Ten weeks later Jane Bicton woke up, opened her eyes and did not move from her bed. She lay staring at the ceiling which seemed to her to be moving in coloured waves, rather like a sea painted by an imaginative child who had never been told it was blue.

She did not remember where she was. She looked around the room and it all seemed new to her. She got out of her bed and walked stiffly to the desk under the window and picked up a felt tipped pen. She looked at it for a few moments, as if wondering what it was, before walking back to the bed and laying down on top of the covers.

Staring at the wall she carefully took the cap off the pen and began to draw the patterns that would make more sense of the wallpaper. The black and green swirls she drew spoke to her of links and connections that no one else would be able to understand.

Then she started to write a series of numbers, 157 342 836 426 777 142 780 535 703 665 281 520 334, a sequence of numbers that seemed to her to make perfect sense. She drew diamonds and triangles, cubes and rhomboids encapsulating the numbers, trapping them so they could not escape.

Then she wrote, in large block capitals, on the wall behind her bed-head I CANNOT BE WHO YOU WANT ME TO BE. Then she carefully blacked in the holes in the As and the Os and the Bs. Then she drew scoll-like lines from the tops of the letters.

When Elizabeth came into the room to nag Jane to get up and get ready for school she stared at the wall.

"Janey?"

But Jane didn't answer, she was lying, her face towards the wall.

"Janey?"

Elizabeth sat on the side of the bed and put her hand on her daughter's shoulder, expecting it to be shrugged off, but there was no response.

She knew Jane was unhappy, she knew she had dreaded starting at the new school, but she had expected her daughter to face up to the challenge, just as she had in the summer when she had started afresh in Ludlow.

"Janey?"

"It is all my fault isn't it?" Jane didn't turn over to look at her mother. "It has always been my fault. Everything's always been my fault." She stared eyes wide open, staring at the wall.

Elizabeth couldn't move. She tried to speak but nothing would come out. She stared at the wall and back at her daughter who was laying on her bed staring at the patterns she had drawn on her wall.

"It really isn't Janey." She whispered. "Honestly. It really isn't."

"It's my fault for being born." Jane said still staring at the wall. "You should have gone and had a knitting needle stuck up you."

"Oh Janey, I couldn't have done that."

Jane ignored her mother. "Then I'd never have existed."

"Janey, darling, I love you. I would never have been without you."

"I should never have been allowed to exist."

In those minutes, as Elizabeth realised Jane was on the brink of a breakdown, she came closest to telling her daughter the truth. But she could not give her the burden that that knowledge would bring.

"Janey. I love you so much. I'm so, so sorry."

Elizabeth sat on the bed for what seemed like a long time but was probably only a few minutes. Jane said nothing, she didn't turn over to face her mother, she stayed staring at the wall just inches from her face.

Eventually Elizabeth left her alone, closing the door quietly behind her and she went downstairs to phone the school.

"I need to speak to someone to ask if my daughter has been having trouble settling in."

"Your daughter?"

"Jane Bicton. She started at the beginning of the term. I need to know how she is getting on."

Jane had always loved going to school, ever since those earliest days in York and even in Ludlow she had settled in quickly and had done well. Elizabeth realised she should have asked the question before but Jane had given her no sign of being particularly unhappy.

"Who?"

"Jane Bicton."

"I'll check."

Elizabeth thought that the woman at the other end of the phone seemed particularly uninterested and it seemed a long time before she came back on the line.

"Her form mistress is not in school today."

"Is there anyone else who might be able to help?"

"I'll ask."

Five more minutes passed before there were a few clicks and then a voice.

"Mrs Bicton? I am Jane's Head of Year. Can I help?"

"I am worried that my daughter may not be settling in." Elizabeth repeated her concerns. "Have there been any problems?"

"She's only been with us for a few weeks."

"Long enough for you to spot any problems I would have thought." Elizabeth responded coolly.

"I've got her file here. All the staff write any issues they may have with a pupil in the file. If there were any problems they would be noted in here."

"What does it say?"

There was a long silence.

"Well? What does it say?"

"Perhaps you could come into school to see me. I think this might be best dealt with face to face."

"Whatever 'it' is I would like you to tell me now. If needs be I will come in later but you need to answer my simple question."

"It appears she hasn't communicated with anyone. She doesn't talk to anyone and doesn't answer the simplest of questions such as what her name is. She says her name is Silver Birch. I have a note asking me to call you in."

"Call me in?"

"Well it appears the exam papers Jane completed over the holidays were excellently done, completely beyond what she is achieving here now."

"So?"

"We have to ask whether she did them herself."

"She did them herself." Elizabeth answered coldly. "We do not cheat."

"Well that is extremely odd because she is showing no signs of anything near that level of understanding. In fact I have a note here asking whether she had any special educational needs."

"Special needs?"

"We need to know whether she has any difficulties with learning."

Elizabeth was angry.

"She's got 9 O levels, she's aiming to get into university. What do you mean 'has she any difficulties with learning'?"

"According to these notes she sits at the back of all classes contributing nothing."

"My daughter had never once had a problem in school."

"Well she seems to have one now."

"I don't believe it. Jane is a clever girl, very bright, brighter than average by a country mile."

"I think you'll find most parents say that about their children." Elizabeth felt like spitting at the supercilious woman at the other end of the phone.

"In this case it happens to be true."

"We wouldn't know. She sits, completely unresponsive, at the back of every class and has made no effort whatsoever to communicate with her classmates."

"Have they made her welcome? I appreciate it's the middle of their year and they will have been together for a long time but has any one of them tried to make her welcome?"

The Head of Year made no answer. Instead, looking at her notes, she repeated the comments written by her colleagues.

She, after all, had no idea who Jane Bicton was.

"She has attended every day up until today, but she has handed in no course work and apparently appears to have answered no questions in class. She appears to be a very disturbed young lady."

"Why haven't you said anything before?"

"It's only been a short time and since she hasn't caused any real trouble…"

"You mean," Elizabeth interrupted, "those who have taught her have gone for the quiet life? Since she wasn't actually pulling a knife in class or threatening a fellow pupil they haven't bothered? Do they even know who she is? Would anyone have mentioned this to me if I hadn't asked?"

"Do you want an appointment with the educational psychologist?" The year teacher asked, having heard the bell she needed the conversation to be over.

"For Jane?"

"Of course for Jane. As I said, it is obvious she is very disturbed."

"No I don't want an appointment. And thank you," she hoped the teacher picked up on the dryness in her tone, "you have answered my question. No. She is not settling in."

Elizabeth put the phone down and stood wondering what she could do to help her daughter. She eventually sat down, feeling defeated.

Nine months ago they had been happy, looking forward to a long hot summer, and for reasons Richard had not fully explained, even to her, their lives had been thrown into turmoil. She knew there was nothing she could say to Jane, she simply had to make her understand that they had to stick together as they faced whatever the future would hold.

"Jane?" She knocked on her daughter's bedroom door but there was no reply.

"Jane?"

When she still got no response she opened the door to find her daughter doodling on an exercise book cover.

"Are you all right Jane?"

"That's not my name."

"Yes it is. Jane…"

"No!"

"Jane?"

"No! No! No! No!"

Elizabeth looked down and saw the scribbles. She looked sharply at her daughter. The doodles frightened her.

Jane had been gripping the pen in a fist and had been scrubbing the pen backwards and forwards across the page. The doodles were black patches of ink with round white areas that could have been faces with mouths and noses but no eyes.

She went to take the pens out of her daughter's hands, for there was one in each hand, but the resistance was fierce.

"Jane. Give me those pens."

"No! No! Mine! No! Mine! No!" Jane screamed.

"Jane. Calm down."

"No! No! No! No! My name isn't Jane!"

"Jane. Stop it!"

"No! No! No! No!"

Elizabeth slapped her daughter hard across the face and was relieved to see her slump into a silent ball, huddled into the corner of her bed, protected by the walls.

"I'm sorry sweetheart. I'm so sorry."

Elizabeth leaned against the wall and sank slowly to the floor. She would never have thought she could have hit her daughter. "Oh Janey I'm so sorry." She whispered.

She stayed for a long time watching as Jane slowly fell asleep, her grip on the pens slowly relaxing.

She had pushed Jane too far and now it was all too difficult. She slowly pulled herself to her feet and edged over to the bed.

She took a long look at Jane's sleeping face and leant down to kiss her gently on the forehead.

Three hours later Richard arrived and took her daughter away.

Jane got into the car willingly, thinking that Richard was going to take her home to the island.

She sat in the comfortable front passenger seat of his car as they drove through countryside. She looked at the trees, the stark outlines of branches and twigs seemed to be trying to tell her something. Neither spoke for the two hours of the journey.

When they drew up in front of a large house, built of red brick that she could just see through the ivy, she realised he hadn't taken her home.

She didn't respond when she heard Richard say goodbye, she just watched him as he shook hands with a man in a white coat and left through the large wooden door.

She knew the men and women in white coats weren't on her side. They pretended to be her friends but she knew they were lying to her. So she answered none of their questions. She knew it was best to stay silent. If she said anything, whatever she said, it would be wrong.

After a while she was shown to her room. This one was larger than her bedroom at home on the island, smaller than the one she had the previous summer, brighter and larger than the one she remembered from that morning.

She looked around the room, walked to the bed and lay down.

Whatever they did to her, whatever they said, whatever they asked her to do, she would do the opposite.

She knew that her mother, Elizabeth or Georgina or whatever her name was, had not told her the truth when she had said she must trust Richard.

She knew that Richard, if that was his name, was not telling her the truth when he said she was with people who wanted the best for her.

Six weeks later Richard called in to see Elizabeth.

"I thought you might want some company."

"Yes, I have been a bit lonely. It's Janey's 17th birthday today."

"Seventeen? It doesn't seem that long ago." Richard remembered the call he had had from the nursing home, telling him of the safe arrival of Elizabeth's daughter.

"I wish she was here to celebrate. We had such a lovely time last year, her 16th, the weather was lovely and she had a party with all her friends. It seems such a long time ago. So much has happened since then."

"She's in the safest place."

"For whom? Her or me?"

"Both of you."

"It seems Jane is the one paying a pretty high price for my actions."

"She's being well looked after, you know. I went there yesterday, and no, I didn't see her, I just wanted to have up to date information for you."

"Is there any change?"

"I'm afraid not, apparently she just sits in her room looking out of the window saying nothing."

"She thinks all this is her fault."

"All what?"

"All the moving, all the disruption and all the unhappiness."

"Are you unhappy?"

Elizabeth didn't have to say anything, her face was enough to tell him the answer.

"It's all for the best, you know." He tried to comfort her. "If Eric found you he would go straight for the jugular. He would present false evidence, he would show doctored photographs, he would pull all the tricks to implicate you and Grahame with the Soviets. Within no time at all you would be being 'de-briefed' and the Americans would be involved and I really don't have to tell you what that would mean do I?"

"But we were never able to find anything on GJ were we? He never put a foot wrong, here or in our trips to Washington and Moscow."

"Not that we spotted. I was always worried about that night in Moscow, you know."

"Worried?"

"Well why did he send you off alone that evening? He must have known we would follow you. What did he get up to?"

"I had never thought of that."

"And I wasn't the only one following you, so were the other minders, and Eric. All our attention was focused on you."

"What could he have done?"

"He could have gone out on his own?"

"Surely he would have been spotted."

"You'd like to hope so."

"Unless there was someone helping him in the Embassy?"

Richard nodded. "Entirely possible. I've always thought we made a big mistake that evening but I've never been sure what it was. Eric has always believed both you and GJ were traitors and that's what he'll still be trying to prove. I just hope we gave him nothing that evening to work on."

"You know I'm not an agent, Sir Michael, all of them know what side I worked for. Why can't they set him right?"

Richard's silence was a second too long.

"They think I was a double?" She asked incredulously. "I would never in a million years betray this country."

"That's not the way it would seem. The newspapers would tear you and Grahame to shreds, they hardly need much excuse the way the world of politics is at the moment. You've really got to keep going with this."

"Why doesn't Grahame give up politics? Surely he's had his taste of power, surely he can't still be ambitious?"

"He has no intention of giving up any day soon."

"Doesn't he realise he's stealing his daughter's most precious years?"

"I don't think he gives that much thought."

"Perhaps he ought to be made to?"

"I don't think that would be a particularly good idea."

"No perhaps not."

"And just as long as she's where she is she's safe and so are you."

"How long will she be there?"

"As long as it takes."

Richard visited again three months later, on 24th June. It was Elizabeth's 54th birthday.

"I never told you did I?"

"What?"

"Your birthday is my birthday."

"Today? How old?"

"49."

"You know it's not really my birthday don't you?" Elizabeth didn't want any celebrations to be under false pretences. "I have no idea when I was born."

"I know. But it's the day in your passport and all your official records."

"True."

"So let me take you out to dinner so we can both celebrate."

"Haven't you anybody closer to celebrate with?" Elizabeth asked, realising it was probably a tactless question.

"No one I'd rather be with."

As they settled at their table Elizabeth started the conversation, feeling more comfortable with Richard than she ever had.

"How long have we known each other Richard?"

"Since 1958, that makes it 19 years. That was when I was seconded to the protection squad and assigned to GJ."

"How old were you then?"

"I was 30, five years younger than you."

He remembered when he had first seen her and had felt an immediate attraction to her that he knew was not reciprocated. He had dealt with it, put it to the back of his mind and got on with his job. Now, as he looked across the crisp white tablecloth he saw an older version of that same woman. And he still found her attractive.

"I thought you must be older than that. You've always seemed so, well, so responsible."

"That has been my job."

"Is it still? Is that why you're here?"

"No. I'm here because I didn't want you to be lonely on your birthday. I knew you'd be missing Jane and I wanted to keep you company."

"That's nice." She said as the waiter left them menus and filled their glasses with water from a jug.

"Tell me about yourself Richard." She continued when they had been left alone. "I know nothing about you at all. You turn up, tell me to do things, drive me to a new house and then I only speak to you on the phone. Who are you when you're not being a policeman? I don't even know if you're married."

"I was."

He could see she was surprised by his answer.

"A couple of years after you were settled on the Isle of Wight I got married. My father and mother said it was time, they wanted grand-children."

"You don't sound like it was really your idea."

"It wasn't really. Susie was married to the only man in the service I called my friend. He was killed, in Berlin, so I married her to look after her really."

She didn't ask if he had loved Susie, it was clear to her from his tone that he had not. And he could not tell her that he might have thought he loved Susie if it had not been for the way he knew he felt for Georgina Carmichael.

"Children? Did you produce those grandchildren your parents wanted?"

"Yes. We did. Two. A boy and a girl."

Elizabeth was surprised at the sadness in his face.

"My son James was 5 years old and my daughter Alice was 3 when they, along with Susie, were killed in a car crash."

"I'm so sorry." It was the only thing she could think to say. "When?"

"It was years ago now. Sometimes I wonder whether any of it happened at all."

"So here we are, me 54 and you 48?"

"49."

"And we've known each other for nearly half our lives. We really should be friends you know Richard."

"Friends?" he asked. She was to his mind still a very attractive woman and in some ways being her 'friend' was the very least he wanted to be. His job though, as he frequently reminded himself, was to be her protector.

He could not let her be exposed as mother of GJ's daughter or as an agent. Eric would sell it to the press, every aspect of her life, her birth, her parents, her work, everything about her would be questioned. She would be destroyed. And he would do everything he could to avoid that.

He was not so fond of Jane.

Jane was a loose cannon, he had no idea what she would do and when. He had no experience of teenage girls and he had no idea what motivated her to rebel and to disobey so he had no means of ensuring she conformed and did as he told her.

She was, he thought, more like her father than her mother and that meant he cared less for her than he might have done.

"I will always be your friend, Elizabeth, always. If that's what you want me to be"

He had been, in a way he felt ashamed of, pleased when Jane had had her breakdown. With her away he had had the chance to get closer to Elizabeth, and when he was close to her he felt she was safer. Richard knew that whatever happened to Grahame and his career, eventually Jane would grow up and leave home. Then he would be able to look after Elizabeth as he had always wanted to, as her husband.

"I could do with a friend." Elizabeth acknowledged as the waiter came to take their order.

"How's Jane?" Elizabeth finally felt able to ask.

"She's reading now."

"Can't I go to visit her? Surely that can't hurt?"

"The doctors say it wouldn't be a good idea. She seems to have channelled all her fear and resentment towards you and me. She needs to overcome all of her anger, well at least a good part of it, before she can take up her old life."

"So she'll be there some time?" Elizabeth asked, unsure which answer she hoped for.

Richard nodded.

"But what about you? What are you doing?"

"There's only so much dusting and hoovering to be done." She smiled sadly. "And there's no point in bothering about cooking for one."

"Why don't you get a job?"

"Could I?" She was surprised. She had thought there would be too many difficulties.

"Of course you could. What would you like to do? Numbers again?"

"Something completely different I think. I'd rather like to be a tour guide. You know, Stratford, somewhere like that, showing American tourists the sights and trying to get them to understand how much of England there is outside London."

"I'm not sure that would be a good idea. Something a little less public perhaps?"

"You're probably right." She smiled. "What do you suggest then?"

"How would you like to teach maths?"

"Teach? I've never thought about it. I'm not really qualified am I?"

"You'd have no difficulty in a private school."

"That would be really good. I'd really enjoy that. Perhaps I'd even be good at it."

Richard watched Elizabeth as her face lit up with enthusiasm.

"A carefully chosen school, references would present no problem, you'd very soon prove your competence." Richard seemed to be ticking off items on a list. "I would plan to start in September."

"Oh thank you Richard! I could kiss you!"

"Then why don't you?"

Richard took every opportunity he could to be with Elizabeth through the summer of 1977. He would not push her, and she neither encouraged nor discouraged him.

There were so many reasons why they should not have allowed that relationship to develop into one of love, but by September it had and Richard spent every weekend with Elizabeth at her house in Sutton Coldfield.

"Jane really is improving." Richard said when he arrived to spend the long Christmas break with Elizabeth. He still visited the hospital on a regular basis and he still discouraged Elizabeth from seeing her daughter.

"When I do get to see her she'll have changed won't she?"

"She's seems a lot older, a child no more."

"When do they think she'll be released?"

"She's not a prisoner."

"You know what I mean."

"Another six months, at least."

"You said she's getting better. Why is it another six months?"

Elizabeth felt guilty that she was in two minds about Jane's recovery. She, of course, wanted her daughter to be well and happy again but she had been enjoying her life free of Jane. For the first time in twenty years she had some independence, earning a salary and having some responsibility for herself. She was also becoming very fond of Richard and the normality their weekends together brought to her life. Everything, she knew, would have to revert to its old pattern when Jane returned home.

"She's getting better but she's still a long way from being cured of her fears. She has so much paranoia still, she still thinks you, and I, and everyone else, do nothing but lie to her. She needs to learn to trust again."

"It all seems so bleak for her."

"It is."

"And I've made a new life for myself. What with the school, and you. Well it hardly seems fair."

"I don't suppose it is, but that's the way it is. Anyway, she'll come through and she'll be the stronger for it."

When Richard made a special visit to Sutton Coldfield on Jane's 18th birthday the conversation turned to Jane's future.

"They say she will be ready to leave soon, perhaps as early as June."

Elizabeth didn't say anything.

"Will you want her back here with you?" Richard asked tentatively and Elizabeth wasn't certain what he wanted her to say. There was no clue in the tone of his question. She had to think before answering.

"She'll have to come back here." She realised she sounded less than enthusiastic. "She'll have nowhere else to go. Of course she must come here."

"She could go to a half-way house."

"A hostel? Oh no Richard that would be awful."

"She might prefer it, you know."
"Doesn't she want to come home?"
"Not at the moment."

Elizabeth was dismayed to realise she felt relieved. "Wherever she goes what will she be able to do?"

"What do you mean?"

"Well, she's 18, she can't go back to school and she's got no real qualifications. She'll need a job, something to use her brain?"

"She's changed, Elizabeth, her horizons are very much narrower than they were. I think something with routine would suit her best."

"Routine? That sounds so un-Jane like."

"Elizabeth, you must realise how ill Jane has been, what she's been through. She will need a great deal of help."

Elizabeth could think of nothing to say. She loved her daughter, she had given up so much because of her and now, just as it seemed she was making a life of her own again she was going to have to give it all up for Jane.

"Jane is not the feisty girl she was. She will need your time, your care. Are you sure you want to take her on again? Are you sure a hostel is not the best answer. For everyone?"

Elizabeth took a long time to answer.

"I used to say that my life was to be all about Jane."

"Yes, I remember, when we left York."

"And again when we left the Isle of Wight."

"But you didn't realise what it would mean did you? Not really?"

"No. I don't know what I thought. I suppose that, once she was older it would be easier."

"It's just going to get more difficult."

"I've got so much more to lose now."

"More than you had back before she was born?"

"Definitely."

"Perhaps you should leave her in the hands of the professionals. They will know what's best for her."

"No. She must come home."

"However difficult it is? Whatever you have to give up? Your job? Us?"

"I'm sorry. She is my daughter and I must look after her. As I've said all along, my life is all about Jane. As long as she needs me it always has been and always will be."

Jane had not wanted to go home, she had wanted to start her life afresh, away from her mother and all that that meant, but no one had asked her.

When Richard dropped her off outside the house she had seen her mother waiting for her at the door and had felt nothing. She had avoided her mother's attempt at a welcome hug and had walked straight up to her old room. Although it had been redecorated, she could still see the vague outlines of the black writing under the pale yellow paint.

"This is a mistake." Were the first words she said to her mother who had followed her up the stairs. "They say you should never go back."

"You'll be all right when you've got used to being home again."

"This was never my home."

"All your things are here."

Jane opened and shut the drawers of the desk under the window, noticed the book with *Silver Birch* written on the cover and still felt nothing.

"Shall we have a cup of tea?" She said, she wanted her mother out of her room. "You go and put the kettle on, I'll be down in a minute."

When her mother had left her alone, Jane sat down on the bed. It was sixteen months and five days since she had last been in the room. Now she was back things would be different. She would do things on her terms, even though she might seem to be doing as her mother and Richard told her.

Sooner or later she would be free of them and that would be easier, she had learned, if she appeared to cooperate.

She realised very quickly that all the people she worked with in the job Richard had found for her had very low expectations of her. Although in her last two months at the hospital she had learned to type and do shorthand she was not asked her to do anything that required those skills. When she completed her first task, ordering files in three filing cabinets alphabetically, in half the allotted time she was told to do it again as she had done it so quickly it was obviously wrong.

She showed no signs of the annoyance and frustration she felt as she accepted all the criticism. She had learned that much at the hospital. It had taken the doctors and therapists months but she now understood that if she did as she was asked without question or argument no one could stop her mind from being somewhere else, they could not stop her thinking and imagining and being the person they had no idea she was.

So Jane said nothing as her competence was questioned again and again. She rose above it all. Let them all believe that she was not intelligent enough to understand the concept of numbers, of the alphabet or of dates. She knew better.

She found the routine of her days vaguely comforting and she was never bored as she played games in her head as she went about the mundane tasks she was given.

After three months, as the summer of 1978 turned to autumn, she began to be aware of more of what was going on around her. She noticed that very few people in the office seemed to enjoy their work, no one seemed to smile or show any enthusiasm, so she decided to be different. From then on she was unfailingly cheerful, showing an eagerness for work that made her even less likely to make any friends.

Since Jane had been back both Elizabeth and Richard had thought it best that they gave her no hint of how close they had become. 'We'll tell her when she's more settled and more ready to accept me as her friend.' Richard had said. 'We'll have many years together, but this one we must put Jane's needs first. Things would have been different if she'd gone to a half-way house, but you made that decision and we'll both stick to it.'

"How is she getting on?" Richard asked when he called Elizabeth on Jane's 19th birthday.

"I don't think she's terribly happy. She doesn't talk much but there's much more of the old her than there used to be."

"Grahame's said he's going to stand again." Richard gave Elizabeth the unwelcome news without preamble. "He's not giving up when the General Election is called in the next few weeks."

"Oh no!" Elizabeth had thought he would finally call a day on his political career.

"He's decided to carry on."

"Where does that leave us?"

"Us as in 'you and Jane' or us as in 'you and me'?"

"Both really."

"Jane's 19. Everything is due to end in two years."

"Everything?"

"Any official involvement with you. Money, protection."

"But surely no one thought Grahame would carry on so long? Surely they'll reassess our position if he's still in the public eye?"

"I doubt it. Times have changed."

"So what are we supposed to do then?"

"Something will work itself out." Richard said reassuringly.

"We can hope." Elizabeth wanted to believe him, but the news that Grahame was selfish enough to want to carry on when she had really thought this was his last parliament depressed her.

"You've still got your job. Are you still enjoying it?"

"Oh yes. And the hours mean that I'm home before Jane. But…."

"But?"

"I miss you."

By simply doing what she was asked to do as well as she could Jane caught the eye of one of the managers and in the assessments of July 1979, marking the completion of her first year in the job, she was promoted to a higher grade. It did not escape those who worked with her that she had been promoted more quickly than others who had been in the department longer and were older. It didn't make her popular but then, Jane reasoned, she had survived without friends for the three years since she had had to leave the Isle of Wight, 'so what else is new?'

Jane felt as alone at home as she was at work.

She had been angry when she first realised that her mother had a job which she enjoyed, teaching in a boys' Prep School. She felt betrayed in a way she could not explain when she realised she was not the centre of her mother's life any more.

Every morning, before she left for the 8.05 bus, Jane had a hurried breakfast with her mother. They didn't talk over their coffee and toast as they each prepared for their very different days.

Every evening, when Jane returned in time for the six o'clock news, she watched television as Elizabeth read piles of identical small green exercise books and made marks in red biro on the neatly written pages.

If Elizabeth asked her daughter how her day had been Jane would reply 'OK', never describing the mind games she played to make her work more interesting. Jane never asked about her mother's days.

The two women shared a house but there was very little they shared in their lives.

"How's Jane?" Richard's first question in his monthly phone call in March 1980 was, unusually, not about Elizabeth.

"I'm not sure. We don't seem to talk very much but she seems to be getting on OK. She goes to work every day and spends her weekends reading. But she's so different from the Jane I used to have before, well, before we had to leave Yarmouth."

"She hasn't told you, then, that she's been doing really quite well?"

"Doing well? No."

"She's been promoted and is showing a great deal of promise."

"You've spoken to her?"

"No. I've seen her personnel file."

"Of course, you would have done."

"She was promoted one grade last July and another on January 1st this year. Didn't she tell you?"

"She hasn't said a word."

"Well, as I say, she's doing really well and I was wondering why we can't sort out some way of getting her back to studying? Then she would be able to be independent, she can't stay living with you forever, and then, with her happily living elsewhere you and I can get together properly."

"Is that a proposal?" Elizabeth laughed lightly. "Get together properly?"

"Then I can protect you properly." He corrected himself.

"But only if we can get Jane settled in something she can enjoy and be happy with."

Richard had spent three years trying to like Jane, without success. But he knew Elizabeth saw more in her daughter than he did.

"I don't think that will be a problem. Underneath everything she's been for the last four years there is an intelligent, sensible young woman. We should give her a chance to be that person."

"What if...."

"What if Eric Atkinson finds her? Is that what you were going to ask?"

"Well yes."

"We'll just have to make sure he doesn't."

"He'd stop looking if only Grahame would give it all up. Couldn't Laura have persuaded him?" Elizabeth asked.

"He and Laura haven't really been close for years. Now their children are at university they live pretty separate lives."

"She'd fulfilled her purpose I suppose." Elizabeth said bitterly.

"Sadly so."

"If only he'd give up. There'd be the initial obligatory flurry of publications of diaries and memoirs, but then he'd fade into the background and anything anyone could say or do would be academic. If and when he finally retires, interest in him and his associates and his past and whatever he may or may not have done in the 1950s and 60s will be forgotten, won't it? People will move on won't they?"

"You might like to hope." Richard's voice implied that he thought that any such optimism was undoubtedly misplaced.

Chapter 11
Birmingham, May 1980

When Jane saw in the papers that her father was addressing a meeting in Birmingham she decided she would go to see him. She had no intention of trying to speak to him, or even seeing him close up, she just wanted to see him as he was, not as he appeared on television or in newspaper photographs, and hear his voice undistorted by a microphone.

When the day came she didn't tell her mother where she was going as she left the house but Elizabeth was not fooled. It was just too coincidental that Jane was going out on a Saturday morning, something she never did, on the one day her father was going to be a bus ride away.

She phoned Richard.

Jane arrived at the Town Hall in Birmingham far too early.

She decided against joining the short queue for public tickets as she had no intention of being in one of the front rows of the audience, instead she would spend half an hour in the library reading what the morning's newspapers had to say about Grahame Johnstone.

When Jane looked up from the paper, which she did every few minutes, she found herself looking vaguely in the direction of a young man sitting at the other end of her table. Whenever she looked up he was concentrating on his book and she was not to know that when she was looking down, reading her paper, he was staring at her, looking down quickly when he saw her about to look up.

She thought, rather vaguely at first, that he looked familiar, like someone from a dream she couldn't quite tie down. Each time she took a glimpse at him she became more and more convinced she knew him from somewhere.

It was several minutes before she realised the man was David Childs.

It was nearly three and a half years since that evening in Ludlow and he did look older. His hair was longer, his chin no longer stubble-free but it was definitely him.

Her first thought was to leave. She didn't want to have to talk to him. He would have done so much with his life, and how could she explain that she had done nothing with hers, that she worked as a clerk in a local authority office. She stood up and headed for the exit. She did not want to meet David Childs. She checked the time on the clock as she left the library, she had half an hour before the doors to her father's meeting would shut.

"Silver." She heard the name called and immediately turned around.

"David Childs?" She asked, as if it were a question. She did not want him to know that she had already seen him and was trying to leave without his noticing her.

"I thought it was you."

"I've got to go." She wanted to get to the Town Hall. She wanted to see her father. She did not want to talk to David Childs.

"Come on Silver, let me buy you a coffee. We've got lots to talk about. What happened to you that day? I went to your house and you'd moved out. I think you owe me an explanation."

"No I don't owe you anything. We moved. It's simple."

"Did you get my note?"

Silver then remembered the scrap of paper that was still tucked into the corner of her purse *David Childs loves Silver Birch* she had never moved it. It had been a kind of talisman through the years, a promise that one day her life would be normal again.

"Come on Silver, let me buy you a coffee."

She looked at her watch and shook her head. "I've got to go."

"Well if you change your mind I'll be over there." He nodded in the general direction of the Town Hall. "There's a pub, The Grapes, just round the back of the station. I'll be there for an hour or so."

"I've really got to go."
"Don't forget."
"I've just got to go."
It had all seemed so innocuous.

Jane had no idea what was she was going to do when she got to the meeting. She just knew her mother and Richard would hate her to be doing what she was doing.

"Hello young lady."

"Hello." Jane replied doubtfully as her progress towards the entrance was intercepted by a respectable looking young man in a suit.

"You're just the sort of person we want."

"Pardon?"

"Would you like to ask our guest a question? We need young people like you. For the cameras you see."

Jane didn't see. If she'd thought about it at all she might have assumed it was a random process. It did not occur to her that the people seen on television asking questions of politicians were carefully identified to fit chosen sections of the population.

"What sort of question?"

"Well do you know anyone who's disabled? We are hoping someone would ask a question that would allow us to praise the new provisions for access."

She shook her head, having no idea what he was talking about.

"Well how about immigration? Do you have a neighbour who is, shall I say, from abroad?"

Again she shook her head. "I could ask him about what he's going to do to help single parent families."

"I don't think so, not the sort of question we need today." She couldn't help noticing the man looking down at her stomach obviously wondering if she had a very personal reason for asking that question.

"Then I could ask him about Russia, you know the ending of the Cold War, the Berlin wall, his foreign policy?"

"Thank you Miss, I don't think we need a question on any of those subjects." The young man was looking over her shoulder, having decided that he was wasting his time and he had only a few minutes to find two other questioners.

Jane joined the line of people waiting to file past the security men to be let into the hall.

She heard someone calling her name quite quietly but she did not respond. Jane was a common enough name and she was sure the person being called must be someone else.

As the name was called again she wondered, since the man's voice was clearer and vaguely familiar, whether she was the Jane being called. But she didn't feel like talking to anyone and no one knew she was here.

She felt a hand on her shoulder and turned around instinctively.

"Jane."

"Oh. Richard. It's you. I suppose Mum told you I was here?"

"She did phone, yes. She was worried you might..."

"Might what? You think I might stand up in front of anyone and say 'look at me' 'look at who I am'. Is that what you really think?"

He went immediately to the point. "No I don't think even you could be quite that stupid but do you really think being here is a good idea?"

"Why shouldn't I be here?"

"I would have thought that was pretty obvious."

"He won't see me, no one will, and I wasn't going to speak to him you know."

"Well that's a relief anyway. Now, come with me."

She had no choice but to let Richard lead her away from the queue, his arm was holding her elbow tightly. As he steered her through the doors of the Town Hall, past security, and into a small room with a Formica topped table and with walls lined with shelves filled with paper files she wondered what the other people in the queue had thought, perhaps they imagined her to be an Irish terrorist.

"I just wanted to see him close up you know."

"I understand that but here is not the place. There are cameras. There will be all sorts of people watching. People who might...."

".... who might what? Recognise me?"

Richard nodded.

"I know you said I was like him but I've changed since then. No one would know who I am." She tried to argue her case.

"That's where you're wrong, Jane." He sat down opposite her, his face serious, hoping she would realise how wrong she had been to come. "There are a few people who know very well what you look like. They may not know where you live, where you work, what you do day to day but believe me, they are looking for the day when they see you at an event like this. There are a great many people who don't want your father to be re-elected and they would try all sorts of dirty tricks."

"And I'm a dirty trick?"

"A photograph of you with him certainly would be."

"Who would do that?"

"You remember the Isle of Wight?"

"Yes." Jane replied doubtfully.

"The reason we had to move you and your mother was because someone had tracked you down?"

"Yes, I remember."

"And then he turned up in Ludlow."

"That wasn't particularly difficult since I managed to get my picture, and name, in the paper."

Richard nodded. "Well that man's here today."

"Here?"

"He's been like a dog with an old bone on this story. He's been with your father every step of this tour, convinced that now you're grown up you will make yourself known to him."

"So what?"

"He's waiting for that one photograph that will be used to ruin your father's reputation. There are a lot of people who would pay a very great deal to make sure your father's career was destroyed."

"So what? His politics stink."

"You haven't thought this through have you? You would be under the spotlight. Every aspect of your life would be splashed all over the newspapers. Not just your father, you, and every single aspect of your life. Believe me, they will find you. You shouldn't have come here. You've known for years to keep your head down. All you've done today is put you and your mother in jeopardy."

"That's all you are about isn't it? Mother. You don't care about me, not even about my father it's all about her isn't it?"

"Both of you. I've been looking after both of you."

"No you haven't. You've been looking after Mum.

"You're not a girl any more so you have to make these decisions for yourself but you must not unravel everything that you and your mother have given up so much for. Don't play into the hands of this man and the press."

"So why shouldn't I let this man find me?" She knew she was being reckless. "Why should I give a shit?"

"You don't owe your father anything but what about your mother?"

"I don't owe her anything either. Between them they've managed to fuck everything up for me."

"She hasn't given up the best part of her life to protecting him just so you can throw it away in a fit of pique."

Something in the way he spoke gave Jane the hint of a suspicion. She said nothing, so Richard continued. "She thought that protecting your father was important enough for her to give up everything she had and go into hiding."

Every word he added made her more suspicious.

"She was very upset when she realised what you might have been planning for today."

What had, moments before, been the slightest suspicion became, in Jane's mind, a certainty.

"Look Jane, I probably have no idea how difficult this life is for you but so much has been invested, and I don't mean in money terms, in keeping you...."

"Secret?"

"Safe. Keeping you and your mother safe."

Jane said nothing for a few moments.

"Why are you so determined to keep my mother out of sight? I can't believe it's just about a few articles the newspapers would print about my father. I don't believe she can possibly care enough about him after all this time to still worry about his career."

Richard said nothing. He could not possibly tell Jane the real reason Elizabeth had to be kept out of the public eye.

"It's got to be something else." Jane said firmly.

Richard spoke calmly and slowly.

"For over twenty years it has been a large part of my job to look after you and your mother. I know you both probably better than anyone else in the world and I care about you both. It matters to me that you are kept out of the newspapers. I know what it would do to you both if you were found."

"So you keep saying."

"I promise you, Jane, you do not want to find out the hard way what it is like to be hounded by the newspapers."

Again Jane was silent for a few moments, muffled applause from the hall broke the awkward silence.

"When I was away you were sleeping with my mother weren't you?"

Jane spoke so quietly that Richard wasn't sure he had heard her correctly. It was not a question he had expected and he couldn't immediately find an answer.

"You wanted me out of the way didn't you? That's why you kept me in that bloody hospital for so long wasn't it?"

"No, Jane, it wasn't like that. You must know how ill you were and how much you needed help."

"And how lonely my mother was and how sleeping with her would help her through all those lonely months. It wasn't just having a job that changed her it was fucking you."

"Jane you will stop this and you will listen to me."

Something in the authority of his voice made her obey.

"I have known your mother a very long time and yes, we are friends and did spend time together when you were away."

"Not very professional."

"Over the years I've grown to care about you both and what happens to you, both of you." He put a great deal of emphasis on the last words.

"Will you be planning on fucking me then?"

She knew she had gone too far and was not surprised when he looked at her long and hard and replied calmly "You are not my type."

"Can I go now?" She asked after a few moments of angry silence.

"No you cannot."

"Why not?"

"Because you need to understand something and now is the time to make sure you do. Before you were born, in circumstances I cannot explain, Eric Atkinson, the man who has been trying to track you down, believed that your father and your mother had done him considerable harm. They had done nothing of the sort but he was convinced they had. That is why he is doing everything he can to find proof of something that will ruin their reputations."

"Why do you care?"

"Because I was responsible for Eric's misunderstanding."

"So everything that's happened to my mum is your fault?"

"No. I didn't say that."

"Yes you did. You said it was your fault this man hates my mother and your fault this man is after us."

"That is not right Jane, you know that's not what I said. I was not responsible for anything other than Eric's refusal to give up."

"And there's more stuff?"

"Of course there is. There's always more. But you will never have to worry about it because you will never know."

"I can't be trusted."

"No."

"I just have to believe that you and my mother know best?"

"Yes."

"And I have to still keep out of sight?"

"Yes."

"So you're saying all this is for my own good? Like some toddler I can just be patted on the head and told the grown-ups know best? Well fuck you."

"Jane, in this particular instance I do know best."

"And you'll carry on following me, making sure every little thing I do is written down and filed away somewhere. In some anonymous building there's a file with everything I've ever done? Everyone I've ever met? Everywhere I've ever been? You follow me around and report back on everything?"

"No. Jane. No. I don't. I'm only with you when it looks like you might be about to do something out of the ordinary. Today I'm here because your mother called me and asked me to be here."

"But you know where I've been, everything I've done since I left home?"

"I do."

"Tell me."

"You caught the 8.15 bus. You arrived in Birmingham too early for this meeting. You stood around for a few minutes obviously wondering what to do to fill in time, you didn't want to queue, so you went to the library. Coming out you were joined by David Childs. I can't imagine you knew he would be there so I believe it was an accidental meeting, on your part anyway, I'm not so sure about him."

"What do you mean?"

"Well, he followed you into the library, he was not there first."

"He couldn't have known I'd be here."

"It is entirely possible that David Childs knows who your father is and was here specifically to meet up with you. It is entirely possible he is the source of the original leak in Ludlow and it is entirely possible he is linked to Eric Atkinson."

"I am supposed to be frightened?" Jane's voice dripped with sarcasm.

"Yes. You should be." Richard was being very serious. "Don't go anywhere near David Childs."

He stood up. "You are going to leave here and go straight home."

He took her by the arm and led her through the long corridors and out of the rear door. "Go home, Jane and if you have the slightest respect for me and your mother you will not go back to see David Childs."

As the door slammed shut behind her Jane turned towards the station.

She had had no intention of meeting David Childs in The Grapes until Richard had told her not to. As she hustled along the streets away from the Town Hall she was filled with a mixture of resentment and anger. Who was Richard to dictate so much of her life? Why should she do what he said when he wouldn't tell her the real story? And he had slept with her mother.

Whatever she did it would be exactly what Richard did not want her to do. If David Childs was there she would spend time with him, she would talk, her head close to his, she would kiss him. She knew Richard would be watching and she wanted to give him something to worry about.

As she turned into Lower Severne Street she saw the pub. She had no doubt David Childs would be there. She looked at her watch, it had only been half an hour. Her interview with Richard had seemed like a great deal longer than that.

He was there, sitting at a table in the window.

"Sorry about that." She said, sitting down next to him, rather closer than she would have done if she hadn't known she was being spied upon.

Perhaps it was her day to be followed.

Perhaps David Childs had been waiting outside the Town Hall, knowing who she was and that she would be there. Perhaps he had followed her to the library and manufactured the meeting. Perhaps she was doing something that would come back to haunt her, but she didn't care.

Many years later, as she sat motionless in the dock during a break in her trial for his murder, she wondered what would have happened in her life if she had not gone for that drink with David Childs. What would have been different if, instead of wanting to stick two fingers up at Richard, she had walked to the bus stop and meekly returned home? Had it all been so much a matter of chance or had it been Richard's fault for being so hard on her and for not telling her the truth?

She spent an hour with David Childs in The Grapes that morning.

When he left her to go to the bar she had reached into her purse and taken out the scrap of paper that had been in it through all her bad times. *David Childs loves Silver Birch.* Quickly turning it over she had written *Silver Birch loves David Childs* and her phone number on the back before slipping it into the top pocket of the jacket he had left on the back of his chair.

As they left the pub she pulled him back towards her and lifted her face towards his and kissed him.

It was not something that she would have done if she hadn't known that Richard would be watching.

She walked away, her head held high, knowing David would find the paper in his pocket and would call her.

And when he did phone she would decide whether she was going to allow him to be more important to her than Richard wanted him to be.

As she sat on the bus she wondered whether she really wanted to encourage David Childs.

She had calmed down as she had waited in the slight drizzle for the bus and she had realised that she didn't particularly like him, he seemed to her to be a bit creepy. She decided that best reason for hoping David would call her was that Richard didn't want her to have anything to do with him and she knew she would always do exactly the opposite of anything Richard ever asked.

But Jane was not given the opportunity to further annoy Richard because David Childs did not phone her.

Chapter 12
West Midlands, July 1980

"You're very miserable darling, what's wrong?"

Elizabeth asked as she watched her daughter hunched up in her chair staring at, but not watching, the television. She had put up with Jane's mood for the six weeks since she had spent the morning in Birmingham.

"Nothing."

But her mother knew her better than that. She turned the television off and insisted that Jane talk to her. She was always watching for any sign that her daughter might be sinking back into that black state she had been in two years before.

"You were OK. You were getting more like your old self."

"Unquestioningly accepting everything you and your lover say and make me do? Is that what you mean?"

"No." Elizabeth answered carefully. She wondered how Jane had found out. Surely Richard couldn't have said anything when he intercepted her at the meeting. "No. I'd just like to see you happier."

"Why is being unhappy with what you make me do so wrong?"

Elizabeth didn't answer directly. "I really don't like the Jane you're allowing yourself to grow into."

"Tough shit."

"Jane! Please. You know the situation. It won't last forever."

"Are you sure? Whatever happens Grahame fucking Johnstone will carry on won't he? He'll carry on because he'll hate to end his career a loser and he'll say his party needs him. Whatever happens nothing will change. Why can't he just retire or kill himself then we can be normal?"

"Jane!"

"He's so fucking selfish! But that's not the point is it? You're the fucking selfish one. You just want me out of the way so you and that policeman can screw each other silly. At your age! I can't believe it!"

"Jane!"

Jane was working herself up into what her mother thought of as 'a state'. She had uncurled herself in her chair and was sitting with her legs and arms stretched out rigid. "No one bloody cares about me do they? Grahame fucking Johnstone only cares about his career, you only care about yourself and Richard, or whatever his real name is, only cares about sticking his cock where you want it to be."

"Jane!"

"Don't 'Jane' me. I'm just a complication in all this aren't I? You don't care what happens to me. No one cares."

"That is not true. We all care. More than you can possibly imagine. Now just calm down, please."

Jane clenched her fists, determined not to do as her mother said. "I don't fucking believe you."

"Jane. Please stop swearing. It doesn't help."

"What doesn't it help? You? I don't fucking care whether you like it or not. It makes me feel better. It's all fucking bollocks anyway."

"I don't understand why you're so angry with the world, so much angrier than you've ever been. The world is not against you so please don't just retreat into yourself. Please don't go back into that dark time."

"Why not? Then you could stick me back in an asylum and screw Richard to your heart's content."

"Grow up Jane. Start taking responsibility for yourself. I have a right to a life. I can't give everything up for you anymore."

"Then don't. I never asked you to, did I?"

"But I can't let go until you're able to look after yourself and you're showing absolutely no signs of being able to do that. I will not let you lose the future you could have."

"What bloody future? Hiding from this stupid man who you say is tracking us because he wants to expose some politician who is no more my father than Richard is. He's never been in my life, he's never done anything for me other than fuck everything up. Why the hell should I do anything to help him?"

"Oh Jane. I promised. It was all agreed." Elizabeth knew it sounded unconvincing. "It was so much easier when you were younger. I had no idea it was going to go on for so long but if we give up now, and let the papers know everything, all those years will have been a waste. Don't you see that? We have to carry on or it would all have been utterly useless."

"It has been. Surely it wouldn't have wrecked bloody Grahame Johnstone's precious bloody career. Perhaps we should have gone public, he deserves it, his career hasn't exactly been an overwhelming success has it? Certainly for the country. Wars? Recessions? Terrorism? Strikes? Maybe we would all have been better off if the man had been exposed years ago for what he is. He's just not much good as a politician."

Elizabeth knew that somehow she had to persuade her daughter to carry on with their charade. And she had to keep saying the reason was Grahame Johnstone, she could not risk telling her daughter the truth. Elizabeth had no idea how her daughter, in her current state of mind, would react if she knew who her mother really had been.

"It's all fucking bollocks."

Elizabeth began to lose control of her temper.

"Grow up Jane, for Pete's sake, and stop swearing, it's so ugly. There are some things you just have to take on trust. You must know that I really would not have done, be doing, this to us if it wasn't absolutely, one hundred per cent necessary."

"So Grahame Johnstone can have his career without fear of some embarrassing bastard daughter."

"You don't understand."

"Then explain so I can."

"I can't. I can't explain any more than I already have. It's difficult to go back 21 years, things were very different then, values were different, life was so different you cannot possibly understand. Perhaps you will understand when you've grown up a bit, when you can put yourself where I was those years ago. For the time being you're just going to have to trust me."

"I'm a bit old to be told 'Mummy knows best' don't you think?"

"Until you show me you're not only old enough in years but adult enough in maturity that's just what you will have to accept."

The phone rang, giving the two women a break from the intensity of their argument.

"I suppose that was your fucking Richard." Jane said when Elizabeth returned from the hall.

"No, actually it wasn't."

For a moment Jane was sure it had been David Childs and her mother had turned him away. "Was it … for me?" she asked.

"No. It was school, nothing important."

"So what you were saying was that I've just got to trust that you are doing the right thing for me? That the truth is too important to be trusted to me? There seems to be an awful lot about trust here. I've got to trust you but you don't trust me. That doesn't seem very fair does it?"

"Answer me some questions and we'll see whether you're trustworthy or not." Elizabeth said, turning her back on her daughter and staring out of the net curtains that she had never wanted hung in the window.

"What?"

"When you went to Birmingham to see your father did you know you'd be meeting David Childs?"

"How do you know about that? Oh Richard told you!"

"Did you?"

"No. I didn't. You can believe me or not I really don't care."

"Did he say he'd keep in touch?"

"No. He didn't."

"Did you give him your address, or the phone number?"

"No." Jane lied.

"I have to tell you that David Childs didn't bump into you by accident. It was no coincidence. He was there quite deliberately to see if you were there too."

"Are you sure?"

"Richard is certain that David Childs knows who we were, are. He thinks, to put it bluntly, that David Childs engineered that meeting because he knows you are your father's daughter and he wants to profit from that knowledge. If he's leading you on by saying he cares for you he's lying."

"He didn't expect to see me. And why should anyone who says they care for me be lying?"

"That's not what I'm saying."

"Yes it is."

"David Childs is not to be trusted." Elizabeth put as much authority in her voice as she could.

"Neither am I, according to you, so we must be well suited!"

Elizabeth ignored the childish riposte.

But a seed of doubt had been sown in Jane's mind.

She began to question whether her memories were accurate.

What questions had David Childs asked? What had he seemed to know about her? Had she told him about seeing her father? She thought perhaps she had. If he hadn't known who she was before that Saturday, she thought, he probably did now. But, she argued with herself, nothing had happened. There were no press door-stepping the house in Sutton Coldfield, there were no lurid articles in Sunday Newspapers. It couldn't be true then. David Childs wasn't a danger.

"I don't even like him. I only met him because I knew Richard would be watching." She realised then how silly and immature she sounded. "Mum?"

"Yes darling?" Elizabeth recognised that there was some attempt at reconciliation in her daughter's voice.

"Is there really no way out of all this?"

"No. There's no way out. For any of us."

"Surely one day that bloody Eric what's'isname will stop hounding after us and we can just live normally?"

"I doubt it. Even if your father ever gives up his political career it'll just go on and on."

"Why?"

"Because mistakes were made and have to be paid for. Some are just more difficult than others to clear from the tab."

For all Jane's anger she heard the sadness and regret in her mother's voice.

"So nothing will ever change?"

"Not really."

"What were the things you 'agreed'? You said we had to do all this because you had 'agreed' to do it."

"I promised that we would stay out of the public eye until your 21st birthday in exchange for protection and financial support."

"And when I'm 21?"

"I suspect it will continue after then because I don't think anyone expected your father's career to go on as long as it has."

"And now I've grown up no one knows what to do about me? Everything was tickety-boo when I was five years old but now no one has the first clue?" Jane's anger was re-surfacing.

"I think a lot of people are playing it all by ear."

"But I can't stay in that dead-end filing job much longer. I want a career, something worthwhile."

"Is that what you want?"

"It's what I've always wanted."

"It's what you used to want, for the past couple of years you don't seem to have been particularly bothered."

"Well I am now."

"You haven't said anything."

"You haven't listened."

"Well I am now. Something will be sorted."

"Just like that?"

"Yes, Jane, 'just like that'."

"And what about you?" Both Jane and her mother knew that the answer was something to do with Richard. "You've made plans for when I'm no longer in your hair?"

Jane didn't give her mother time to answer as she stood up, walked over to the television, turned the set on and the volume up before pointedly sitting down, bringing the conversation to an unsatisfactory close.

Three weeks later Jane arrived home from work to find Richard sitting in the kitchen with her mother.

Usually when Richard visited it meant they had to move and there was usually crying and shouting but Jane was surprised to hear laughter.

"Hello." Jane said with as much suspicion and resentment in her voice as she could raise.

"Hello Jane." Richard was smiling. "You look well. A tan has always suited you"

Jane ignored the compliment. "What are you doing here? Have I interrupted something?"

"No." Richard answered carefully, glancing at Elizabeth for a hint of what Jane might know.

"So you haven't spent the afternoon screwing each other?"

Richard cast a sharp glance at Elizabeth who shook her head.

"So why are you here? Are we moving again?"

She had to ask even before she had sat down pointedly at her place at the table.

"No. It's not that." Elizabeth answered swiftly. "Apparently that man has known for a few months where we are but he hasn't taken his pictures and written his story."

"Why not?"

"He's biding his time. He wants the right picture, the right story, the most lucrative story." Richard sounded tired, and rather cynical.

"But he could have made a real splash couldn't he?" Jane asked what she thought was a sensible question.

"He wants to make more of a scandal. He's waiting for what he sees to be the most damaging moment." Elizabeth added.

Since that day in Birmingham Jane had been thinking that there was more to it than just trying to protect a politician nearing the end of his career from an ancient scandal but she had never had any idea of what the true story could be.

The fact that the man knew where they were, had probably seen her in Birmingham, probably followed her day in day out, and yet still had not broken the story, made her even more sure there was more to it. One day, perhaps, her mother and Richard would trust her enough to tell her. In the meantime she would just have to go along with their story, as if she believed it.

"So we've been living on borrowed time?"

"Pretty much. But we felt we couldn't change your life again, not after the problems the last move caused you. But we felt, as long as we could prevent a really embarrassing photograph..."

"Such as me with him in May?"

"Just such as that, as long as we could prevent that, it would be OK."

"So if we don't need to move again so why are you here?"

"I'm not saying that change isn't going to happen but this time it's not going to be because of Eric Atkinson. This time I've come with some good news."

"Good news?"

"Yes. At least your mother thinks so and I hope you do too." He paused, before continuing as if remembering a script he had rehearsed many times. "You have always been good with numbers and enjoy working with them.

Your mother tells me that you're unhappy and unfulfilled in your job, you're sticking with it but feel bored and wasted. She tells me that..."

"She seems to tell you a lot about me. Didn't you ever think to talk to me directly? I am able to answer for myself and perhaps I know me better than Mum does?"

"There's no need to be like that, Richard doesn't deserve that." Elizabeth seemed embarrassed as she told her daughter off. Jane looked at her mother and then at Richard and she wondered why she hadn't seen years before that there had always been more to their relationship than his just being their minder.

"Jane." Richard's voice was the firm one that was difficult to argue with. "We've been thinking about you all the time but now you're an adult we realise that you must have some independence."

"And what about Eric Atkinson? Are you going to leave me to get photographed and splashed all over the newspapers?"

"No! Not for a moment! It's just that you can have a life that's a little less claustrophobic."

"Our life hasn't been claustrophobic."

"Hasn't it?"

"Think about it Jane." Richard answered Elizabeth's sad question. "Your mother has had to pay all these years for loving a man she shouldn't have loved. Now she loves me, and yes, she does love me, you've seen that, and she has a chance to be happy and free. But she will not take that chance for happiness, not if the price is your security and privacy. So, next year, you will be able to leave home....."

"Home's going to leave me you mean." One minute facing the idea of life without the security of her mother was enough for Jane; the whole idea terrified her even though it was what she had thought she wanted for years.

"Yes. I'm afraid so."

"Most young people of your age are leaving home...."

"Flying the nest." Jane interrupted, trying to put a mixture of sarcasm and irony in her voice.

"..... and making their own lives. That is all your mother and your father wish for you."

Mention of her father silenced her.

"He knows about all this?"

"Yes, and he wants to help you find a career you will enjoy and that will stretch you. He understands how disrupted your childhood has been and he understands something of the costs to you and to your mother. He was so disappointed that you didn't get to go to university but understood the reasons."

"You talk to him about me?"

"Of course I do. He has said if you want to go to university now it would not be impossible."

"He'd pull strings?"

"It would not be too difficult for him for he has many friends as well as enemies."

"University? There's not much I'm qualified to do."

"You're intelligent and you have a good, logical mind. You could do a maths degree or you could go into the statistical office."

"Like where Mum worked years ago?"

"Similar. There's all sorts of changes going on as technology is changing so fast. There are boundless opportunities to be had, for someone with the right sort of mind and the right qualifications."

"I've always loved maths and logic." She admitted reluctantly.

"So you should when you think about who your mother and father are."

"I'd like you to do that, go to university I mean." Elizabeth finally spoke, up till then she had let Richard make all the running.

"But how? I've got no A levels and by the time I got those I'd be 22. Most people are graduating at that age, not just starting out."

"That's all been worked out." When Richard saw the look on her face he added quickly "just in case you wanted to choose that option. We have a cover story….."

"Not another one."

"Listen, Jane, this is important." Richard was business-like. "If you want to do this you must listen. We will say you have been living abroad, probably East Africa, we'll have to fill you in with what growing up there would have been like, but no questions would be asked, you could make your own history, and your own future."

"I think I'd like that. Will I still have to be Jane Bicton? I hate that name."

"What name would you like?" Richard asked gently, suspecting that the battle had been won.

"Why not Jane Carmichael?" She knew she was being provocative.

"I don't think so." Her mother said coldly.

"Well I'd like something that I can have for the rest of my life. And something that is part of my history. I really want to be Jane Carmichael. You say that man knows who and where we are so it's hardly going to make a great deal of difference."

"Not Carmichael." Elizabeth said firmly.

"It's either that or going back a generation. What was your mother's maiden name Mum?"

Jane noticed the quick glance that passed between Richard and her mother.

"What's the problem? Aren't I supposed to know?"

Elizabeth was horrified to realise she could not answer her daughter's question, not because she didn't want to, but because she didn't know the answer. "I never knew it." She answered simply. "All our family papers were destroyed in the raid that killed them. I never knew my parents well enough to ask them about their lives."

"Cavanagh." Richard said, plucking a name out of mid-air. "How about Cavanagh?"

Jane thought about it for a few moments and then nodded.

"If I can't be Carmichael then Cavanagh seems OK. Jane Cavanagh seems actually quite distinguished."

Elizabeth and Richard exchanged a smile of relief. So many problems could have arisen from any conversation about Elizabeth's past.

"There's lots to do." Richard was again business-like. "You'll have to go and meet the College tutors, then there will be a lot of cramming over the summer to make sure you aren't out of your depth, then there's getting you familiar with your back story."

"You make it sound so exciting."

"Be excited, Jane, it's important to your Mother that you are excited by life."

So Jane Cavanagh was to go to university, as Silver Birch had aspired to and as Jane Bicton had been unable to because life had just been too bloody difficult.

Chapter 13
Birmingham, 1980

David Childs watched the girl he had always, and would always, think of as Silver Birch, walk away. He moved his tongue around his mouth tasting the last remnants of her kiss. He wondered about going after her, stopping her somehow from leaving him again. Instead he watched her until she was out of sight and then turned and went back into the pub. He intended to get very drunk.

He sat at the same table in the window he had shared with Silver and stared at the pint of bitter and the glass half filled with whisky deciding which to drink first. After a full minute of indecision he decided on the whisky but as he went to pick it up his thoughts were interrupted.

"Mind if I join you David?"

It had barely registered that the stranger knew his name before a chair had been pulled out and a man sat down.

"Mind if I call you David?"

"Who are you?"

"My name is unimportant, but if you want to call me anything you can call me Eric."

"Well Eric, how do you know my name?"

"I know you from Ludlow."

"I don't remember you."

"We probably didn't mix in the same circles."

"Probably not." David looked more closely at Eric. He was probably in his late 40s, though he looked a lot older. The description that first came to mind was 'weasely' as he watched Eric light a cigarette without offering him one.

They sat in silence for at least a minute as David wondered what this man wanted and Eric enjoyed the young man's discomfort.

"What do you want?" David eventually asked hoping he had put enough in his voice to make Eric realise he would rather be on his own.

"I rather think I can help you."

"Help me?"

"Well you don't seem to be very happy. I reckon you'll soon be looking for a job, from what I hear you aren't cut out for lecturing. That is what you were thinking of doing wasn't it?"

"You seem to know a lot about me. I've made no decisions about a career yet. I've got to get past finals first."

"I've made it my business to know about you."

"Why?"

"Because I think we can both be useful to each other."

"Useful?" David drained the glass of whisky and then finished his pint in one.

"Another?" Eric picked up his glasses and went to the bar. David thought he might as well listen to the man if he was going to buy him drinks.

"Here." Eric placed the replenished glasses on the table and sat down, pulling his chair a little closer to David's.

David drank the scotch without a word of thanks and began to down the beer.

"Not too fast boy." Eric said, still speaking with a pleasant, unthreatening tone.

"How do you think we can be useful to each other then?"

"Simply you need a job and I need a job doing."

"A job?"

"It's nothing illegal and you might find it interesting."

"What is it?"

"The young lady you were drinking with a few moments ago...."

"Silver?"

"Silver?" The name was not what Eric had expected.

"I know that's not her name but I call her that."

"No it isn't her name. Do you know what her real name is?"

David Childs thought for a moment, and found he couldn't remember. He shook his head.

"Her name is Jane."

"I prefer Silver."

"Well we'll call her Silver then. What do you know of Silver?"

David thought. What did he know about her? When it came down to it he knew very little. He suspected a lot but he had no proof of anything, he never had had. But after their conversation this morning he knew a little more than he had before. He decided to say nothing to this stranger.

"Not a lot. We went on a couple of dates."

Eric knew it had only been the one date but he didn't contradict the young man.

"Did she say anything about her family?"

"She lives with her Mum. I don't think there's a dad around."

"Her mum. Did you meet her?"

"No. Look, what's this all about? Do you know where she lives? Have you got an address?"

"It's very simple. I have, shall we say, an interest in your friend Silver and I'd like someone, you, to keep me up to date with what she does. I think you'd be good at that."

"I'll probably never see her again."

"Oh I doubt that very much." Eric had seen Jane put the scrap of paper in David Childs' jacket pocket. There would be a phone number. He had watched them kiss as they left the pub and saw in that kiss more than perhaps there was. He knew perfectly well where Silver Birch and her mother lived but he would wait for David to tell him as a test of the young man's trustworthiness.

"Are you something to do with her father?" Eric had expected the question and was quite happy for David Childs to think that so he said nothing, instead making an expression that could have been taken for assent. "You aren't the man she came into Birmingham to see though are you?" Again Eric said nothing, if David wanted to believe that then it could do no harm. "OK. I'll do it. What do you want me to do?"

Eric tore off a corner of a beer mat and, after writing his phone number on it, handed it to David. "Get in touch with her and when you've done that give me a call. We'll meet again and make sure you're sober."

"I'm not pissed."

"I think you are. Remember, call me when you're in touch with the little bitch."

Eric stood up and by the time David had drained his pint he had gone.

Without looking at it David put the scrap of card in his pocket and went to the bar. "Same again."

Ten minutes later he was joined by a friend who unobtrusively handed him the small packet of tablets. 'Here you are Davy boy, no need to count them, they're all there. That's ten quid you owe me.' David handed over the money.

The next morning he remembered very little of what had gone on the day before. He remembered seeing Silver and he thought he remembered kissing her but then he decided he must have dreamed it. He had no idea how he had got home. He had no idea where he'd been all day. He could remember nothing clearly after he had left the library.

The day got worse when he had a massive argument with the girl he had been living with for a year and she spent the morning clearing everything that was hers from drawers and cupboards.

"Don't touch any of my stuff." He followed her around the flat sulking as she put her things in boxes.

"Why would I?" She asked rhetorically as she pushed all his things to the back of the cupboard and out of her way.

When she had finally gone the flat seemed so empty he went out to buy more pills. He was going to get stoned.

In the weeks that followed he spent too much time drinking and popping pills and not enough studying. As he daydreamed in the library he tried to draw from his subconscious every detail of that Saturday morning and meeting Silver. He was not sure that everything he remembered had actually happened. The boundaries between his imagination, his memory, things he wished had happened and events he remembered from reading about them in books and seeing them on the television were very blurred.

All he knew was that he really wanted to find her.

He went back many times to walk around the Cathedral gardens or, when it rained, to sit in the pub going over and over what he knew about her. And what he didn't. He went back to the library every day for a week, and then every Saturday for months but he didn't see her again.

He decided that the only explanation for her behaviour, for taunting him and then leaving no way for him to get in touch with her and not being anywhere they might meet, was that she was being deliberately provocative. Perhaps, he persuaded himself, she wanted him to chase her, to earn her by solving the problem of finding her.

But he could think of no way of doing that.

He had no phone number, no idea where she worked or even where she lived.

He achieved the degree he needed to take up his job in the university and through that first academic year he concentrated some effort on his career. He contributed to the publication of two papers in 1981, neither of which was particularly original, and he achieved some popularity as a tutor with his students, if not with his professor. He had a short-lived relationship with one of his students, then another with a fellow junior lecturer, then another with another student. None of the girls mattered to him because they were not Silver. At Christmas 1981 he was briefly engaged to a girl in Ludlow but she called it off before too many people were aware of their intentions. He knew his life was going nowhere.

At the end of May 1982 David Childs decided he had had enough of Birmingham. A second engagement had come to nothing after a period of endless bickering and brutal sex but it was the interview with his Professor who had asked, not very kindly, whether he really thought he was suited to academic life which led him to offer his resignation which was unflatteringly accepted.

As he set about packing up the flat he had lived in for four years he blamed Silver Birch.

Without her he would have been able to concentrate on his work, without her he would have been able to hold down a relationship. Without her he wouldn't be the failure he knew he was turning out to be. It had taken two years but he understood that everything that was wrong with his life was her fault. He no longer wanted Silver as a lover or even as a friend.

He wanted to make her pay for all the suffering she had caused him. He had no idea how he would do it. He had no idea where she lived or where she worked. But he would find her. And he would make her pay.

As he put clothes he would never wear again in boxes to give to charity he checked through the pockets of a long unworn and decidedly unfashionable jacket.

There he found a piece of paper.

'*Silver Birch loves David Childs*'

He sat down, staring at the scrap of paper. He wondered how it had come to be in his pocket. She must have put it there, sometime that Saturday morning.

And it had been in his cupboard all that time.

He turned it over in his hands and saw his own scrawled note. As he read it he was remembering how he had felt sitting on the wall outside her home in Ludlow.

'*David Childs loves Silver Birch*' He read the words he had written and then he saw the telephone number.

He sat on the edge of his bed looking at the number for a long time filled with self-pity and regret. He would have given anything in the world to have seen that two years before.

Why hadn't she told him she'd given him her phone number? Why hadn't she said something like 'give me a ring' when they had kissed outside the pub? Then he would have looked for the number. He would have called her.

And everything would have been different.

He reached over to his phone and dialled the number, having no clue what he would say when it was answered.

He counted the rings that told him the number was still active, two years wasn't such a long time, and was about to hang up when a man's voice answered.

"Yes?"

"Hello. Is this the right number for Silver Birch?"

"Who?"

"Silver Birch. That might not be her real name." He didn't remember Eric reminding him her real name was Jane.

"Well there ain't no Silver Birch 'ere."

David knew the man was about to put the phone down.

"Where are you?"

"Pardon?"

"Where are you? I mean I'm trying to track down an old friend and I don't even know where she lived."

"Sutton Coldfield mate."

"Thanks."

He put the phone down knowing he would never find her.

He had hoped she hadn't moved on again, that she hadn't disappeared overnight as she had done from Ludlow. He'd hoped the phone number was a small village where someone might have known where she had gone.

"Shit!" He shouted at the phone. "Shit shit shit."

He sat down on the side of his bed. What must she have thought when he didn't call? How long did she wait before she had given up on him? "Shit."

He went back to the jacket and felt again in the pockets, perhaps Silver had left another slip of paper.

Instead he found the beer mat.

"Christ!" He had forgotten all about the man who had got him drunk that afternoon. David looked at the beer mat but could remember nothing of the conversation. He went back to the phone and dialled the number written on the mat.

The phone was picked up remarkably quickly.

"Atkinson."

"Who?"

"Who's asking?"

"My name is David Childs. I've just found this phone number on a beer mat in my pocket."

"That was two years ago."

"You know me?"

"You've forgotten how much I know about you?"

"Sorry?"

"Meet me in The Grapes in an hour."

Before David could say he had other things to do the phone went dead.

"Oh sod it." He threw the jacket on and left the flat. Perhaps this man could give him something to do with his life that would let him make Silver suffer as he had done.

Eric Atkinson was sitting at the table in the window as David walked in.

"Sit down." David sat. "First tell me why you have taken two years to call me."

"I forgot all about you."

"Have you forgotten my name?" David shrugged so he continued. "My name is Eric Atkinson."

"Ah yes. Eric." David tried to sound as if he was remembering.

"I should have known you had had too much to drink that day, and drugs too I shouldn't wonder. Anyway, I hope you've changed as I can't use you if you are unreliable."

"If you know so much about me and you wanted me why didn't you get in touch with me? You must know where I live."

"I'm not going to pressgang you into anything. A drunk or a druggie is no use to me."

David looked at the pint on the table in front of him. "You got me this."

"One or two don't do any harm but I suspect you were well out of it that morning. Drink and drugs are out from now on if you are to be of any use to me."

"Use?"

"The girl you call Silver."

"Silver." David looked down into his beer. "I haven't seen her since that Saturday. I have no idea where she is."

"I do."

It took a moment for David to register what Eric had said.

"You know where she is?"

Eric nodded and then took a long time drinking very little beer waiting for David to ask for more detail.

"Where is she? What's she doing?"

"She's in Cambridge."

"Cambridge?"

Eric pushed a card across the table and David read the address. And then he continued. "Which is where you are going to be very soon."

"Me?"

"Come on David, I thought you were brighter than this."

"What?"

So many things were running through David's head. He would see Silver again. Soon. This Eric man wanted him to work for him. He had something to do with his life, something that seemed to be quite exciting.

"You can't be of any use to me if you're as dim and slow-witted as you're being today. I thought you were a bright lad."

"Sorry. It's just that I'm so... so ..."

"So what?"

"So fed up that I didn't find your number sooner."

"That's past now. Do you want to help me or not?"

"It depends."

"On what?"

"On what you want me to do."

"I want you to tell me everything about her life. I want to know who her friends are, if she has a relationship I want to know who with, if she meets anyone new I want to know the lot. I don't just want words I want photographs, photographs of her on her own, with friends everything."

"You want me to spy on Silver?"

"I suppose that's a simplistic way of looking at it."

"Why?"

"Pardon?" For the first time David felt he had Eric on the back foot. Surely he should have realised he would want to know why he was being asked to do all these things but Eric didn't seem to have an answer prepared. It seemed a simple enough question.

"We need to know."

"We?"

"Me and the people I work for."

"Who are they?"

"You don't need to know that."

"Oh not that God-awful thing about 'if I told you I'd have to kill you'?" David joked.

"Something like that." Eric's serious answer stopped David in his tracks.

"Really?"

"And don't think I won't. If you get on the wrong side of me or the minute you're a threat to me."

"Come on! Be serious." David tried a laugh but there seemed to be no humour in Eric Atkinson's eyes.

"I am taking a risk asking you to do this. I don't know whether you are up to it. You've got a brain but you don't seem to want to use it that often but you do have a thing about the girl you call Silver Birch. So, as I say, I'm taking a risk but I want you to prove me right. I'll get you a job, see you're OK for money and then I'll wait for your reports. If they're useful we'll carry on with the arrangement. If they aren't then you'll be on your own."

"If you haven't killed me!" David tried to joke but still Eric showed every sign of being serious. "If you're so interested in her why don't you do all this surveillance yourself?"

"I have other fish to fry."

"You can't be in two places at the same time? Is that what you're saying?"

"Exactly right."

"But up until now you've not needed me?"

"Up until two years ago. Since then I could have done with you, or someone like you."

"It's her Mum isn't it?"

"What's 'her Mum'?"

"You've been trailing after them both which was OK when they lived together but Silver's left home hasn't she? That's why you need someone else?"

"Don't ask questions you wouldn't understand the answer to."

"And her Dad? It's all about her Dad isn't it?"

"And who do you think her father might be?"

"Well it's obvious isn't it?" David took a punt.

"Yet you haven't been to the press about her?"

"I couldn't prove it could I? I only had that photo from the local paper in 1976. The press would have laughed at me."

"You're right there," But Eric was careful not to say whether David Childs had been right in his guess.

"Your job will be to tell me all about Jane, you must concentrate on her. At least for a few months until I see whether you're up to it or not."

"I'll be up to it."

"Keep in the background, don't get to know her or she'll be suspicious, meeting you here may well be put down to coincidence, they do happen occasionally, but if she saw you again she might begin to suspect you were stalking her."

"What am I looking for?"

"Everything. As I said, everyone she meets, everything she does."

"Why do you want me to do this?"

Eric took a long draught of his beer and put his empty glass down on the table before answering.

"One day you may find out. But then remember, when you do I will have to kill you."

Chapter 14
Cambridge 1982 to 1986

"Bye Mum."

"Bye darling. See you at Christmas. And remember, if you need anything just call."

"Bye Jane." Richard had his arm around her mother's shoulders as the taxi drove away.

As she drove away from the house she had always hated she knew she was being unfair. Her mother was going to be happy with Richard. They were going to get married and make a life together and they didn't want her around.

And she didn't want to be around.

She wrote the letter on the train and posted it when she arrived in Cambridge.

'Dear Mum. I think it's best if we make this a clean break.' Jane knew it sounded as though she was writing a 'Dear John' letter to a boyfriend rather than leaving home. *'You and Richard want to be together and you don't need me around.'* What did she need them for anyway? All they had ever done was mess her around. It was her dad who had got her the place in Cambridge, it was her dad who had promised to pay her an allowance that would see her comfortably through until she was earning enough to live on. She could have no idea how hard Richard had worked to persuade a number of people that she was worth investing in. *'You get on with things. I don't want to come to the wedding so don't invite me. And I don't really want to hear about your life together. We can't play happy families can we?'* She looked at the words on the paper as soon as she had finished the sentence and wondered whether she was being a little too harsh. But, she remembered something her mother had often said, 'you have to be cruel to be kind'. *'Let's just have each other's addresses so we can get in touch if we ever need to.'* Was that really a clean break? She asked herself but decided it was only fair to keep the possibility of future contact open.

They would know where she was until she graduated anyway. *'Let me get on with learning who I am and what I am capable of without always having to worry about stuff you did or my Dad did. All that has got nothing to do with me and I don't want any part of it.'*

She watched the countryside passing by quickly, taking her to a new life and she decided she would only write again to her mother if there was something really important to tell her.

She was certain they could get reports on her progress if they wanted them.

Jane soon settled into what she thought of as a normal life. Protected by the strictly enforced routines and regulations of her college she found a security she realised she had not known since leaving the Isle of Wight more than six years before.

For the first term she rarely ventured out of the small area bounded by her room, the lecture theatres, her tutors' rooms, the library and the refectory. She did not go out of her way to avoid socialising with her fellow students, it was just that they were a lot younger than she was and seemed to be far more confident and she was happy with her own company. She was content to work. She had found something she enjoyed and was good at. It was not easy, despite all the preparation she had done through the summer but she relished being tested.

She met Matt Greenaway in the university bookshop during the long summer holiday at the end of her first year.

"Hi." She had asked. "I'm looking for a book."

"We have a few." He had said drily, looking around them at the walls lined with shelves packed with nothing but books.

"A particular book." She answered coldly. "*A Russian Childhood* by Sofia Kovalevskaya. I would have thought you would have had it in stock but I haven't been able to find it."

"A little light reading for the summer?" The man smiled what Jane reluctantly thought was a rather attractive smile.

"Yes actually."

"Are you a mathematician?"

"You know Sonya Kovalevskaya was a mathematician?"

"Does that surprise you?"

"Sort of."

"It's just a coincidence really. Someone asked for the book last year and I remember it."

"You remember a book someone asked for a year ago?"

"It's just the sort of memory I have."

"Wow."

"I'm nearly finished here. Would you like to share my end of shift drink with me? It's a lovely day we could go and sit by the river?" Jane didn't particularly want to get involved with anyone but he had impressed her so she agreed.

She would not allow Matt to distract her from her studies so at first she limited their meetings to weekends. On the first anniversary of their meeting Matt asked her to move in with him. She had argued that it was her final year and she would have little time to do anything but work but he had said he wouldn't get in her way. She had argued that she wasn't much of a housekeeper and he said she shouldn't worry he was used to doing the shopping and cooking and cleaning. He'd lived on his own for years. In the end his persistence wore her down and she moved in on July 4 1982. They celebrated by opening a bottle of wine and watching Jimmy Connors beat John McEnroe for the Wimbledon title.

Matt's house was one of the semi-detached houses that lined one side of a pleasant avenue. The pavements were wide, the grass verges carefully mown and there was still evidence of fruit on the cherry trees. On the opposite side of the road there were rather larger, detached houses with net curtains in their windows. Jane knew it was not the part of the city where a third year student would expect to live but she was older than most students and Matt, several years older still, had been ready to settle down.

She wrote a brief note to her mother to tell her that she was living outside college. She did not say why and she did not mention Matt. There was no reply.

Jane was as content as she had ever been through the summer of 1982. Matt gave her free rein to make his house as much hers and she spent most of July decorating and moving furniture.

At the end of the month they went to Brighton for a week's holiday and Jane realised it was six years since she had swum in the sea. Six years since spending that day on the beach at Colwell and returning home to be told she had to leave the island. She had been 16 years old then, a child. She had been through so much since she had tasted the salt in the wind and heard the cries of seagulls wheeling and darting above the waves. As they sat together on the beach she told herself that she was a different person now. Jane Somerset had been happy and she was determined Jane Cavanagh was going to be too.

She would forget about ever being Jane Birch and Jane Bicton, they no longer existed.

As their taxi drew up outside their house bringing them home at the end of their idyllic week together neither Jane nor Matt noticed the man sitting on the wall on the other side of the road. It was a bus-stop, there were frequently people waiting there.

Three days after meeting Eric Atkinson in Birmingham David Childs was sitting at the bus stop looking across the road from the house where Silver now lived. He expected to see her any moment but he waited all through the afternoon and into the evening and there were no signs of life in the house.

On the third day, with still no sign of activity at the house, David chatted to the milkman who had said yes, milk had been stopped for a week but that they'd be back at the weekend. 'They?' David asked suspiciously. 'Yes a nice young couple, he's been there a while but she's just been there a month or so, doubled the milk order.'

'They're a couple'. David Childs thought, fighting back the jealousy. 'Silver's living with someone, perhaps she's even got married.' 'But,' he countered to himself, 'Eric would have said something if she had.'

He waited all the following Saturday and was beginning to think the milkman had been wrong when the taxi drew up.

She hadn't changed.

Still shorter and plumper than was attractive, her hair tied behind the nape of her neck in a ponytail he thought she looked no older than she had when he had first seen her, six years before, in Ludlow. In Birmingham two years ago she had been too thin, too gaunt, but now she looked a lot better. He was not sure how he felt but he would have to report to Eric that she looked happy.

He looked carefully at the man she was with. He would tell Eric that he looked quite a bit older than Silver. He wasn't particularly attractive, David thought, not particularly anything. He wondered what she saw in him. Surely she could do better.

He was wondering whether there was any point in hanging around any longer that evening when, about an hour after they had arrived, the front door opened and the man walked out and turned towards the city.

David was unsure what he should do.

He could knock on the door. She was alone and he could talk to her. He could tell her what she had done to him. How his life had gone to hell because of her, but how they had another chance now. He would tell her about not finding the note in the jacket pocket, how fate had kept them apart, but how it had now brought them together.

But Eric Atkinson had said she was not to see him. And, David had to admit, he was afraid of Eric Atkinson.

And Eric would not want him to let Silver know he was there.

He decided he would find out more about the man. Perhaps, if he got to know him, he would get to know about her through him. Perhaps he was going to the pub, that is what David would have done after having been away for a week, so David followed him and was unreasonably pleased when he realised his presumption had been right. The man had gone to the pub.

David was even more pleased at the fact that he was no stranger in the pub either, it was just over the road from his flat and he had already spent a few evenings there.

As David got to the bar it was obvious Silver's friend was a regular. He was poured 'the usual', he leant against the bar as if he owned it and talked to one or two other drinkers, laughing at the landlord's feeble jokes.

David sat at a table with a pint in his hand watching the man, who he now knew to be called Matt, and decided he would be happy playing the long game.

As he kept an eye on Matt at the bar he thought of where he had been less than a week before. Then he had been packing up his flat, jobless and homeless, about to return, a failure, to his father in Ludlow. Finding that scrap of paper and the beermat in that long forgotten jacket had changed his life. Now he had a flat, paid for by Eric, he had a job and he would be seeing Silver every day. Sooner or later he would see a way to hurt her.

David made The Anglesey Arms his local and he began to spend at least an hour there every night. It was some time before people began to nod to him when he walked in, then the regular barmaids told him their names and asked for his. Soon they were pouring his usual drink as soon as he walked through the door.

Every little thing he heard about Silver and Matt and their life together he reported back to Eric but there was little out of the ordinary.

He soon discovered that she never went to the pub with Matt. She didn't like pubs and Matt was happy to let her stay at home. 'Time off for bad behaviour' he joked. Through the Autumn and Winter David learned that Silver was working hard for her degree as she wanted to stay on at university to do a Masters. Then, Matt let slip, she wanted to collaborate in the writing of a book on something so obscurely mathematical that no one would ever read it. Sometimes, David noted to Eric, Matt was quite rude about Silver and, although he still wanted to hurt her for ruining his old life he accepted that it was because of her he was now doing so well.

Just hearing about Silver's life was not enough for him and in the Spring of 1983 David moved into a flat in one of the large Edwardian houses opposite the house where she lived.

From his bedroom window he could see into her lounge and her bedroom. On a few evenings she didn't draw the curtains fully and he could watch her as she sat, with her legs up on the settee, reading. On the few nights she didn't draw her bedroom curtains he could watch her undressing and then making love.

Although his weekly reports to Eric were largely repetitive and contained little of interest his album of photographs of Silver grew.

When Eric asked for information on Matt's politics David had a lot to say as Matt would happily discuss anything with anyone over a pint. He couldn't stand the Prime Minister who he said, at length and many times, was ruining British industry. He wasn't a pacifist in all circumstances but he was anti the war over the Falkland Islands. He thought Michael Foot brave but dangerous and he thought he'd probably vote Conservative in the coming general election because he liked his local MP, Grahame Johnstone.

David hadn't known that Grahame Johnstone was the local MP, but he thought it an interesting fact which he didn't pass on to Eric because he must have known already.

When he followed Matt and Silver to Brighton for the Easter weekend of 1983 David thought he might have something more interesting to report to Eric but even though he tailed them everywhere on their walks along the sea front and through the Lanes, they didn't seem to meet or talk to anyone else.

He was very careful not to let them see him as he walked behind them and took photographs, his presence in Brighton would be difficult to explain, and so he was quite relieved when they returned to Cambridge and he could get back in his usual routine.

David often wondered whether Matt ever told Silver of his mate 'Dave' who he met most nights in The Anglesey Arms, but since she never joined him he decided that Matt kept the two parts of his life very separate.

Jane's three years of undergraduate study were over and on the day after the results were published Jane was grinning as she walked past the porter's lodge to meet with her tutor to discuss a fourth year and a Masters degree. Her results had been as good as she could have hoped for.

"Miss Cavanagh?"

"Yes Harry."

"May I offer my congratulations? We will be seeing more of you next year?"

Jane simply smiled and said she hoped so.

"I have two letters for you." Harry handed the two envelopes to her but didn't leave her to read them in peace.

He had been intrigued as one was no more than five inches by four, far smaller than modern envelopes, and it had the embossed portcullis on the back flap showing, to Harry's experienced eye, that it came from the House of Commons.

"Friends in high places Miss?" He asked, probing for information. He prided himself on knowing everything that it was necessary or interesting to know about every one of his students and Miss Cavanagh had been one of his for three years and he had had no idea she might have had what he called 'connections'. "Handwritten from the House." He added prodding her to explain.

She decided, quickly, that an enigmatic smile was the best answer. She thanked him and walked no quicker than she normally would across the Quad.

Sitting down, carefully choosing a bench out of Harry's sight, she opened the small envelope and extracted the piece of paper unfolding it to see in the top left hand corner a small blue oval seal. 'House of Commons' she read, surprised. 'From the office of The Right Honourable Grahame Johnstone" There were ten hand-written words on the page. *You must know how extremely proud I am of you*.

She carefully folded and replaced the note in its envelope.

"So you didn't forget." She said, then realised she had spoken out loud.

"No he didn't."

Jane looked up sharply to see a man, about her age, looking down at her.

"Don't worry. My name is Nick and I work for Grahame Johnstone. He asked me to find out who picked up the letter from the Lodge and to bring that person upstairs."

"Pardon?"

"I'm GJ's private secretary and by private I mean private. So don't worry, there isn't going to be any fuss. He would just like to meet you and congratulate you in person."

"Grahame Johnstone's here?"

"Yes."

"Here?"

"Well yes. You father's here. This is his old college remember. He has every right to be here."

"You know me? And he wants to see me?"

"He does indeed."

"I'd better come with you then."

She had no idea what to expect and she had no time to think how she was going to approach the meeting. Nick ushered her into a study and there, standing by the window, was her father.

"Dad?"

He turned and she had a moment to think how old he looked, far older than on television or in newspaper photographs.

"Is that how you think of me? I'm so glad."

"How else should I think of you?" She asked rather too defensively. "Sorry, I didn't mean that to sound like that."

"I probably deserve it."

"Do you think of me as your daughter?"

"Laura, that's my wife, she remembers you on your birthday and at Christmas and has made sure that you have never been forgotten in our household."

"Do your children know about me?"

"Yes. No specifics of course, but they do know they have an older half-sister. We, well, Laura really, didn't want it to be a shock to them if it ever came out in the newspapers. She thought the best way to deal with it was to make it a perfectly normal part of our lives."

"It?" Jane asked carefully.

"Sorry, it's my turn to say I didn't mean that to sound the way it probably did."

"So you're not ashamed I exist?"

"Of course not. I loved your mother and would have married her."

"Then why didn't you?"

"I, well, the PM really, said it wouldn't be a good idea."

"The PM?"

"Look I don't know how much you know about your mother, her family, that sort of thing."

"Not a lot."

"Well her family background made it impossible for her to be the wife for a politician."

"How do you mean 'her family background'?"

"What has she told you?"

"As I said, not a lot. She told me her parents were killed early in the war, in an air raid."

"She has never said anything else?"

"No. Should she have done?" Jane asked suspiciously.

"I've said too much. If Georgina hasn't told you….."

"She did say her real name was Georgina Carmichael. I remember that much."

"Well. If your mother hasn't told you then it is not up to me to break her confidences. You must ask her yourself."

"I don't have any contact with her now."

"Since she married Richard?"

"You know Richard?"

"Of course I do. I've known him for almost as long as I've known your mother."

"There's so much about you all I don't know."

"She will tell you one day. I'm sure she will."

"But something in her 'family background' meant you couldn't marry her?"

"It was the middle of the Cold War. Although the dreadful 'McCarthy era' was passed, anyone with the remotest of connections to anyone who had ever been a communist was off limits."

"And my mother had connections to someone who had been a communist?"

"I was told so." Grahame Johnstone was thinking on his feet. He had rather assumed that Georgina would have told Jane of her family history and she had obviously said nothing. "There was a connection between your grandfather and communists in the Spanish Civil War." He trusted that was obscure enough for Jane never to be able to check.

"Lots of people were communists then weren't they?"

"Yes, my dear girl, lots of people were."

"But you would have married her if you hadn't been a politician?"

"Yes, I would have. But I was a politician. And, I'm rather ashamed to say, I was an ambitious one. Today, knowing what I know now, I would make a different decision, but then? Well I wasn't strong enough and I did as I was told."

"You're very trusting, telling me all this."

"I trust you. You are my daughter."

He said it in such a way that Jane believed in his sincerity.

"Yes. I am."

"You are my daughter in more ways than one, Jane. Not only have you inherited something of the way I look you have also inherited my love of mathematics."

"And my mother's?"

"Yes. She had a wonderful brain too. But talent such as yours cannot come only from what you have inherited from your parents, you have worked hard. After I sent that letter I knew it wouldn't be enough. I had to be in College today so I thought it would be an opportunity to meet. I'm only allowed a few minutes to myself but I couldn't miss telling you how proud I am of you and how sorry I am that it has all been so difficult for you as well as for your mother."

"Difficult?"

"It can't have been easy moving around and I heard about your breakdown. Yet you have turned out remarkably well. Are you staying on? Doing your Masters, eventually a doctorate?"

Jane was unsure whether her father was showing real interest in her or just wanted to be sure she would be out of his way for a few more years.

"I haven't decided. Probably."

"It was all such a risk three years ago, you know. Richard Mackenzie was adamant you would repay the investment and he was right."

"Richard stuck up for me?"

"You owe him a lot young lady. Not only is he making your mother very happy but he persuaded me that you had so much locked up potential. You owe him everything."

"No. It was you. I owe you."

"But I would have done nothing if it hadn't been for him."

"Oh." She hadn't known and it made her feel guilty.

"Jane?"

She waited a few seconds for him to continue, but he was just looking at her rather sadly.

"Yes?"

"You must never think I didn't love your mother and never think that I would have abandoned you. And you must always remember how much I regret not having known you as you grew up. I had my own children but somehow, well they are like their mother."

There was a knock on the door and Jane's father smiled a rather wan smile and left the room.

Jane sat down and tried to remember the conversation, perhaps the only conversation she would ever have with her father. Her grandfather had been a communist? It didn't really seem enough to end a relationship, and it wouldn't have been if he had really loved her mother. There were so many questions she wanted to ask him, so much she wanted to say, but he had gone and she would probably never have the opportunity again.

When she got home she would write this in the book she still kept, the book with *Silver Birch* on the cover.

She remembered the other envelope. She had known it would be from her mother and Richard and had not wanted to open it but after what her father had told her she felt she owed it to them to read what they will have worried about writing. *"We really are very proud of you. You have done just what we would have imagined for you, what we all hoped for you."*

"Oh shit." Jane swore as she screwed up the letter. She thought better of it a moment later and straightened out the sheet and put it in her bag with the other. Perhaps, she thought, I should let them know how I am. Then, she told herself harshly, they would already know wouldn't they.

After her interview with her tutor Jane walked back home thinking that her future seemed secure. The route through to her PhD plotted and the area of research planned. There was even talk of collaborating on a book. It would be completely academic and rather selfish since it wouldn't advance the sum of human knowledge nor would it improve the lot of humankind but it would be something she would do well.

When Matt had asked her to marry him on the night of her last exam she had said she needed some time to decide, a statement that he had taken to mean she was saying 'no' and which had led to something of an argument but as she walked home she thought that perhaps she should accept.

Then her future would be really settled.

"OK." Jane said as she and Matt had finished their dinner.
"OK what?"
"You asked me to marry you, remember?"
"Oh yeah."
"Well don't sound so ruddy enthusiastic."
"Sorry. I hadn't forgotten, I just thought perhaps you had."
"Well OK then."
"You're saying yes?"
"Don't sound so surprised."
"Well that's great."
"You mean it?"
"Of course I mean it." Matt took hold of Jane's hand and squeezed it. "Of course I did, do." He managed to sound convincing. "Come on, let's open a bottle of something and celebrate and plan."

As she handed Matt the corkscrew she gave him a hug. "Mrs Jane Greenaway. I really like the sound of that."

"Here's to Mr Matthew and Dr Jane Greenaway. It won't be long you know, you'll get that doctorate."

"Cheers."

The next day neither Jane nor Matt said anything to each other about the night before. Jane cleared up the wine glasses and as she put the bottles in the rubbish she decided not to say anything until Matt did; perhaps he had changed his mind, he hadn't seemed very enthusiastic. Matt ate his breakfast in silence wondering if he should say something but since Jane didn't, he didn't either.

And it went on like that.

By the end of the summer Jane decided he hadn't meant it and they fell back into the routine of their first year together. Matt was still working in the bookshop and it looked like he would never leave. His money, topped up by an allowance Jane received, was good enough for their needs and he saw no reason to push for something better. Matt loved books and he loved his job. He was content and he couldn't understand why Jane was always pushing herself to do things more difficult than she had ever faced and to a higher standard than she had ever reached.

"You put so much stress on yourself Janey. Chill. Relax. Enjoy life. We're only here once."

"But I like pushing myself. I just always want to be better."

"Better than who?"

She corrected his grammar as she often did. "You should say 'whom, better than whom' not 'who'." Then she answered more thoughtfully, "Better than me." But she knew what she meant, and could never admit, was 'better than my mother'

Jane hardly noticed the passing of the year of her Masters and the three of her PhD. Time didn't seem to be important. She was comfortable enough with Matt, they were, if not what she thought of as 'honeymoon happy', they were content with their lives together. They never again discussed marriage or the possibility of a family, they both just assumed it would happen 'sometime'. Jane's focus was on her work and she had no intention of changing anything in her life that would prejudice that.

David Childs, still living in the first floor flat opposite, sent his reports to Eric though he was able to say very little that justified the monthly cheques he received.

After the first year Eric had suggested David Childs join the police and an interview was set up. Eric said he could do the job as long as he continued to keep a close eye on Matt and Silver and he needed no encouragement to do that.

He was so familiar with their routine that most weeks he was able to let himself in through their back door, using a key Matt had carelessly left lying one evening on the bar, and he would look around Silver's house.

Being very careful not to disturb anything he would check the piles of post and papers that were always strewn across the kitchen table for anything that Eric might find interesting. He would look in the fridge to see what food was there and imagine sharing the cottage pies and chicken casseroles that she would cook. He would climb the stairs and look in their bedroom, opening the drawers of the dressing table and touching her underwear. He would go into the bathroom to see what pills were in the cabinet, and to confirm that she was still taking her contraceptives. He would never spend more than half an hour in the house but that half hour was the best half hour of his week.

There was nothing about Jane's life that David did not know.

The photographs he had taken of her covered his bedroom wall, and when there was no more space he put them on the walls of his spare room and his bathroom.

He knew even more than he passed on to Eric especially after he had found an exercise book in a drawer with ornate lettering *Silver Birch*. He read and re-read what she had written in that book but kept the information to himself.

He would know when it would be useful. He was learning how to make best use of any piece of information as he progressed in the police. After two years pounding a beat he had moved to plain clothes. He liked to think he was good at the job and others seemed to agree with him though none of his colleagues liked him. They teased him cruelly about his not having a girlfriend. There were times with some unpleasantness that they accused him of being gay, but then he just said he had had a girlfriend once who had died and he had never found anyone to match her. He talked about Silver, how beautiful she was and how imaginative she had been in bed, with such conviction that those who heard left him alone.

Every night David lay on his bed trying not to think of Silver in bed with Matt. He could never understand what it was about Matt that had attracted her, Matt was an old man, a drunk, a waster, a good for nothing. As he lay in bed David's imagination was very vivid. With his eyes closed every night it was Silver who did all the things to him that gave him pleasure as if she wasn't in the bedroom across the road. With Matt.

In the Summer of 1987, Dr Jane Cavanagh's first book was published. At the launch party Matt had too much to drink and interrupted the speeches by announcing "Jane and I are getting married."

"What?" Jane concentrated hard on Matt's face to see if he knew what he was saying.

"Jane and I have been engaged for four years but we're finally going to tie the knot. Now she's had her baby, the book I mean, she will have time to concentrate on me. So we're getting married. It's all arranged. St Mary's on 1st August. Don't look so surprised Janey, we've been engaged for far too long. Time to settle down and have proper babies."

It was that that made Jane realise he was drunk, or high on something. She knew he would never talk like that under normal circumstances.

"And another thing...." Matt hadn't finished. "I'm opening my own shop. I've always wanted to and now it's going to happen."

He sat down and finished his glass before immediately pouring another. Jane got him home as soon as she could.

"What the fuck was that all about?"

"Don' you wanna marry me Janey baby?"

"No."

"No?"

"No. Not when you're like this."

"I've waited ages and ages and ages Janey." Then he fell asleep.

The next morning Matt, nursing his hangover, was apologetic.

"I'm sorry, I didn't mean to say anything in front of all your colleagues and people. I just got carried away. But I do mean it. I've told my parents....."

"You've told who?"

"Whom?" He smiled but she ignored his attempt at making up by using their familiar in-joke. He realised Jane was not smiling in response so he continued. "I've told my parents. And they're thrilled. They said it was about time. They're looking forward to grand-children. They've waited long enough. How long have we been together? Five years? Six?"

"Something like that."

"And we love each other?"

"Probably."

"So why not? You're not getting any younger and ..."

"What?"

"We're not getting any younger and if we're going to have a family we'd better get started."

"I'm 27."

"Well that's getting on for having a baby isn't it?"

"I've got years before I've got to worry about that."

She didn't think now was the time to tell him she had no intention of having children. Why would anyone want to bring another human being into the world as it was?

"You don't want to marry me?"

"Of course I do." She didn't think she sounded convincing.

"Then what's the problem?"

"I don't suppose there is one."

"So let's go out and buy the ring."

"Today?"

"Yes. Why not?"

Jane sat staring into her coffee while Matt did the washing up. Perhaps, she thought, her lack of enthusiasm the previous night was because it had been a surprise. For months, years, she had assumed things would just go on as they had since they had started living together. It was comfortable living together, she was as happy at home as she had ever been and that gave her the confidence to become engrossed with the book. The writing had been interesting, time consuming and challenging and it had taken much of her time and concentration. Perhaps she had taken Matt for granted. Perhaps it had been his way of sharing her big night. She hadn't been pleased that he had stolen her co-authors' thunder but she tried to understand how Matt felt and she began to warm to the idea.

"Can I have a nice, subtle, nine carat diamond?"

Matt turned round and grinned. "I really thought you'd gone off me."

"Don't be so daft!" And she relaxed as he wrapped his arms around her and she laughed as his wet and soapy hands pulled down the shoulder straps of her t-shirt. "Come on, the jewellers can wait."

That evening Matt went to the pub, as he always did, and it wasn't long before David joined him at the bar, as he so regularly had done for five years.

"Hiya Matt."

"Wotcha Dave I've got some news."

"Yeah?"

"I'm getting married."

"Yeah?" David Childs tried to be non-committal. "You sure you want to get tied down?"

"Why not? She's beautiful, my Janey."

"You've been together for a long time." David was thinking fast. He could not let Silver get married. Not to this man. There was only one person she was going to marry, ever, and that was him. He had accepted that she was living with Matt but it didn't really matter as long as he could keep an eye on them and as long as she wasn't married.

He could not allow Matt to marry Silver. He really couldn't.

It was quite easy to make it look like an accident and no one seriously doubted the facts.

Matt was drunk, it had been a long session, he was staggering, he walked into the path of the bus. It was all over in seconds.

Chapter 15
London 1989 to 1993

David waited at the scene as police and ambulance arrived to take Matt's body away. He gave his details, as the only independent witness to the accident, then he walked quickly back to his flat.

He watched from his window as the two policewomen approached Silver's front door. The curtains weren't drawn and he was able to watch as Silver sat down on the sofa. He found it strangely satisfying watching her calmly accept the news. He could see no evidence of tears or cries of disbelief. The policewomen didn't stay as long as he thought they would, they didn't even make Silver a cup of tea. Perhaps, he thought, she was quite pleased Matt was dead. Perhaps he'd done her a favour.

He stayed watching as she picked up the phone. He wished he had set a microphone in the house, it was something he had meant to do. Whoever it was she was talking to seemed to have made her angry as she stood staring at the phone for several minutes before she replaced the receiver. She then closed the curtains and he could see no more.

Jane poured herself a large glass of whisky and sat back in the settee. 'You're not his wife.' Mr Greenaway had told her, 'Mrs Greenaway and I will go to the hospital. We will identify our son. You can't sign anything since you never bothered to marry him.' He had told her that she was not a member of the Greenaway family but they would let her know when the funeral was in case she wanted to attend.

Jane was excluded by Matt's parents from all the mundane bureaucracy of death that would have helped keep the grief and loneliness at bay through the first few days.

She had not realised quite how important to her Matt's just being there had been.

She had been annoyed by him so many times, she had wanted to be left alone when he had wanted to do things, she had wanted quiet music when he had wanted lively, and she had lost count long ago of how many times she had sworn at him for leaving his clothes lying around the bedroom floor and how many times she had badgered him because he never put away the dishes even when he did do any washing up.

But he had always cheered her up when she was sad, and encouraged her when she was sure that everything she did was wrong.

He had been so annoying at times but she missed him dreadfully.

The day before the funeral Mr and Mrs Greenaway arrived at the house that had been Jane's home for five years and, barely speaking to the woman who would have been their daughter-in-law, cleared out the wardrobes and shelves and cupboards and chests of drawers of everything that was their son's.

Jane sat in the kitchen fuming that she was not even allowed the catharsis of going through the things that were so familiar.

'You weren't married to him so you have no rights.' She was told firmly, 'you have no rights whatsoever to anything. You should know that the house is up for sale. You'll have to leave sharpish.' Jane tried to explain that she had paid half the mortgage for five years and had some rights, but Mr Greenaway was dismissive 'you expect us to believe a student could afford to pay half the mortgage'. Jane argued that Matt wouldn't have wanted her thrown out into the street and it was reluctantly agreed that she could stay in the house until September as long as she kept it tidy.

After she had watched them drive away Jane sat down at the kitchen table and wrote to her mother and Richard.

There's some good news and some bad news. Good news 1. I've had my first book published, you won't have seen anything about it in the press as it's not really a book for the general reader but I'm told it'll be on the undergraduate reading lists in a number of universities so may bring in a penny or two now and again. Good news 2 would have been that I was getting married. I've been with Matt for six years or so and we always meant to get married. We got engaged last month and finally set the date but then there is the bad news. Matt was killed. It was an accident, three weeks ago. So here I am, 27 years old with the beginnings of a career but alone. I suppose that's why I'm writing to you. I'll be leaving Cambridge as soon as I can. One of the collaborators on Good News 1 has suggested I join his department in London so I'll probably go there. His name is Peter Carmichael (funnily enough, though I suspect no relation) and perhaps he is interested in more than my brain but it is far too soon after Matt to even think about that. Though it would be convenient, wouldn't it? I could, after all, be Jane Carmichael. I'm not getting any younger. I promise I'll keep in touch and let you know what happens in the next instalment in my life.

I've loved Cambridge. It was an inspired choice. Was that down to you Richard or was it GJ? I met him by the way, he came to College when I graduated. It seems years and years ago.

I don't know why I've written this letter. I expect you knew everything anyway through your network of spies. Perhaps, after being away for a quarter of my life, I'm missing you.

Just two days later Jane received a reply.

Darling. So good to hear from you. So glad to hear your Good News items but saddened beyond words about the Bad. You say nothing about Matt so we can only assume it is all rather raw. We would love to have met him but then life is always so full of regrets is it not? You are right in assuming Richard and I have followed your successes but will always remain at arm's length as long as that is your wish. You should, by the way, know that

Cambridge was initially Richard's idea but it was your father who made it happen.

Jane was surprised at how easily her move to London fell into place. Peter Carmichael was very helpful in what Jane thought was a rather pedantically tactful manner and it was only nine weeks after her book launch, and Matt's exuberant announcement of their engagement, that Jane left Cambridge with little more than her clothes, her books and two boxes of bits and pieces. The only tangible reminders of her life with Matt were in her photograph albums.

Detective Constable David Childs had to work quickly to get a transfer from Cambridge to the Metropolitan Police but Eric had contacts and within a month of Jane's move David had a flat and a job in London.

"Why did she move?" Eric asked David Childs when they met for the first time in seven years.

"Matt died and his parents chucked her out." David answered as if he was stating the obvious.

"I don't believe that the death of her fiancé was reason enough. From what you have reported it seemed more of a liaison of convenience. And she could have stayed in Cambridge couldn't she?"

"She seems quite friendly with Peter Carmichael, he was one of her co-authors on her book. Have you read it?"

"Mathematics isn't my subject." Eric answered drily. "Is there anything between her and this Peter?"

"I don't think so. She never saw him socially outside the university."

"I'll find out more about him." David waited while Eric wrote in his notebook.

"I thought she was about to leave Matt anyway."

"Really?"

"She'd been working on that book with people from a university in London for years so I think she was heading out of Cambridge anyway."

"Really?"

"I think she'd told him she was leaving. That last night in the pub he was very depressed. That's why I think he walked in front of the bus."

"Really?" Eric commented coldly. "I'd rather assumed you'd pushed him."

David said nothing. He had been the only witness to Matt's death. The bus driver couldn't have seen anything. No one could prove he had done anything.

"I want to talk about Silver not Matt." Eric continued. "When someone changes their life so significantly it's for a reason."

"Like what?"

"Have you never wondered why I'm so interested in your Silver?"

"Not really. It's your business. As long as you keep paying me I don't need to know do I?"

"It's time you knew a little more about what to watch out for. Now she's made a move we need to be more on our guard."

"What do you mean she's made a move?"

"It's the way they work."

"They?"

"For years they do nothing, fit into society, have careers, relationships, have a life. And then, when no one is expecting it, they get a call or have a chance meeting or receive a letter and they have a task to perform. They are wakened from their sleeping. You mustn't give up. One day her call will come. I know it."

"Sleeping?"

"That's what spies do."

"So you think Silver's a spy? I didn't think it could all be about her father. Can't you tell me all about it?"

"As I said in the beginning, if I told you what it's all about I'd have to kill you."

"But you were joking weren't you?"

"No." Eric enjoyed watching David Childs' face as he realised something of what he was involved in.

"But Silver? A spy? Who for?"

"As I say. If I tell you....."

"I know. But if she's a spy do you think there might be some sort of message or code in that book of hers? Russians are good at maths aren't they? Perhaps Peter Carmichael is involved as well."

"I think you're being a bit far-fetched there Dave."

"It was just a thought. I mean she's done nothing all these years to make anyone suspicious apart from writing that book. There's got to be something in it, something that's telling something to someone somewhere, hasn't there?"

"I doubt very much any message would be in the complexities of a mathematical textbook." Eric was not going to tell David Childs that he had wondered the same thing. "Just keep telling me who she comes into contact with and let me do the rest."

On 1st April 1990 Jane Cavanagh married Peter Carmichael.

She wasn't in love with him and he wasn't in love with her. She knew that even as they had the conversation in the wine bar in Covent Garden when he had suggested they get married. It had all been very matter of fact. They got on well enough and Jane couldn't think of any particular reason why it wouldn't work. Her biological clock was ticking and, apart from thinking that perhaps now was the time to have a child, she loved the idea her name would be 'Carmichael', her mother's real name.

The wedding was a more formal affair than she would have liked but Peter had a large family and, after more than two years in London, they had a wide circle of mutual friends. Jane invited Richard and her mother but they thanked her and said it was probably better if they didn't make the journey up to London. Jane was not disappointed. They weren't part of her life any more.

As she walked back up the aisle, her hand lightly resting on the arm of her husband of twenty minutes, she knew she had made a dreadful mistake.

She smiled as she thought a bride should and throughout the reception said all the right things to their friends and to Peter's family. As they walked to the taxi Peter told her he would try to make her happy and she said nothing as she held her smile. She looked out of the window as they were driven onto the Strand and had she been focused on the people milling around she may have recognised David Childs. But she was concentrating on the rivulets of rain running down the window and wondering how on earth she had got herself into this situation.

David had watched Silver as she walked along the Strand to the church. He had thought she looked beautiful, as she always did when she made the effort. He had walked into the church behind a very smartly dressed group and sat down, unnoticed, at the back. He had slipped out of the church before the final blessing and was standing with a group of people by the railings as she emerged from the church. He had felt certain she wouldn't have seen him behind his camera's lens. He had followed the wedding party as it walked to the hotel for the reception and two hours later he had seen her face through the wet taxi window and known that the man she had married could not make her happy.

With the right woman Peter would have made a thoughtful and considerate husband and with the right man Jane might have made more effort to be the wife that was expected of her but he was wrong for her and she was wrong for him and from the beginning they made each other unhappy.

Every day they commuted together into London to work in the same department at the University but they rarely spoke about anything other than the day to day administration of their lives. Their conversations rarely went beyond what shopping was needed, what bills had to be paid and whether the train to work would be delayed.

They both had their work to concentrate on but it did not help Peter's temper that Jane was the more successful of the two. Her most recent book, written without her husband's collaboration, was well received and when people spoke in glowing terms of 'Dr Carmichael' it was more often than not Dr Jane that they meant, not Dr Peter.

Peter reacted to his unhappiness by spending any free time he had in the local pub drinking while Jane responded by having an affair.

"She's meeting someone."

David reported to Eric in one of their regular phone calls.

"Do you know who?"

"I know he's married and his wife is Indian. He works in the City."

"How did she meet him?"

"I'm not entirely sure. Probably at one of the seminars she gives, he's an economist."

"Name?"

"Simon Ackroyd."

"His wife?"

"Amisha."

"Hindu or Moslem?"

"God knows! Does it matter?"

"You never know. Anything might matter."

"I'll find out."

"Don't. I'll be checking anyway."

"Where do they meet? Silver and Simon."

"During the day mostly, lunches, hotels."

"Sordid. I would have thought better of her."

"So would I."

"Are you sure it's an affair, not just a friendship?"

"I'm sure. I followed her two weeks ago. And then last week. I checked today that there was a pattern before bothering you with it. She meets him at The Tower Hotel and they're there for two hours or more. What else will they be doing but shagging?"

"That we need to find out. Let me know if the pattern changes. I'll find out about this Simon Ackroyd."

And the conversation was over.

After she had been married for a year, and after six months with Simon, Jane decided it was time to be open with Peter.

The conversation began in civilised fashion.

"I've been having an affair." Jane said as she put his plate of sandwiches on the kitchen table. "I thought you'd like to know."

"I thought you might be."

Jane thought Peter didn't sound very interested. "You knew?" She asked. But he did not catch her eye. She sat down opposite him and watched as he concentrated on his lunch.

"Well I assumed. Tuesday's was it?"

"Mostly." She wondered how he had known.

He looked up and asked her directly. "Are you in love with him?"

"No. I don't think so."

"Just sex then?"

"Pretty much."

Jane didn't hear that the pitch of Peter's voice was getting higher. "Aren't I enough for you now?" He asked, putting his half-eaten sandwich down on the plate.

She couldn't answer. She couldn't tell him that he had never been enough.

"Or are you just trying to get back at me, trying to hurt me?"

"Why would I want to do that?" She asked him calmly. "Do you really think I care enough about you to want to hurt you?"

Perhaps, she thought afterwards, she had gone too far. At the time Jane did not recognise the rising levels of his anger and self-justification.

They had argued many times before. On almost every occasion Jane could remember their voices would gradually get louder until they were shouting then Peter would leave, slamming the door behind him before going out to the pub. When he returned nothing would be said and the air was never cleared.

"You're incapable of caring about anyone but yourself."

"That's not fair."

"You've never given yourself to me in the way you should have."

"What?"

"You've never let me use you in the way you should have."

"What are you talking about?"

"I'm talking about the way a man should be able to rely on his wife, the way I've never been able to rely on you."

"What for? Sex? If you'd ever been remotely loving I might have responded!"

"Loving? Sex is not about love you stupid bitch."

"You've never loved me."

"No. I haven't. But I always thought you might be OK to fuck."

"Then why did you marry me?"

"I can't think of one good reason." Peter shouted.

Jane waited for the slam of the door and the hours of peace she would have until he returned, drunk. But his voice suddenly went quiet and she found that disturbingly threatening. "You have never, ever, allowed me to enjoy you the way I wanted to."

"What do you mean?" Jane was beginning to get frightened.

He didn't answer her question. He stood up, grabbed her by the arm so hard that the skin pinched. She screamed at him to let her go.

"Let you go! Oh no, not yet." He held onto her arm and as she tried to lash out with her free arm she was dazed when she felt the full force of his fist on her cheekbone.

She could not resist as he tore at her clothes and forced her onto the kitchen floor.

Jane had read reports about marital rape and through that afternoon with Peter she wondered dispassionately why she hadn't taken the reports more seriously.

She gave up fighting after a few minutes, realising she could never win against the strong and angry man. She detached herself from what was happening, making herself believe it was not happening to her.

She did as she was told. After the initial assault she let him pull her up the stairs to their bedroom. There she put on and took off her underwear as he told her. She posed as he directed while he took photographs. She said nothing knowing that the slightest resistance from her would lead to a repeat of the vicious and unnatural assault. Through the afternoon she filled her mind with thought of numbers and sequences and problematic equations as he did what he wanted with her.

"Is that it then?" She asked him when he finally left her alone.

"It's all you're good for."

She closed her eyes knowing, by the sounds, that he was dressing and knowing from experience that he would be going to the pub.

After he had left she stood under the shower for a very long time but she could not wash away the dirt she felt. The bruises would die away, she told herself, the throbbing pain would ease but she knew she had reached rock bottom in her life.

Every morning they left their house in Surbiton and took the train into London. During the day Jane thought of nothing but her work. Every evening they met up and returned to the house in the suburbs. She told Peter one evening that she had stopped seeing Simon but he said nothing and it made no difference to the humiliation Peter meted out to her every Saturday afternoon.

Week after week, relentlessly and inevitably, Peter raped and assaulted her. She knew it was not normal. She knew she should not have to put up with it, but somehow it seemed impossible to face up to fighting back.

She didn't ask what he did with the obscene photographs he took. She assumed they were hidden somewhere as she couldn't find them in the drawers and cupboards she searched. It did not occur to her that he was selling them to men he met in the pub. One man, who Peter knew only as Dave, bought quite a collection of the more intimate ones.

In July 1992 Peter was out when Jane returned from shopping to find they had been burgled.

The back door was damaged but still locked, the front door untouched, but some of her washing had been removed from the clothes line in the back garden. She phoned 999 but she didn't think they had taken her seriously.

"Underwear you say? And what else?"

"Some t-shirts."

"Anything valuable madam?"

"Not that I can find, I don't think they got into the house."

"So you won't be bothering with insurance then?"

"I shouldn't have thought so for a moment. I just thought you might be interested that a crime has been committed."

"I'll send someone round to check for fingerprints if you want madam but I can't hold out great hope on a washing line. Underwear you say?"

She could hear the vulgar laughter.

"I'm sorry to have bothered you with such a trifling matter." And she hung up.

Perhaps it was trifling, the theft of her bras and pants from a washing line, but it disturbed her and it was some time before she forgot about it.

Peter didn't tell her that Dave, one of his mates from the pub, was a detective and had called round one day the following week when he had had the day off to take more details of the theft and had spent a long time checking through the house to make sure that nothing else had been taken.

The divorce went through as easily as any divorce could. They had been married three years and one month when the *Decree Nisi* came through. Jane agreed to be the guilty party. It had been Peter's price for him to finally let her go.

Chapter 16
Isle of Wight 1993

It took a while for Jane to pluck up the courage to write to her mother and Richard but she did, the week before the absolute was due.

You must know when you get a letter from me there is some trauma going on in my life. Well this time it's divorce. I should never have married Peter, nor he me. Anyway, here I am single again. I'll have to sell up as I hate this house and I hate Chessington. I'm not sure what to do now. I have thought about going freelance, doing some writing, travelling, learning more about other stuff. Perhaps even visiting you! What has it been? 13 years? Perhaps that's enough water under the bridge for us to make up? Be friends again? Have I forgiven you? I've probably realised there wasn't anything to forgive. So am I asking to come and visit? Probably. Will it be easy? Undoubtedly not. Let me know what you think. I finish in London mid-June. I've handed in my notice so am free pretty much any time after the end of May. Will you let me know?

It had taken a lot out of her to write the letter and she waited, more worried than she wanted to admit to herself, for an answer.

When it came she wished it hadn't.

Jane, Forgive me for not having written before, I probably should have, but I have not wanted to burden you. Your mother is not well, she has not been well for some time. I would love to see you, of course, but you should be aware your mother probably won't know you. Dementia is an invidious disease and at 70 she is too young but when you do come to see us you must realise she isn't the Mum you knew any more. Come to see us, by all means, but you should know it won't be easy. Please do come, I would love to see you."

Jane looked again at Richard's letter. She was surprised to see from the address at the top of the letter that they lived in Freshwater, on the Isle of Wight, barely three miles from where she had been so happy so many years before.

When Jane had left the Midlands for Cambridge she had left her mother to Richard. She had wanted a clean break and had written a letter she sometimes regretted and somehow the separation had taken on a life of its own. Being independent from her mother and her father's selfishness had been more important than anything else and then her independence from them had become an end in itself.

She decided that she would go to the Isle of Wight and see her mother and Richard. She would try to rebuild bridges with them while the house in Chessington was sold and then she would travel.

In some ways she knew she was lucky. She had made a career for herself. She had written papers that achieved acclaim and recognition, she had published text books which were becoming considered standard texts, to many she would appear successful. But she had never been good with people and she knew that she was a failure at the only thing that was important.

"Thanks for coming Jane."

"Hello Richard. Mum?"

"Hello." The face showed no recognition so Jane looked to Richard who shrugged. "Hello. I'm Elizabeth, at least I am today."

"Hello, I'm Jane."

"I had a daughter called Jane. Once. Yes. I did. I had a daughter called Jane. Are you my daughter Jane?"

Jane looked to Richard for help. He had warned her that her visit would be difficult but she had had no idea how bad it could be.

"Yes Mum. I'm Jane."

"Jane was very clever." Elizabeth smiled grimly up at her visitor. "Are you clever?"

"I'm Jane, Mum." She looked despairingly at Richard as she realised there was no point in looking at her mother.

"Jane? Jane? I had a daughter called Jane. She was clever. Yes. She was clever. Are you Jane? Hello!" Elizabeth smiled an open, guileless smile at Richard as if she had only just seen him enter the room. "This is my daughter Jane. Have you met Jane? This is my darling, darling daughter Jane."

Jane looked at Richard for help.

"Come on dear." He said to Elizabeth, "Let me settle you in and then I'll make Jane a cup of tea."

"Tea? Yes. I want a cup of tea."

Richard wheeled Elizabeth in her chair into the front room and sometime later joined Jane in the kitchen. The kettle was on the boil and Jane had put tea bags in mugs and was looking at the tidy kitchen and the well-tended garden of the old-fashioned bungalow in a road of identical old-fashioned bungalows.

"Has she been like this for long?"

"It's getting worse. The drugs help but it's only a matter of time."

"She isn't Mum any more is she?"

"No, though some days are better than others."

"Did you have some good times together?"

"Oh yes. We had some good years. We've been together twelve years now."

"Were you happy?" It was suddenly important to Jane that they had been.

"Oh yes, though she was always concerned that she had let you down."

"I was always worried I had let her down."

"There you go then."

Richard busied himself making the tea and carefully placing the mugs and a plate of biscuits on a tray to carry into the front room.

"Jane was a very clever girl." Elizabeth said conversationally as they sat down.

"Yes Mum."

"She's her father's daughter."

Jane looked at Richard but he didn't seem to mind.

"You're Jane?" Elizabeth asked holding out her hand and grasping at Jane's.

"Hello Mum. Yes. I'm Jane."

She turned to Richard. "This is my darling daughter Jane." She said and then sat back grinning.

Jane concentrated on her tea, wondering how it was possible that her intelligent, infuriating Mother had come to this. Richard saw how upset she was and signalled for her to follow him back to the kitchen.

"She's still so young." Jane said sadly, "How could this happen to her?"

"No one ever said life was fair."

"She told me that once, when we were upping sticks sometime. I've not been a very good daughter have I?"

"How do you mean?"

"Well as soon as I could I left her. I never tried to see what life was like from her perspective. I never tried to listen to her side of things."

"All children are selfish. That's what she used to say. You were no better and no worse than she'd expected."

"Ouch."

"But she's been very proud of you, you know. Very proud indeed."

"Janey?" The thin voice from the front room of the bungalow interrupted. "Janey? Did I imagine you or are you really here?"

"I'm here Mum." Jane looked at Richard and left the kitchen.

Her mother was a completely different person.

"Janey. I hear you're getting divorced. Tell me about it."

Her mother looked bright and alert. Jane looked, again, to Richard for help. This afternoon's visit was turning out to be altogether too confusing. He smiled weakly and explained quietly that the medication had just kicked in. She would be more able to cope for an hour or so.

"Peter was a shit Mum. I should never have married him."

"I blame myself. If I had given you some idea of a sensible ordered life you wouldn't have jumped into bed with the first man you met and expected him to look after you as I never did."

"Peter wasn't the first person I jumped into bed with."

"No? Oh yes. There was that man in Cambridge. He got run over by a bus didn't he? What was his name? Matt? Yes that was it. Neither of them was right. And then there was that first boy, the one in Ludlow? What was his name? David? I remember more than you think you know. Whatever happened to David? Matt died and Peter got set aside in divorce but what happened to David?"

After the rapid outpourings of her damaged mind Elizabeth fell silent.

"Whatever did happen to David Childs?" Richard asked Jane, looking with perhaps more intensity than she noticed.

"I haven't a clue." She answered brightly. "I haven't seen him since that morning in Birmingham."

"Are you sure?" Richard asked, attempting levity.

"Absolutely. Why on earth would I?"

"No reason. It's just that he had seemed important to you at the time."

"I can't say I've thought of him since."

Richard wasn't sure that he believed her.

"Mum?"

"Yes dear?"

It was obvious from Elizabeth's voice that she had no idea that she was talking to her daughter.

"Mum. Do you know how I am?"

"You're a friend of Richard's, a nice young friend of Richard's. Are you Claire? No. You can't be Claire. Claire's still a baby."

"And who is Richard?" Jane asked carefully.

"Richard is my friend too."

"Isn't he your husband?"

"Husband! Oh No. I never married. I had a boyfriend once. I had a daughter once. Oh she was a lovely little girl. You'd like her. She had lovely brown shiny curly hair. Yes, you'd like her. I wonder what ever happened to her. I haven't seen her for years." Jane saw the light disappearing from her mother's eyes. "I wonder where she is now. My daughter. My little Janey."

"Is she always like this now?" Jane asked Richard as they watched her mother close her eyes and sleep.

"I'm afraid to say this is a good day."

"I'm so sorry. I had no idea."

"Why would you? I never told you and no one else would. Now let us talk about you? What are you up to?"

"Well I'm writing a book."

"Another one?"

"I've just started it and it's going to be slightly out of my comfort zone this time."

"Sounds interesting."

"It's still maths related as it's a biography of a mathematician, a woman called Sofia Kovalevskaya. In fact I'm hoping to go to Moscow sometime to do some research there."

Jane was looking at her mother so she could not see the look that crossed Richard's face. If she had she would have seen a moment, quickly overcome, when his eyes opened wide with interest.

"I might be able to help you there." He said quietly. "That is if you really want to go."

Three weeks later Jane walked through the arrivals hall of Moscow airport.

She had had no difficulty getting a visa. Her name was known amongst those academics who mattered and her interest in Sofia Kovalevskaya was well documented as there were many references to her work in Jane's publications. No suspicions were raised about her visit and she had even received an invitation to a meeting with eminent mathematicians from the University.

'I am on holiday.' She explained as she sized up the men and women. Under normal circumstances she would have enjoyed their company; their names were known to her, as hers was to them, but for a reason she could not put her finger on these did not feel like normal circumstances. 'I have left London and am going freelance.' She wondered if they would believe her but there seemed no reason why they shouldn't. 'Kovalevskaya was a remarkable woman, a comrade socialist before her time' they said, 'and a remarkably clever person' Jane agreed.

She spent a tense but interesting afternoon with the men from the university and they seemed to accept her for what she purported to be, an academic on holiday, taking the opportunity to learn more about their country. 'Enjoy your stay in our remarkable city. Make sure you visit our university library. I am sure you will see it is better stocked than any in Cambridge or Oxford or in London' the leader said as they left, apparently satisfied that she had no other motive for her visit to Moscow than the one she had given.

The next day Jane went for a walk in the hot sunshine. When she left the hotel she passed the British Embassy and headed across the river to Alexander Garden. She could not know that the route she took was almost identical to that taken by her mother thirty-five years before.

"Dr Carmichael?"

She turned to see a grey haired man not old, but past middle age.

"Yes?"

"Forgive me for interrupting your sightseeing but I understand we have mutual friends." Without giving her a chance to ask who they might be he continued. "Please meet me on Saturday morning in the University Library. They will allow you in when you give your name. I will be on the third table to the left of the entrance. Now I will not keep you from your sightseeing. It's a beautiful afternoon and the city is at its best." The man tipped his hat in an old fashioned gesture of respect and walked swiftly away.

Jane sat down on a bench to think about the strange encounter. How did the man know where she would be? Who were their 'mutual friends'? Who was he? He had spoken very good English but with a strange accent. She had worked with men and women from Eastern Europe and from Russia in the previous ten years and she thought the accent was not pure Russian, nor German nor Polish. She decided that it was not a genuine accent, the man was English, pretending to be Russian.

She was intrigued and decided that on Saturday, the day before she left for England, she would meet him.

As she approached the University Library she had been prepared to be rebuffed but she was handed a visitor's pass without query. They had obviously been expecting her.

"Dr Carmichael." The man pushed his chair back as he stood to welcome her to his table. "I am sure you have many questions for me. I will do my best to answer them."

"*Kak tebya zavut*? What is your name?" Jane tried out her Russian.

"My name is Berndt Schreiber. That will mean nothing to you I am sure." He paused, waiting for Jane to answer, wondering whether she would, after all, recognise his name.

"No, it doesn't mean anything to me."

"Nor should it." He sounded relieved.

"You said that we had mutual friends. May I ask who they are?"

"I knew a woman called Georgina Carmichael very briefly….."

"Mother? You knew my mother?"

"I'm not sure I can say I knew her. I met her, once, many years ago, remarkably enough in the same gardens in which I met you earlier this week."

"I didn't know she'd ever been to Moscow."

"I don't think she ever came a second time."

"And how did you know I'd be in those gardens when I was?"

"I was there every day since you arrived in Moscow."

"You waited for me?"

"Richard told me he had told you to go there."

"Richard? You know Richard too?"

"I have known Richard far better than I knew your mother. He has been a good friend to me."

"How? How do you know them?" Jane had so many questions to ask. Her mother, when she was Georgina Carmichael, that is before Jane was born, had been here in Moscow. So had Richard. Had they been here at the same time? For the same reason? Was this the reason for all the secrecy over the years?

Had all the hiding been nothing to do with her father at all? Berndt's answer did nothing to allay her suspicions.

"I'm not sure that is something I can answer, Jane. I'm sorry. You must ask Richard."

"Will he be able to answer the question?"

"Better than I, my dear girl, better than I."

"I will ask him then."

"Only ask questions for which you are prepared to get the answers."

Jane laughed. "That's very cryptic."

Berndt smiled. "Sometimes it is better not to know the truth of things."

"I'm not sure I would like to live in ignorance."

"Sometimes it is more comfortable."

"You may not have known my mother well but you know of her don't you?"

"Only what Richard has told me over the years. He was in love with her for a long time you know, many years before they married. He never had eyes for any other women."

Jane had thought as little as possible about the love her mother had for Richard and he for her but as she listened to Berndt Schreiber's gentle speech she realised that she knew nothing. She had judged them as only an angry teenager can judge her parents and now it was this stranger who was telling her how unnecessarily harsh and unyielding she had been. She would have a different attitude towards Richard when she returned to England.

"I hope you don't mind my taking up your time."

"Not at all this is fascinating. It is so difficult to know about people close to you isn't it? I have no family to ask, no grandparents, no cousins or aunts or uncles so it has taken a stranger to tell me things I really should have known."

Jane could not see the man's smile as he had turned away from her, towards a satchel that had been slung on his chair. By the time he turned back towards her his face was as inscrutable as it had been before.

"I have something here I think will interest you."

He pushed two books across the table and Jane looked at them. They were rare first editions. She had read them in modern format but had never thought to handle them in their original binding.

As he watched her reverentially brush the covers of the volumes Berndt asked her quietly. "Will you give a message to your mother from me?"

"She isn't well so a message is unlikely to register."

"I understand. Then will you give it to Richard?"

"Of course."

"Will you tell him that I did meet with you and that I am well?"

"I will, of course I will."

"Will you also tell them that I hope to visit England soon?"

"Of course I will. No problem."

"I would be most grateful. I know he worries about me. And you are to keep those books."

He must have registered Jane's look of surprise as he hurriedly added "I have every right to give them to you. I have followed your work and know of all the people in the world who should have them it is you."

"You've followed my work? Are you a mathematician too?"

"Of sorts. I have long had an interest in patterns and numbers."

"I will tell him I have seen you and what a kind and generous man you are Dr Schreiber."

"You credit me with a title I have not earned. I am simply Mister but I would like to think that you will think of me as Berndt."

"Well thank you Berndt. I have so enjoyed meeting you. Perhaps we will meet again, when you come to England?"

"I do hope so too."

"And I cannot thank you enough for these."

"Cherish them."

"I will."

As she stood to leave he stood too and as she held out her hand he took it and kissed it gently in another of his old fashioned gestures.

"Goodbye Berndt."

"Au revoir Jane Carmichael".

When a few minutes later in her hotel room she opened one of the books and found a small white embroidered handkerchief she resolved to ask Richard to tell her everything about the charming, but mysterious, Berndt Schreiber.

David Childs had followed Silver to the Isle of Wight and reported immediately to Eric that she had gone to see her mother and Richard Mackenzie.

"This could be it." Eric said trying not to sound triumphant. "For all these years she's ignored them. There will be a reason why she has finally gone to see them."

"Her mother is ill."

"An excuse only."

"She's just gone through a divorce and may be lonely and unsettled." David tried to make excuses for Silver. He did not want her to be the person Eric implied she was.

"Mark my words, David, she will be travelling abroad in no time."

"Perfectly understandable since she hasn't done any travelling before."

"Don't let her get away, David, we've been on her trail for too long to let her get away now."

Three weeks later David Childs phoned Eric again.

"She's going abroad, just as you said." He reported reluctantly.

"Where?"

"It looks like she's going to Moscow."

"I bet she is!" Eric could not keep the excitement out of his voice. "Leave this with me now Dave. I still have friends over there. You have done your job now. Well done. We have her!"

Eric was more disappointed with the report he had from Moscow a week later.

He was told that she met no one of any interest whatsoever. When he pressed for more detail his contact said that she had simply spent her time doing what she had said she would do, research some unknown nineteenth century mathematician.

The only people she had met, the man reported, were academics who were all beyond reproach. He was not told of the meeting in the library with the man named Berndt Schreiber.

Jane phoned Richard on her return to Chessington.

"How's Mum?"

"Not good."

"And you?"

"As well as could be expected I suppose. Did you have a good time?"

"It was all extremely useful."

"Did you meet anyone?"

"I did actually, a lovely man who said he knew you. His name is Berndt Schreiber and he said to tell you he was well."

"Anything else?"

"He said he hoped to visit England soon."

"Anything else?"

Richard wanted to be sure that the man Jane had met was Berndt and there was only one way that could be proved.

"Well yes, actually. He gave me two books and in one was a small white handkerchief."

"With or without embroidery?"

"With. But…"

"Look Jane, your mother's calling. I've got to go. Let us know what you're up to."

Jane could hardly say 'bye' before the line went dead.

"Well," she said to the dead phone receiver. "What was all that about?"

In March the following year, 1994, Dr Jane Carmichael moved into her cottage in Yarmouth, just three miles from Richard and her mother, on the Isle of Wight.

There she settled into a routine of caring for her mother, and, when she had time, writing.

Her trip to Moscow faded in her memory and she never found the right time to talk to Richard about Berndt and ask him the questions that had seemed, at the time, important.

Every day was the same and the days, months and years went by too quickly as her mother's condition deteriorated, stabilised, appeared to improve, then deteriorated further.

'Procrastination isn't the thief of time,' she told Richard more than once, 'routine is.'

Chapter 17
Isle of Wight 2014

The vicar was young and sympathetic. He took his responsibility at funerals seriously and since he had never met Elizabeth he spent an hour talking to Richard and Jane to find out what he could about her. He wanted to do her life justice in the funeral service. 'Can you tell me about her?' he asked and Jane looked at her step-father and shrugged. 'There isn't much to tell' Richard had lied. 'She lived a very straightforward life.' 'I'll talk about her being a loving wife and mother then shall I?' The vicar asked, wondering how he could make that in any way special.

The woman at the funeral directors was very helpful as she suggested the wording for the notice in the newspaper. Richard could not find an answer then asked what his wife's maiden name was. 'It's usual to say Mackenzie née Smith or whatever' the woman had said and was surprised at how difficult it was to get an answer from the bereaved man. In the end Jane took the initiative and insisted on Carmichael. '*Elizabeth Mackenzie née Carmichael*' she said firmly.

'Then it's quite usual to say 'wife of' 'mother of' that sort of thing. You should keep it short as it can get quite expensive' the woman said kindly, as if cost had to be a problem. Jane dictated: '*Dearly loved wife of Richard and mother of Jane, died 29th July 2014, peacefully at home on the Isle of Wight aged 89.*' 'That bit is quite simple.' Richard said but Jane had wanted more. 'Can't we say something about what she achieved in her life, other than just being a wife and mother?' 'Like what?' Richard had asked sharply, instantly regretting his words as they seemed to imply that he thought his wife of more than thirty years had achieved nothing of note in her life. 'I mean' he had continued quickly, 'how can we say what she has done and who she has been in a few lines in the newspaper obituaries column?' 'You could add that the funeral is on the 20th August in Yarmouth and that all enquiries should come via us?' The woman asked encouragingly after several moments of awkward silence. They accepted that and gave up on anything more creative.

Nothing in the bland clichés even hinted at the truth of Elizabeth's life.

The obituary notice, when it appeared, was one of the shortest that day. As Richard read it he wondered who else would see it and what the ramifications would be. He knew he should have said no when the woman had asked whether he wanted to put anything in the newspapers. It had been a bad idea to mark his wife's death in this way. He just felt she would have expected it.

Early the next Sunday, six days after the obituary was printed, Richard phoned Jane and told her he needed to see her urgently. As she drove the three miles to his bungalow she had no idea what to expect. Was he ill? He had sounded very agitated on the phone.

As soon as she arrived Richard made her sit her down and he handed her the newspaper.

"Read." He said without preamble.

"*The Fifth Man?* This article?" She asked, bewildered by Richard's fidgeting. He was normally so calm and controlled.

"Read it. I wanted to be with you when you read it. I didn't want you to read it without me being with you." His agitation showed.

She picked up the paper and began to read.

In the dark days of the Cold War when nuclear annihilation was a real and ever-present threat the industry of espionage was, arguably, at its most effective.

This country had our spies whose names will never be publicly acknowledged but whose work has never been forgotten. A long list of authors including Ian Fleming, John Le Carré, Len Deighton and Graham Greene have fictionalised and glamorised those men and women who worked for our country in those literally dreadful times.

Jane looked up to see Richard staring at her, obviously trying to gauge her reactions as she read the article. He frowned. She said nothing and looked back down at the paper to continue reading.

But there were Englishmen and Englishwomen who were not fighting the Cold War on their nation's side. The 'Ring of Five' and the 'Cambridge Five' are terms applied to men, highly educated and intelligent men, whose allegiance was to our principal enemy at the time, the Soviet Union. Through the Forties and Fifties several traitors were unmasked. Maclean and Burgess were the First and the Second Men. Kim Philby most probably the Third and the Fourth, revealed years later, was Anthony Blunt. The name of the Fifth man has never been identified.

Many have made their suggestions as to who this Fifth Man might have been, a simple search on the internet will suggest three or four candidates.

Today this newspaper suggests another: Lord Grahame Johnstone.

Jane again looked up. Richard was still staring at her. "Really? Are they joking? They can't possibly be serious."

"I suspect they are moving to their end-game."

"They?"

"Eric Atkinson and the men who have been funding him all these years. Your father's enemies."

"End-game?"

"You and your mother have been loose ends. They couldn't publish anything while your mother was alive because she may well have known things they didn't know she knew. But now she's gone they have a free field of action."

"Action?"

"They will try to discredit your father. This article is their first salvo, the first of many I suspect. They will force him into discussing their accusations openly and if he denies them he will be accepting that they have some validity."

"You mean all he has to say is 'I was not a spy' and they will edit out the 'not'? That's what they do isn't it?"

"Perhaps not so blatantly, but in the public's mind the words 'Lord Grahame Johnstone' and 'traitor' will form in the same sentence. It's the way the media works."

"There's something in it though, isn't there? I mean that trip I made to Moscow. That man I met. I had so many questions but somehow I never got round to asking them."

"Such as?"

"Well, who was Berndt Schreiber, I've never forgotten his name and his generosity to me. And how did he know you and my mother?"

"Time enough for all that when you have read more."

"And how do Mum and I come into all this? They can't know we've anything to do with Grahame Johnstone, can they?"

"Read on."

For over fifty years my informant has followed this man's story.

It begins during the 1930s when GJ, as he is familiarly known, was at Cambridge University. At the outbreak of the Second World War, when he was 21 years old, he did not volunteer for the armed forces to defend our country instead he joined the Civil Service. Undoubtedly he was a gifted mathematician and the job he did in the Ministry of Fuel and Power certainly was of some importance but it is hard to admire a man for manipulating numbers in the safety of an office in Whitehall at a time when young men his age were fighting and dying for our country's very survival.

During his time at the Ministry he met a young woman, we will call her, as she called herself, Georgina Carmichael even though that was not her real name. Georgina was also a gifted mathematician and the two worked well together. Perhaps too closely.

After the war GJ was persuaded to enter Parliament and such was his party's faith in him that he quickly advanced. The young woman he had worked with through the war years became his PA.

Although the exact path of their relationship cannot be known it was an open secret in Westminster that Grahame Johnstone and the woman known as Georgina Carmichael were lovers.

Perhaps he never expected to be successful in his career and privately hoped that one day he would return to his life as an academic mathematician, but that was not to be. He did well, perhaps rather too well.

Perhaps we should give Grahame Johnstone the benefit of the doubt. Perhaps we should believe that, through all the years of their relationship, he never learned his mistress's true identity. That is possible. But it is also possible that he had known all along. And it is also possible that that was precisely why he had fostered their friendship. Perhaps Grahame Johnstone sought out the company of this woman simply because she was who she was.

And who was that? Who was the woman who called herself 'Georgina Carmichael'?

Lord Johnstone's lover throughout the years of the Cold War was Russian. She was born in the Volga region of Russia in 1923. She emigrated to England with her parents when she was a young child but, as a family, they retained much of their culture, their language and, most importantly, their communism. There was no such person as Georgina Carmichael only Selina Schreiber.

Jane looked sharply up at Richard.

"Schreiber? That man in Moscow? Berndt? You must tell me who he was."

Richard did not reply so she looked back at the paper and continued reading.

As many immigrants from Europe did in those years they changed their name to something more English. Selina Schreiber became 'Georgina Carmichael'. Luckily for 'Georgina' all the records of her family and her birth were destroyed in the early air-raids on London. When she applied for a job in the Ministry of Fuel and Power in 1942 it was only her skill with numbers that the authorities were interested in. Perhaps in the need to defeat fascism her communism and false background were overlooked by the authorities.

It is possible Grahame Johnstone knew nothing of this.

Perhaps he did not know his mistress spoke fluent and colloquial Russian, perhaps he did not know that the woman who regularly accompanied him on his official trips to Moscow and to Washington in the height of the Cold War was a Russian Communist?

There are questions that Lord Johnstone must answer.

How much did this rising star on the political firmament know of the woman with whom he frequently shared a bed? What was their pillow talk? Was it of personal matters, was it of the trivia of day to day life? Or was it of the secrets of England as we faced Nuclear War?

Having read the evidence this newspaper believes that Grahame Johnstone knew everything about his lover's background. We suggest he not only knew of her allegiance to the Communist System but he shared that loyalty.

We cannot ignore the possibility that Grahame Johnstone himself was that final member of the Cambridge Five.

"Was he a spy? Was Mum a spy? Is that what it's all been about?" Jane asked with as little emotion in her voice as she could possibly show.

"Read on. I'll answer all your questions when you have read it all."

We all know what happened to Grahame Johnstone. In 1960 he was married, but not to Georgina Carmichael, and had a son and a daughter. His career in active politics was long and successful though he never climbed to the absolute top of that greasy pole. He is still referred to as one of the best Prime Ministers this country never had. His career is the subject of almost reverential study. Now in his 90s he lives a reclusive life on his estate in the New Forest and is seldom heard of.

But what happened to the woman who called herself Georgina Carmichael?

In the Autumn of 1959 she simply disappeared from the face of the earth.

There is no record of her death but neither is there any evidence of her continued existence. There is no record of a passport being issued to anyone of her name and birth date. There is no record of her claiming a pension of any sort despite the fact that if she still lived she would be nearly ninety years old. There is no record of anyone with her national insurance number ever working, paying tax or claiming any benefit of any kind after 1959. It is as if she never existed.

It is possible she could have escaped back to Russia. She may have had connections, relatives, still there.

But information that has come into the hands of this newspaper shows that she never left Britain.

On 15th March 1960 a daughter was born in a nursing home in York to a woman going by the name of Elizabeth Wright. Information has been given to this newspaper that 'Elizabeth Wright' was 'Georgina Carmichael'. The daughter was named Jane, and the father was Grahame Johnstone.

The security services, whose job should have been to expose the undoubted risk to national security caused by this relationship, were pressed into keeping it, and the daughter born of it, a secret.

We owe knowledge of this to the perseverance of a man who has kept the woman Georgina and her daughter Jane in his sights through all the years. He has followed their progress around the country as they have, with the connivance of a rogue member of the secret services, changed identities to maintain their anonymity. They have been the Wrights, the Somersets, the Birches and the Bicktons. And at every turn he has followed them; from York to the Isle of Wight, to Shropshire, to the East

Midlands, to Cambridge and back to the Isle of Wight where, in 1980 Georgina married that same rogue member of the security services.

Selina Schreiber who became Georgina Carmichael and finally Elizabeth Mackenzie, died last week so her story is ended, but her husband, Richard Mackenzie, and the father of her daughter, Grahame Johnstone, must be made to answer questions that this newspaper must be allowed to put to them.

This newspaper has not published all the information it has been given. We have handed much to the authorities but there is more we can publish and in the weeks to come we will be telling you more details of the lives of Selina Schreiber and her daughter Jane.

But we demand that those authorities launch a thorough investigation into the actions of Lord Grahame Johnstone before he is no longer subject to the laws of this world.

Jane had so many questions she wanted to ask but her overriding feeling, as she carefully folded the newspaper and put it down on the sofa next to her was resentment.

"So it was never about me." Jane spoke carefully, keeping her tone to one of calm regret.

"No, Jane. It was never about you." Richard spoke matter-of-factly.

"It was about my mother and my father?"

"It was about protecting you all."

"Protecting us from what?"

"Protecting you all from false accusations."

"Accusations by whom?"

"By, amongst others, the man called Eric Atkinson."

"Who was he really? Obviously he wasn't the newspaper man you always said he was, was he?"

"He was a man I worked with many years ago. He has done everything he can to acquire evidence to destroy your father and with him you and your mother. I suspect he is Ms Camilla Moore's source for all this."

"Camilla Moore?"

"She wrote the story."

"I didn't notice. But surely she's scraping the barrel here. Surely it's all old history now? I mean my father retired from active politics long ago."

"If I know anything about politicians, even those whose careers are ostensibly over, it is that they care about their legacy. They are, every single one of them, concerned with what posterity will think of them."

"So?"

"Other news agencies, TV and radio stations, phone ins, they'll all pick up on this article and he will be made to answer the accusations. He is still a big name. To some it'll be as bad as saying Maggie Thatcher was a Russian spy. He may not answer himself but he will have people who will answer for him, his son, his daughter and his grand-sons probably."

"And what do you think they'll say?"

"I think they'll say he was completely innocent and that, if there was any espionage going on, it was by your mother and he knew absolutely nothing about it. He will say their relationship was not one where they lived in each other's pockets, they will say that if he was guilty of anything it was being a little too unworldly and a little too trusting. She is dead. He knows he cannot hurt her. So he will throw her memory to the wolves. He will be the innocent, trusting, trustworthy man who was seduced by a young, attractive, communist sympathiser who, as soon as he discovered her inclinations, had her removed from public sight. The fact that she was pregnant was incidental."

"How will he explain the secret service's part in hiding us? I mean your part?"

"He will say that it wasn't a formal 'witness protection', he will say, as the newspaper has said, that it was me, a rogue agent acting alone, who organised it all using procedures and funds without authority. He will say

I was her lover and that the child Jane was probably mine."

"Were you? Am I?"

"No Jane. Until you left for Cambridge I had no relationship with your mother other than being assigned to looking after her, and your, safety. Grahame Johnstone is undoubtedly your father."

"But his family will deflect all the press flak onto us."

"Most likely.

"And he'll do that because he wants to protect his legacy?"

"I think that is highly likely. If any evidence comes to light he will say he is completely innocent and that it was Georgina Carmichael, your mother, who was guilty. He'll say she seduced him and by becoming pregnant had tried to trap him into marrying her. But, they will say, he was too clever for her. Instead of being trapped into a marriage he had her quietly removed from circulation so that he was free to marry an eminently suitable woman and have eminently suitable children who will look respectfully defensive as they lie to the cameras."

Jane looked across the outspread newspapers at Richard.

"They were spies weren't they? It's obvious now. All the trouble you've gone to all these years, the money to keep us, the safe houses, the identities, that man in Moscow somehow related to my mother. It's so obvious! They were spies. Who's been paying for it all? The Russians? All this newspaper is saying is true isn't it?"

Richard said nothing as he let Jane vent her resentment and her fears.

He looked out of the window at the bright sunlight and shadows on the lawn in the garden Elizabeth had tended when they had first moved there thirty years before. Fleeting memories of good times were pushed away by darker ones of the first years he had known Georgina Carmichael. Memories of long weekends in country houses in the Home Counties as Georgina used her training and her language skills in de-briefing defectors from the eastern bloc; memories of hurriedly passed messages and complex set-up situations where arrangements were made for those men and women to leave their homelands; memories of conspiracies and plans, some successful some thwarted.

"It's not quite that simple." He answered reluctantly, gauging how little of the truth he could get away with telling Jane.

"Simple? I hardly think any of this is simple."

"They are right. Your mother was an agent. Your father too." Richard spoke so quietly Jane wasn't sure she heard him correctly.

After a few moments of silence, he continued. Despite not thinking it safe for her to know any more than was absolutely necessary, he decided that it was only fair that she should know the reasons for so much that had happened in her life. He decided to tell Jane the truth about her parents.

"Your mother was an agent, but not of any enemy security service, she worked for MI5. After the war we worked together, our assignment was to keep an eye on your father because of his school boy flirtations with communism. Through the late Forties and Fifties it was our job, between us, to identify everything he did, everywhere he went, everyone he communicated with. It was a time where everyone suspected everyone else. McCarthyism was running riot in America. Anyone who even spoke a single word of Russian was suspected of being a 'commie spy'. Funnily enough, although she spoke fluent Russian, and was, indeed, born in Russia, your mother was trusted by everyone. Perhaps no man, in those days, could really believe a woman could be that clever. I have always thought the Americans, the Russians and the British authorities always underestimated her."

Jane tried to remember the things her mother had told her about those years and could remember nothing that hinted at her ever having played such a role.

"OK." She had to choose her words carefully. "So Grahame Johnstone was under suspicion, under continuous surveillance, no doubt there was a fat file on him somewhere in the dark recesses of Whitehall, but that doesn't mean that there was ever any truth in the suspicions does it?"

"Nothing was ever proved."

"But you're not saying he wasn't guilty?"

"You're right, Jane, guilty men escaped because there was nothing substantial enough to set out in a court of law or, more frequently, there was sufficient proof but it couldn't be used because in the use of it the source of it would be exposed, and in many cases that could not be allowed."

"In my father's case?"

"I can't say. Not because I know and couldn't tell you, I just don't know. As they say these days 'that was beyond my pay grade'."

"But you think he was, don't you?"

Richard slowly shook his head and for a moment Jane thought he was denying such a thought, then she realised he was shaking it because he really could not answer her question.

"I really don't know, Jane. It wasn't my job to judge him. I never saw him do anything that would have been the actions of an agent working for the Russians. I don't believe he was. I know your mother wasn't. But others believed they both were."

"Eric Atkinson?"

"Definitely Eric Atkinson did."

"And others?" Jane prompted.

Richard paused for a few moments before answering indirectly.

"At the time your father was in a position where he had to work with the Americans and with the Cold War raging, he was trying to work with the Russians as well. War, nuclear war, seemed very close at times. It was actually very, very close at times, much closer than the public was ever allowed to know. News was managed very carefully, even more carefully than during the war and certainly more carefully than it is now. Politics at that time was on a knife-edge and a scandal would have caused all sorts of problems nationally and internationally."

"So Mother said, the one time she deigned to talk about those times." Richard accepted the bitterness in Jane's voice. He could say nothing that would comfort her, she had every right to feel hard done by.

"There was a lot of talk about Russian spies and Grahame was linked to them. Most of the men being talked about as The First Man, The Second Man, The Third Man etcetera all went to university together and they weren't all spies, though some undoubtedly were. I have no doubt they tried to recruit your father. Eric Atkinson was not alone in his suspicions, a number of people thought he might be. All the secret services; the CIA, Mossad, the Stasi, KGB, the lot, they all had files on Grahame, believing he might be one of the 'university set'. It was my job to keep an eye on him, as it was the job of your mother. Amongst other things."

"Was Mum sleeping with him then?"

Richard nodded.

"She was sleeping with him to keep a closer eye on him?" Jane could not keep the cynicism from her voice.

"She was sleeping with him, yes, but I believe she was genuinely fond of him."

"That doesn't really answer my question. Did she have the affair with him so that she could keep a closer eye on him or because she loved him?"

Richard knew how much the answer would mean to Jane and so he told her what he knew she wanted to hear.

"She loved him. It hurts me to say that because I loved her all that time but, yes, I'm sure she loved him. It was not easy for her when she had to leave him."

"Did she have to be sent away?"

"Unfortunately yes, for more than one reason. Firstly, it was seen by our side that she had 'gone native'. She had allowed herself to become pregnant by the man she was supposed to be looking after. It would not do. Secondly, it would have been the last straw in taut negotiations with the Americans if one of the main men they were dealing with was all over the papers because of an affair. The Americans are, at heart, a very moralistic tribe even if that morality is usually tinged with hypocrisy. And can you imagine what would have happened if they learned that the woman he was involved with was born a Russian?"

"I don't suppose it would have gone down well."

"It most certainly would not have done."

"So my mother was being used to spy on my father. Did she do anything else?"

"That really isn't important."

"That's a yes then."

"She was, but not in the sense you mean."

"Well in what sense was she a spy?"

"She was never what this paper is implying. She was never a Russian spy acquiring British secrets…"

"She was a British spy acquiring Russian secrets? American secrets?"

"It really wasn't quite that straightforward."

"She was a British spy pretending to be a Russian spy feeding lies and secrets to anyone and everyone?" Jane suggested facetiously.

"You've read too many trashy novels Jane. She was, in truth, only a very small cog in a very big wheel."

"But still a spy."

"That would be a very shorthand description, a lazy description, of what she did and who she was."

"She was a spy who was sleeping with a man who was suspected of being a spy who was also a rising star in the political world?"

"Those two professions are not always mutually exclusive."

"And then she fell pregnant."

"May 1959 was not a good time. China was unsettled, the Middle East was unsettled, Germany was unsettled. Grahame could not be seen to have a flaw."

"And I was a 'flaw'?"

"You certainly were." Richard's voice was harsher than he meant it to be.

"So we had to be got out of the way? Out of sight?"

"Your mother had to be removed and, as they say in bad jokes, where she went so did you." He tried to speak lightly but he knew he had not succeeded.

Jane stood up and walked to the window, staring out through the raindrops running down the glass to the familiar garden and the chalk downs beyond.

She felt immensely sorry for herself.

Her mother had never told her much about her past life and everything she had said had been a lie. She had lied by omission if not commission, but she had lied. She had never done anything but lie. And now she was dead it was too late for her to answer any more questions.

"I've lived here for nearly twenty years." Jane said thoughtfully. "I've seen her pretty much every day and she wasn't out of it all the time. Why couldn't she have said something? Why couldn't she have explained? And why couldn't you? Whenever I asked her about the past she said it was all in the past and we were different people now and then she would change the subject. And now it's too late."

"She couldn't tell you, Jane. We did talk about telling you more about everything but she kept saying that it would not be fair for you to have the weight of that knowledge. That's what she always said, 'the weight of that knowledge'. She truly believed that you were kept safer by knowing absolutely nothing.

"But she could have told me about her family couldn't she? She could have told me where she came from? I mean where she came from is part of me isn't it? And she was never Georgina Carmichael, that was a fabrication, she was Selina Schreiber." She stopped short. "Who was Berndt Schreiber? Who was he really?"

"He was your mother's brother, your uncle."

"Her brother? She didn't have one. She told me she was an only child."

"She wasn't lying deliberately, Jane, she never knew him as her brother. When her parents left Russia in 1923 they left the boy behind. He was a baby, they knew he would die on the journey out of Russia so they left him with members of the family who stayed."

"Did he know who I was? When I met him?"

"Oh yes. He knew."

"But he never said anything."

"He couldn't."

"I wish he had." She was quiet for a few moments before adding. "Did he work with you too?"

Richard didn't say anything. He stood up and busied himself doing nothing that was necessary around the basin.

"I'll take that as a yes then." Jane said, her voice low with resentment. "So I come from a family of spies; spies and liars."

"That is harsh, Jane, harsh and unfair."

"I wish she could have said something to me. She really, truly, never did anything but lie to me."

"Listen Jane, it was a complicated time when it all started."

"Yes that was one thing my mother did tell me." There was bitterness in her voice.

"And lies, once started, tend to grow a life of their own."

"So all that moving about, all that secrecy and changing names was never, ever about hiding me from the press to save Grahame Johnstone's career? It was all about her."

"I'm afraid it has been."

"Telling me it was because I was the illegitimate daughter of a major politician, blaming me for being born, was always a lie. Making me feel, all these years, that it was my fault was a lie."

"We never meant to hurt you."

"Well you did."

"You should never have blamed yourself."

"Well I did. What else was I supposed to think when it was all about the bloody reporter and my father? Except it wasn't was it?"

"It all seemed to be the only thing we could say at the time."

"Well it's all been an utter waste of time because now it's all over the papers."

The next day Jane picked up all the newspapers early and drove with them round to Richard's bungalow.

She spent the morning reading every word though she really didn't want to.

The woman they wrote about was not her mother. It was as if the reporter was documenting another, parallel, world that had nothing to do with them at all. She was appalled to see pictures of herself, as a toddler, splashing naked in a paddling pool in a garden of a semi-detached house that must have been in the house in York, though she had no memory of the garden, or the summer's day.

"How did they get that photograph?" She asked Richard.

"That would be Eric."

"He must have leant over the next-door's fence."

"When would it have been? 1963? 1964? Cameras were big then. I'm surprised he could do it without anyone noticing."

Other pictures were as intimate, some, she recognised, she had taken. "How had the paper got hold of all these photos of me? There's me on the Yarmouth Pier when I was about 10 and they've picked up on that one from the Ludlow News and these with Matt in Brighton? How have they got all this Richard?"

He didn't answer.

"And this article here on my career. Look, because I was interested in Russian mathematics makes me a spy too according to this stupid person."

A few minutes later. "This is just too awful! Look they're going through all my relationships. They've said I lived with Matt for years without bothering to marry him and they've dredged up the divorce papers from Peter. How are they allowed to do this? Aren't they supposed to get in touch with me first? Ask me if it's all true?"

"Well it is isn't it? It's all pretty much 100% accurate."

"I don't know why they're doing all this stuff on me."

"But it's nothing terrible is it? Just the facts of your life."

"It's a bit intrusive don't you think?"

"Your mother always knew this would happen one day. She had always known that one day your existence would come to light and I'm afraid to say she always hoped that the press would focus on that. Isn't that what they say 'it's sex that sells newspapers'. She hoped they would focus on your existence and then they wouldn't look too closely at anything in her past."

"Well that didn't work did it? They're doing both."

"She always knew when someone looked into her background, into that of her parents, it wouldn't look good. She knew no one would believe she wasn't a traitor."

"I don't think I like the idea that she was happy that I'd take all the flak so she would be protected."

"That's not the way I'd have put it but I suppose yes there is some truth in that. She didn't want the papers looking into anything other than the fact that Grahame Johnstone had an illegitimate daughter."

"Tell me more about Elizabeth." The vicar repeated on the visit he felt he had to make, after having read three days of newspaper reports. "So I can do her justice in the funeral. She's not quite the traditional wife and mother you described the other day was she? And I gather there's going to be quite a congregation, the funeral directors have told me there have been quite a few enquiries."

"You've read the papers?"

"I'm afraid I have to say, yes, I have. It appears your wife has some notoriety."

Jane answered brusquely. "My mother had an affair with a prominent politician and I am his illegitimate daughter. It was, obviously, a long time ago. The papers say they were Cold War spies but that is complete nonsense, though, of course, people will always look for the most salacious of details however inaccurately reported."

The vicar looked sheepish. He was young and inexperienced, but also ambitious.

After his first visit to the Mackenzie household immediately after Elizabeth's death, he had been expecting a low key funeral where his main job would be to give comfort to an unexceptional elderly widower and middle-aged daughter. He had thought that the service would be sparsely attended. But after having read the papers he realised the funeral would be the centre of attention from the newspapers, radio and television and it would be an opportunity to make an impression.

"Will Lord Johnstone be attending?" He asked rather too enthusiastically.

"I can't see him coming over to the island." Jane answered dismissively. "Not at his age." She didn't like the anticipation the vicar appeared to be showing at being the centre of attention.

"Have you any idea how many will attend? I mean, the church is small, we cannot accommodate more than a small number."

"We will put a notice in the papers to say that the funeral is private. We will tell the funeral directors to say that no one other than close family is welcome. We will change the time. We want to be as private as possible."

"Nasty little man." Jane said after she had shown the vicar to the door. "I really think we should get everything speeded up and done quietly. I'll talk to the funeral directors. See what I can do. I'm sure they'll understand in view of all this." She spread her arms out to encompass the newspapers that were still laid out around the room.

Richard nodded his agreement.

"It'll be OK." Jane said as she said goodbye to Richard. "It really will be OK won't it?" She said it as if she needed reassurance but he gave her none.

Richard sat down wearily in his familiar sitting room, trying not to notice all the things that reminded him of Elizabeth. He knew what would be in store for him and for Jane in the coming days. Old wounds would be re-opened, old scores settled.

He recognised, even if Jane didn't, that she was in more danger than she had been in all her life. She was a loose end and people like Eric Atkinson didn't like loose ends. He would find a way of getting rid of her. Or of using her. Somehow.

The pain in his chest was sharp and he could think of nothing other than that for some time Gradually, as he regained control of his body, he accepted that he wouldn't be around long enough to make a difference. Jane would just have to deal with whatever Eric Atkinson had in mind by herself.

There was, after all, no service in the Parish Church for the press to disrupt or for the young vicar to fuss about. Jane had driven Richard across the island to the crematorium where there was a simple ceremony which passed without interruption or incident.

"Come in for a while?" Richard asked as it seemed that Jane was simply going to drop him off at his house. She wanted to be in the safety of her own cottage.

She had been moved more than she had thought as her mother's coffin had disappeared behind the crimson curtain as tinny recorded music had broken the heavy silence of the almost empty chapel. She no longer trusted Richard and she wanted to be alone.

"No, thanks. I'll be getting back. I'll come round tomorrow if you like."

"Only if you want to."

It seemed that their familiarity had disappeared along with the reason for it.

"I'll pop round in the afternoon to see if you're OK."

"You don't have to if you don't want to."

She was unsure whether she would or not, 'after all', she thought as she drove away, 'what loyalty can I possibly owe him after all he and Mum did to fuck up my life?'

Richard sat back in his chair in the empty lounge and took a long draught of the generous scotch he had poured himself.

The house was quiet apart from the low hum of traffic from the road outside and the loud ringing in his ears. He wondered how long he would have to put up with being alone.

He hoped it would all be over quickly whenever the end came.

He had spent so many years looking after Elizabeth, one way or another, and now she was truly gone. There was nothing of her to care about. And he knew he had failed her. She would never know, but everything they had tried to keep secret was in the open, her reputation torn to shreds, her character dissected and discussed by people who had never known her.

At least, he thought, there had been some respect shown. No newspapers had door-stepped the bungalow in Freshwater, no one had phoned him or tried to contact him for a story. Someone, he assumed it had to be Grahame Johnstone, still cared enough and had sufficient influence to protect Elizabeth's reputation. For that he was grateful.

The story would die down, he told himself, the press would move on, Elizabeth and Jane would soon be forgotten.

He had almost fallen into a fitful doze when he heard his front door opening.

"Jane?" He called out, instantly aware that Jane always called out 'It's only me' on her visits.

He hadn't had time to stand up when the man appeared in the doorway.

It had been many years since the two men had been in the same room together and they had both changed. The years had not been kind to either of them.

"Eric."

"Richard."

"For God's sake don't say you're here to tell me you're sorry for my loss. I hate the phrase and every single person seems to say it. It's horribly American and completely insincere."

"I wasn't going to say that."

"Well what do you want?"

"Well I certainly haven't come here to give you your ten quid."

"What ten quid?"

"You've forgotten our bet? I'm disappointed in you Richard old boy. A tenner on GJ making PM? You've forgotten? Moscow? July 1958? Well he didn't make it did he so I owe you a tenner. But I'm not going to pay up."

Richard said nothing. He remembered much about that trip to Moscow but had no memory of a bet.

"I want to give you the opportunity to earn back your stripes."

"What on earth does that mean?" Richard tried to understand what Eric was getting at.

He should have stood up to Eric, but he couldn't think of the best thing to say as he watched Eric sit down in what had been Elizabeth's chair and pull out a packet of cigarettes.

"Please don't smoke in here." But he had to watch as Eric carefully took out a lighter and defiantly lit up.

"You were always a bit prissy about cigarettes weren't you?"

"Please go." Richard felt tired, too tired to be the equal of the man who had been his nemesis for over fifty years. He was far too tired to be able to outwit him.

"Me and my friends are going to give you the opportunity to redeem yourself."

"Redeem myself?" Richard tried to understand what Eric wanted of him.

"You have protected the little shit all these years while we've all known he was as guilty as hell but now you will be forgiven if you help in finally nailing Grahame Johnstone to the wall."

"Nail him?"

"All you've got to do is say you knew all along that your precious Grahame and his tart were traitors. All you have to do is agree with what's been written in the press, say it's all true. Agree that you went native and fell for the object of your surveillance. Admit you turned a blind eye to what was going on because you fancied the knickers of his bit on the side."

"Remember you're talking about the woman who was my wife for more than thirty years."

Eric ignored the interruption.

"If you talk to Camilla, tell her all this, then I'll leave off the girl."

"What are you talking about?"

"Admit you have known all along that Georgina and Grahame Johnstone were traitors, tell Camilla about all the meetings in Moscow, the messages passed, the sharing of secrets about the American negotiations, tell her everything and then I'll leave the girl alone."

"The girl?"

"Try not to be too stupid Richard. The girl. Grahame and Georgina's baby daughter. Jane Carmichael I think she calls herself. She's followed in her parents' footsteps hasn't she? Little Fraulein Schreiber's bastard daughter has followed her mother into the trade hasn't she?"

"Of course she hasn't." Richard was forced onto the defensive.

"Well that isn't what Camilla's going to write in next Monday's paper."

Richard tried to think clearly but found he couldn't, the pain in his chest was taking most of his concentration.

"She's already had a go at Jane." He said, determined that Eric would not see that he was on the defensive as the pain subsided. He tried to divert the conversation. "I understand how you got those photographs of Jane in York but how did you get the more, shall I say, intimate ones? That intrigues me. Did you bribe her fiancé or her husband? I can't imagine you were in a position to take them."

"No." Eric smiled a knowing smile that Richard did not like. "No I didn't take them."

"Are you going to tell me who did?" The pain in his chest had eased and he began to think more clearly again.

"You don't know?"

"Don't know what? There are undoubtedly many thousands of things I do not know but one of the impossibilities in life is knowing what it is you don't know."

"You don't know that I've had an accomplice all these years?"

"An accomplice?"

"When Jane grew up it was very difficult to cover them both. I mean I had my suspicions that your fraulein had passed on her beliefs and possibly her job to her daughter but I couldn't keep an eye on both of them could I? Especially as the girl grew up and left home. So I recruited a willing if rather unimaginative assistant."

"Don't tell me. David Childs."

"The very one."

"I really should have known." Richard felt defeated. He really should have guessed. His life on the island and his concern for his wife, his care through her illness, had made him ignore the possibility that they were still objects of interest to Eric and his friends.

"Yes you really were quite dense about that."

"Dense? Why should I ever suspect you of spying on Jane via some boy who met her once or twice?"

"You remember David Childs then?"

"His name is impressed in my memory though I had thought never to hear it again."

"He's been closer to you than you think for a long time."

"I beg your pardon?"

"Wherever Jane Cavanagh then Jane Carmichael lived so did David Childs, first Cambridge, then London, then that sojourn in the leafy suburb of Chessington and finally here on the Isle of Wight. For an insignificant little shit he really has been incredibly resourceful."

"No doubt providing you with a relentless supply of photographs."

"And a lot more besides."

"But I suggest never anything that could remotely incriminate her in anything illegal or suspect."

"She has been extremely discreet but I don't believe she is innocent. God only knows what coded information she's put in those books of hers and then in 1993 she went to Moscow on some flimsy academic pretext and who did she meet there? Surprise, surprise, she met the same man her mother did forty odd years earlier. And, to add yet another remarkable coincidence, that same man fetches up in London three months later and is given protection. What the fuck is anyone supposed to think?"

"The Soviets haven't existed for years, Eric, you are deluding yourself. I find it all rather sad that you have hung on to this fantasy all these years."

"How do you explain why the daughter went to Moscow then? And it was just coincidence she meets up with her uncle in a place no one can see them? Of course they're all in it together, living out their lies.

"You are the one who has lived a lie Eric. You've wasted so much effort on a complete nonsense. The Schreibers may have had certain, completely understandable and I would stress legal, political sympathies and their daughter may have helped them when she was a youngster but she did not continue with those allegiances after they died. She chose to be an Englishwoman and that was who she was. She fell in love and had a child, the father wanted her out of sight so he could pursue his career, she did as he requested. That is it. Is it so difficult for you to accept?"

"I will not accept it because it is a lie. She managed to hoodwink you for all these years. That is what you have to accept."

"There's no evidence. There can't be any evidence because she has never been involved in anything like that."

"No?" Eric answered, taking a long drag on his cigarette and blowing the smoke very deliberately into the middle of the room. "Never?"

"No. Never."

"So what was she doing with Herr Schreiber in Moscow? We know he sent a message back with her."

Richard had to give an answer. "She didn't know what she was doing."

"You used her?"

"I'm not saying I haven't used people, just as you have Eric, the difference is that I have used people who haven't been told what they're doing and who maybe helped once or twice. But your David Childs seems to have been pathetically enthusiastic in his pursuit of non-existent evidence for most of his life."

Eric nodded. "Yes, and now his usefulness is over. He's read the papers, he knows why he has been doing what he has been doing all these years I fear I will have to go through with the unpleasantness of ending his involvement."

They both knew what that meant.

"Does he know how ungrateful you are?" Richard asked

Eric smiled, took another drag from his cigarette and dropped it in a coffee cup. "And I don't think he ever will. Now, Mackenzie, when do I get Camilla to pop in to see you and hear all about the secrets you have hidden all these years?"

"You don't. I'm not going to give you anything, or your tame reporter, Camilla what's-her-name. I'm saying nothing. You have done enough harm. Let Jane be."

"Is that it then? You're going to abandon her."

"Abandon?"

"Well, Dicky boy, you are in between a rock and a hard place where your dear Georgina's daughter is concerned. Either you come clean and say I've been right all along and the whole family were Soviet spies and Camilla writes all about it next week or I will get her in another way."

Richard made the mistake of seeing that as an empty threat.

"I'm not going to tell the papers anything that is a complete lie. They were never what you think. You have been wrong all these years."

"Is that your final answer?"

"Of course it is."

"Don't ever say I didn't give you a chance for things to be different."

Still Richard believed it to be an empty threat.

"Give me what I need then and I'll leave."

"I've told you. I'm not giving you anything."

"I think you will be giving me your service revolver."

"My gun?" Richard was confused. "I have no gun."

"Of course you've kept it. And I bet I know where you keep it." Eric stood up and walked purposefully to the bungalow's only bedroom, followed by an agitated Richard.

"Not very imaginative old chap." Eric opened the drawers of the bedside table on the side of the bed that still showed the signs of someone having slept there the night before. "But I bet it's in one of these….. ah here we are….." He checked whether it was loaded before pointing it at Richard. "Now I cannot imagine for a moment you have a license for this? No? Well I think I can make use of it. Don't worry about reporting any theft. Ah, but no, you wouldn't since you aren't supposed to have it in the first place."

Richard knew that thirty, twenty, even ten years before he would have had the better of Eric but now the pain in his chest was stopping him. He could not think quickly enough. He had no response.

Eric raised the gun towards Richard and clicked the trigger. Then he laughed. "I'll take this with me. Perhaps you'll get it back on Sunday lunchtime."

"Sunday lunchtime?"

"You will meet me for a drink in the pub in town, the Queen's Head? Is that what it's called? Be there at twelve fifteen and I will return this to you. Perhaps." And he smiled.

Eric had always disliked Richard. For over fifty years he had dreamed of being in a position of power over the man he thought of as a supercilious, arrogant fool. He was going to enjoy every minute.

"Sunday?" Richard asked, the strain of the past weeks evident in his voice and in his face.

"Yes. Twelve fifteen. Sharp."

"And you will give me back my gun?"

"I will relinquish it." Eric chose his words carefully. "Yes then I will surrender your gun."

As Richard watched Eric walk down the path away from his bungalow his old instincts made him uneasy.

They seemed odd words to have used.

Eric was smiling as he took out his mobile phone from his pocket and chose a number near the top of his contact list.

"David?"

"Yes Eric. What can I do for you?"

"I have just been to see Richard."

"Was Silver there?"

"No. I missed her. Now listen carefully. There will be a break in at Silver's cottage this evening. When this is reported you will investigate. You hear me? You must make sure you attend the crime scene. You may make yourself known to Silver. Then you will make sure she accepts your invitation to a drink on Sunday lunchtime. Say it's for old time's sake or whatever but you will make sure you meet her to the Queen's Head in town at twelve thirty on Sunday. I am sure you will be able to persuade her. Have you got all that?"

"Yes. Break in. Ask no questions. Pub Sunday twelve thirty pm. Do you want me to find anything in particular when searching her house?"

"You will find no evidence of a break in. You will find that she is wasting police time. Explain away anything she says. Make sure there's no official record"

"So there is a break in reported but we are to find no evidence of a break in and nothing will be recorded. How can I make sure that my fellow officers see nothing as well?"

"You are the DI you make sure they only see what they are supposed to see. And make bloody sure you are in that pub come twelve thirty on Sunday with the girl."

"Silver won't want to come."

"I'm sure you'll be able to persuade her."

"Is all this to do with all that stuff in the paper? I've been reading everything. Those pictures came out really well didn't they?"

"We could not have done it without you, Davey."

"So this was what all these years have been about. Nothing to do with Grahame Johnstone being her dad. Just about her mum and her being spies?"

Eric didn't answer.

Years before he had told David that if he ever learned the real reason for their tracking Silver he would have to kill him. It was an old joke, used frequently in spy novels, and he hadn't expected David Childs to take him seriously.

Eric knew the time had come, he could not allow David Childs to go to the press or to the authorities who he knew would be following up on the newspaper story, but he knew he would not be the one to take responsibility for the pulling of the trigger.

He was going to kill two birds with one stone.

He smiled as he pressed the screen of his phone and ended the call.

Chapter 18
Sunday lunchtime

The burglary had been an unpleasant experience though Jane never considered herself in any real danger.

She had been in town all afternoon shopping and having a quiet tea and scones in the café by the pier. She felt no pressure on her for the first time since she couldn't remember when. She had no responsibility for her mother any more. Richard seemed to prefer to have some time on his own. The stories in the paper would eventually die down, they always did when something else took their attention. She would just ride it out and then everything would be calm and peaceful again. She would do some more writing. Her time would be her own.

She was almost happy as she walked along the common, sitting for a while watching the yachts on the blue waters of the Solent before reaching her cottage just after six o'clock in the evening.

She was letting herself in the kitchen door when the two boys rushed passed her and ran away down the road and out of sight. She had shouted at them but she couldn't follow them and watched helplessly as they disappeared round the corner. She had been burgled once before, many years before though the unpleasant memories came flooding back to her, and it took her some time to face looking around the house to see what was missing and what mess had been made. And then she called 999.

She hadn't expected anyone to turn up after the disinterested response to her call and had been surprised when two police cars arrived within a few minutes of her call. She had always understood from the newspapers that the police rarely had any real interest in a simple domestic break in.

She didn't recognise David Childs, he was just the first of the three policemen who arrived.

Then he introduced himself.

"DI David Childs."

The name surprised her. She looked directly at him trying to see whether this man could be the David Childs she had once known.

"Jane Carmichael." She answered confidently as he, somewhat unexpectedly, held out his hand for her to shake. She was concerned when he held on to it for a fraction longer than was necessary. "Dr Jane Carmichael."

"Hello Silver." He said over-familiarly. She looked about her for his colleagues and realised there was no one else in the room.

"David?" She asked tentatively. It was more than thirty years since she had even thought of him. He was part of a past she had long ago put behind her. Why was he now appearing in her life, the week the newspapers gave so much coverage to her mother?

Richard's past suspicions began to surface in her thoughts. Richard had said that David had known who her father was since their time in Ludlow, Richard had believed that he had deliberately met her in Birmingham. But since then there had been nothing.

The way he had said 'Hello Silver' made her think, fleetingly, that he hadn't been surprised to see her.

Other police entered the room and said something to David Childs that Jane could not catch.

When he turned to her she didn't like the look on his face. It was, she thought, as if he had won something. He seemed jubilant, superior. Untouchable.

"It appears there is no sign of any intruder." He said with something she could only think of as smugness.

"I told them on the phone that whoever had been here left as soon as I arrived home."

"They just left?" He asked doubtfully. "Oh dear, that isn't very helpful is it?"

There was something about the informality in his manner that made Jane wary. He sat down on the settee, pushing out of the way the newspapers that were on it. She felt he presumed too much. She had not asked him to make himself at home and she was still standing.

"Can you give me a description of your assailants?" David Childs looked at Jane giving no sign that he intended to take any notes.

"They didn't assault me." She said rather sharply. "As I said they ran away pretty much as soon as I arrived home. They looked like youngsters, possibly barely in their teens."

"Did you get a good look at them?"

"Apart from seeing they were identically dressed in faded and ripped blue jeans and grey sweatshirts, despite the weather, and they both wore baseball caps pulled right down to their eyebrows. So no, I wouldn't be able to recognise them. As I said, they ran away as I arrived."

"Can you tell me what, if anything, appears to be missing?"

Jane tried to ignore the doubt in DI Childs's voice. "Nothing's gone. Everything seems to be here, everything's still here."

"Can you show me around and we can check together that nothing is missing?"

At the time she thought he was just doing his job, but later she realised it was an excuse for something else.

He stood up and she reluctantly showed him around. No drawers or cupboards had been opened, no papers or files in her office disturbed. In a strange way she felt more violated by his intrusive peering into everything in her house than she had by the original break-in.

She just wanted him to leave.

"What about these?" David Childs opened a drawer of her desk, apparently at random, and pulled out a handful of old photographs.

"Please put them away, they could be nothing remotely of interest to anyone."

"Are they of you?"

"Yes." She didn't want him to be interested in her photographs and she didn't want him looking at the pictures of her. "Please put them back."

He did, but immediately opened the drawer below it and checked the contents. She saw her book, with the words 'Silver Birch' carefully written on the cover. Nothing was said, and he made no sign, as he closed the drawer, but she knew he had seen the book. She had only kept it through all those years so that she had something to remind her of how unhappy her childhood really had been.

"Can I have a cup of coffee?" DI Childs asked, "Just while my people check all the locks and windows and make sure the house is secure. I'll see you down there, I just need to have a word with one of my colleagues."

He gave her no choice so she reluctantly left him alone in her office as she went down to the kitchen and put the kettle on. He was a policeman, she told herself, she could trust him, surely. She tried to reassure herself that there was nothing suspicious about David Childs as she made the mugs of tea.

It was ten minutes or more before he joined her in the kitchen just as she heard a car drive away.

David Childs made himself at home at the kitchen table and Jane sat down opposite him.

"What a coincidence that you live on the island." Jane said trying to make his presence in her house seem normal. She hoped that he would leave soon so she could set about checking that nothing had been taken, by either the intruders or the police.

"Yes. I've been here some years, since 1994."

Jane had moved from Surrey to the Isle of Wight the year in the autumn of 1993 and she was unsettled at the coincidence.

"And have you always been a policeman?"

"No I taught in Birmingham for a couple of years but joined in 1982. But I'm due to retire soon. I've done more than my time."

As they waited for their coffees to be cool enough to drink Jane wondered what it was about the man that made her feel afraid; not just wary, absolutely afraid. Everything he was doing and saying seemed designed to disconcert her.

And as he watched her across the table David Childs wondered why he had not gone against Eric's instructions and made sure he had had a relationship with the woman.

He saw her as the 16 year old in Ludlow and he wanted her. Just as he had always wanted her since that first day he had seen her in the summer of 1976 and as he had dreamed of taking her through those Cambridge years when he had observed her, through net curtains, from across the road, and through the Surrey years when Peter had shown him those photographs and he had imagined it was he who had made those marks on her body.

"Come and have a drink with me? Sunday lunchtime? At the Queen's Head?"

"I'm not sure." She said. She wanted to keep her distance from David Childs.

"Go on. We can talk over old times."

"We have had no 'old times' to talk over" She said firmly with a great deal of suspicion in her voice.

"Just a drink. I'd love to hear what you've been up to since Birmingham."

"From the sound of it you've known pretty much everything and even if you didn't before you've probably read it in the papers."

"Come on Silver, what harm can having a drink with an old friend do?"

She wanted him out of her house. Perhaps if she agreed to meet him on Sunday he would leave. Perhaps it seemed to be an easy way to get rid of him.

So she agreed and he left.

She immediately went upstairs to her office to check that everything was still there. She opened and closed the drawers one by one then sat down.

She was being paranoid, she told herself. Everything was still there.

Jane arrived at The Queen's Head just after half past twelve that Sunday.

It was one of the better pubs in the town but still one she rarely went into. It seemed that David Childs was a regular as the bar staff called him 'Dave' and a few of the other customers said 'hiya Dave' as he walked past.

She felt uncomfortable. She could not imagine why she had agreed to meet him as he put his arm around her shoulders and shepherded her to a table by the window.

Concerned as she was with detaching herself from his arm she did not see Richard at the bar.

"Sit yourself down. I'll get a bottle and a couple of glasses."

Jane Carmichael was becoming increasingly certain that she had made a bad mistake by agreeing to this meeting.

David Childs sat down opposite her at the table in the window by the door.

"How long is it since I last bought you a drink in a pub?"

"I don't know." She answered quickly, trying not to remember that day in Birmingham.

"I checked it out. It's exactly twelve thousand five hundred and ten days. Thirty four years, three months. To the day."

The precision frightened Jane and she was even more certain she should not have accepted his invitation. "I've been thinking...." She was going to make her excuses and leave when he interrupted.

"So have I, Silver, so have I. And no, you are not leaving. You are going to listen to what I have to say."

She did not ask him to stop calling her Silver. It hardly mattered what he called her.

They sat opposite each other as he talked about himself. She was uncomfortable and nervous. She fiddled with her glass, barely touching the wine, as David Childs told her more than she wanted to know about his life.

He told her, as if she should be interested, that he had never married, he said that was because he had never found anyone who could live up to his expectations of what a wife should be. She thought about telling him that perhaps he would have been more successful in finding a wife if he had thought about 'who' rather than 'what' a wife should be. But she didn't.

He told her how he had had girlfriends for the sex but they had all let him down, one way or another, leaving him before he was ready to end the relationships. Again she thought about suggesting that perhaps they had realised that he wasn't interested in them, just in their bodies. But she didn't think it worth the bother.

He told her how he had taught for a while but had disliked both the staff he had to work with and the students and felt, after two years, he should try something else.

As he talked she wondered what other unwelcome revelations he would make about his life.

"After that I moved to Cambridge."

Jane shivered. Why, she thought, would he have gone to Cambridge? "When was that?" she asked, but he didn't answer. He just continued telling her about his life and the more he told her the more frightened she became.

He told her how he had enjoyed his time in the force as much as he would have enjoyed any other job but, after initial promotions he hadn't advanced as quickly as he believed he should have. Something, or someone, had kept him back.

He told her how he had moved around a bit and ended up on the Island.

She wondered, but didn't ask, whether he had been in London and in Surrey before coming to the island. Somehow she thought he probably had.

His voice changed and he hunched down over his glass as he told her that now he was 55 and should be retiring he had no idea what he was going to do with his life. She almost felt sorry for him as he told her how he dreaded growing old alone, how everything about his life had been a great disappointment to him. Until he told her that it was all her fault.

As David talked Jane wondered what he wanted from her. He had to want something. This lunchtime drink couldn't possibly be just to tell her about what he had been doing with his life for the past forty years.

"Now look at your life." He looked up from his glass and into Jane's eyes. "Despite all that trouble about the people who were your parents you have been successful, you have achieved things. You turned yourself around didn't you? You were ill when I met you in Birmingham, you weren't well and you were in some dead end job, yet, you turned it round. You went to university, you found something you were really good at and you did it."

Jane began to feel uncomfortably certain that he knew everything there was to know about her, especially when he began to tell her things that hadn't been splashed all over the papers.

"You never found the right man though, did you Silver? What was his name? Matt? In Cambridge? I knew he wasn't right for you so it's a really good thing that bus came along. And what was the name of that man you married? Peter? What a shit. If only you'd asked me before that fancy wedding in the Strand, I could have told you that would be a disaster. You knew it was, didn't you? Even as you drove away from that posh hotel for your honeymoon. No wonder you had that affair. Tuesday's wasn't it?"

"How do you know all this?" She finally asked, a chill passing along her arms and to the tops of her fingers.

"You'd be surprised what I've always known about you Silver Birch. You and your mother and father, and that man your mother married. The papers haven't got it all yet have they? No, not by a long chalk. But there isn't much about you that I don't know, Silver."

"Stop calling me that. You know it is not my name."

"You'll always be Silver to me, whatever name you've called yourself over the years."

"Tell me. How did you find out about me?"

"Funny. I thought your first question would be 'why?'"

"That will come later. How?"

"It wasn't difficult."

"I didn't ask if it was easy, I just want to know how."

"I was intrigued. After Birmingham I was bored and aimless. As I said I taught a bit and then I met Eric."

"Eric Atkinson?"

"The very same. You know him?"

"Of him." So that was it, Jane realised. That was the connection.

She had her back to the man leaning against the bar ten feet behind her who turned his head slightly as he heard his name spoken.

"Eric Atkinson paid you?"

"Yes. Over the years he saw me right. He got me the job in the force and he arranged my moves around the country."

"He did all that?"

"He really wanted to nail your mum. He knew what she was, what your father was, and he really wanted to nail you all."

"And what could you give him. There was nothing. We did nothing."

"We had enough, between us. You read the papers, all that stuff about the Schreibers. Now the whole world knows. Because of us everyone in the world knows them for the traitors Eric always knew they were. But there's more of the story to come."

"What do you mean?"

Surely, she thought, there couldn't be anything else to expose.

"I think that people will be really interested to know what your father has cost them. How, because he couldn't keep his dick to himself, it's cost the proverbial taxpayer millions of pounds. All that security, all that maintaining secrecy costs money you know. And then there's all the other costs. You and your mother have lived off taxpayers' money since before you were born. What's that? Fifty five years or more? At what? In today's money? Fifty grand? That's nearly three million."

"I beg your pardon?"

"Since she fell pregnant your mother has had every house, every bill, paid by the government. By us. The taxpayers. I'm getting a pension when I retire next year but it's a fraction of what you've been given over the years because of who your father is. That man has arranged everything, including the generously stocked bank account given you in 1983, the pension you have been paid since 1995. Everything is provided by the state because of who you are. I've got all the account details, all the dates, all the sums. I don't give a shit about spies or illegitimate bastards. What I resent is that you've never had to do a day's work in your life."

"I'm leaving. This was a terrible mistake."

"You can't run away from this."

"Tell me what you want."

"I want some of the money."

"Blackmail?"

"Not a nice word. I've told you. My pension is a pittance. And I've worked hard for it. I just want a sub approaching the tax I've paid over the years returned to me. You've done very nicely out of all this over the years. You've got a nice house, nice things in it, you haven't had to work for years. All on the taxpayers money. Well I'm a taxpayer. I want that money. I reckon I've paid about one hundred thousand pounds in tax over the years. That should do. For starters."

She couldn't believe it was, after all, all going to be about money.

She stood up and bent down towards him. "Absolutely not. No. Never." She turned and walked as quickly as she could through the door.

She felt the premonition of fear she had experienced for most of her childhood. She was 16 again, 16 and angry at leaving the town, this town, that had been her home. She was 20 again, in Birmingham, scared, disappointed, depressed. She did not want these feelings again, in the town that had been her sanctuary, but now, with David Childs, she knew she would no longer feel secure. She just wanted to be home, to get over her mother's death and then she would start her life anew.

She knew he would follow her and, with the streets crowded with trippers and cars she knew he would catch up with her.

She heard him calling her. She could pick out the word 'Silver' from the other sounds in the bustling street, but she pressed on.

She had managed to cross the square, dodging between cars moving slowly as drivers looked for parking spaces, when David caught up with her, pulling her arm so she had to turn to face him.

Two things happened then but however many times she relived the moments she was never able to determine exactly in what order they occurred.

Somebody, it could have been a man or a woman, brushed against her, nearly knocking her over so she put her hand out to steady herself and felt something placed in it which she instinctively gripped.

And she heard two sharp cracking sounds.

She had months to try to work out whether the sound had come before the unsteadiness or after it.

She could never be sure but she was certain of what came immediately after.

She watched mystified as David Childs slid down to the ground, looking at her with an expression she thought of as confused and bewildered.

The trickle of blood sliding from the edge of his mouth and the emptying look in his eyes told her that he was dying.

But she had no idea why.

She stood there, shocked, looking down at him, his face bathed in sunshine. She couldn't move. She stood there looking down at his face with the staring, empty, eyes.

Dr Carmichael had seen dead people before but not many, and certainly none so ghastly. She could not stop staring at him. One minute ago he had been so alive and so threatening. And now there was nothing to him.

She knew someone had said something. Was it before or after the unsteadiness and the noises? Was she supposed to hear? 'Two birds, one stone'. In a rather detached way she wondered what that meant.

She was aware that there were people staring at her. It was a sunny afternoon, the town was crowded with trippers and shoppers, some brushed passed her as they seemed to try to get away from what was happening.

She thought she saw Richard on the other side of the road.

Then she looked down at her hand.

It was holding a gun. She wondered in a detached fashion how it came to be there.

There was a crowd around her. There were people screaming and tugging their children away from her.

And still she stood there, unable to move, staring down at the gun in her hand.

Chapter 19
An interview

She stood, bewildered, looking down at the man who had been David Childs while a circle of people formed around her and then they were gone.

She looked at a man in uniform, registering that he was a policeman, as he took the gun from her hand.

She felt as if she was in a bubble. No one was in that bubble with her; she was alone, everyone else was outside, she could not be a part of whatever it was they were doing or saying.

It was some time, she had no idea how long, before she realised that they we accusing her of murder.

She tried to say the words 'It wasn't me' but no sound came.

The siren of an ambulance made her look up, away from David Childs and all she could see were people looking at her.

"I was going home." She said, quietly, almost to herself, as if it wasn't important to anyone else.

She tried to remember what had happened. Some part of her understood that it would be important for her to remember as much as she could.

"Where's Richard?" She asked, but no one seemed interested in giving her an answer. "He was there. I saw him." She told the policeman, but he didn't seem interested in talking to her.

She had to remember everything she could. She had been walking home, she had left David Childs in the pub. He had been talking about….. What had he said to her? She couldn't remember. She had left to go home. Then she had heard him calling 'Silver'. He had caught up with her. People were brushing against her.

Then there was a noise. Was that before or after the man had brushed against her? She couldn't remember.

Then David Childs was lying at her feet and he was dead and she had the gun in her hand.

She had no idea where that gun had come from.

David Childs had looked at her in surprise. She remembered that. But whether it was before or after the noise she couldn't say. And when did she hear that whisper in her ear about two birds and one stone?

It had all happened only minutes before and she had no idea exactly what had happened and in what order.

"Do you understand?"

"What? Sorry? What?"

The police officer repeated the words Jane had half listened to in so many police dramas on the television. Her mother had watched them every day, or at least they had been on the television as her mother sat in front of the set. How much she watched or understood Jane had had no idea. Now she felt as detached as she had then from what was going on.

"Do you understand? I am arresting you on suspicion of the murder of Detective Inspector David Childs. You do not have to say anything, but it may harm….."

Jane knew what was going on but it seemed as though it had nothing to do with her.

In the twenty minutes it took to drive along the familiar road to Newport she sat in silence in the back of the car trying to remember what had happened. The shots, the gun, the voice in her ear, David Childs staring at her in surprise as he fell, they were all a blur and could have happened in an instant or over several minutes, and in any sequence.

When the car stopped she was pulled out and led to a claustrophobically small room by a grim looking policewoman who, as she turned to leave asked, almost as an afterthought, if Jane wanted to make a phone call.

Who could she call? Fear was crowding everything from her normally logical mind. She thought she should call a solicitor but she didn't have one; she had had no need of one since she bought her house nearly twenty years before. There was only Richard. She gave the police woman his number.

The room was windowless and all there was to look at was the Formica topped table, three uncomfortable looking chairs lined up against one wall and a clock half way up another. The room reminded her, unexpectedly, of the time Richard had shouted at her in the Town Hall in Birmingham.

As she sat in the empty room she began to see what had happened more clearly. David Childs was dead and they thought she had killed him. While she waited for Richard, or for anyone, to come she wondered what the press would make of the day's events following, as they did, so soon after the revelations about her parents' lives. It was, she knew, going to be a sensation, and not just in the tabloids. Everyone who read a newspaper or watched a news bulletin or listened to a radio phone-in would assume she was as guilty as hell.

Perhaps, she thought as she sat waiting in the empty and depressing room, she was the only person in the world who knew she wasn't.

No, she corrected herself, someone else did, the person who had actually pulled the trigger.

When the clock read 6:51 pm, after she waited alone for more than three hours and twenty minutes, the door opened and a man in a suit and shirt, but no tie, came in and introduced himself as the duty solicitor.

"You asked us to contact a Richard Mackenzie." He said without looking at her, checking the name on his tablet computer.

"Yes?" She asked hopefully.

"Not possible. He had a heart attack. They took him to Queen Mary's."

"He's OK?" she asked.

"No. He's dead." The solicitor was not interested in making anything easier for the woman who, to his mind, had killed David Childs, a man he had often worked with, exchanged banter with on an almost daily basis and with whom he had frequently shared a pint or two. She had murdered Dave and there was, everyone in the station agreed, no possible doubt about it.

"Dead?" She asked. "No. No. That can't be right. He was fine this morning. I phoned him. I spoke to him on the phone. He was fine."

"Richard Michael Mackenzie, born 24th June 1928 in Romford Essex?" The man read the words on his tablet.

"I didn't know he was born in Essex." But she knew that that was his birthday. She was strangely comforted that Richard Mackenzie also appeared to be his real name.

"Well he was DOA this afternoon. A heart attack."

"No. That can't be right." It was all she could say.

The solicitor asked her no questions and concentrated on swiping through various screens on his tablet computer that Jane strongly suspected had nothing to do with her.

"I didn't do it." Jane said after they had sat in silence for eight more minutes. As she watched the second hand go round on the clock on the wall she thought dispassionately of the clocks she had watched in school classrooms and university lecture halls and libraries.

"No?" He asked doubtfully without looking up from whatever it was he had been reading.

"No."

"There seem to be a number of people willing to give sworn statements that they saw you do it."

"Then they're either lying or simply mistaken as to what they think they saw."

"You had the gun in your hand."

"Yes, but I have no idea how it got there."

"It is your step-father's gun."

"Richard's?" That did surprise her. "I didn't know he had a gun."

"Well he did."

"I didn't know he had a gun." She repeated. "But of course he would have done wouldn't he?"

Jane looked urgently around her in the hope that the dreary walls would give her some explanation as to what had happened.

When the solicitor didn't reply and just continued looking at his computer she repeated. "I didn't do it. I know it looks dreadful but I didn't. I really didn't."

He didn't seem interested in finding out why she kept protesting her innocence when it was obvious to him that she was guilty.

They sat in silence for another 23 minutes until the second hand of the clock worked its way up to the 12 and it was exactly 7:25pm.

Jane was tired, she was frightened and her need to go to the lavatory was becoming desperate. She waited as long as she could and, a further fourteen minutes later, she asked if she could relieve herself.

Without replying he stood up and left the room. Four minutes later a policewoman came in and wordlessly gestured for Jane to go with her.

They walked down the drab corridor and at the end was a Ladies.

"Leave the door open." She barked as Jane went to shut the cubicle door behind her. The policewoman stood staring as she pulled up her skirt and sat. Jane had always had a thing about people hearing her pee and the indignity of being watched by the unsmiling, angry, miserable woman was unbearable.

"Am I to be allowed to wash my hands?" Jane asked as she headed for the row of basins.

The policewoman moved her eyes towards the basin, a sign that Jane took to mean agreement that she could perform this basic act of hygiene.

As she held her hands under the dribble of lukewarm water she realised that in the hours she had been at the station no forensic officer had taken a swab of her hands. And she was still wearing her own clothes. She had not been stripped and made to wear a sterile jump suit while her clothing was taken away for analysis. As she was ushered back to the interview room she wondered whether all the procedures in all the television programmes she had watched with her mother had been wrong or whether she was being treated differently for some reason.

As Jane sat back at the table in the interview room the clock showed it was 7.51. A few minutes later the door opened and a woman and a younger man who she presumed to be the detectives who would finally conduct the interview entered the room, drew up two chairs and sat down.

The woman looked at Jane with something approaching loathing as she pressed the button on the tape recorder.

"Eight pm Sunday 24th August 2014. Detective Sergeant Anne Hill, Detective Constable Ian Spalding present with Mr George Green Duty Solicitor. Interview of suspect going by the name of Dr Jane Carmichael."

"Why do you say that, as if it isn't my name?" Jane asked.

Anne Hill answered "We know it is only one of many aliases you have used."

"I beg your pardon?"

"Have you not, at various times, gone by the name Cavanagh, Bickton, Wright, Somerset and Birch?"

Jane looked at the solicitor but he appeared to be showing no interest at all.

"Yes, anyone who read last week's newspapers knows that about me and knows the reasons."

"David, that is Detective Inspector Childs, first met you when you were Silver Birch and that is the name he knew you by."

"I was Jane Birch, he decided to call me Silver. No one else did. But that was a very long time ago. My name is, and has been since my marriage to Dr Peter Carmichael in April 1990, Jane Carmichael and since I hold a PhD in mathematical and statistical sciences I am also entitled to being called 'Doctor'. My name, therefore, is Doctor Jane Carmichael."

The Detective Sergeant ignored her.

"How well did you know DI Childs?" The young man who sat next to Anne Hill spoke for the first time. "What I mean is how well did you know the deceased?"

Anne Hill cast him a sideways look and he said no more.

"I didn't 'know' David Childs at all." Jane answered firmly.

"I find that very difficult to believe."

"Well I knew him many years ago, briefly, and then I met him again on Wednesday, when he came to my house after I had been burgled."

"Burgled?"

"On Wednesday afternoon I returned home to find two young men in my house but they ran off as I approached."

"Two young men?"

"No more than boys really. I phoned 999 to report it and your people turned up to investigate."

"I was on duty on Wednesday. There was no report of a burglary in West Wight that evening." She nodded to her DC who checked something on his tablet.

"There are no reports of a burglary. The call appears in no log."

"But that's ridiculous. I called 999 and David Childs and two other policemen turned up to investigate"

"There is no record of this alleged burglary."

"It was not 'alleged'. It happened. I got home and two young lads pushed past me. I called 999. Two police cars turned up within minutes. David Childs was there with two others."

"There is no record." Ian Spalding repeated slowly.

"There must have been. Though nothing was taken my home was broken into. Two young men, boys, were in my house. I called 999. Three police officers arrived. David Childs was one of them."

"Anyone can claim anything." DC Spalding spoke quietly, as if to himself. Jane wondered irrationally if the tape would pick up his comment.

"Are you saying there was no burglary? That I made it all up for some reason?"

"Now why would I think that?" Anne Hill asked in a tone of voice that indicated that was exactly what she thought.

"Perhaps you wanted some attention." Ian Spalding suggested with a smirk.

"Attention?"

"Because you're a lonely old woman?"

"I beg your pardon?"

"It isn't unknown for lonely old women to claim they have been burgled when they themselves have roughed up their houses, just so they can have the company and the excitement of being the centre of attention for a few hours."

"Well not in this case. I am neither lonely nor a fantasist." Jane was indignant. "Nor," she added tartly, "am I old."

"Perhaps you wanted to make contact with DI Childs?"

"That's ridiculous! I had no idea he was on the island."

"But if you had known he was on the island you would have wanted to make contact with him?"

"That's not what I'm saying. I barely remembered David Childs existed until he turned up at my house to investigate the burglary."

"Oh I think we shall see that that isn't quite the truth is it?" DS Hill looked down at the bundle of papers and plastic bags she had placed on the table in front of her.

"We have been quite busy since your arrest. We have been to your house. And we have found a lot of evidence that you knew David Childs really quite well."

She picked up one of the plastic bags and turned it round so Jane could see the contents. Inside the bag was a photograph of a man, smiling at the camera. It was a photograph of David Childs looking a few years younger than he had that afternoon.

"If you didn't know him how do you explain this?"

"I've never seen that photo before in my life."

"Well it was in a frame in the room you use as your office."

"It couldn't be. I've never seen it before."

"You will see there's writing on the picture. Would you read it out for the benefit of the tape."

Jane looked at the writing and reluctantly read it. She could not understand how it came to be in her house.

"For the benefit of the tape I have never seen this photograph before."

"Please read the inscription."

She reluctantly read it. *"To darling Silver, to remember the summer of '94, With all my love David."*

"The summer of '94?" The woman asked pointedly. "You obviously had a memorable time with DS Childs as he would have been then."

"Whoever took that photograph it was not me. And I have no idea how it came to be in my house. I have never seen it before. I can only imagine, for the benefit of the tape, that someone has planted it in my house to incriminate me."

"That's a very serious accusation. You should think twice before making it." Ian Spalding spoke menacingly.

"Don't you think being seen to shoot DI Childs and being seen by many witnesses standing over him with the gun that killed him, your step-father's gun by the way, to be sufficiently incriminating?" Anne Hill added.

"I don't know how that happened."

"You didn't take your step-father's gun with you when you went to meet with your lover with the express intention of killing him?"

"I did not."

"You admit you were his lover."

"I absolutely do not. I am not, was not and never have been David Child's lover."

"Then can you explain this? Also found in your office, in one of the drawers of your desk."

Anne Hill pushed a plastic bag across the table top and in it Jane saw the scrap of paper. She didn't have to read it;

as soon as she saw it memories flooded back and she knew exactly what was written on it.

"That was a very long time ago."

"So you're not denying that you did know David Childs."

"I knew him when we were 16 years old."

"But you wrote him love notes?"

"That was a stupid note on a scrap of paper. I gave it to David Childs years ago. I haven't seen it since and I have no idea, for the benefit of the tape, how it came to be in my house."

She was beginning to feel not only frightened but also violated.

She remembered scenes from the countless television episodes of Midsomer Murders and Inspector Morse and Miss Marples and Hercule Poirot that she had watched with her mother. Surely the police should have had a warrant, or her permission, before rifling through her property.

Who, or what, was to have stopped them putting whatever they wanted in her house in order to back up their theory that she had been David Childs' lover and that that somehow gave her a motive to kill him.

"You're a lot older than 16 in this."

Anne Hill pushed over another plastic bag in which was a photograph. Jane judged from the hairstyle and clothes it had to have been taken when she was in Cambridge; she would have been about 25.

"Please read the inscription."

"*To darling DC your SB.*" Jane spoke reluctantly. "For the benefit of the ....."

Ian Spalding interrupted her. "That is you isn't it?"

Jane nodded. It was undoubtedly her.

"Can you explain how this came to be in DI Childs' house? We've been there too."

"I didn't give it to him. Anyway, that isn't my writing. I have no idea how he got that. I hadn't seen him for years before then."

"You hadn't seen him since you were 16 yet he has this photograph of you when you say you were 22?"

"25. I would have been 25 when this was taken."

"That would have been when?"

"1985." She repeated carefully, knowing they were trying to trip her up and find inconsistencies in what she was telling them. "I did not know David Childs then. I have no idea how he got this photograph, which I think was taken by my then fiancé, and I did not write those words. For the benefit of the tape."

Ian Spalding then pushed another clear plastic bag across the table top.

"This exercise book seems to indicate you were quite happy to be called 'Silver Birch', a name you said only David called you."

"How did you get that?" Jane asked.

"We have been investigating the links between you and your victim and this was found in David Child's house, in his bedroom to be precise."

"It was not. It couldn't have been. It was in my desk drawer at home. I saw it there after the break in."

"It was found in David Child's bedroom. You must have given it to him. Now why would you give him such a personal thing if you didn't want to be in a relationship with him?" he asked knowingly. "It's full of very intimate things, very personal things."

"You've read it?" Jane was appalled.

"Enough to see you were fantasising about David Childs."

"I was a silly romantic and disturbed teenager when I wrote those things. And it wasn't for anyone else to read."

"Yet you kept it all those years. And why would you want to do that if you didn't have feelings for him?"

"I kept it to remind me how lucky I was to have left those days behind." She looked from the woman to the young man to her useless solicitor and tried to remember what else was in the book. She had written about her mother, and Richard and her father. She tried to remember what secrets they would now know.

"And then you gave it to David Childs. Now why would you do that if you didn't know him?"

"I most certainly did not give it to David Childs."

She knew they had made up their minds about her. They were not going to believe anything she said. "I did not give that book to David Childs." She repeated lamely.

She was beginning to understand that she would not be able to make them realise that she was telling the truth.

The solicitor was no help to her. She kept looking at him and he was always either reading something on his tablet computer or tapping away at the screen. He didn't seem to be listening to anything that was being said and he certainly never intervened to say she didn't have to answer a question or suggest that the detectives were being unreasonably illogical or harsh.

Jane had never enjoyed films or television programmes or novels of injustices and mistaken identities. She had always wanted to believe that justice would prevail but as the night went on she began to think that she was in the middle of one of those stories where the truth would not win through.

The murder weapon was a gun she had had access to, though she had never known of its existence. She had, unarguably, been with David Childs when he had been, very publicly, shot.

She was not sure she would have believed in her innocence had she just been given those facts.

"Why would I want to kill a man I hardly remembered existed?" She asked trying to sound sensible. "I have no motive."

"You had the oldest motive in the world. Revenge."

"I beg your pardon?"

"There has been a great deal in the papers recently about you and your family has there not?"

"Yes but....."

"And you believed David Childs was involved in passing information to the press, something, by the way, that as a senior and long-standing detective he would never have dreamed of doing. You felt betrayed by the man who had ended your relationship and who you still loved so you killed him. That seems to me to be a very strong motive."

Jane listened carefully to what the detective said then, as calmly as she could, began to rebut each statement in turn.

"Firstly I did not know, until this lunchtime when he told me, that he was involved in providing information for the story. Why would I? I only knew it was a man called Eric Atkinson who had a vendetta against my mother and step-father. Secondly, sad as it may seem, it is not unknown for police to pass on information to the press. Thirdly, I have never been in any kind of relationship with David Childs. I have never been in love with him. If there was any obsession in all this it was his for me not mine for him."

"You keep saying that you were never in a relationship with DI Childs but how do you explain these?"

Ian Spalding pushed a number of sheets of paper across the table.

"How do you explain these?" he repeated.

Jane looked at the photographs. They all appeared to be of a small room, the same room from different angles. The walls were covered with photographs.

"These are all photographs of you. There are small square and faded ones, which must have been taken in the 1980s. There are hundreds of photographs of you, right up to what look like very recent ones. And you still say you don't know David Childs and never had an affair with him?"

"Surely all that those photos show is how obsessed he was with me?"

"They are the record of your long standing affair."

"No."

"I find that very difficult to believe."

"Well it's true. Until last Wednesday when he came to my house, I hadn't seen him since the early 80s. He's taken all these without my knowledge."

"Every single photograph is of you. And all the other things. Look."

There were other things in that photograph of David's room that she recognised, a scarf she could remember her mother gave her for her birthday when she was 16; newspaper cuttings of the death of her fiancé Matt in Cambridge, cuttings of reviews of her published books and copies of every book she had written. When she saw her biography of Sonya Kovalevskaya she remembered again meeting that man in the library in Moscow; her uncle.

It was all so complicated and so unfair.

What was becoming clear to Jane was that David Childs had been stalking her. For more than thirty five years he had been obsessed with the life of a girl he had hardly known. For a fraction of a second she almost felt sorry for him then she began to remember some of the things he had told her that lunchtime and she shivered.

"This room is a shrine to the woman he knew as Silver Birch. Do you still say you did not know DI Childs?" Ian Spalding pressed her.

"It depends what you mean by 'know'. I told you, I knew him a little when we were at school. I went on a date with him when I was 16. One date."

"Tell us about that then." Anne Hill's voice made it eminently clear she was going to interpret anything Jane said in the worst possible light, having already made her mind up about her

"It was in 1976."

"Where were you?" She interrupted.

"In Ludlow, in Shropshire." Jane answered calmly. She had a feeling there was going to be a lot of interruption and she had no intention of rising to the provocation.

"How old were you at the time?" Anne Hill asked, though she had Jane's birthdate on the file in front of her.

"16."

"Just tell us about how you met David Childs."

"I first met him when I was in the town shopping in the summer. I'd just moved there. I didn't know anyone."

"He picked you up?"

"I wouldn't describe it like that. We just started talking."

"Did you lead him on in any way?"

"It was not in my nature to lead anyone on though I can't imagine why you can think a casual meeting all those years ago has any bearing whatsoever on what's happened today."

"You seem to have made some impression on him."

"Well I can't imagine what I might have said or done that could have led to all that."

"So you let yourself be chatted up and then you went out with him?"

"One date. But that was months later. We met up again at a school debate. He asked me to the pictures and I went. One date. I have absolutely no idea why he seems to have been obsessed with me."

"Obsessed with you?"

"Well what would you call it when a man I barely knew, a boy I barely knew, has a room plastered with my photos, a map of every place I've ever lived, some bits and pieces I thought I'd lost over the years. What else could you call it?"

Neither Anne Hill nor Ian Spalding answered.

Jane tried again "You're saying this obsession of his is my fault? That my 16 year old me brought this on myself?"

Neither of the detectives said a word.

At last the solicitor spoke.

"I think, Detective Sergeant, that my client could probably do with a cup of tea, I know I would like one, it's been a long evening."

The young detective stood up with some reluctance after speaking to the tape. "Detective Constable Ian Spalding leaving the room."

"How much longer is this likely to take?" The solicitor spoke again.

"Sooner or later she is going to admit that she knew DI Childs very well indeed, that they fell out, perhaps over those newspaper revelations or maybe something a bit more personal, and that she killed him." Anne Hill answered as if Jane wasn't present.

The three sat in silence until the young DC came in with a tray and three paper cups of very milky tea that had bits of tea dust that had escaped from the tea bag floating on the surface.

"DC Ian Spalding returning to the interview room."

"Let me summarise." DS Hill spoke with condescension, as if Jane was incapable of remembering what had been said just a few minutes before. "You moved to Ludlow in Shropshire. One day you were chatted up, you went on one date, and that's all there ever was to your relationship with David Childs?"

"I might have seen him once or twice around the town. I can't remember. But I didn't know him for long. My mother and I moved away after a few months, certainly before that Christmas."

"You moved a lot then?"

"Yes." Jane didn't think she needed to say any more. They had obviously read all about her in the newspapers. "There were reasons. As you probably well know."

"So you may have gone out with David Childs one or more times but you only knew him for a few weeks? In 1976?"

"Yes."

"Let me read you from one of his diaries."

"He wrote a diary?" Jane was surprised, and frightened. If he had been mad enough to have written on photographs to give the impression they were lovers what fantasies might he have put in his diary?

"Not a diary as such, more writings, jottings, his thoughts and beliefs, his inner self."

The detective picked up an exercise book and opened it near the beginning. "How about this for starters? *'She looked up at me and in the dark of the gateway I put both arms around her and kissed her properly. Tongues. Deep throat. Her hand on me told me she wanted more. So I gave it to her. I fucked her hard in the dark of the archway.'* Are you saying you never had sex with him? This seems pretty unambiguous to me."

"I might have kissed him, I mean. I can't honestly remember. But I never did anything else. I was a virgin until I was 22. He's fantasising. That's all. These are the fantasies of a sad young man."

"Then how do you explain all these pages describing how you went out together and snogged each other and touched each other and 'did more'? A lovely euphemism don't you think?"

"I can't be expected to explain the fantasies of an adolescent boy."

"Fantasies? They're very clearly written. Very explicit. Lots of details of where and when and what you did with him."

In the silence that followed Jane realised how desperately tired she was.

The solicitor, George Green, looked like he wanted to be somewhere else, but then, Jane thought, he had since the moment he had arrived. Even DC Spalding seemed to be losing interest. It was DS Anne Hill who was driving the interview. Perhaps, Jane wondered dispassionately, she had fancied David Childs and she was making this investigation a very personal issue.

"So how did you get back in touch with David Childs after you left Ludlow?" DS Hill asked but didn't wait for Jane's answer. "He writes here that he didn't have your address or phone number so you must have got in touch with him somehow."

"I didn't."

"You're saying you lost touch?"

"Absolutely I'm saying that. I've already said that."

"But you did see him again. You made sure you saw him again didn't you?"

"How could I do that?"

"You knew where he lived. It would be easy enough. Especially since you wrote in Silver Birch's exercise book how much you 'loved' him and how much you wanted him to make you feel again the way you had felt with him and how much you missed him. You wouldn't have wanted to lose touch would you?"

"But I did. Lose touch I mean. When we met again it was years later and completely by chance."

"So where was it you met again?"

"In Birmingham."

"It's a big city to meet someone by chance."

"The world, they say, is but a village." Jane immediately regretted her facetiousness. She should have known that smart remarks were not a good idea under the circumstances. The detective and her silent colleague did not look amused. Neither did Jane's equally silent and unsupportive solicitor.

"When was it you met David Childs again?"

"I don't know, three or four years later?"

"Don't ask me. I'm the one asking the questions." Anne Hill snapped.

"It was in Birmingham, anyway. I was in the Central Library."

"And he just walked in?"

"Yes. He came to sit at the table I was at. Or was he there first? I can't remember. I didn't recognise him. Three or four years at that age makes a great difference. I think I'd changed a lot. I'd been ill and had lost a lot of weight. I was surprised he recognised me."

"And you went for a drink with him?"

"Probably. I can't really remember."

"You don't seem to remember much." Jane could hear the disbelief in her voice.

"It was nearly 35 years ago for Pete's sake!"

"There's no need to get aggressive."

"I'm not getting aggressive. I just want to know why you're asking me all these questions about my past, my long, distant past. You're trying to make out that I had a relationship with this man who is obviously completely deranged."

"Was. The man is dead."

"And you think I killed him?"

Neither detective answered.

"Well I didn't kill him. Why would I?"

They ignored her question saying, wearily. "Let us return to Birmingham in 1980."

"Was that when it was?" Jane's patience was wearing very thin.

"Saturday the 24th of May 1980 according to his writings."

"Well it must be true if he's written it." Jane tried to put all her anger and frustration into her voice but all three sitting with her around the table looked at her, disapproving of her inappropriate sarcasm.

She knew she was doing herself no favours but she was nearing the end of her tether. The injustice of it all was overwhelming her.

"So, again, let me summarise the story you have been telling."

Jane looked at her solicitor, was he going to let the detective get away with the implication that she was lying. He didn't seem worried about it.

"It is not a story. It is true. For the benefit of the bloody tape."

Jane's intervention was ignored.

"Up until last week you say you had met David Childs three times in 1976 when you were a schoolgirl, once when he chatted you up on a hot summer's day, once at a school debate and once when you went to the cinema with him. You met him again, by chance, some four years later in Birmingham when you coincidentally were using the same library at the same time. You met him last Wednesday when you say he attended your house to investigate a burglary of which there is no official record and you met him in the Queen's Head for a drink earlier today, within a few minutes of his murder. So you are saying that in all your life you have met him on only these six occasions?"

"Yes. That is what I am saying because it is the truth."

"You are asking us to believe that you never met him in the intervening thirty five years?"

"Absolutely. I did not."

"What about in Cambridge?"

"Cambridge?"

"Didn't you meet him in Cambridge?"

"When?"

"In 1987."

"No. I did not meet him in Cambridge or anywhere else for that matter."

"You're saying you didn't meet him, know him intimately, continue your affair, in Cambridge in 1987."

"Absolutely not. I was engaged and about to marry."

"But you didn't marry?"

"Not then. No. My fiancé, Matt, was killed."

"Killed. How unfortunate." There was no sympathy in Anne Hill's voice.

"When Matt died I moved to London, where I did marry and lived for a few years before getting divorced, giving up my career and coming to the island to look after my mother who was too ill for my stepfather to cope with alone. In all that time I neither thought of, nor saw, David Childs. Not once."

"Then how do you explain all these photographs and the letters?"

"What letters?"

"These."

She pushed several sheets of paper onto the table. There were no envelopes. They were letters in her handwriting; and a quick glance showed her that they were love letters.

"Yes. They are my letters. But I didn't write them to David Childs."

"No?"

"I wrote them to Peter, my husband, ex-husband. When he was away from home, before we married. How the hell did you get hold of them?"

"You are admitting that you wrote them but you say David Childs was not the addressee?"

"That is exactly what I am saying."

"Then how do you explain how they came to be in his room, with all the other mementoes of your love affair?"

"There was no affair."

"How do you explain his being in possession of them then?"

"I can't."

As Jane put her head in her hands she saw the triumphant look on Anne Hill's face

The world, her world, was going mad. Nothing had made any sense since that morning when she had been reading the papers which were still dragging up stories about Grahame Johnstone and her mother and thinking she really ought to walk into town to meet the rather odd man who had insisted on inviting her for a drink.

She was exhausted. She had no idea how David Childs had got hold of those photographs, those letters, so many personal bits and pieces of hers.

She could not think of any sensible explanation and, tired as she was, she understood that her situation was bleak.

Ian Spading continued to badger her with the same questions. "You never saw him?"

"No. I did not. I have told you I did not."

"You never spent time with him?"

"Never."

"You were never his lover?"

"Absolutely not."

"As we have seen he has, had, quite a collection of photographs of you. Perhaps you can explain how he came to have them in his possession if he did not take them."

He showed Jane yet another photograph. It was of a younger, slimmer version of Jane lying on a tousled bed, posing seductively for whoever was taking the photograph.

"Are you saying that you didn't see David Childs as he took this photograph?" Jane thought the look on the detective's face as he spoke could only be interpreted as a malicious leer.

"David Childs did not take that photograph." Jane said as firmly as she was able.

"Then who did?"

"Matt, my fiancé, did."

"If your dead fiancé took it how do you suppose it came to be in David Childs' possession?"

"I have absolutely no idea how he could have got hold of it."

"When was it taken?"

"I don't know exactly. 1987? It must have been a day or so before he died."

"Where were you?"

"That was in our house in Cambridge."

"And how do you think it came to be in the hands of David Childs if he didn't take it or you didn't give it to him?"

"I have absolutely no idea."

"I have a suggestion to make. The photograph was, indeed, taken in your house in Cambridge, something we can of course check, but it was taken by David Childs. While your fiancé was out you 'entertained' David Childs, you fucked him and afterwards he took this photograph."

"Absolutely not."

"What about this one?"

The detective showed Jane a photo of her leaning against the promenade railings in Brighton. She remembered Matt taking it. It had been very windy and she was barely able to stand upright.

"That again was taken by my fiancé, Matt."

"You will be able to date this photo?"

"Yes it was Easter 1987. We spent a weekend away."

"In Brighton?"

"Obviously."

"Not very adventurous."

"I seem to remember we had a very nice time."

"How did your inconvenient fiancé die?"

Jane ignored the implication. "He was run over walking home from the pub."

"Hit by the proverbial bus?"

Jane looked at the detective trying to understand why she was being so provocative.

"Yes." She answered as coldly as she could. "He was. This was taken only a couple of months before that. Matt was a lovely man. I was with him a long time. I loved him."

"So you say. And in all this time you spent in Cambridge you never saw David Childs?"

"Of course not. I have said so many many times now."

"Yet he was living in Cambridge then."

Jane remembered something of what David Childs had been telling her that lunchtime. "So he told me this lunchtime, but I had no idea until today."

"He lived in Cambridge. Quite close to your home, conveniently close, opposite in fact. David Childs joined the police force in Cambridge in August 1982. He lived, first as a lodger with a Mrs Williams and then he rented a flat in the house opposite yours."

"I didn't see him."

"Not once?"

"Not once. It wasn't the sort of area where everyone knew each other and neighbours lived in each other's pockets. I went to work every day and spent every evening at home."

The detective looked disbelieving.

Jane was at a loss as to how she could make this obdurate woman understand that what she was saying was the truth. It seemed that she had already decided what the truth was going to be.

"Let's leave Cambridge behind. We can come back to that later if you want to change your story in any way. I mean just in case you are able to remember more accurately what happened."

"I did not see David Childs in Cambridge, nor in London or any time after that one time in Birmingham."

"So how about this picture?"

The detective placed the photograph on the table in front of her and swivelled it round to face Jane. It was her wedding day. She was wearing a pink silk dress. It was a rainy morning in early April and she was smiling a thin, strained smile.

"Yes. My wedding. The church was in Central London so it was unsurprising there had been people around as we left the church. I wouldn't have worried about people with cameras but I find it really weird to think that David Childs was there, taking a photograph."

"The marriage didn't last?"

"You know it didn't or you wouldn't ask."

"Can you tell me the reason for your divorce?"

She looked again at George Green who was making notes and failing to catch her eye. "Do I have to answer all these questions? They're hardly relevant? This was years ago."

He looked up and nodded.

"Adultery." She answered shortly.

"Whose?"

"Mine."

"With whom?"

"No one was ever named. I admitted it. It wasn't a problem. Peter and I hadn't been happy for a long time. We both knew our marriage was a mistake so we agreed to divorce. I wanted out of the marriage marginally more than he did so I agreed to be the guilty party, though I found out later that he had been screwing around and I had only that one lover. I never did think that was fair."

"Was that lover David Childs?"

"Of course it wasn't."

"Then who was it? Perhaps we can trace him to corroborate?"

"It was years ago for God's sake!"

"Then, if you refuse to cooperate, we can only assume it was because the man involved was David Childs."

Jane looked at George Green. Surely he couldn't let the detective get away with that but he didn't appear to be listening as he touched out words on the screen of his tablet computer. She spoke as firmly as she could.

"For the benefit of the tape I wish to register that I don't think that that is, in any way, a reasonable assumption to make."

"Then how did he get hold of these? Also found in David Child's house" Ian Spalding pushed a number of photographs across the table.

Jane could not believe that they still existed.

She had known Peter had taken photographs of her in that time he had felt he needed to impose himself on her but she had no idea how they came to be in David Childs' possession. She saw the bruises Peter had inflicted and she saw the outfits he had made her wear and she felt again the fear and the disgust she had felt in those months when she had had to do as he insisted. He had been so careful that none of the damage he did to her would show when she was dressed and in public but he had enjoyed making her strip so he could record the dark bruises on the intimate parts of her body.

She shuddered at the memories but could not look away.

"They are me, but they were taken by Peter, my then husband. I have no idea how they came to be in David Childs' possession."

"It is obvious isn't it? You and David Childs were lovers, he took these photos of what can only be described as extremely kinky sex. That is how they come to be in his possession. It is the only explanation."

"He did not take them. Peter did."

"I don't think so." Ian Spalding said dismissively. "I don't think these are the photos a husband takes of his wife. You and David Childs have been lovers all along haven't you? It started in Ludlow, continued in Birmingham, in Cambridge, in London and here on the island. You have followed each other through life so that you can be together. He has recently rejected you, you think he has betrayed you, so you took your step-father's gun and you killed him."

"No. You are wrong." Jane said, despairing that they would ever listen to her. "Until this morning I had no idea whatsoever about any detail of where David Childs lived or what he did. I couldn't have cared less about him. I can't have spent more than six hours with him in my entire life."

"He seems to have known exactly where you were most of the time."

"Well that isn't down to me. I had no idea. Everything you're showing me is just weird."

"Yet he has all those photographs, all that, how can I describe it, memorabilia, all relating to you. He has been in the same place at the same time as you many, many times." The detective spoke wearily.

"So you keep saying."

"And you have no explanation?"

"None. Other than that the man has been stalking me all these years." Jane was close to tears. The frustration of not being believed had become too much. Unwisely, she reacted by losing her temper. "And will you both stop bloody banging on and on about what you are imagining to be the truth. Watch my lips. I did not kill the man. I had no idea whatsoever that he was anywhere near me. At any time. Ever. He's made the whole thing up. He's completely mental. Isn't that obvious? God only knows why but he's made it all up. Why can't you open your minds and understand that?"

She stopped, realising she had made a mistake. She looked at George Green and managed to catch his eye. "Can't you see I need a break. I'm desperately tired and confused and frightened."

"I suggest you calm down while the police complete their interview." It was not the intervention she had hoped for from the solicitor. She stared at him, her lips pursed, then turned her gaze back to Anne Hill. The look on the woman's face showed something approaching triumph.

Jane looked down at her hands then back across the table at the two detectives and spoke slowly and clearly. "I suggest you believe me because what I say is true. I did not kill him. Until today I did not know he lived in Cambridge and I did not know he lived in London."

"Surrey." Ian Spalding corrected her.

"I did not know he lived here on the island until he turned up on Wednesday." Jane continued. "What do I have to say to make you understand that nothing you have suggested is anywhere near the truth?"

But even as she asked the question she knew what the answer was.

She could do or say nothing to make them change their minds.

"It would be easier for you if you just admit to your relationship with David Childs." The detective spoke as if she had not heard anything Jane had said.

"I have never had a relationship with him."

"He has lived within a few miles of you for the past thirty five years. Whenever you moved he moved."

"And I did not kill him."

"He was your lover all those years and when that article in the papers told the world your family's secrets you felt, without any evidence whatsoever, that David Childs had betrayed you. You wanted revenge for the hurt he was causing you so you took your step-father's gun and you killed him."

"Yet again. He was not my lover. I had no idea he was here on the island. I did not see him between 1980 and last

Wednesday when he came to my house to investigate the burglary. I had no reason to link him to the stories in the newspapers and I did not kill him."

"He was your lover, has been your lover for many years. You argued and you killed him."

"No. You are wrong on so many levels."

"You decided, because of the revelations in the newspapers, that the time had come to rid yourself of another inconvenient lover. You met him in the Queen's Head. You argued, and we have many witnesses for that. You left him. A few minutes later you shot him with the gun you had stolen from your step-father for that exact purpose. It was a very public murder, Ms Carmichael. Witnesses saw you leave the pub. Witnesses saw David Childs leave the pub and follow you, apparently trying to be conciliatory after your argument. Witnesses saw him fall to the ground. The gun was in your hand. Why don't you save us all a lot of trouble and admit it?"

"I did not kill David Childs." Jane spoke clearly and deliberately.

"No?"

"No. For the benefit of the tape and anyone else who may be listening I did not kill David Childs."

Jane knew what the Detective was going to say when she stood up.

"Doctor Jane Carmichael, I am charging you with the murder of Detective Inspector David Childs."

Jane wondered what would happen now.

"Have you finished?" She asked wearily. "Can I go home?"

"Oh no. Not a chance. We'll hold you and oppose bail. Killing a police officer is a very serious offence."

"But what will happen to it?" Jane asked. "I've left windows open. The plants will die without being watered and what about my car? It's not locked. I was only going into town for an hour."

Somehow focusing on the unimportant things helped her as she faced the fact that she was on her own.

The police had decided she was guilty and she would never be able to prove them wrong.

There was no Richard to come to her rescue and there could be was no one else to help her.

Chapter 20
A Defence

When Jane Carmichael first met the man who was to defend her in court she liked him immediately. He was the first person she had spoken to in the six months since her arrest who seemed to be on her side.

Without introducing himself and before he sat down he spoke directly to her. "Answer me one question truthfully. Did you murder David Childs?"

"No. I did not." She answered, rather surprised at his bluntness. She watched as he sat down opposite her and placed a file, which he did not immediately open, on the table between them.

He smiled broadly showing her what she noticed was a perfect set of even white teeth. "Right then, let's see how we can get you out of this mess. By the way my name is Gordon Hamilton and I will be leading the team defending you in court."

Jane had been desperate with the utter uselessness of the solicitor the police had supplied immediately after her arrest and she had little faith in the legal profession as a whole. 'Overpaid and opportunistic parasites' would have described her feelings about all lawyers, until the day she had that first interview with Gordon Hamilton.

Every visit she had had from her court-appointed lawyers in the months she had been remanded in prison had been a frustration to her. They all seemed uninterested in her case, making no sensible argument for bail, seemingly having accepted her guilt. In the months she spent in jail awaiting her trial she had felt alone and powerless although she had tried to resign herself to the sheer injustice of it all. She had spent the long days remembering as much as she could and trying to identify what she would have done differently since her first memories of her life in York and on the Isle of Wight.

'If only I had refused to go into town to meet him that Sunday' she thought many times.

There were so many if onlys.

As the date of her trial drew closer she began to focus her mind on coping with being in the public eye, having her history and that of her parents exposed, again, to public dissection and then living with what seemed to be the inevitable verdict and sentence.

Two weeks before the court date she had been surprised when a new solicitor had visited her. He had been business-like but friendly and she allowed herself to hope that he would be better than his predecessors in putting forward her side of the case.

The next day she had another visitor, a young man who eventually introduced himself as Gordon Hamilton.

The small room set aside for such interviews had few comforts. There was a window which looked out onto an ivy-covered wall. On the remaining three walls there were only a clock and two framed certificates to break up the grim grey paint. For furniture there was only a small table and two chairs. It was the same room she had been in on every meeting with her solicitors and every time she had been in it she was reminded of the police interview room and of the store room in Birmingham Town Hall where Richard had lectured her.

She had lost count of the number of times she had wished she had listened to him that day.

"Now tell me what happened in the days leading up to that afternoon."

"You've seen all the statements I've made?"

"Yes, but I'd like to hear it all from you. I find the spoken word less ambiguous than the written."

Jane took a deep breath before beginning to tell again the story she had already told many times. "After my mother died there were some incredibly detailed and hurtful reports about her and my father in the newspapers." She paused, waiting for the inevitable question 'were the reports true' but Gordon Hamilton gave no indication of wanting to interrupt her. "A few days later, the day of my mother's funeral, my house was burgled. One of the detectives who came to investigate was David Childs, someone I had known many years before. He invited me to meet him for a drink the following Sunday and wouldn't take no for an answer. I really didn't want to go but he was very insistent and then, when I got there I didn't much like what he was saying so I left as soon as I could. He followed me and was shot."

She stopped and looked across the small table that separated them awaiting the inevitable questions. "The gun was in your hand when the police arrived. How long after the shooting would that have been?" He wasn't reading from notes, Jane was impressed that the young man had obviously done his homework.

"I have no idea really, it's all a bit of a blur."

"Seconds? Minutes?"

"It could only have been a very short time."

"Since you didn't use the gun why do you think were you holding it?"

"I have no idea how it got there. Someone was standing close to me at some time, pushed me, I overbalanced and reached out but I don't know who and I don't know whether it was before or after the shots. And there was a voice in my ear saying 'two birds one stone.' I don't know who said it but someone did. And Richard was there, on the other side of the road."

"Richard Mackenzie?"

"Yes."

Gordon Hamilton looked down at his notes and turned back several pages before filling three lines with what Jane could see was small, neat and almost childlike handwriting.

"So, Dr Carmichael, you were at the scene of the crime and holding the weapon in your hand. This gives the prosecution what might be called a head start." Unexpectedly he smiled. "I like a challenge."

Jane allowed herself to return his smile.

"One thing that will help our case is that the police appear not to have followed normal procedures after your arrest. There appear to be no swabs of your hands, no forensics were done on your clothes. They are claiming that you were hysterical and uncooperative, soiling your clothes and deliberately contaminating your hands but it at least gives me something to work on."

"I was not hysterical and I did not soil anything."

"No, somehow I didn't believe you would have."

"I wondered at the time why they didn't do anything like that. I rather assumed they thought they didn't need to."

"They should have done and they appear to be trying to cover up their failure. I will just have to make sure they are not successful won't I?"

"I didn't kill David Childs. Why would I? I had no reason to kill him. I hardly knew him."

"Ah the motive!" He was still smiling. "In my experience there are perhaps only four categories of motives for murder and we need to explore all of them, certainly the prosecution will. First there is the sex-love-jealousy group. This is the one they seem most keen on with their emphasis on your supposed long standing affair with the deceased man. Sex, in one way or another, is probably the most common motive for doing away with someone." Jane was surprised to see Gordon Hamilton smile and she noticed that the tone of his voice was almost conversational. "I love that phrase don't you? 'Doing away with'. It so well describes the action. What is your answer to that possibility?"

"I never had a love affair with David Childs. I had only met him once since I was a schoolgirl. I was not and never had been in love with him, anything I may have written that implies I was involved with him would be the ramblings of an immature and very confused young woman."

"Very succinctly put." He paused and smiled reassuringly at her again. "The next most common reason for murder is money. This, I believe can be discounted in your case. You had nothing financial to gain from the death of David Childs, I assume you hadn't taken out a life insurance policy. No? No, somehow I doubted you would have done. One looks, in such cases, for *cui bono* 'who benefits'. I cannot see the possibility of any financial benefit to you brought about by the 'doing away with' of David Childs."

"I could not possibly have benefitted in any way."

"Are the prosecution going to find any hidden secret in your bank accounts?"

"What I have has come from my own earnings as an academic and a writer and from an allowance paid to me by my father."

"Ah yes, your natural father. I understand that he has been generous to you and your mother over the years."

"He has."

"So you have no money worries?"

"No. None." She said firmly. "I have continued to write through the years of looking after my mother and my books are on many university reading lists so there is some small income from royalties, not a lot, but then my needs aren't great."

"So we can discount money. The next group of motives is usually something to do with fear. The perpetrator fears disclosure of some secret. In short murders are committed to shut the victim up. Is it possible that you have anything more in your past that you needed to keep secret, a secret so important to you that the only way to keep your privacy was to kill David Childs?"

"Such as?"

"You tell me."

"My past, as I'm sure you are well aware, was plastered all over the newspapers in the days before that Sunday. My parents, my step-father, my parents' careers and histories, their parents, everything, absolutely everything, about me and those I have loved is in the public domain. There was nothing left to be disclosed. I had nothing more to be afraid of."

"Ah yes. I have seen the newspaper articles. They weren't kind to you were they?"

"They weren't kind, especially as none of it had anything to do with me really."

"You were the innocent party?"

"Exactly. How could I have been anything otherwise?"

Gordon Hamilton smiled and wrote another line in his neat, small hand-writing.

"There is, of course another motive." Jane volunteered.

"Yes?"

"The police seemed to be convinced that I wanted revenge."

"Ah. Revenge." Gordon sat back in his chair, clasped his hands together over his chest and twiddled his thumbs. "Yes, that was the fourth and final category."

"They said, right from the start, that I murdered him out of revenge for being betrayed to the newspapers."

"Nonsense! You would not have killed David Childs for revenge."

Jane was surprised at the vehemence in the young man's voice.

"No, of course not, I had nothing to be vengeful about."

"Of course you didn't. And I believe the prosecution will find it difficult to prove you had. Let me tell you something about revenge, Dr Carmichael. Only people with no imagination and no intelligence kill quickly if the motive is revenge. Those who really want revenge make it a longer lasting, more strung-out event. The need for revenge burbles under the surface of a man's mind for years, decades even and then they want their victim to suffer. As far as I can see David Childs didn't suffer. He was shot, he wondered what the pain was and then he died. Sorry to be blunt. But if it was a revenge murder it was a bit of a failure. Unless......" He stopped himself and looked across the table at Jane Carmichael, an idea forming itself very clearly and very precisely in his mind. He wrote for several seconds.

"Unless?" Jane prompted.

"Just a thought, nothing to worry yourself about."

He continued to write for a further minute as Jane tried to read his writing upside-down. It was too neat and too small and she wasn't able to make anything out.

"Now, I need to ask. Is there anything, anything, in your life that would be embarrassing to you and your case if it came out in court?"

"You mean did I have a secret affair with a politician? No. Did I cheat or plagiarise any of my publications? Have I ever shop-lifted or broken laws? Was I a spy like they say both my Mother and Father were? No, no and no. I am as blameless an individual as you are ever going to find."

"So you didn't kill him out of revenge for the pain he had inflicted by betraying your mother and your father?"

"Of course not."

Gordon Hamilton looked through the notes he had written and carefully inserted a word Jane could not read.

"That's good. Now let's look at what the prosecution will say. They have indicated that they can prove that you and the victim were long-term lovers, that he had ended the relationship and had given a great deal of information about you to a reporter, one Camilla Moore. They will say you found this out and, distraught at his betrayal of your shared secrets to the newspapers, killed him."

"Well they are wrong in so many ways. They are wrong on just about everything."

"They seem to think they have a great deal of evidence to suggest that they are not."

"Evidence?"

"Photographs, his diaries, well not so much diaries as scrapbooks. I won't ask you to read them, much of it will be easy to explain away as the sexual fantasies of a lonely man."

"In which case I don't think I do want to see them."

"They do not make pleasant reading, but what I get from them is that either you had a relationship that lasted through many different stages of your life or he made it all up."

"That's simple. We had no relationship. He has made it all up."

Gordon Hamilton nodded and looked down at some papers in his file. After a minute he looked back at Jane. "There are three matters I would like to clarify from your perspective."

"Only three?" She smiled back at him. She was beginning to trust him. He seemed very young, perhaps too young, but he was the first person who seemed to believe her.

"Firstly. Did you at any time in your life suspect that the moves in your childhood and early adulthood were for any reason other than that if your existence was publicised it would be an embarrassment to Grahame Johnstone? You are, after all, his illegitimate daughter?"

"No. Once I was old enough to ask why we were being moved around I was told it was because the newspapers were looking for anything that would expose my father for what he was."

"And what was that?" Gordon asked innocently.

"He was an immensely sad and hypocritical man whose ambitions for power far outweighed his responsibilities to the women he had once loved and his illegitimate daughter."

"Harsh."

"But true I think. For my whole life after that I felt guilty for being born, for causing so much trouble to everyone. I only learned none of it was about me when I read it in the papers after Mum died. It was only then that Richard told me, though it seemed pretty bloody obvious from the newspaper stories, that it was all to keep her history hidden. Apparently it had all been about someone wanting to find proof that she and my father were Russian spies." Jane paused, looked across the desk at Gordon Hamilton and sighed. "God that sounds so melodramatic doesn't it?"

He ignored her question. "Were you ever told the name of the man who was trailing you?"

"Not for a long time. Richard told me his name was Eric Atkinson, Mum never said anything."

"She wouldn't have done. She was bound by many promises, not least the Official Secrets Act."

"I wish she could have talked to me about it."

Gordon was sensitive to the wistfulness in Jane's voice. "She undoubtedly wanted to protect you. It seems Eric Atkinson always believed that you would follow in what he was convinced were your mother's footsteps."

"Yes, I read that too."

"He might have thought you would, eventually, be of use to someone."

"Have you spoken to him?"

"I'm afraid that hasn't been possible. He died soon after you were arrested."

"Died?"

"Yes. He had a stroke. Did David say anything to you about Eric Atkinson at all?"

"How do you mean?"

"When he came to your house, or in the pub that lunchtime, did David mention Eric Atkinson at all?"

"I don't know. I've never really been able to remember much about that."

"Anything would be useful."

Jane closed her eyes.

"He wanted money. He wanted me to give him money."

"Did he say why?"

"Something to do with not having enough money to retire on."

"Did he mention Eric Atkinson at all?"

"Honestly, I can't remember."

"If you remember anything more you will let me know won't you?"

Nobody else had asked her about Eric Atkinson; not the police nor any of the solicitors she had seen.

"Why the interest in Eric Atkinson? What's he got to do with this?"

"He was there."

"There?"

"In the pub, with Richard."

"Bloody hell!"

"You didn't know?"

"I had no idea."

"It appears that for the past ten years, and quite probably for far longer, Eric Atkinson paid small but regular sums of money into David Childs' bank account. Also he was named as a referee when Childs first applied to join the police force in Cambridge in 1980 and again when he requested a transfer to the Met in 1987."

"No!"

"My interpretation of much of the evidence I have been able to unearth is that Eric Atkinson kept a close eye on you and your mother until 1980. He may not have known exactly where you were at all times but I believe that, despite the best efforts of Richard Mackenzie, he knew where you and your mother were most of the time. In those years he was able to keep an eye on both of you at the same time. But then you left home. He wasn't going to be able to keep tabs on both of you both so he carried on checking up on your mother and he recruited David Childs to keep an eye on you and report back to him."

"That's a bit far-fetched isn't it?"

"Dates and places match up."

"Really?"

"They do. I am not alone in believing an entirely plausible explanation is that Eric saw in David someone who would see tracking you as far more than just a job and would therefore stick at it far more than any other, more reasonable, person would. We believe he recognised that David was somewhat obsessed and Eric used that obsession to his own ends. Unfortunately, with all the protagonists dead, it will be impossible to prove. But I would say it adds to our conviction that what you say is true."

Jane did not think to ask who the others were who Gordon included in his reference to 'we' and 'our'.

"Thank you." Jane now was convinced that, at last, she had someone on her side. "I knew about Eric but it never occurred to me that David might ever have known him. Why would I?"

"He might have told you? That lunchtime in the pub?"

"I can't remember."

"If he had have done would you have been angry?"

"I'm not sure I would have been angry, saddened perhaps, and not a little afraid. But even if he did say anything I wouldn't have known any of that when I left home so why would I have had taken Richard's gun with me? Which I didn't by the way."

"The prosecution will say that you meant to kill him and that is why you took the gun with you that day."

"If I was going to kill him, and I wasn't, but if I had planned to do it why would I choose to shoot him in a crowded town on a hot summer's day?"

"Well of course, if you were planning to kill him there would have been far better places, places where there was the slightest chance that you might have got away with it."

"But the prosecution don't see it that way?"

"Apparently not. They will argue you were so incensed, so angry, felt so betrayed, that you wanted the act to be a very public one."

"The action of a mad woman?"

"Precisely. You must try to remember what David Childs said to you that lunchtime. Anything would be helpful."

"I will try but I think I've probably shut it out of my mind."

"Now to my second question, this relates to your fiancé, Matt Greenaway, and your ex-husband, Peter Carmichael. Were they both what might be termed 'pub people'?"

"Yes. They both were."

"Did you join them?"

"No. Matt always went on his own, so did Peter, except for odd Sunday lunchtimes. I've never really seen the attraction of spending time in pubs. If I wanted a gin and tonic or a wine after work I'd have it at home. I found that far more pleasant. I just left them to it."

"Were they alike? Matt and Peter I mean."

Jane thought he asked as though he was really interested. "I suppose they were, in some ways."

"Tell me about Peter."

"Don't you want to know about Matt?"

"I'm sure he was a very interesting and nice man but it is Peter we are interested in."

"Well, although originally an academic he did a lot of work with city firms, actuarial statistics, that sort of thing. That was in the early Eighties when it seemed that most work was done in wine bars."

"Did he have a drink problem?"

"I don't think so, no more than most city types of the time at any rate. He did drink an awful lot."

"An awful lot?"

"I don't know really, but I can't imagine it was less that six or eight pints at lunchtime and the same in the evenings."

"That is a lot."

"But he seemed to be able to handle it. Well, most of the time anyway. He wasn't often what you'd call out and out pissed."

"And you didn't go to the pub with him in the evenings?"

"No. I had better things to do with my time. If I wasn't working I was sorting out the house. You know, the washing, ironing, cleaning, that sort of stuff."

"You disapproved of his drinking?"

"I'd never say anything, it wasn't worth it, but yes, I probably disapproved. It was just that I didn't see that it was a good use of time."

"So he spent a lot of his time in pubs?"

"Yes. He did."

"So he would have had friends you knew nothing about"

"Of course he would have done. We didn't really have any friends. We weren't very good at socialising as a couple. We weren't very good at doing anything as a couple really."

"I want to explore this avenue as the way in which Childs got hold of those photographs he had in his possession. Have you any theories?"

"I've thought about this for months. It must have been the break-ins."

"I wondered if you might have seen their relevance to your case."

"There was the one the Wednesday before, well before David Childs died. And there was one, years ago, just before I left Chessington."

Jane watched as he Gordon Hamilton wrote several lines of notes in his careful and very neat handwriting.

"Were there any common factors in the burglaries?" He asked without looking up from the paper.

"There were actually. Not much was stolen. In the first one it was only silly bits and pieces and in the second I couldn't find anything missing."

"You say 'silly bits and pieces' were stolen in the 1982 Surrey break in Surrey? Such as?"

"Well they stole some of the washing off my line."

"Underwear?"

"Well yes."

"And would it have been possible that photographs were taken from albums and letters from desk drawers that you may not have noticed were missing?"

"That's definitely a possibility, certainly in the break-in last year. The police were in my house when they came to investigate the burglary and then after I was arrested. They could easily have put things in the house or taken them out."

"This is something I've had looked into and I've found two interesting facts. A common denominator if you like."

"Yes?" Jane prompted him after he had paused for some moments. "What?"

"Who. The common denominator is a 'who'." He was enjoying the luxury of teasing his client. He wanted to see her reaction when she heard. He watched her carefully as he said. "David Childs." But she had guessed and as he spoke he saw she was mouthing the name.

"Yes." He continued. "David Childs. He was the investigating officer in Chessington."

"Oh God. Really? That's actually quite frightening."

"You had no idea?"

"None at all. I didn't see the police, Peter dealt with it all."

"I'm afraid I took the liberty of getting a colleague of mine to check out whether there is anything at all to link your ex-husband with David Childs."

"Peter and David?"

"Pub memorabilia is an interesting source of information." Gordon said, smiling, as if changing the subject. "Some pubs keep photographs of their customers for years. Photos of events like Christmas parties, darts matches, pub football matches that sort of thing. Well David and Peter knew each other quite well it seems."

"That really is quite frightening."

The young lawyer pulled out a photograph from a folder and showed it to Jane.

"I think it's entirely possible that David got to know Peter because he was your husband and he used Peter's unhappiness with you to his own end."

"Oh shit."

"I also asked my young pub-going assistant to take a trip to Cambridge. Unfortunately there were no surviving photographs but he talked to someone who remembered Matt Greenaway and who recognised the photograph of David and, yes, they were drinking mates there too."

"He knew Matt? And he knew Peter?"

"I think this is interesting but it doesn't prove anything. It is not impossible to imagine that, had you been having a long-term affair with David Childs, he would make an effort to get to know the other men in your life."

"It may tell you that but it tells me he was obsessed with me because I know I never met him, not in Cambridge nor in Surrey."

"Unfortunately we can't prove that you didn't meet him, though we can prove the friendships with Matt and Peter."

"It explains everything though, doesn't it?"

"It explains everything, but unfortunately it proves nothing. We have David Childs knowing Eric Atkinson, working for him over a number of years, tasked with following you and presumably reporting your movements, your friendships and anything that might link you to people connected with your mother's possible role with a secret service. To this end he befriended the men you were close to and he used those friendships to obtain embarrassing, intimate, photographs and other personal items belonging to you."

"But none of that proves I didn't kill him."

"No. It doesn't. But bear with me." Gordon wrote another neat line of notes on a sheet of paper before he continued. "The prosecution have indicated, from their initial questioning and in everything they have done, that they believe it was you who was obsessed with David Childs not the other way round. I think we have enough to be able to show that is not the case. We can explain how he came to have those photographs and the love letters by the Chessington burglary and we can readily explain the only evidence they have that you were the obsessive by the Isle of Wight burglary."

"You mean he planted that stuff in my house?"

"Someone did. It's unlikely to be David, after all, he didn't know he was going to be killed did he? Someone else did the planting."

"So the stuff was planted in my house during or after the burglary? Not by the police? I suppose I have always been assuming it was them."

"Someone who knew David was going to be killed. Someone who knew you were going to be the main suspect, someone who wanted you to take the blame. The only candidate for that is Eric Atkinson."

Jane sat for a few moments in silence.

"Someone who wanted revenge, not on David Childs but on Richard, and me."

"Revenge is best served cold. This may, after all, turn out to be a revenge killing, Dr Carmichael, but revenge by proxy."

She had always hoped for an explanation and had never been able to find one. But it seemed that Gordon Hamilton had. Her immediate relief at knowing that what she had been told was the truth of the matter was tempered when she realised they could do nothing with the knowledge.

"But Eric's dead. You'll never be able to prove anything."

Gordon Hamilton didn't answer directly. He was following his previously organised lines of thought.

"We need to look more closely at your Isle of Wight burglary."

"Did they ever catch the intruders? You know they said I made the whole thing up to get David Childs into my house."

"There is that inference, certainly, though how they could have expected you to know it would be David Childs responding to the call I have no idea. Another thing that bothers me about their interpretation of that day is that it is highly unusual for a DI to follow up a simple break in, especially a break in that was never formally logged as a call. Luckily your phone records prove you made the call even if their logging system has no record."

"I've been thinking that he arranged the break in so that he had an excuse to visit my house."

"Certainly that is a possibility but I think it far more likely that it has Eric Atkinson's hand behind it. It's the only explanation that works. David Childs wasn't clever enough. Someone else told him what to do and that 'someone else' could only be Eric Atkinson." Without changing his tone of voice in any way Gordon continued. "Tell me. Why did you keep that scrap of paper *'Silver Birch loves David Childs'*? It does rather back up the prosecution argument that you felt strongly about him."

The change of tack threw Jane. She had been allowing herself to think that Gordon Hamilton could prove her innocence and now he came across reasons why he couldn't.

"But I didn't keep that scrap of paper."

"It was found in the drawer of your bed-side table."

"So the police say."

"Because they will say it was found there we have to say why it couldn't have been there."

"He wrote his side of the note when I left Ludlow. He put it in our stuff when the removal men were emptying the house. I kept it then because I was a confused and lonely romantic. I was ill. I had a breakdown. I suppose I kept it because it was something that reminded me of a better time. I know I was only in Ludlow for a short time but it was a normal time. Mum and I lived the nearest we could do to a normal life. It was our last 'normal life'. When we left Ludlow it all changed, everything went pear-shaped as they would say today. I suppose that scrap of paper reminded me of that time. Not of David Childs in particular."

"You had it in your pocket when you met David Childs in the library in Birmingham?"

"Yes, it was in my purse."

"You kept it in your purse for four years?"

"It was a difficult time. I had problems. I told you, I was young and unhappy."

"And obsessed with the idea of David Childs."

"No I wasn't. I barely thought of him."

"I wonder if we can persuade a jury that that is true."

"I hope so because it is the best I can do."

"So how do you think it came to be in your desk drawer when the police checked your house last summer?"

"I had written my phone number on it so I put it in his pocket that day in Birmingham, thinking he'd find it and ring me."

"But he didn't."

"No. He didn't."

"So the last you knew that scrap of paper was in David Childs' jacket pocket, in Birmingham, in 1980?"

"Yes. He must have kept it and then someone put it in my drawer during the burglary."

Gordon Hamilton wrote another neat line on the sheet of paper.

"Now I come to my third question, Jane. What did you feel when you saw what the newspapers wrote about you when they broke the story of your family's colourful history."

Gordon's voice was kindly but firm. He sat back in his chair, his hands resting on his chest, his fingers meeting in what Jane thought of as a church steeple. She took a deep breath and tried to put into words the mixture of pain, distaste and confusion she had experienced.

"You have to understand that for all of my life I had blamed myself for all the upheavals we had been through. I had thought, for over fifty years that all my mother's problems were my fault. It was my fault for being born, my fault my mother was hounded around the country, my fault that that had made her so ill. Then I found it wasn't."

"You were hurt?"

"Hurt and confused. Most of what I read was complete news to me."

"Yet what was written was accurate?"

"Apparently so. Richard said it was and he was probably the only person who could know. He said dates and places were right. There were lots of photographs to back it all up. I hated seeing the photographs of me as a child. It seemed horribly creepy that Eric Atkinson must have been so close when he had taken them and I hadn't known. I also thought the way they characterised my mother was awful when she wasn't there to be able to defend herself and there would be no one with the facts to argue, except my father of course, and he wasn't going to say anything was he? Though, if what was written in the papers was right, she never actually lied to me."

Jane paused and looked down at the floor. Gordon made no move to hurry her. He wanted to hear what she had to say. It was a long minute before she continued. "My mother once said something I've never forgotten. When we left one of our homes in a hurry she told me not to say anything to my friends as they would be in danger if they knew the truth. She said it was better for them not to know anything even if it meant they thought badly of me. I suppose that was her philosophy with me. What I didn't know couldn't be dragged out of me, and I wouldn't be hurt by, even though her silence led me to think badly of her. I'm really sad that I didn't hear all those things from her but I understand why she never told me. You ask what I felt when I read those reports? Overwhelmingly I felt disappointment that I had to learn about everything from badly written, sensationalistic newspaper articles."

"And who were you most angry with?"

"Angry? I don't think I was angry at all. Anyway, if I was there was nobody to be angry with."

"Your mother?"

"She was dead. You can't be angry with dead people."

"Richard?"

"No. I don't think so. I think I realised how much he had cared for my mother and for how long."

"Your father?"

"How can you be angry with someone you don't know? I suppose if I have any emotion about him it's that I despise him."

"Despise?"

"It seems that he was a bit of a weak man, to give up the woman he loved for his career? I mean what sort of person does that?"

"Many more than you could possibly imagine."

"He had another family, a wife, a son and a daughter. What must it have been like for them? No I'm not angry with him. I just think he can't be a very nice man."

"Have you ever met him?"

"Once. In College in Cambridge. We talked for a few minutes."

"What did you think of him?"

"Does it really matter?"

"No. I don't suppose so." He paused, looked as if he was thinking about something for a few moments before continuing. "So, if you weren't angry with Grahame Johnstone, with your mother or with Richard were you angry with Eric Atkinson?"

"Eric Atkinson? Am I angry with him? I've a lot of questions I'd like to have asked him if he were still alive. I'd ask him whether she was proud of being such a despicable little toe rag."

"And David Childs?"

"I had no reason to even think about him at the time."

Gordon looked down at the page of notes he had taken then looked at her and smiled. "You have answered my three questions very honestly I think. Thank you for your time, Dr Carmichael. You have been very helpful, and with a little necessary research going our way, I think we may have your defence."

"My defence?"

"I won't say any more than we have a number of avenues to work with. I can make no promises other than that I will do my level best to make the jury see the truth of what you have told me."

"Before you go can I ask you a question?" Jane asked tentatively.

"Fire ahead."

"You're not a legal aid lawyer are you?" Gordon Hamilton smiled as he slowly shook his head from side to side. "No. I didn't think so. Will you tell me who hired you to take my case and who is paying your probably not insubstantial fee?"

"Ah. I wondered if you'd ask me that. All I can say, Jane Carmichael, is that you have many friends who are looking out for your best interests."

"Can I ask who they are?"

"You may ask but I will give you no satisfactory answer."

"My father?" She asked with some incredulity in her voice. But Gordon Hamilton had no need to lie as a knock on the door was followed immediately by the appearance of a warder who told him brusquely that his time was up.

"My time is up now Jane. I will see you in court. Remember. You are not alone. You have friends and we will do our damnedest to see you right."

Jane had no way of knowing that within an hour Gordon Hamilton was at his desk talking to two elderly men.

Even had she been a fly on the wall she may not have recognised one of the men as Berndt Schreiber, her uncle, the man she had met in Moscow twenty one years before, who had presented her with the most valuable books and whose messages she had repeated to Richard.

She would most certainly have recognised the frail elderly gentleman with whom he was chatting amiably as her father.

Chapter 21
The Trial concludes

Gordon Hamilton had not cross-examined any of the police witnesses. He had let the reports of the three policemen who had attended the scene and the detectives who had conducted the interviews go without comment. He had not questioned the absence of forensic tests. He hadn't intervened as Camilla Moore had described the scandals, both sexual and political, that she had been able to expose that had caused Jane Carmichael such distress that the prosecution said could only be resolved by the revenge murder. He had asked no questions of thirteen of the fifteen witnesses who had told the same story, they had seen the accused standing over her victim with the gun in her hand.

Only two of the prosecution witnesses remained, sisters who had been sitting on the bench by the church. They had been held to last by the prosecution because they were the only two witnesses who felt able to give evidence relating to the moments leading up to the murder.

Vanessa Woods enjoyed her time in the witness box. She had been looking forward to the day for weeks and was disappointed that it was all over so quickly.

"No questions My Lord."

When her sister Louise was called the prosecution barrister asked her the same questions and they were answered identically. They had been sitting together, she said, and so had seen exactly the same events.

"Now Mr Hamilton, I have to ask, have you any questions for this witness?"

"I have My Lord."

There was a buzz around the court at the unexpected reply.

Jane watched as Gordon Hamilton stood up, fastidiously adjusting his black gown.

Louise Woods was nervous. Why had this nice young man picked on her to be asked more questions? Why hadn't he asked Vanessa? Vanessa would have loved to be the centre of attention for longer. She had tried to answer the nice lady barrister's questions correctly and even though it had only been that morning she wasn't sure she'd remember the exact answers she had given. The young gentleman appeared kind but she was afraid she would say the wrong things.

"Firstly, Miss Woods, may I ask if you were alone when you were watching the drama you described this morning unfold?"

"No. I was with my sister. I told the police this. She told you this. I told you this. Here, this morning." Louise looked nervously about her, wondering if it had been a trick question and she had answered it wrongly.

"There was a group of you?"

"No. It was just two of us."

"You were together?"

"Yes. I just said that."

"So you both saw the same thing."

"Yes. Obviously we would."

"So you were both facing in the same direction?"

"Yes. We were sitting on the bench by the church looking out across the square towards the pier."

"You weren't facing each other? Perhaps gossiping, chatting about the weather?"

"No. We were both looking out over the square. Watching people making a mess of parking I remember."

"You are very definite about that?"

"Yes."

Louise looked about her, looking for her sister in the public area, but she couldn't see her.

"So what you saw you would say that your sister also saw?"

"Obviously." Louise Woods said, wondering why the young man was making such a thing about how and where they were sitting. The judge and the other lawyers, on the other hand, saw that by making that point very clear

Gordon Hamilton could discredit the evidence of both witnesses.

"And what was it that you both saw?" Gordon Hamilton continued.

"As I said, we saw her killing him."

"How?"

"Pardon?"

"How? How did she kill him?"

"She shot him didn't she?"

"Since you ask me I would say that David Childs did, indeed, die of gunshot wounds. And I would agree that the gun was seen in her hand but I believe it has yet to be proved to the satisfaction of our jury that Dr Carmichael fired that shot."

He paused to allow the seed of a doubt to plant itself in the minds of the members of the jury. The pause unsettled Louise Woods still further.

"Can you tell the court when it was that you first noticed my client?"

"What do you mean?"

"What I mean is did you see Dr Carmichael walking into the square? It has already been established that there was quite a crowd that day, what was it about Dr Carmichael that drew you to look at her?"

"I don't understand what you're asking."

"It really is quite simple Miss Woods, there would have been how many, twenty, thirty, maybe forty people in the square at that time, what was it that made you notice one of them in particular? Was she wearing anything particularly colourful? Maybe she was waving her arms around? Was she shouting out to someone? There must have been something about her to make her literally stand out in a crowd."

"I don't know. I just noticed her. You do sometimes don't you?"

"And your sister just happened to notice her at the same time?"

Gordon didn't wait for an answer that he knew would not come. He looked down at his notes, appeared to pick up a pen and write something, then, after carefully replacing the pen on the desk, he looked back across the courtroom at Louise Woods. He knew she was unsettled. It was something he had been banking on.

"Can you tell the court what Dr Carmichael was wearing?"

"Wearing?" Louise was confused. She hadn't expected to be asked that question, her sister hadn't reminded her.

"You noticed this woman across the crowded square, what clothes was she wearing?"

"I can't remember."

"Perhaps I can help. She was wearing a white tee-shirt and a blue denim skirt. Where was the gun?"

"It was in her hand." Louise Woods answered.

She knew that was the correct answer.

"Are you saying you saw Dr Carmichael walk along a crowded street with a gun in her hand? I have to say that no other witness has mentioned that."

"She must have had it in her hand."

"No other witness has mentioned this, Miss Woods. I would have thought it would have been fairly obvious. The gun is quite a large one is it not? Could the court be shown the gun again?"

There was a slight delay as the court usher found the relevant exhibit and eventually held up a clear plastic bag containing a sizeable revolver.

"Not something that is easily secreted. Can you honestly say you saw the gun in Dr Carmichael's hand as she crossed the square?"

"I don't….. Well no. Sorry. No. I can't say that."

Louise Woods looked up at the judge who did not meet her eye. She looked across at the members of the jury who seemed to be staring intently at her. She looked away hurriedly as the young barrister began his questions again.

"Dr Carmichael was wearing a blue denim skirt that day. May we see the skirt? Usher?"

The skirt was displayed to the court.

"Has the skirt any pockets Miss Woods?"

"I don't think so."

"The court can see that the skirt has no pockets. If Dr Carmichael did not have the gun in her hand and her skirt had no pockets where might the gun have been as she crossed the square?"

"I don't know."

"Miss Woods, I hate to badger you on this point but it is an important one. You testified earlier to having seen the gun in Dr Carmichael's hand as she stood over Detective Inspector Childs but the court really does need to know how it got there. Was Dr Carmichael carrying a shopping basket, or perhaps a handbag?"

"Yes. She was definitely carrying a handbag. She must have got it out of her handbag."

"There is no 'must' about it Miss Woods. Now can you tell me what sort of handbag she was carrying?"

"What?"

"What sort of handbag? Was it a small clutch bag? A bag hung over the crook of her arm? A shoulder bag?"

"I don't know. I can't remember."

"I can tell you it was a shoulder bag. Now did you see Dr Carmichael remove the gun from the bag?"

"I don't know. I can't remember." Louise Woods wanted the whole ordeal to be over. She had never wanted to come to court in the first place. She wasn't sure she had really seen anything clearly. It was all so long ago now.

"If Dr Carmichael didn't have the gun in her hand as she crossed the square, and no witness has ever mentioned she did, and there were no pockets in her skirt, as we have seen there weren't, the only place it could have been was in her bag. Did you see her remove the gun from her bag?"

"No. No. I didn't. There were lots of people, lots of cars." Louise Woods knew it was an inadequate answer.

"My Lord, may I ask that Dr Carmichael place the bag over her shoulder."

The judge nodded and the bag was passed to Jane in the dock who slung it over her shoulder.

"Now, Dr Carmichael, imagine you have something in the bag you wish to remove. Please go through the motions."

The court watched as Jane looked under her shoulder to find the zip that held the casual bag shut. She opened the bag and put her hand inside.

"Thank you Dr Carmichael. Now Miss Woods that was quite a cumbersome operation wouldn't you agree?"

Louise Woods nodded.

"Can you speak up for the court?"

"Yes."

"Now did you see Dr Carmichael perform that operation either standing still or walking across the square?"

"She must have done. Perhaps it was open. The bag must have been open."

"We have already heard testimony from the arresting police officer that when she was arrested Dr Carmichael was wearing this white t-shirt, this pocket-less denim skirt and that her shoulder bag was fastened closed. I ask again. Did you see her opening her bag?"

"No."

"Or closing it again?"

"No." Louise Woods sounded defeated. She had let her sister down. Vanessa would have been able to answer all these extra questions. She would have known what it was best to say.

"Could it have been that you only saw her with the gun in her hand after the shots had been fired?" Gordon Hamilton continued relentlessly.

Louise Woods looked at the judge to help her with the answer but he was looking at her and raised an eyebrow and gave a slight nod of his head to indicate that she should answer.

"I'm not certain." Louise Woods eventually spoke. "I certainly saw her standing over him."

"Did you not see her before that?"

"Well. I thought I had. I can't be sure. No. I can't be sure. But I saw her standing over him. I saw the gun in her hand."

"So you didn't see whether she had a gun in her hand before the shot? You couldn't say that she had the gun in her hand as she walked across the square. Nor can you say you saw her open her shoulder bag and remove it. So when did you first see the gun?"

"I saw her with the gun."

"Did you or did you not see Dr Carmichael with the gun in her hand before you heard the gunshot?"

"I saw her with the gun." Louise Woods repeated. She looked up again at the judge, wishing it was that nice Judge John Deed from the television. He would stop this young man haranguing her with difficult questions.

"I'm sorry, Miss Woods, I don't mean to repeat myself, but this really is quite important. Could you please confirm when you first saw Dr Carmichael with the gun in her hand? Was it before or after the sound of the gunshot?"

"I don't know what you mean."

"I'm not sure how I can be any clearer but I will try." Gordon Hamilton was not being sarcastic and he was not being harsh on the witness, his voice was kind, helpful even. He felt sorry for Louise Woods, the police had depended on her testimony too much. And he knew he had to get the answer from her without seeming to bully her. The jury would not like him if he did that. "When you first saw the gun in the defendant's hand was it before or after you heard the shots?"

"I..... Well...... She was with him, she had the gun in her hand. She was standing over him."

"If she was 'standing over him' as you have just said surely the shots would already have been fired and David Childs would already have fallen to the ground."

It took a while before Louise Woods answered. She looked across the court at all the faces staring at her and felt afraid. She hadn't wanted to get involved in this. She had told Vanessa she hadn't and Vanessa had taken no notice. Now she was being made to look like a foolish old woman.

She shook her head.

"What is your answer, please Miss Woods?" Gordon Hamilton's voice was still gentle and sympathetic despite the persistence of his questioning.

"It must have been after. I didn't see her before. I'm sorry." She looked at the judge who, she was pleased to see, was not looking at her.

Gordon Hamilton looked down at his notes hoping the judge would not call for a break in proceedings. He was coming to the main questions in his interrogation.

"Now Miss Woods, can you say whether there was anyone else close by when you first saw Dr Carmichael?"

"Anyone else?"

"Perhaps I need to be clearer. Was there any other person standing close by the accused?"

"There were lots of people around."

"Was there anyone particularly close to her?"

"I don't know. I can't remember. I saw her with the gun. She must have killed him. Right in front of us she killed him, she must have." Louise Woods heard the panic rising in her voice. She had not been prepared for these questions and she didn't know how she should answer them. She wondered what Vanessa would say.

"Please Miss Woods, could you answer the question. Was there anyone standing particularly close to Dr Carmichael?"

Louise Woods looked around her again. Vanessa hadn't said anything about anyone else.

"Yes please, Miss Woods," the judge repeated "it is a perfectly reasonable question."

"I don't know. I can't remember. I didn't notice anyone in particular. There might have been. There were lots of people around, someone might have been closer than others. I don't know."

"Was there not another person, an elderly gentleman, who was jostling against Dr Carmichael, as if pushing to get past her?"

"There might have been, I don't know, I didn't see."

"Is it possible that in those seconds after the shot and before you could focus on Dr Carmichael that someone could have placed the gun in her hand."

Gordon Hamilton waited for the prosecution to intervene, he knew he was asking a question that the witness could not possibly answer, but neither Maria Stanley nor the judge said a word. The thought crossed his mind that they were beginning to see what had seemed to him to be obvious flaws in the prosecution argument. Everything, Gordon Hamilton believed, came down to the details, the precise details, of how the murder was committed. And when the details were examined it seemed to him impossible that Dr Carmichael could have been guilty.

Louise Woods could not think what the right answer should be so she spoke quietly, saying dejectedly. "She must have done it."

"Must have?"

"Well how else could it have happened? She must have killed him."

"Must have?" Gordon Hamilton repeated.

"She was right with him when he fell, and she had the gun in her hand. She had the gun in her hand." Louise Woods repeated, increasingly unsure that she had, in fact, seen anything.

"Now, Miss Woods, can you honestly say that you saw the gun in Dr Carmichael's hand before the shot that killed David Childs was fired?"

"Well that's what must have happened."

"Or did you, perhaps, only see what happened after you were alerted by the loud cracks of the gunshots, and that there were therefore several moments after the shots before you saw anything clearly and that in those moments it is entirely possible that someone placed the gun in Dr Carmichael's hand?"

Louise Woods looked at Gordon Hamilton and at the lady barrister who had asked her all the questions she had been prepared to answer and then she looked at the jury who were all staring at her.

It was all too much for her. She knew she had sworn the oath to tell the truth, the whole truth and nothing but the truth and now she knew she had to say what she had known all along.

"I wasn't looking!"

She looked across at the barrister, and at the defendant, and then to the jury and the judge and then down at her feet in the shoes she had bought specially for her day in court.

"I beg your pardon?" Gordon's voice was still gently enquiring, exhibiting mystification rather than condemnation. "You say you weren't looking? But you have been brought to this court as an eye-witness. You have answered questions from my learned friends, you have indicated all through the investigation and these proceedings that you had seen Dr Carmichael shoot David Childs. How can you now say that you weren't looking?"

"We weren't. We were looking at someone parking. We noticed it because there were two yellow cars next to each other." She looked at the judge and then back at the jury. "You don't often see yellow cars, let alone two together, so we were looking at that. Then we saw the man on the ground and the woman with the gun."

"We?" Gordon prompted.

"Vanessa and me, we were looking at the two yellow cars. I'm sorry."

"You cannot say, then, as you have testified earlier, that you saw her kill him." Gordon Hamilton turned to the jury though still talking to the witness. "You, and your sister Vanessa, both saw only the aftermath of the attack, as did every other eye-witness called to give evidence. In the time between the shot and your view it is entirely possible that someone placed the gun in Dr Carmichael's hand is it not?" He didn't give the witness time to respond, or the prosecution to make objections before concluding "Thank you Miss Woods."

"Mrs Stanley?" The judge prompted the lead barrister for the prosecution. "Do you wish to come back on anything?"

"I think Miss Woods has probably had enough. I have no further questions My Lord."

Gordon Hamilton glanced at Jane Carmichael. He felt everything was going quite well, and all according to his plan.

The case for the prosecution ended and as the session began the next morning the Judge smiled wryly down at Gordon Hamilton. "You have been remarkably quiet up till now Mister Hamilton. I trust you will have more to say in your client's defence."

"I have, thank you My Lord." Gordon Hamilton "We will not argue many of the facts that have been presented by the prosecution but we will disagree vehemently with their interpretation for, we believe, there is considerable doubt about that."

He looked across the courtroom at Jane Carmichael who sat, as she had done throughout the trial, with an unreadable expression on her face. He was to begin to give the case for the defence happy that doubt was beginning to form in the minds of the jury. He and his team had been given sufficient funds to spend a great deal of time on the case and he was confident he could not only prove Jane Carmichael's innocence of the murder of which she stood accused but also, in so doing, go some way to exonerating her parents, who had been accused and found guilty in the print and broadcast media and over the internet of betraying their country.

Gordon Hamilton turned to the jury. "Certainly Dr Carmichael was apprehended with the murder weapon in her hand, we cannot disagree with that fact, but we will ask the question 'Does that mean that it had to be her finger that pulled the trigger?' Unfortunately no forensic tests were performed at the time to discover whether or not there was any residue on Dr Carmichael's hands or clothing. We cannot disagree that the murder weapon, the service revolver, had belonged to Richard Mackenzie, Dr Carmichael's step-father, but we will ask the question 'Was Dr Carmichael the only person with access to that gun?' We will not disagree that the defendant knew of the victim's existence but we aim to show to your satisfaction that theirs was only a brief acquaintance and that was many years ago. My client will deny absolutely that she had any relationship with David Childs, she will testify that she bore the victim no animosity whatsoever as she barely knew him and could have no motive to do away with him. And we will show that there were others who did have such a motive."

He paused to take a sip from his glass of water and glanced back at Jane Carmichael who returned his look without displaying any emotion. He had to admire her, she had obeyed his instructions to the letter and had given the press nothing to work with, even when her character was being so maligned.

"Although the witnesses brought by the prosecution undoubtedly are honest in their memories, and we have no doubt of their good faith, you will recall that not one could say they actually witnessed the moment the gun was fired. Not one of the many witnesses for the prosecution can testify to the location of the gun prior to its being fired and ending up in Dr Carmichael's hand. I will come back to those points later but first I will address the 'relationship' Mrs Stanley has suggested existed between Dr Carmichael and the deceased and upon which the prosecution depends heavily for providing my client with a motive. We ask Dr Carmichael to the witness box."

Jane Carmichael was ready. She had spent half an hour that morning preparing. She stood up and was ushered to the witness box, she took her oath and for the first time was able to see the public sitting in the gallery. She recognised no one.

"Dr Carmichael. Did you ever have an affair with David Childs?"

"No."

"Dr Carmichael. To your recollection how many times, in your life, did you meet David Childs?"

"Seven." Jane spoke firmly and clearly, addressing her answers to the jury, just as Gordon had instructed her.

"Would you care to give the court details?"

"I first met David Childs in the market square in Ludlow, Shropshire, when I was 16. I had just moved there and he started talking to me. The second time I met him was at an inter-school debate when he asked me to the cinema that weekend. The third time was that date. The fourth time was four years later when I bumped into him in the library in Birmingham. The fifth time was an hour after that when I met him in a pub and we had a few drinks and talked for an hour or so. The sixth time was more than thirty five years later when he investigated the break in at my house and the seventh was the following Sunday lunchtime when, at his insistence, I met him for a drink."

"And that's it?"

"It is."

"That's the sum of your 'relationship' with David Childs?"

"It is."

"Did you have any reason to kill David Childs?"

"I hardly knew him."

"Did you kill David Childs?"

"I did not."

"Thank you Dr Carmichael." Gordon Hamilton sat down.

For the remainder of that morning Jane Carmichael could not be shaken by Maria Stanley. She answered the increasingly aggressive questions with patience and calmness. She was totally consistent and completely confident in her answers.

That afternoon the defence called Miss Emily Richards. There was a buzz around the court as Miss Richards took the stand as no one other than the defence and the prosecution had any idea who she was. There had been much unsubstantiated speculation in the press that Lord Johnstone would be called to support his daughter in some way and the public gallery was disappointed with the plump, grey haired and rather nondescript woman who took the oath.

"You are Miss Emily Richards, sometime barmaid of the Anglesey Arms, Cambridge?"

"I am."

"Did you know the victim, David Childs?"

"I did."

"Can you elaborate Miss Richards?"

"Between 1982 and 1987 Dave Childs was a regular in my pub. He drank with us most nights."

"It's a long time ago, yet you remember him?"

"It was a long time ago, yes, but he was such a fixture in the pub and you remember men like that however many years pass."

"I understand. Do you remember if David Childs had any particular friends? Were there any particular people he met, men and women who stood in the same places every day at the bar?"

"Yes, David was part of a group of four. All men, they weren't the sort to drink with women if you know what I mean."

"Did you ever see David Childs drinking with a woman?"

"Oh no, never. He was a man's man was Dave. Only drank with the same group."

"Do you know any of those other men's names?"

"Certainly first names, we never really worked with surnames if you know what I mean. Anyway there was George and Malcolm and Matt. There were the four of them, always stood at the same part of the bar and always had the same drinks. I worked in that pub for years but you always remember the groups."

"May we focus on Matt? Did you know Matt's surname?"

"No. Not at the time. But I learned it when he died. He was Matt Greenaway. He fell under a bus on his way back from the pub one evening."

"For the benefit of the court I would confirm that Matt Greenaway was engaged to be married to Dr Jane Carmichael. According to the records of the Coroner's court the only witness to Mr Greenaway's fatal accident in August 1987 was PC David Childs."

There was a murmur from the gallery interrupted by the judge. "Mister Hamilton please do not let me think you are making any insinuations."

"No, My Lord, certainly not. I am merely stating fact."

"Good. I'm very glad to hear it. Continue."

"Now Miss Richards, did the defendant ever venture into your establishment?"

"Not that I ever saw."

"So as far as you know the defendant and PC Childs never met in your pub?"

"I never saw her."

"But it was a female friendly environment?"

"Oh yes. Lots of men drank with their wives and girlfriends. It wasn't one of those places women didn't like to go in."

"Thank you Miss Richards."

Maria Stanley's questions allowed the ex-barmaid to explain the long hours she worked, the many shifts and that, had Dave Childs ever been in her pub, it would have been such an odd occasion one of the other staff would have told her. She was also able to explain that her memory for names and faces was excellent, as it had to be in a well-run pub and that Matt Greenaway's death had been part of the pub's history ever since 'falling under that proverbial bus' so she could never have forgotten Dave Childs.

Gordon paused, waiting until the judge had finished making notes and the now elderly Cambridge ex-barmaid left the court.

"The defence calls Miss Charlene Eastwood."

Again there was a murmur through the court as another woman took the witness stand.

"You are Miss Charlene Eastwood, sometime barmaid of the Dog and Duck, in Chessington in the county of Surrey?"

"Another barmaid Mister Hamilton?" The judge asked and Gordon nodded with a smile, repeating his question.

"I am."

"Did you know the victim, David Childs?"

"I did."

"Can you elaborate Miss Eastwood?"

"I knew Dave well."

"What years are you referring to Miss Eastwood?"

"He first came in in the autumn of 1988."

"That is a long time ago, can you be sure about your memories?"

"Oh yes!" Charlene Eastwood laughed. "Once known never forgotten!"

"In what ways, Miss Eastwood?" Gordon Hamilton continued in his calm, reassuring, almost conversational, tone.

"He was always very chatty, he was. I wasn't so sure about him at first, him being a detective an' all, but he was a lot of fun. He joined in everything, darts, footie, quizzes, everything. Very gregarious our Dave."

"Did he have any particular friends? People he met, men who stood in the same places every day at the bar?"

"One particular I remember. Him and Dave were great mates."

"Do you know the man's name?"

"Certainly, it was Pete Carmichael."

"You are very certain?"

"Oh yes, There's loads of photos of them on the wall. Still, after all this time."

"Photos of Pete Carmichael and David Childs together?"

"Yes."

"May I see?" The judge asked and a photograph was passed across the court to an usher who handed it up to the judge. "Carry on Mister Hamilton."

"Did you know Peter Carmichael was married?"

"Oh yes. But his wife never came to the pub. He said she didn't do pubs, he was actually quite rude about her. They didn't get on at all. He was screwing, sorry, I mean he was in a relationship with my boss, the pub landlady."

"While he was still married to Dr Carmichael?"

"Yes sir but they got divorced."

"Did you see much of Peter Carmichael after the divorce?"

"Oh yes. He moved into the pub. That's why I remember him and Dave so well. He moved in with the landlady, you know what I mean?"

"Yes I think we know what you mean Miss Eastwood, thank you. Now did you see much of David Childs after the divorce of Peter and Jane Carmichael?"

"No. Soon after that he got transferred. We missed him, he really kept us doing well in the quiz league, we were never as good after he left."

"When would that have been?"

"1993."

"Thank you Miss Eastwood."

"May I ask where this is taking us Mr Hamilton?" The judge asked.

"I am establishing that, contrary to the evidence of the police stating that my client had a long relationship with David Childs, it was actually the case that David Childs was obsessed with my client. We are showing that he followed her around the country over a period of many years, establishing a pattern of becoming friends with the men in her life but never seen with her. We will show that he was, therefore, in a position to obtain the photographs and the private articles belonging to the defendant that the prosecution has used as evidence for the non-existent close relationship between the two."

"You have made your point I think."

"I would now like to call Miss Camilla Moore."

"Not another barmaid I trust?"

"No, My Lord, a journalist."

Camilla Moore took the oath and looked around the courtroom. She looked particularly at the members of the press who were sitting in the gallery and smiled a broad smile of something approaching triumph.

"You are Miss Camilla Moore?"

"I am."

"Can you tell the court how you came to write about the defendant in an article published just days before the death of David Childs?"

"I've been putting together the piece for a while."

"The piece?" Gordon Hamilton prompted.

"It was an exposé of the activities of Lord Johnstone."

"Of Lord Grahame Johnstone?"

"Yes. Him."

"And what did this 'piece' expose?"

"That when he was first in government, during the 1950s, Grahame Johnstone had a lover, a colleague of his who happened to be Russian and who was quite probably an agent for the Russians during the Cold War, and that relationship resulted in the birth of their illegitimate daughter, Jane Carmichael."

"We do not need to go into the details of your report. We have heard more than enough of its content from the prosecution. What the court does need to know is whose idea was it to write this article."

"Sorry?"

"Did you, off your own bat, and without any encouragement from anyone, decide to write this article about a respected elderly statesman?"

"Well, no."

"Then who encouraged you?" There was no reply as Camilla looked across at the judge so Gordon continued.

"Will you tell the court who it was that suggested the article?"

"Do I have to answer this?" Camilla Moore looked across at the judge. "Freedom of the press and all that?"

The judge looked across at Gordon Hamilton and raised an eyebrow.

"It is pertinent My Lord."

"Then please answer Miss Moore." The judge insisted.

"It was years ago. My grandfather talked about it often before he died."

"Your grandfather being?"

"Sir Michael Fox."

Gordon Hamilton looked down at his notes. "For the benefit of the court Sir Michael Fox was a Member of Parliament attached to the Ministry of Defence and was a participant on the trip to Moscow the details of which we have heard about from the prosecution when Jane Carmichael's mother was supposed to have passed information to a Russian Agent." He turned towards Camilla Moore though his eyes were not focussed on her. "And can you tell the court who it was who gave you much of the information that was included in the article, much that is nowhere in the public record?"

"Do I have to?"

"I think so." The judge replied.

"It was a contact of my grandfather's." Camilla Moore said reluctantly.

"And who was this contact of Sir Michael's?"

"He is my source. I don't have to name him."

"A man then."

"I don't have to name my sources."

"In the interests of justice it might be helpful if you did."

"I hope this is going somewhere Mister Hamilton." The judge intervened, realising the drama of the moment but determined to keep control of proceedings.

Gordon Hamilton looked up at the bench. He was disappointed that the build-up of pressure on Camilla

Moore had been interrupted but he was grateful that his line of questioning had not been stopped. "Yes, My Lord. The prosecution have used this past scandal to build the chimera of a motive for my client. I am showing that Dr Carmichael had, in fact, no motive to murder David Childs, but that others, present on the scene that Sunday afternoon, did."

The judge looked down at the row of lawyers. Gordon Hamilton stood only feet away from where Maria Stanley was sitting. Both were staring at him, awaiting his judgement on the line of questioning. "Mister Hamilton, you may continue, but please be careful you do not overstep the mark. Miss Moore, you will be helpful to this court."

Gordon knew the importance of maintaining a relationship with the judge and nodded towards him. "Thank you My Lord, I will be careful." He turned back towards the witness. "I ask you again, Miss Moore, who was this contact of your grandfather's?"

When there was no answer Gordon Hamilton persevered. "Who was this person who was in Russia and who fed you with all this information about Lord Johnstone and his daughter?"

Camilla Moore had been weighing up the advantages and disadvantages of giving an answer to the question. On the one hand she would be giving away the name of her source, but she knew he was dead so it probably didn't matter that much. On the other hand she would be the centre of much speculation and that would do no harm to her career. She answered carefully. "It was the man called Eric Atkinson."

"Eric Atkinson. Thank you." Gordon Hamilton looked down at his papers, though he had known the next question without any reference to his notes. "Now Miss Moore can you tell the court whether or not you dealt directly with this Eric Atkinson?"

"Oh no. I never met him."

"You never met him?"

"No. I always met with his side-kick."

"His side-kick?"

"That's how he was described."

"And what was his name, this 'side-kick'?"

"I always knew him as David."

"David? Only David? Did you never know a surname?"

"No."

"If I were to show you a photograph would you be able to recognise the man called David?"

"Oh yes, I'd recognise him all right."

"Let the court note that I am showing a photograph of the deceased, David Childs."

"Yes that's the man."

"So you met David Childs and he gave you information from Eric Atkinson that enabled you to write your article about Lord Johnstone, his Lordship's erstwhile mistress known then as Georgina Carmichael and their daughter Jane?"

"Yes."

"Yet David Childs was a policeman, a long-serving detective inspector, he really shouldn't have been passing information to you should he?"

"I didn't know that at the time."

"Did he ever receive payment from you?"

"Oh yes. I always gave him money."

"Were these large amounts?"

"Several thousand pounds over the months."

"And this money was yours?"

"No, of course not!"

"It was your newspaper's?"

"Of course not!"

"Then can you please tell the court whose money was used directly to pay a member of the police force for information that was prejudicial to Lord Johnstone, to the late Mrs Elizabeth Mackenzie and to the defendant Dr Jane Carmichael?"

Camilla Moore looked around the court and knew she would cause something of a furore in certain circles if she answered honestly.

"Do I have to answer this, My Lord?" She looked up at the judge, a man she had known much of her life as he was a friend of her father's.

"You do, Miss Moore, I find it a perfectly reasonable question." He looked at Maria Stanley who shook her head and looked down at her papers.

"Well Miss Moore?" Gordon Hamilton prompted.

"It was my grandfather's money."

"That would be Sir Michael Fox?"

"It would. I took over paying them after he died."

"He left you the money specifically to pay them?"

"I'm afraid he did." She looked at the judge and smiled mischievously but turned away when she saw he was not amused.

"Did Sir Michael ever tell you why he was prepared to pay these men, Eric Atkinson and David Childs, to provide you with the history of Lord Johnstone and his connections and with their alleged perfidy?"

"He never told me why. No."

"Then we can only speculate about his motives."

"So far I have been very lenient Mister Hamilton." The judge said "But I must remind you that speculation should play no part in these proceedings."

As Gordon Hamilton bowed his head in acknowledgement many in the court saw the smile in the judge's eyes.

The judge had been surprised when he had learned that Gordon Hamilton was to be defending Jane Carmichael. He had discussed with several of his fellows in chambers whether the blood relationship between the barrister and his client was too close to allow the young man to take the case but it had been agreed that it could be allowed since the defendant was unaware of the connection. They were all interested in how a defence could be mounted and would watch with interest. They all knew that success in this case would do the young man's career no harm at all.

"Please continue."

"I have no further questions for Miss Moore."

"Mrs Stanley?" The judge asked.

"No My Lord." Maria Stanley was beginning to realise that was losing the jury.

"Then you may stand down Miss Moore."

The first witness the next morning was Miss Claire Tompkins.

"Miss Tompkins. Will you tell the court what your job is?"

"I am bar manager at the Queen's Head."

The judge intervened again, with an indulgent smile. "Yet another barmaid Mister Hamilton?"

"Indeed so, My Lord, it is a fact that David Childs spent a great percentage of his leisure time in public houses."

"Carry on. Carry on."

Gordon Hamilton thought the judge was rather enjoying the case and judged that to be a good sign for his client. He turned to the woman in the witness box. "Miss Tompkins, will you tell the court where you were on the afternoon that David Childs died?"

"I was working."

"Did you know my client's step father Richard Mackenzie?"

"I did."

"Was he a regular at the pub?"

"No, sir, he wasn't. He came in occasionally over the years but not what you could call a regular."

"May I ask how you knew him then?"

"He lived next door to my Gran."

"And you visited your grandmother regularly?"

"Yes, sir, a couple of times every week."

"And you got to know Mr Mackenzie?"

"Yes him and his wife, though she was ill and I didn't talk to her much I'd always say hello to Mr Mackenzie and we'd chat about his garden. It was always beautifully kept."

"Can you tell us where Richard Mackenzie was during the lunchtime of the Sunday in question?"

"He was in the Queen's Head. I was quite surprised to see him but his wife had just died and I thought maybe he needed to get out of his house for some company."

"Was he with anyone?"

"Yes, he was with another man."

"Did you know that man?"

"No."

"Was he this man? Usher, exhibit D15B please."

"Yes. That was him. I remember him because he got to the pub really early that morning, before we were open for drinks."

"Let the court know that the witness has recognised the man in the photograph and that that man is Eric Atkinson."

"Now Richard Mackenzie and Eric Atkinson were drinking together at the same time as the defendant and the victim?"

"Yes, but they were at opposite sides of the room."

"The two couples didn't speak?"

"No. Not that I saw."

"Was that the first time you had seen the man you identified as Eric Atkinson?"

"No. I saw him the day before and earlier that week."

"Where was that?"

"When I was visiting my gran. I saw that man go in to Richard's house."

"You have a very good memory for faces?"

"You have to in my line of work. If you want to be good at it that is."

"And on what days did you see Eric Atkinson at Richard Mackenzie's house?"

"The day of Elizabeth's funeral and then the day before the shooting, the Saturday."

Gordon Hamilton turned to the jury. "So Eric Atkinson was in the house of Richard Mackenzie and could have had access to Richard Mackenzie's gun, the gun that was used to kill David Childs."

"My Lord you cannot possibly allow that! The witness could not possibly know the answer to that question." Maria Stanley stood, her hands on her hips emphasising her righteous indignation.

"Mister Hamilton, you continue to push your luck. The jury will ignore that last statement from the defence."

"I apologise My Lord." But all the lawyers in court knew the damage had been done and another seed of doubt about the prosecution's case had been planted in the minds of the jury.

Gordon Hamilton turned back to the witness box. "Miss Tompkins, can you tell the court whether you saw these four customers, Eric Atkinson, Richard Mackenzie, David Childs and Dr Jane Carmichael, leave The Queen's Head that Sunday lunchtime and, if you did, in what order?"

"I did notice it particularly because Richard knocked over his drink. He and the other man left in a real hurry."

"What did you see that precipitated that rush?"

"When Dr Carmichael got up to leave she was followed by Dave Childs and then the man with Richard, that man in the photo, almost ran out followed by Richard. Richard was really distressed, he seemed to be reaching out to the other man."

"You seem very certain of all this. Is it possible to have seen it all in a busy and crowded pub?"

"I was worried about Richard and was keeping a special eye on him."

"Worried?"

"He'd only just buried his wife and he was behaving oddly."

"Oddly?"

"He was having a drink with this man but they really didn't seem to be friendly. And after all the unpleasantness in the press about him and his family, well I was worried about him. I thought the man might be a reporter or something so I was keeping a special eye on him and on Jane. There were lots of odd things about that lunchtime."

"Odd things?"

"Well for a start why didn't Richard talk to Jane? I mean he just stood there watching her and Dave Childs. I wondered if they'd fallen out but they seemed fine the day before when Jane visited him."

"And anything else?"

"I knew Jane from all the times she visited her mum and Richard but I'd never seen her in the pub before. Not The Queen's Head or any other one. She just wasn't the sort. She'd always visit the tea rooms but never the pubs. And there she was having a drink with the detective."

"So you saw these four all leave at about the same time?"

"Yes. Jane left first with the detective right behind her though they weren't leaving together if you know what I mean."

"Can you explain?"

"Well she got up and said something to him and left. He got up and followed her. They weren't leaving together."

"And then who left?"

"The man with Richard Mackenzie followed. He didn't finish his drink and he didn't say anything to Richard. He just pushed his way to the door."

"How far behind Dr Carmichael do you think this man was?"

"Only a few seconds. And he was moving ever so quickly for an old man. He was hurrying after her."

"Could he have been hurrying after Detective Inspector Childs rather than Jane Carmichael?"

"He could have been. Yes."

"Thank you."

Claire Tomkins was a good witness, as Gordon Hamilton had known she would. She had known Richard, Elizabeth and Jane since she had been a child and she had been in the perfect position to view the pivotal events that Sunday lunchtime.

She was also a strong woman and her evidence stood up well under Maria Stanley's cross-examination.

In their final summing up the prosecution held to their story that Jane Carmichael had killed David Childs through anger that the man she had loved for so long had betrayed her to the media but Maria Stanley sounded less than convinced as she repeated the propositions that made up the prosecution case. It sounded to her, what it was, a hastily contrived and unconvincing case brought to support the preconceptions of the police. She had always known there were flaws in the case, especially relating to the procedures immediately after Dr Carmichael's arrest and the gathering of scene of crime evidence and had never been convinced that the police were being entirely honest with her when they described Dr Carmichael as being hysterical and un-cooperative.

When Gordon Hamilton stood to give his summing up he told the story of a girl trying to make her life in the most difficult of circumstances. A girl whose mother had been hounded through her life for one short meeting in Moscow in 1958; a girl who was made to feel guilty for having been born; a girl who had been followed throughout her life by men who wanted to trap her into incriminating herself in treachery. He told of the words Jane had heard at the time of the shooting 'two birds with one stone'. He explained that to Eric Atkinson the first 'bird' was David Childs, the man who knew too much about him and his paymasters and who was no longer useful to him and, by handing Jane the gun, she would be the second bird, imprisoned for the rest of her life for a crime she didn't commit. The injustice didn't matter to his warped mind as he was a man obsessed with the idea that she, and her mother, had got away scot-free with the crimes he probably truly believed they had both committed.

Jane watched as Gordon talked to the judge, to the jury and to the prosecution team exuding a confidence in her story that was compelling. He was a charismatic man and she was aware of how much she was indebted to whoever was paying his fees.

Jane spent the hours that followed believing that the argument had been lost. She persuaded herself that being found guilty would not be the worst thing that could happen. She would be incarcerated for years but she began to convince herself she could cope with that. After a few months she would be sent to an open prison where she would have space for herself, she would be able to write, even perhaps, to do some good by teaching other inmates the joy to be found in manipulating numbers.

She knew she would get a life sentence, automatically, but would probably serve no more than 15 years in prison. She wondered whether she would be allowed to rent out the cottage with the income being paid into an account to await her freedom. She would be an exemplary prisoner and she would, in the worst case scenario, be no older than 70 when she was released. She told herself it could be worse; sixty years earlier and she would have been hanged.

She dared not allow herself to think she would be found not guilty.

"I am confident we have done your case justice, let us hope the court delivers it." Gordon Hamilton reassured her as they waited for the jury to come to its conclusion.

"You sound optimistic."

"I am. After all is said and done I am the best defence barrister money can buy." He smiled a self-deprecating smile to show he wasn't being entirely serious.

"Was it only the money made you take my case?"

He looked at her before giving her the answer he had been told to give. "No. I won't deny I'm being well rewarded but I took the case on because of the challenge. If we win it'll be a real bonus to my career." He saw the look on her face. "No seriously, Jane, We have always believed in you and believed the truth of everything you have told me. Honestly, it's never been about the money."

"The jury's back." The cue for Jane to return to the courtroom came after two days.

She watched as clerks and lawyers stood up and sat down, as people left and entered the courtroom performing she knew not what tasks.

She tried not to think too much as the jury filed in and sat in their customary seats. She tried not to look at them, the nine women and three men who held her fate in their hands. But then, she told herself, her fate had already been decided. She made herself sit up straight, her shoulders back and her chin up as she waited for the man who had always occupied the right hand most seat of the bottom row of the jury box to stand up.

She allowed herself to listen as the question was asked 'has the jury reached a unanimous verdict?' and the answer given 'yes, My Lord.'

She had been told that if the jury foreman couldn't look at the defendant then the verdict was guilty. If he was able to face the person whose fate depended on his words then the verdict was likely to be in the defendant's favour. She then thought that perhaps that was only in American courts but she looked, quite deliberately, directly at the jury foreman as he stood answering the court's question.

He was looking at her.

She would allow herself to feel no elation until the words 'not guilty' were spoken. She had to hear those words. Then, and only then, would she be able to relax. David Childs and Eric Atkinson would have been defeated, their minds and their motives the subject of investigations by others. The reputations of her mother and her father would be restored in the very same media which had torn them to shreds.

"What is the verdict of this court?"

Jane watched the foreman. If he said 'guilty' she thought they would undoubtedly appeal. There would have to be some grounds for appeal. Perhaps one of the main points of law raised through the proceedings had been erroneously decided, perhaps the judge's directions had been too precise, perhaps they had been incorrectly based on a misunderstanding of some obscure legal precedent.

So much could go wrong.

Time stood still. Jane thought that minutes must have passed since the foreman had answered the judge's question when in fact it could only have been a few seconds.

She heard the word 'guilty' but could have told no one whether the word 'not' preceded it. She looked down at the jury and saw that they were smiling in her direction. Surely that meant 'not guilty'. She reasoned that they wouldn't be smiling if they'd condemned her to life imprisonment.

She looked at Gordon Hamilton who was smiling up at her. The prosecution lawyers were shuffling papers on the table in front of them.

It was all right after all. Gordon Hamilton had won.

"You are free to go Dr Carmichael with no stain whatsoever on your character." The judge spoke with a smile.

"Free?" She asked the police women who still stood on both sides of me.

"You got away with it." One said resentfully.

"I did not kill David Childs." She replied.

"We know you did." The other police woman said with spite.

"I did not. I did not kill him in fact and now in law."

She knew they didn't want to walk her out of the dock to freedom. But they were going to have to watch her leave.

She had been found not guilty and was free to go.

Chapter 22
The Letter

The taxi dropped Jane at her garden gate. She opened it and walked the ten yards to the front door she had left nearly a year before.

She should never have gone for that drink with David Childs. Never in a thousand years.

She opened the door immediately aware that someone must have been in to clear the hall of the mail that would have been delivered in those months. It had carefully been sorted into piles and laid out on the dining room table. There were piles of bills, junk mail and personal correspondence.

She first looked at the personal pile.

There were Christmas Cards. Christmas seemed so long ago. Obviously these people had had no idea that she was in jail awaiting trial for murder.

One of the letters stood out. It had been delivered by hand, there was no postmark.

She opened it, almost reluctantly. There was a date and a time written at the top. It had been written that morning, within an hour of the verdict.

My dear Jane Carmichael

When we met twenty two years ago you did not know who you were. And now you do. Now you also know something of who your mother was.

She and I were just very small cogs in a complex wheel but she helped this country enormously during those drear times of the Orwellian Cold War. She was never, she could never have been, a traitor to this country. And neither, and you will have to take my word for this, was your father.

You will now understand that what is called 'espionage' is not as the more sensational films will have it, as it is often simply a matter of a message being passed from one person to another. Your mother, your father, myself, none of us were innocent of espionage, but you must believe that everything we did was always for the good of this country, in one way or another.

I must tell you that when I met your mother, in the months before you were born, she did not know who I was. She did not know the importance of the envelope I gave her nor of the words I spoke. But she will have known they meant something and she did as she was asked without question. Your mother may have known what she was doing, passing that information on willingly, but you did not. When, that afternoon in Moscow in the University Library, you gave me an innocent message and took my reply to my old friend and colleague Richard Mackenzie you too were involved. Does that make you a spy too? Of course it doesn't. But yes, dear Jane, we used you and I am sorry for that.

I also regret the trouble that Eric Atkinson has caused you through your whole life. I should have killed him when I had the chance. Richard told me that he had also had an opportunity and had also forsworn it. You must know it was an error of judgement that haunted him for many years.

So much for the past.

You must know that, although Atkinson is now dead, there are others who will take up his cudgels, men who believe, as he did, in the guilt of your father and who will want to succeed where he and Childs failed. Eric himself was but a pawn in the game played by more powerful men. These men have long memories and, some would say, live in the past. These men have wide ranging influence so the need to protect you is as great as it ever has been.

I have spoken with your father, yes my dear niece, we have known each other for many years, and we have nominated his daughter's son as your protector.

He will be your 'Richard', the man to whom you may always turn when you are in need. In a way he is your nephew (being the son of your father's daughter how complex some families are…) and you already owe him a great deal. His name is Gordon Hamilton.

We all have a great admiration for your courage and wish you many peaceful years.

It was signed with the initials *BS*.

Jane re-read the letter and took it, with a box of matches to the grey fireplace.

She slowly took a match out of the box and struck it. She waited as the flame caught hold and then slowly, deliberately, carefully, put it to the corner of the letter.

As the words slowly disappeared she allowed herself, finally, to cry for all that she had never had and all that she had had but had lost.

Lightning Source UK Ltd.
Milton Keynes UK
UKOW02f0653130914

238478UK00001B/4/P